BUT NOT FOREDOOMED

A CLINT WOLF NOVEL
(BOOK 25)

BY

BJ BOURG

WWW.BJBOURG.COM

TITLES BY BJ BOURG

LONDON CARTER MYSTERY SERIES

James 516
Proving Grounds
Silent Trigger
Bullet Drop
Elevation
Blood Rise

CLINT WOLF MYSTERY SERIES

But Not Forgotten
But Not Forgiven
But Not Forsaken
But Not Forever
But Not For Naught
But Not Forbidden
But Not Forlorn
But Not Formidable
But Not For Love
But Not Forborne
But Not Forewarned
But Not Foreboding
But Not Forespoken
But Not For Blood
But Not Foreknown
But Not Fortuitous
But Not For Fear
But Not Foreseen
But Not For Lust
But Not Forspent
But Not Forsworn
But Not Foregone
But Not For Vengeance
But Not Foregathered
But Not Foredoomed

BUT NOT FOREDOOMED
A Clint Wolf Novel by BJ Bourg

This book is a work of fiction.
All names, characters, locations, and incidents are products of the
author's imagination, or have been used fictitiously.
Any resemblance to actual persons living or dead, locales, or events
is entirely coincidental.

Cover design by Christine Savoie of Bayou Cover Designs

PUBLISHED IN THE UNITED STATES OF AMERICA

CHAPTER 1

"For to him that is joined to all the living there is hope; for a living dog is better than a dead lion." – Ecclesiastes 9:4 (The Bible, KJV)

3:13 a.m., Monday, September 19
Mechant Loup, Louisiana

Andy Verdin stared mournfully through the darkness at the seat across from him in the pirogue. It's where T-Bill, his great-grandson, used to sit and help him haul in a mess of catfish early every morning before T-Bill had to go to school. They used to run more than a hundred jugs up and down Bayou Tail, but now that T-Bill was gone and Andy was alone, he was forced to scale back the operation to thirty jugs. Even that seemed a bit of a challenge for him these days.

At ninety-six, Andy could feel his body slowing down almost by the minute, and it scared him. As he had approached ninety, he'd had a lot of people around him mention that they were wishing to make it to that age, and how they would be satisfied to live that long, but he was not. Sure, he had lived a good, long life, but he was not ready to leave just yet. There was still so much left to be done, and in his mind he felt so young. He couldn't believe he was ninety-six. It seemed like just yesterday he had turned fifty, and that had freaked him out a little, because back then he still felt twenty.

Andy slowly worked the paddle and moved the pirogue toward the western bank of the bayou, where the old bridge used to be. The pirogue didn't slice through the water like it once did. In fact, it seemed as though he were paddling in mud. His muscles burned from the effort. How much longer would he be able to continue doing this? The thought caused that burning fear to creep back into his belly again. Sometimes, he would lay awake in bed wondering if that night would be the night he would drift off to sleep and never wake up again. That very thing had happened to many of his friends, all of whom were younger than him, so he figured it would be a matter of time before he caught up to them in the afterlife. While he felt fortunate to have escaped the grim reaper's scythe so far, he knew there was nothing special about him. He thought he was healthy enough to reach a century, but he knew there were no guarantees in life, and that was why he never subscribed to things anymore. Why pay for a year's worth of magazines when you might not live to read the first two? He didn't even read the expiration labels on food anymore, because there was a chance he might be gone before the food went bad.

Andy paused to give his arms a rest and to catch his breath. He shook his head as he remembered how easy it used to be to cross the bayou with T-Bill's help. Although only seven, T-Bill had been coming out on the water with him since he was five, and he was stronger than most teenage boys twice his age. T-Bill was Andy's first great-grandchild and the pride of his life. Andy was sure there would be many more great-grandchildren to come, and he would love them all equally, but at that moment, T-Bill was everything to him. He prayed every day that he would be able to watch T-Bill grow into a man and get married and have kids of his own. Ah, the thought of great-great-grandchildren.

He frowned, remembering that it would be hard to watch T-Bill grow up now, considering his dad had been forced to move him and his mother to Texas for work. Sure, Andy and Donna, his wife, had vowed to make as many trips out west to visit T-Bill as possible, but it wouldn't be the same. There was a hole in Andy's heart the size of the Lone Star State to which T-Bill had moved, and the emptiness he felt out here on the water was downright depressing. In recent days, he had considered giving it all up, but only for a moment. He knew the hard work was what kept him alive. If he quit moving, it would all be over...and he wasn't ready to surrender the ghost. He had too many things left to do with his life. Besides, he and Donna needed the food.

Andy finally reached the other side of the bayou and glided up beside the first milk jug in his line. It wasn't moving, but that didn't mean anything. A catfish could've gotten hooked earlier in the night and grown tired of fighting.

Andy placed the paddle beside him in the pirogue and reached for the jug. When T-Bill was with him, one of them would check the jug while the other would hold the pirogue steady, but now it was all up to him. He gave the line a gentle tug and smiled as he felt some resistance from the other end. He had one.

The glow from the new moon above illuminated the area and he was pleased to find that he had a three-pound fish on the line. With deft fingers, he removed the fish, placed it inside the small ice chest, and was about to bait the hook when he heard a noise from somewhere above him. He glanced up and cocked his head to the side.

Andy's primary language was Cajun French, and in his native tongue, he asked out loud, "What was that?"

No one answered, but he wasn't expecting a response. There was no one around. He studied the shadows along the wall of the bank, but he could detect no movements from there. The smell of dank earth clung heavy to the moist morning air, and it was a scent he knew well.

Andy went back to baiting the hook, but he heard the sound again. He stopped what he was doing. The sound had certainly come from somewhere above him. When he glanced skyward, all he saw were stars, the jagged edges of the raised bank, and creosote pilings that made up the remnants of the old bridge that used to cross the bayou in that area.

"Hello?" Andy called in French. "Anyone there?"

Suddenly, there was a flash of movement above him and something fell from the sky. It was bright and dark all at the same time, and it confused Andy. He was still trying to figure out what was going on when the object struck the front of his pirogue—right where T-Bill would have been sitting—and sent him soaring violently through the air.

Andy didn't have time to reflect on the meaning of what was happening. There was a brief moment where he was temporarily suspended in the air, and then he came crashing down. Branches and leaves whipped angrily at him like blows from an angry mob, but it didn't last long. He suddenly jolted to a halt, landing heavily on the back of his neck and shoulders. His body bent back and then something smacked him in the face. He fell again, but this time it wasn't as far of a drop. Everything went hazy as he tried to understand what had happened. His body relaxed into his new position and went limp. He tried to maintain some level of consciousness, but he felt himself slipping into a black haze.

As pain enveloped him and the moon above slowly began to fade from his view, Andy tried to get his bearings while simultaneously making a plan to extricate himself from his situation. He knew he was somewhere along the banks of Bayou Tail, but he didn't know on what side of the bayou he lay. His body was twisted into a pretzel and he could feel dull pain in his nose, jaw, and all four limbs. He thought that one or both of his legs might be broken, but he couldn't be sure, because the sharp pain in his back drowned out the other injuries and made it difficult to determine the extent of the damage.

Andy tried to move his left hand, but he realized the arm was trapped under his body, so he tried to lift his right one. As he did so, his back shifted and a wave of intense agony swept over him and his eyes rolled back in his head. He almost passed out, but somehow managed to stay somewhat alert.

Trying not to move his back again, he tilted his head from side to side to check out his surroundings. As near as he could tell, he had fallen deep into a stand of trees. The green leaves and thick branches from above would completely obscure his body from the view of anyone who might come out to search for him. Of course, he wasn't expected home until daybreak, so Donna wouldn't begin to worry for at least another hour or two afterward. He realized it was not at all impossible to think that he might remain here for at least four or five hours before help would arrive, and even if searchers found his damaged pirogue in the water, would they even think to look in the underbrush along the banks of the bayou?

He thought not, and realized that if he were to escape this, it would have to be under his own power. Only, he was powerless. He couldn't move a muscle without causing great pain in his back. There was no telling how bad he was hurt. He had lived a long time and had been involved in a number of accidents over the past nine decades, so he was pretty astute at assessing personal damage—and this one, he knew, was one of the worst.

Andy tried to shift to a more comfortable position, but quickly realized that such a position was unattainable, so he just lay there in twisted agony. He opened his mouth to holler, but even that motion brought pain so great that he nearly passed out.

Not sure what else to do, his mind wandered to all the people who had gone before him—both, young and old, known and unknown—and he reminded himself that he knew this day would come. It would come for everyone. No one could escape it and no one knew how or when it would be their time to go.

Lying there in that desperate moment, he had to acknowledge that he had been one of the luckier ones. Rarely did anyone live to reach his or her nineties. He and Donna had made a habit of late out of checking the obituaries on a daily basis to see if anyone they knew had gone on to a better life, and he had been astonished to see how many young people lost their lives on a regular basis. He'd heard that most of those deaths were a result of drug usage—apparently, there was some new and deadly drug called fentanyl that was wiping people out on a daily basis—but he still found it very sad.

Andy set his throbbing jaw. He was being selfish. He had lived five times longer than some of those poor kids. He had enjoyed a good and long life. Instead of feeling sorry for himself and wishing for more time, he decided at that moment to leave everything in God's hands. That's what Donna would have done. Never having been an overly religious man, he mumbled through a silent and awkward prayer, trying to remember some of the things he'd heard Donna say when she spoke to the Lord. He thanked God for the time he had spent on earth, and asked Him to look after everyone he was leaving behind. As he finished, he wondered if God understood Cajun French. Donna had always said her prayers in English. Was that because God only spoke English? He began to shake his head dismissively, but the sudden movement caused him to gasp in pain, so he resigned himself to lying still. He would accept whatever happened next.

Oddly, as time drew on and birds began to sing, he felt a warm sense of peace begin to spread across his body and he closed his eyes. It was the first time in years he was able to close them without feeling a rush of panic as he wondered if they would ever open again. At that moment, he was as close to death as he had ever been, and there was a real possibility he had closed his eyes for the last time, yet he didn't panic. He accepted whatever fate might befall him.

Andy exhaled a deep breath, relaxing into his tangled and twisted position amongst the unforgiving underbrush. The pain continued to attack his every fiber with the ferociousness of a relentless army trying to seize control of a coveted city, but it didn't last long. Slowly, his body began to grow numb, and his mind slipped into a merciful sea of unconsciousness.

CHAPTER 2

5:42 a.m.

Takecia Gayle was running radar on the southern end of town in the final minutes of her shift, but she wasn't having much luck. The vehicles that did drive past her location had either been warned by vehicles traveling in the opposite direction or they had found religion, because everyone seemed to be observing the speed limit on that morning.

She glanced wryly up at the sign under which she had parked her marked patrol cruiser, a police-package Chevy Tahoe. The sign read, *Mechant Life Church,* and it was brand new. The compound that now housed the new church used to be an abandoned car dealership. It had been empty as long as Takecia had been in town.

Maybe people in town are finding religion, Takecia thought. After all, this church had only sprung up in town a few months ago, and the parking lot had been completely full yesterday morning and evening for the two Sunday services.

Takecia was about to call it a night when a truck pulled into the church parking lot and drove straight for her Tahoe. Although there was nothing overtly threatening about the action, she twisted in her seat and placed one hand on her pistol and the other on her steering wheel, ready to jump into immediate action should the need arise.

A man with blonde hair and a pale face grinned at her from the driver's seat of the pickup.

"Good morning, officer," he said warmly. "I'm Father Reggie Hamilton. Would you like some coffee? My secretary will be here any minute, and she makes the best brew anywhere this side of the Mississippi."

Takecia smiled and relaxed. "Thank you, but I've got to head in for shift change. I hope you don't mind that I used your parking lot to run radar."

"Not at all." The preacher waved a dismissive hand. "I feel safer having you here." He then cocked his head to the side. "Your accent, um…you're not from here, are you?"

Takecia smiled. Her parents were Jamaican nationals, but had migrated legally to the United States nearly sixty years ago. While Takecia would turn thirty next month and the U.S. was the only country she had ever called home, she had picked up the accent from her parents.

"I am from the U.S.," she said, "but my parents are from Jamaica, and they have had a great influence on me."

"Oh, wow, I've been to Jamaica a few times," he said. "Beautiful place. How'd you find this little paradise in the swamps of southeast Louisiana?"

As a teenager, Takecia had won gold in Judo at the Pan American Games representing the United States, and she had been expected to be the first American in her weight class to take the gold in judo at the Summer Olympics. However, fate had other plans for her, because a training injury had crushed those dreams. She later went on to college, studied criminal justice, and eventually became a police officer. She had met Chief Susan Wolf at a mixed martial arts gym in New Orleans, where the two had become fast friends. Susan had offered her a job, she had accepted, and the rest was history. That had been seven wonderful years ago. While a lot had happened in town since then, every challenge had brought the officers closer and closer together, and Takecia considered them all family.

As for the man in the pickup next to her, he was a stranger, and the details of her personal life were none of his business.

"How did any of us find this place?" Takecia asked with a shrug.

The preacher was about to respond when a Jeep Wrangler turned into the parking lot, momentarily splashing its headlights across Takecia's windshield.

"Oh, there's Laurie," he said. "Are you sure you don't want a hot cup of coffee?"

Takecia shook her head. "Positive. If I drink coffee this late in the morning, I'll never get any sleep."

"Well, I'd like to extend an invitation to you and the other officers in your department to use the parking lot anytime you like," the preacher said as he reached for his gearshift. "Also, feel free to attend our services here. I think the members of the congregation would feel secure having officers of the law in the building. I preach sermons here on Sunday mornings, Sunday nights, and Wednesday nights."

Takecia thanked him and watched as he followed the Wrangler to the building.

"Father Reggie," she said with a grunt. "What kind of name is that?"

She headed out the parking lot and was still two blocks from the police department when the nighttime dispatcher, Karla McBride, contacted her on the police radio.

"Takecia, we've got an overdue fisherman," Karla explained apologetically, recognizing it was nearing shift change. "Shade called to say he'll be a little late, because he drove up on a deputy needing assistance in Chateau Parish. I would've waited until Shade got to town, but the man's ninety-six and his wife sounds really worried. I can call out Melvin if you like."

"Negative, I've got it," Takecia said, and waited for the address.

Shade Rankin was the newest member of the police department. Formerly a corrections officer with the Empyrean Parish Sheriff's Office, he had come to work for Mechant Loup ten months ago, but he still resided in Empyrean Parish and had to cross two parishes to get to work. Shade was a conscientious worker and Takecia knew he would feel bad for missing shift change—especially since they were shorthanded—but there was no way any police officer worth his or her salt could drive past an officer in trouble and not stop.

"The complainant's name is Donna Verdin," Karla called over the radio, "from 100 Bayou Tail Lane. She had a hard time hearing me, so you'll have to speak up."

Takecia confirmed that she'd received the traffic and headed for the address.

CHAPTER 3

The Verdins lived at the corner of Jezebel and Bayou Tail, and Takecia arrived within two minutes. Before she even stepped out of her Tahoe, she saw the complainant standing on the front porch of the gray house staring toward the boat launch, which was about five blocks to the east.

"Morning, Mrs. Verdin," Takecia said when she stepped out of her cruiser. She made sure to speak in a loud and clear voice so the elderly woman could hear her. "I understand your husband is late coming back from the water."

"Oh, dear, I'm afraid something bad happened," Donna said, clutching at a rosary that dangled from her fingers. The words that spilled from her mouth were a mixture of broken English and Cajun French, and Takecia had to listen carefully to understand what she was trying to convey.

"He was supposed to be back an hour ago," Mrs. Verdin continued. "I know something bad happened to him. He was complaining he was getting more tired lately, and I told him he needed to stop cat-fishing since T-Bill's not here to help him anymore, but he's hard-headed. You can't tell him nothing."

Takecia frowned as she studied the worry lines on Mrs. Verdin's face. She appeared to be in her late eighties and Mr. Verdin was ninety-six, but it was painfully evident how much this woman still loved her husband. She allowed herself to secretly wish she would find a love like that as she asked her next question.

"What's your husband's name?"

"Andrew Verdin," she said, not taking her eyes from the east.

"We call him Andy. He's ninety-six. The doctor says his heart's still strong, but he's been having trouble catching his breath lately. I'm so, so worried about him."

"What time did he leave to go on the water?" Takecia asked.

"He leaves at two o'clock every morning, and he's back at four so T-Bill can get dressed for school."

Takecia cocked her head to the side. "Who's T-Bill?"

"That's our great-grandson."

"Did T-Bill go on the water with him?" Takecia asked, confused. "You said T-Bill's not here to help him anymore, but you also said he gets back at four so T-Bill can get dressed for school."

"What?" Donna turned to look at her. "What you said?"

Takecia repeated her question, and Donna explained that T-Bill had moved with his parents to Texas, but that Andy decided to stick to that routine in case T-Bill ever moved back to town and was able to help out again.

"We hope they come back," Donna said. "We miss them so much. I wake up every morning and make Andy coffee before he leaves, and this morning he told me his chest was hurting because he missed T-Bill so much. I'm so worried about him. You gotta find him."

Not wanting to stay there longer than was necessary, Takecia asked Donna to describe what Andy was wearing, and also what type of vehicle and boat he would be occupying.

"He was wearing his pants and shirt like he always does," Donna explained. "He's in his pirogue."

"Where did he launch the pirogue?"

"What?"

"Where did he put his pirogue in the water?"

Donna pointed east toward the boat launch. "He drives his lawnmower to the boat dock and that's where he goes in the water."

"Does he pull it on a trailer?" Takecia asked.

"Oh, yeah, he connects the trailer to the lawnmower and pulls it that way," she said. "Gas is too expensive to use the car."

Takecia nodded her agreement, and then asked, "Do you know where he goes in the pirogue?"

"Yeah, he goes in the bayou."

"Where does he go from there?" Takecia pressed. "Does he head toward the lake or does he stay in the bayou?"

"I...I don't know. He never told me where he goes. He just goes catch catfish."

Takecia sighed inwardly. Without a direction, it might be next to impossible to begin looking for him. She was hoping against hope that she would find him at the boat launch and this would end quickly.

"Do you have a picture of your husband?" Takecia asked. Donna looked confused, so she explained, "It's so I can recognize him when I see him."

"Oh, yeah." Donna hurried into the house and returned with an eleven-by-fourteen frame that held a picture of a bronze-skinned man leaning against an old wooden garage with his hands in his pocket. He wore khaki pants, a long-sleeved navy blue shirt, and a straw hat. "That's the last picture I got of Andy. The kids have some that was taken closer, but that's all I got."

Takecia pulled out her cell phone and snapped a picture of Andy Verdin. His physical features favored those of another Verdin family with whom she was familiar, and they were of Chitimacha blood. If this man was kin to them, then Takecia knew he was tough and highly skilled on the water, like all Chitimacha Indians were.

"What about a cell phone?" Takecia asked. "Does he have one that we can call?"

Donna shook her head. "He doesn't know how to use them. I don't have one neither."

Takecia nodded and smiled when she handed back the portrait. "I'm sure your husband is fine," she said, trying to ease the woman's worries. "He's probably just catching a lot of fish and doesn't want to stop while they're biting."

"I don't know. I have a bad feeling about this."

"Hasn't he ever been late before?"

"One or two times, but that's it."

"Look, he's made it to ninety-six, so that means he's seen a lot and done a lot. I'm sure he can take care of himself."

"He ain't no spring chicken no more!" Mrs. Verdin scowled and shook her head in disapproval. "As much as he likes to think he is, he ain't! He should know better than to go out there by himself. I keep telling him something bad's gonna happen, but he won't listen."

Takecia touched her shoulder. "I'll let you know as soon as I find him."

"Please do, and thank you, dear." The elderly woman stood there wringing her hands. "I don't know what I'd do without him."

Takecia frowned as she walked away. Would she ever find a man about whom she would feel the same, or was it too late for her? While she didn't need a man to be happy, she surely needed one to start a family, and it would be best if she were happy with him. But where were the good men? Had they all been taken? All the good men she knew certainly were. Amy had taken Baylor off the market, Susan had taken Clint, and Claire had taken Melvin. Hell, even young Shade was taken. He had only been dating Alice Pierce for about six months now, and they looked as serious as ever at Amy and Baylor's wedding Saturday night.

Takecia fired up the Tahoe and headed toward the boat launch. She glanced at her cell phone as she drove. She'd received two text messages from the date she'd taken with her to Amy's wedding, but she hadn't responded. She had been eating alone at a restaurant a few weeks earlier when this stranger had walked to her table and struck up a conversation with her. He had seemed interesting at first and they'd exchanged numbers. She had spoken with him several times over the phone in the weeks that followed. They seemed to have a lot in common and he had made her laugh, so she'd invited him to Amy's wedding. That had been a mistake.

"Oh, shit," Takecia said when she arrived at the boat launch and saw a lawnmower with an empty boat trailer parked near a tree. "This old man might really be in trouble."

She parked near the lawnmower and looked it over. There was no evidence to suggest that Mr. Verdin had been attacked at this location, and the fact that his pirogue was gone indicated he had at least made it into the water. She turned and strode toward the boat ramp.

It was early on a Monday morning and there weren't many trucks in the parking lot, so that meant there wouldn't be many people out on the water. That didn't bode well for Mr. Verdin. If he were to run into trouble along an empty bayou, there would be no one around to witness it and call for help.

Takecia sighed as she glanced up and down the bayou. The water lapped lazily against the bulkhead along the opposite bank. All seemed quiet, except for the roaring of a truck engine approaching town from the north. She turned and headed back to her Tahoe. She would have to get a boat and come back.

Since Amy and Baylor were on their honeymoon and Susan was about to burst with a new baby, there was only her, Melvin, Regan, and Shade left to cover the town, with Clint handling all of the detective cases. Melvin would be covering the night shift for Baylor that night, so she wasn't about to bother him with this overdue boater. Although she had worked all night, she felt energetic and strong.

If she hadn't found Mr. Verdin by that evening, then Melvin

could take over the search. Of course, if that happened, Mrs. Verdin would be a nervous wreck, and she would be thinking the worst. Practically speaking, he couldn't have gone very far in a pirogue in only a few hours, so a quick search in either direction should turn him up. If she didn't find him right away, it could mean that he had wandered into one of the many canals that branched off from the bayou and simply gotten lost or lost track of time. If she found his pirogue and not him...well, she didn't even want to think about that scenario.

Takecia had just opened the door to her SUV when the truck she'd been hearing had finally reached town. She looked up as it drastically reduced speed on its approach to the Mechant Loup Bridge. She smiled. It was Shade's personal vehicle. With him in town, she could get on the water and not worry about any complaints going unanswered.

CHAPTER 4

Paradise Place, Mechant Loup

It was a little after six in the morning and I was already dressed for work. Susan had tossed and turned all night, and I'd felt bad for her. She was still a few weeks away from having our son, but it looked like she could give birth at any moment.

"I'm ready to meet our baby boy," she'd said last night before bed. "And when I do, we're gonna have a conversation about a few things."

"Like what?" I'd asked, scooting closer to her and rubbing her bare belly gently.

"First off, I'm gonna ask him why it is that he decides to start kicking me in the bladder the very moment I decide to go to bed," she said. "When I'm awake, I can't get him to move sometimes, and it scares the crap out of me, but right when I lie down to sleep, he starts throwing kicks like he's training for a cage fight."

I had laughed and said, "Come on, Baretta, give your mom a break."

Instead of arguing about the name, she had simply turned onto her side and tried to get as comfortable as possible.

Although I normally slept like the dead, I felt every move she made on the previous night and had frowned every time I'd heard her take a deep breath. I was forever awed by the sacrifices that women made to bring a baby into the world. It was the most selfless thing I had ever witnessed with my own two eyes. I often felt guilty for not being able to share in the pain and suffering that went into carrying and delivering my child. I mentioned it once to Susan, but she had only smiled, touched my face, and said, "I consider it a tremendous blessing to be able to bring a child into this world. It makes me feel lucky."

And despite having had a rough night, she was smiling when she walked down the stairs a few minutes after I'd begun preparing breakfast.

"Smells like beignets," she said with a pleasant wrinkling of her nose. "Is Gracie up yet?"

I nodded my head and moved the container of powdered sugar to the table, while trying not to get any on my shirt. "She should be getting dressed," I said. "I woke her up ten minutes ago."

"Are you bringing her to school or am I?" Susan took a seat in front of a plate that was piled high with beignets. Without waiting for my answer, she heaped a spoonful of powdered sugar onto one of the beignets and took a bite. Her eyes half closed as she savored the sweet flavor.

Grace was nearly four and a half years old—according to her, that half was important—and she had started Pre-K a month ago. There had been no adjustment period. She had transitioned smoothly from staying with my mom or Susan's mom during the day to hanging out with a dozen other kids her age, and she had loved it from the moment she stepped foot in the place.

"I'll drop her off on my way to the office," I said as I pulled another batch of beignets from the hot oil. "Why don't you take it easy today? You had a rough night."

Despite how tired she must've been, my wife smiled her lovely smile. "With Melvin covering Baylor's shift, he doesn't have time to assume my duties, so I need to keep things up-to-date until the baby's born. It'll be fine. I'll pick up Grace and come home early."

I didn't argue because it wouldn't help. Once Susan made up her mind, she usually stuck with her decision.

I finished the last of the beignets, turned off the fire, and pushed the hot pot toward the rear of the stove. Grace appeared from upstairs with a bright smile and a small backpack on her shoulders.

"I'm ready for school, Mommy," she said. "Are you bringing me today?"

I glanced at Susan, who melted in front of Grace's eyes.

"Absolutely," Susan said, pulling herself to her feet. "Come eat your breakfast while I get dressed."

Before I could object, my cell phone rang. I didn't have to look at the screen to know it was the radio room.

"What's up, Karla?" I asked.

"Hey, Clint, do you mind coming in early today?" she asked hesitantly. "Takecia's heading out on the water to look for an overdue fisherman who's ninety-six years old. I just dispatched Shade to a burglary down at Spearmonger's Dive Shop, so he won't be able to help out with the search."

"Did you say *ninety-six*?" I asked incredulously.

"Yep."

"Is he alone on the water?"

"Yep."

"Wow, good for him." I nodded in admiration. "Yeah, I'll be there in a few minutes."

"Takecia's already heading for the boat launch."

Susan had stopped at the landing to the stairs and turned to look at me. "What's going on?" she asked when I'd ended the call.

I explained all that I knew as I dialed Takecia's number. When Takecia answered, she provided even more details.

"As soon as this boat's in the water I'll be heading west toward the lake," she said after providing everything she'd learned from Mrs. Verdin. "If you can head east, that'll be great. He's in a pirogue so he couldn't have gone far, but I'm worried that if we don't find him soon it might turn out bad."

I agreed and told her I'd have a boat in the water within ten minutes.

"Are you gonna at least eat breakfast?" Susan asked.

"No time."

She nodded and met me halfway across the room for a kiss. I then quickly bent, kissed Grace on the forehead, and hurried outside to hitch my boat trailer to my Tahoe. It would be quicker to take my boat than stopping at the police department to grab one of the town's vessels and, at the moment, time seemed to be our enemy.

CHAPTER 5

Once I'd made it to the boat launch and had backed my trailer into one of the slipways, I quickly dropped from my SUV. Achilles, my one-hundred-pound German shepherd, had insisted on tagging along when I'd left the house, and he had been riding shotgun in the front seat. He hadn't learned how to open the door for himself yet, so I held my door long enough for him to jump from the passenger's side to my side and then out into the warm morning air.

I launched my boat and then secured it to one of the cleats while I parked my Tahoe. Even if there would've been a gang of thieves nearby, I would not have had to worry about it being stolen while I was halfway across the parking lot. Achilles was perched proudly on the hull of the boat, and he would've eaten anyone dumb enough to try to board it.

As promised, I was in the water within ten minutes of ending my call with Takecia. Since she had headed west, I headed east up Bayou Tail, carefully scanning the banks on either side of the bayou as I travelled along the center of the waterway. Achilles didn't understand a lot of English, but when I told him to search, he knew what I meant. His ears were high and his eyes sharp as he tested the wind with his nose. I knew he would alert me to the slightest sound, sight or scent, and I was happy to have him with me to help in the search.

We had probably gone a hundred yards when I noticed something floating on the water along the opposite bank. Unable to discern what it was, I pushed the tiller and made my way toward it. I watched Achilles as I approached. His ears were up and he was staring intently at the object. When we were within reach, I killed the engine and waited for the boat to glide up beside it.

We were close enough by then that I recognized it for what it was—an empty milk jug with an apparent length of string attached to the handle. It was used for catching catfish. Most fishermen marked their jugs in a way to be readily identified, and this jug was no different. From what I could see, this jug was yellow, and a red and blue stripe had been painted around the belly.

I plucked it from the water and saw that a white "X" had been painted across the bottom of the jug. I tested the length of string and found that there was a little weight to it, but there didn't appear to be a fish on the other end. I pulled it in and found that I was right. The hook was void of bait or fish. I wondered if this was an old jug, or if it had been lost by Mr. Verdin. It was right up against the bank, which was not the ideal spot to place the jug for cat-fishing.

According to Takecia, Mr. Verdin had been out there checking his catfish lines, and I figured he would've been checking them and then collecting them to be put out again later. Most fishermen didn't leave their jugs out on the water when they weren't fishing, and the information Takecia received was that he fished at night. I wasn't sure if this jug was connected to the case or not, but I didn't believe in coincidences, so I pulled out my cell phone and called Takecia. As the call rang, I hoped she was still within range of the nearest cell tower. She was.

When she answered, I told her what I'd found, and I asked if she knew if Mr. Verdin's jugs had any identifying marks on them.

"I didn't even think to ask his wife," she admitted. "To be honest, I thought I'd get to the boat launch and find him picking up his pirogue, or I would find him on the water in his pirogue. I never thought I'd have to identify his catfish jugs."

That was a fair answer. I described the marks on the jug I'd found—just in case she found a similar one—and told her I'd call if I found anything more.

"Do you want me to call his wife and ask her about the jugs?" she offered.

I thought about it for a second, and then told her no. Even if Mrs. Verdin could identify the jug, it wouldn't help at this point to ask. The only thing we'd accomplish was increasing her anxiety, and I didn't want to cause her more distress than was absolutely necessary. As it stood now, we might have to deliver to her the worst kind of news she would ever hear, so I wanted to keep the torture to a minimum.

"We need to find this man alive," I said softly to Achilles after ending the call with Takecia. "For the sake of his poor wife, we need to find him alive."

We continued our slow trek to the east, but we didn't find any more catfish jugs by the time we'd reached the bend in the bayou, where it continued to the south while another section flowed to the north. I figured Mr. Verdin would be heading deeper into the swamps, rather than farther to the north, so I decided to head south. I was just rounding the bend in the bayou when I noticed something in the water that turned the blood in my veins to ice.

"Shit, Achilles," I said in a low voice to my dog, "this ain't good. It ain't good at all."

Sensing that something was very wrong, Achilles let out a low whimper and edged closer to me, as though trying to decide what he was supposed to do about my problem. I dropped a hand to his head and rubbed his ears. "It's okay, boy."

I steered the boat in the direction of the raised bank, trying not to disturb anything. Over a dozen pieces of splintered wood and other debris floated on the water. Some items had drifted toward the bank near the bend in the bayou and were dancing on the waves that my boat had made, while some of the lighter pieces had been carried farther down the channel.

I had helped my grandpa build a couple of pirogues when I was a kid, and I'd spent lots of time in them over the years, so I was able to easily recognize the pieces of wood scattered on the water as the wreckage from a pirogue. I wasn't positive what had happened out there, but something had torn the small wooden boat apart at the seams. Both sides had been ripped from the bottom, and the cypress boards that had made up the ribs were floating around me. It appeared that two wooden chairs had been built onto the pirogue. One remained attached to the bottom of the boat, which was made up of plywood and was partially underwater, while the other chair had split apart. Portions of the second chair were dangling from either side of the pirogue.

I frowned. Cajuns in southeast Louisiana made their own pirogues, so, while they were all similar in construction, they were also unique. I wasn't familiar with Andy Verdin's craftsmanship, but unless there were two men lost in their pirogues, I was fairly certain I'd narrowed down our search. My only hope was that he hadn't been sitting in the front seat. The damage that had occurred to his pirogue had occurred toward the front, and if someone had been sitting in that chair, they were definitely dead.

CHAPTER 6

After a careful and thorough scan of the surface of the water and the edge of the banks all around me, I shut off my motor and listened. Although I felt foolish doing so, I called out Mr. Verdin's name. Had he survived the damage to his pirogue—which had likely been caused by a motor boat speeding through here—he would've tried to get my attention when I first arrived in the location. I hollered his name again for good measure, but the only sound I heard was that of my own voice reverberating across the water.

I sighed and settled into my seat to call Takecia.

"You can start heading this way," I said. "I found the remnants of a pirogue."

"What?" I heard her engine die. "What'd you say?"

"I found a pirogue destroyed on the water. It's gotta be Mr. Verdin's pirogue, unless we have another missing man out here." I took a breath and glanced at the wreckage. "The rear seat on the pirogue is still attached to the bottom, but the sides have been blown off. The front of the boat took some heavy damage. It looks like a speed boat drove right through it. If you ask me, Mr. Verdin never knew what hit him."

"Oh, no." I could hear the despair in Takecia's voice. "I promised Mrs. Verdin that I would find him."

"Well, you most likely will, but he might be in pieces," I mumbled idly, searching for blood among the remnants of the pirogue. I didn't see any, but that didn't mean there hadn't been any. The water that had poured over the broken boards would've washed away any blood that might have been there. We could use luminol later to determine if the presence of blood had been there at some point, but it would do us no good at that very moment.

"I'm pretty sure I promised to find him alive." Takecia was silent for a long moment. "Do you see a life vest?"

I twisted around in my seat and searched through the debris. There were at least a dozen empty milk jugs scattered around on the water, and they were all painted similarly to the one I had found earlier. A seat pad had drifted across the bayou, as had a small Styrofoam ice chest. I turned in the opposite direction, and that's when I saw it. My shoulders drooped.

"Yep, I see a life vest, but he's not in it." It was too far for me to reach, so I decided to get it later. I tried to penetrate the depths of the water around me, but it was impossible. Louisiana bayous were dark green to black and, with only a few exceptions, it was almost impossible to see even several inches under the water.

"Can you tell how fresh the wreckage is?" she asked. "What if he just got hit? Maybe he can still survive. Maybe we can jump in and rescue him."

"I've been in this area for a few minutes now," I explained. "Even if he went under right before I got here, it would be too late for him. He would've been under for too long. Besides, you know it would be impossible to locate his body without knowing exactly where he went down. Even then, this current is pretty swift, so he could've been dragged away from this spot."

"Is it possible he swam away from the wreckage?" Her voice betrayed the dread she felt, and I detected a hint of desperation. "This man spent his whole life on the water. I'm sure he can swim like a muskrat. Maybe he crawled up the bank somewhere and he's walking home right now."

I scanned the shoreline around me. I saw nothing even resembling a human along the water's edge. The banks were raised in that area and I couldn't see what was above us, but it didn't appear that anyone had clawed their way through the mud to gain the high ground. I turned to Achilles. He was testing the wind with his nose, but he was also coming up empty.

"It looks like his pirogue was struck right where the bayou curves to the west," I explained. "It's the farthest point from any of the banks. With that kind of collision, there's a good chance he was unconscious or even dead when he hit the water. Even if he wasn't unconscious or dead, he was probably too banged up to swim very far. This was a violent crash. It demolished the pirogue."

Takecia was silent on the other end of the phone. Finally, she let out a curse. "I don't want to have to tell Mrs. Verdin that her husband is gone. It's going to kill her."

"I'll do it," I offered.

"No, it's mine to do." She took a breath. "But I'm not telling her anything until we find him or his body. I still think there's a chance he survived."

I scowled and surveyed my surroundings again. From what the old timers had told me over the years, the very spot where his pirogue had been hit was where the old Main Street Bridge used to connect Mechant Loup to the rest of the world, and it was reportedly the deepest part of Bayou Tail. If Mr. Verdin's body was down there, we would need divers to recover him.

Over my cell phone, I heard Takecia's boat engine fire up.

"And if he is dead," she said with a growl, "God help the person who did this to him."

Takecia ended the call and left me to wonder what might have happened and who might have crashed through Mr. Verdin's pirogue. While the crash might have initially been an accident, the moment the operator of the boat had driven away from the crash site, he or she had committed a crime. We were no longer working an overdue boater. At a minimum, we were working a hit and run, and possibly even a negligent injuring or homicide case.

Although I was pretty certain Mr. Verdin had been lost in the crash, I decided to conduct a thorough search of all the banks of the bayou just in case he had miraculously made his way out of the bayou. I began by heading toward the eastern bank of the bayou and working my way to the north along the shoreline. I hadn't travelled a hundred feet when I heard Takecia's boat approaching from the west. I turned and gave her a wave when she drew nearer.

I could see that her jaw was set, and the muscles of her dark arms rippled as she gripped the steering wheel. She shut off her motor when she reached the crash site and then sat there staring over the wreckage for a long moment. Finally, she turned in my direction. Achilles and I were only ten yards away, but she spoke so quietly that it was hard to hear her.

"Someone's gonna pay for this, Clint," she said through gritted teeth. "Whoever did this *had* to know they hit another boat. They intentionally fled the area and left him here to die."

I nodded my agreement, but didn't say anything while she visually examined our surroundings.

"There are no witnesses out here," she finally said. "No cameras on the water. No fingerprints or DNA left behind. How on earth will we get down to the bottom of this?"

That was a great question. Outside of finding Mr. Verdin alive and having him identify the person or persons who hit him, I could think of only one other option.

"I know of at least one person who has cameras facing the boat launch," I explained. "I'll pull them and see who came and went while Mr. Verdin was out here. We're so close to the launch that they must've come and gone from there. Whoever they are, we'll catch them and they'll pay for what happened here—this, I promise you."

"Okay." She shot a thumb over her shoulder to indicate the western shore. "I'll start searching that side."

I nodded and turned back to my work. We kept our engines off and maneuvered our way along our respective banks using long push-poles so we could hear if Mr. Verdin called out for help. There was a light breeze blowing in from the south, and it helped to push us along our way.

Once we'd travelled a quarter of a mile, I decided to turn around and head back to the crash site and beyond, just in case our victim had headed in that direction. I glanced over at Takecia, and saw that she was also turning around.

The wind was in our faces now, and the breeze felt nice. Achilles was perched on the bow, his ears straight up and his nose turned to the sky. I'd told him we were searching for Mr. Andy Verdin, but I wasn't sure he understood me. He definitely knew we were searching for something, and he was doing his part to find whomever or whatever he thought it was.

I grew more and more worried the closer we got to the crash site. The longer it took for us to find Mr. Verdin, the better the odds were that he would be dead when we reached him—that is, if he had survived the crash and made it to shore. The longer we searched, the more I thought he had died in the initial crash. I was about to holler over to Takecia and let her know I was calling out some divers from the sheriff's office when Achilles' head snapped around.

"What is it, boy?" I asked, following his gaze. He was looking toward the opposite bank, near where Takecia was approaching.

"Takecia," I said, dragging my boat to a halt with my push-pole, "Achilles sees something near you."

Takecia lifted her head and scanned the bank directly to her right. I was searching the area, too, trying to penetrate the foliage with my eyes, but I saw nothing that would indicate a person had been through there.

Achilles barked and stood to his feet, still staring at the same area. I adjusted my gaze a little to the left and squinted. Before I could say anything, Takecia spoke up.

"I think I smell smoke," she said.

"I see it." I pointed toward where I saw a thin layer of smoke rising up through the underbrush. "It's over there."

It was an odd place for a fire, and I knew it had to be related to our search somehow, so I cranked up my engine and crossed the bayou in a hurry. Takecia had already pushed her boat up to the bank and was climbing out when Achilles and I reached her.

Achilles bounded from the boat and dashed through the shallow water after Takecia. He overtook her and disappeared into the heavy underbrush, but Takecia was hot on his heels.

I was delayed for a second as I secured my line to a nearby tree. Before I could join in on the hunt, Achilles let out an excited bark. Takecia's voice sounded almost immediately afterward, but there was nothing excited about her tone.

"Clint, call for an ambulance!" she hollered. "And hurry!"

CHAPTER 7

I immediately pulled out my cell phone and called dispatch to request an ambulance. Lindsey Savoie, our daytime dispatcher, had recently gotten on duty and she jumped into immediate action. Even as I was ending the call I could hear her on the phone with the ambulance service. I then rushed toward the sound of Takecia's voice. She was speaking in a low and comforting tone, and I thought that was a good sign. She wasn't prone to talking to dead people, so it must mean Mr. Verdin was still on our side of the grave. Thinking of the way Takecia had described Mrs. Verdin, I said a silent prayer that her husband would remain with us.

Although Takecia didn't sound very far from me, I had to push through a dense wall of blackberry bushes and a thick growth of saplings. After some effort, I broke through to the other side and found myself standing over the twisted body of an elderly man. His eyelids fluttered for a brief moment when Takecia repeated his name, but then they slid shut. The smell of smoke was heavy in that location and I glanced around for the source.

I whistled softly when I noticed a cigarette lighter dangling from the man's right hand. A disorganized pile of smoldering leaves was situated on the ground near his hand. The sleeve of his shirt was also burnt, and even his hand appeared to have been touched by the flame. I glanced at the pocket on his pants and saw that it was turned inside out. Apparently, he had removed his lighter and started a fire to get our attention—and he had done so at the risk of burning himself up.

"That was a smart move on his part," I said in a low voice to

Takecia. "I just hope it wasn't for nothing."

"Me, too." Takecia put two fingers to Mr. Verdin's neck and then sighed. "His pulse is weak. I guess that's to be expected for someone his age and in this condition."

I couldn't tell what all was wrong with Mr. Verdin, but his body was twisted around the branches like a pretzel. I studied the ground around him carefully, but couldn't find a single shred of evidence that would suggest he had crawled or walked into that location. Not a boot print, not a rub mark on the ground, not a snapped twig—nothing.

"How in the hell did he get here?" I asked.

Takecia only shrugged. She didn't take her eyes off of the elderly man as she continued speaking softly to him. I saw that she was gently rubbing his shoulder as she spoke to him. Every now and then, his eyelids would flutter, and I knew he heard her.

Still confused about how he had gotten there, I told Takecia I would head back to the boat launch to meet the ambulance, and I called for Achilles to follow me. He hesitated, apparently not wanting to leave the man's side, but he did. We hurried back through the underbrush and jumped into my boat. As I backed away from the bank, I estimated the distance from the crash site to where we had found Mr. Verdin. It had to be at least fifty feet.

"Damn, boy," I said to Achilles, "that must've been one hell of a crash."

I'd worked more than a few boating accidents, and we'd oftentimes recovered bodies great distances from where the crashes had occurred, so I knew it wasn't impossible to think that Mr. Verdin had been launched through the air upon impact. However, what seemed surprising to me was that he had been launched up and over the underbrush and young trees, rather than directly through them. If he survived this ordeal, this fact would prove fortunate for him.

Had his body been propelled from the pirogue and directly through the trees and underbrush, he would've slammed into multiple trees and the force of those impacts would've probably killed him instantly. Although he had been launched high into the air, the many branches and thick leaves through which he had descended had helped to break his fall, and thus saved his life. Had he landed on solid ground, the impact from the fall might have killed him. He was lucky on a number of fronts, and I was happy for him. I just hoped he was strong enough to make it to the hospital, where he would receive excellent care.

I could hear the ambulance sirens even before Achilles and I reached the boat landing, but they weren't in sight yet, so I hurried to my Tahoe and grabbed my crime scene kit. I had just returned to my boat when they raced up the street. Once the ambulance was parked near the slipway, the medics—a young woman and a middle-aged man—scrambled out of the vehicle and gathered up their gear. The man ran up carrying a large bag and the woman followed closely behind him with a spine board. The man's feet dug into the shells as he stopped in his tracks before jumping onto the wooden dock.

"Um…does he bite?" he asked, indicating Achilles with a nervous nod of his head.

"He won't hurt you," I said, and quickly waved him forward. "We've got to hurry."

The young woman wasn't bothered by Achilles' presence and had vaulted past the man and claimed a seat beside me, the spine board resting across the bench seats.

"I've got a white German shepherd," she said once they were both onboard and I was backing away from the dock. "I call her Siberia, because it's always snowing there."

"Cool name," I muttered, and then began to fill them in on what we knew so far about Mr. Verdin and his injuries. From what I had been able to tell in my earlier assessment of his condition, at least a few bones in his legs and arms were broken, possibly even some ribs. His torso was twisted into an odd angle, and I told them it was possible his back had also been injured.

"Is he alert?" the woman asked.

"He was for a brief moment, but then he passed out," I explained. "I think he's going in and out of consciousness."

"Was he able to move his limbs?"

I nodded and told them how he had used his right hand to set fire to the leaves beside him in order to send us a smoke signal. "It looked like the fire burned itself out, but not before causing some minor burns to his flesh."

"He's lucky he didn't start a forest fire and burn himself up," she said in exasperation.

I nodded and began describing the terrain and position in which we'd found Mr. Verdin. I had barely finished by the time we reached Takecia's boat. I grabbed my camera and waited while they offloaded their equipment. I then told Achilles to guard the boat while I led them to Takecia.

I snapped a few photographs of the area while they assessed Mr. Verdin's condition, and then I asked if they needed me.

Takecia shook her head. "I'll get them back to the launch and follow them to the hospital."

"Are you sure?" I asked, cocking my head to the side. It was well past knockoff time for her.

"I'm seeing this through to the end," she said with her jaw set. I knew better than to argue.

Once I'd returned to my boat, I headed back to the crash site and shut off the engine. I took some photos of the overall scene, and then began focusing on smaller details. While I knew I couldn't recover every piece of the wreckage at that moment, I did go about collecting the pieces that might later tell a story. There was a crack on one of the side boards, a gouge on the rub rail, a black mark on one of the end blocks, some rust marks on the front chair, and a break where the bottom had been ripped away. I retrieved a few of the other larger sections of the small vessel, hoping to piece them together later if necessary.

As I surveyed what I had found, I couldn't make sense out of what had happened, mainly because I had no idea which direction he was facing. Whatever had taken place appeared to have occurred to the front of the pirogue. If I could find out in which direction he was travelling, I might be able to figure out the direction from which the vessel had come that had hit him, and perhaps where it had headed after the crash.

Before leaving the area and heading back to the boat landing, I gave one last look around, hoping to find a piece of debris that would have come from the other vessel, but I had no such luck. That puzzled me, because I'd always been able to find some evidence of both vessels involved in the crash. To my way of thinking, it could only mean one thing—the vessel that had hit the pirogue was so big that it wasn't fazed by the impact.

"Let's go, boy," I said to Achilles. "Time to pull some tape."

CHAPTER 8

My mind was racing on the ride to the boat launch, trying hard to figure out what could have happened to Mr. Verdin. I hadn't seen a single boat on the water all morning and, while it didn't mean there hadn't been any earlier, it sure would be difficult to identify any witnesses. Thanks to the condition Mr. Verdin was in, he wouldn't be talking anytime soon, so he was of no help. Hell, even if he could talk, there was a good chance he hadn't known what hit him, but he might be able to identify others who were on the water during the night.

Absent any witnesses coming forward or information directly from Mr. Verdin, I was left with only one option—I needed to check the footage from the only surveillance system in the area that was facing Bayou Tail, and it belonged to Mr. Sam Beard.

I made quick work of pulling my boat onto the trailer and driving across the parking lot, where I parked across the street from Sam's house. With luck, I would be able to use his equipment to identify a suspect vessel, which needed to happen as quickly as possible. If nothing else, maybe I could identify other boaters who had launched during the night or the early morning hours, and they might be able to point me in the right direction. Sam's surveillance cameras had helped on more than one investigation, and I was hoping they would come through for me once more.

Within minutes, I was standing on the steps of Sam Beard's house. I'd left Achilles in the Tahoe with the windows down, a bowl of water on the floorboard, and the engine running. My dog had a reputation around town, so no one with bad intentions would even attempt to approach my vehicle with him inside. He was tolerant of children and friendly folks, but he was a terror when it came to criminals and evil people. Somehow, he could distinguish between the two.

Even before I'd reached the steps, I could smell fried bacon wafting through the cracks in the windows. It was a pretty day out, and Sam and his wife had opened up the house to allow some fresh air in. Now that I was on the steps, I could hear the bacon frying in the pan.

"I'm coming," Sam called when I knocked.

I waited patiently. When the door opened, he smiled and extended a hand.

"Detective Wolf, how the hell are you?"

"You know it's Clint," I said, shaking his hand. "And you probably already know why I'm here."

He shot a glance toward the boat launch and saw the ambulance waiting. "Trouble on the water?"

"Yeah, we had a collision," I explained briefly. "It looks like a large boat ran over a pirogue. I need to see who launched here yesterday and into this morning."

Sam grabbed his beard near the chin and pulled his hand downward along its length, nodding as he did so. "You know you're always free to access my cameras," he said, "but I don't know how much luck you'll have this time. I don't remember hearing much traffic out here last night or this morning. Things have been quiet."

I nodded and followed him through the house. His wife was moving around in the kitchen, but she took the time to look up and smile a greeting. There were three fires going on the stove at the same time, and each pot or pan was sizzling with mouth-watering greatness.

"Would you like some breakfast when it's done?" Sam asked as he pointed to the small office on the right side of the hallway. "Have your way with the system and I can bring you a plate."

I hesitated, but only briefly. I'd turned this nice couple down in the past and it seemed to have hurt their feelings. In Cajun country, it was almost viewed as an insult to refuse to break bread with a fellow human.

"Sure," I said with a nod. "I would appreciate it very much. And would you have a few pieces of bacon to spare for Achilles?"

Even through his thick beard, I could see Sam's face beam. "Absolutely!"

When he walked off, I quickly took my seat and began perusing the video files on his surveillance system. I began with the previous evening and searched until I found Mr. Verdin approaching the boat launch on his riding lawnmower.

I couldn't help but smile as I watched his mower putter down the road pulling a boat trailer with a pirogue strapped to it. He sat straight and proud in the seat, and it was at that moment that I realized this man would survive. I could see it in the way he carried himself. Despite his advanced age, he had the heart of a lion. In his younger days, I was positive he would've thrown the pirogue on his back and carried it to the boat launch, or swam through the bayou to check his catfish lines.

I watched as Mr. Verdin backed his lawnmower into the first slip and released his pirogue. He tied it to one of the cleats attached to the dock, parked his lawnmower in the shell lot, and then strolled back to the water. With the deftness built of a million repetitions, he mounted the pirogue with the soft touch of a panther creeping across the forest floor, and he was soon gliding on the water. He turned his pirogue east and disappeared from view on Bayou Tail.

"Here ya go," Sam called from the doorway.

I turned and saw that he was holding a plate topped with eggs, bacon, grits, and two slices of buttered toast. I gratefully accepted it and thanked him. He also handed me a plastic baggie filled with bacon.

"This is for Achilles."

I thanked him again and began wolfing down the food as I continued searching through the surveillance footage. It was easy to see cars coming and going from the boat launch, so I was playing the footage at top speed. Every time a set of headlights would whizz by, I'd stop, back up the footage, and watch it in normal speed. Each time I did, it turned out to be nothing worth noting.

From the time Andy Verdin had appeared on his lawnmower to the time Takecia had arrived at the launch, not a single car had turned into the parking lot. I backed to the footage that was recorded an hour before Mr. Verdin had appeared in view, but still got nothing. I didn't even detect a boat passing by on the water in all of that time.

I was finishing up my breakfast and winding down my search when Sam reappeared in the doorway to the small office.

"Any luck?" he asked.

I frowned and shook my head. "You were right. It was quiet out there last night and into this morning."

I copied the footage of Mr. Verdin arriving on his lawnmower to a flash drive and shoved it in my pocket. I handed Sam the empty plate and thanked him again.

"I had to leave home without breakfast," I explained, "so this was a Godsend."

"You're welcome here anytime," he said warmly. "I think you know that."

I waved goodbye to Sam's wife, Heidi, and made my way back to my Tahoe. It had taken about thirty minutes to search through the footage, and it was just then that Takecia was returning to the boat launch with Mr. Verdin and the two medics. I plucked a few pieces of bacon from the baggie that Sam had given me and handed them to Achilles, as I steered my vehicle across the street.

Takecia was pouring sweat and her dark arms glistened in the sunlight.

"How is he?" I grabbed a corner of the spine board and helped them carry Mr. Verdin to the ambulance. His neck was wrapped in a cervical collar and his eyes were closed.

"He's in a lot of pain, but his vitals are good," the female medic answered. "He's a tough one, that's for sure."

I sighed in relief.

Once Mr. Verdin was in the back of the ambulance, I turned to Takecia.

"Are you following them?" I asked.

"Yeah, but first I'll return the boat to the office and then I'm going get Mrs. Verdin," she said. "She needs to be with her husband. What about you?"

I looked up and down the street, running through my options. I didn't have many. "After I bring my boat home, I guess I'll check the residences and businesses along the bayou and see if any of them have surveillance cameras facing the water. Our suspect didn't pass by the launch, so they must've headed south toward the coast or north into Chateau Parish."

"Good luck with that," she said.

"Yeah, I'll need it." I gave a solemn nod. "Call me when Mr. Verdin's alert enough to talk."

She nodded and we both hurried off to our vehicles.

CHAPTER 9

The Verdin Residence

Mrs. Verdin was sitting on the porch swing looking to the north when Takecia pulled into her driveway. The elderly woman seemed paralyzed with fear, because she didn't move. She simply sat there clutching at a quilt that rested across her lap.

Takecia quickly smiled and stepped out of her Tahoe, and she noticed Mrs. Verdin take a huge breath and exhale it forcefully.

"You found him?" she asked, standing shakily to her feet.

"Yes, ma'am—"

Before Takecia could say another word, Mrs. Verdin threw herself against her and squeezed for all she was worth. Takecia smiled and returned the hug. While she was happy for Mrs. Verdin, she also felt a tinge of sadness. Would she ever find someone to love her as this woman loved her husband? She was fine with being alone. She didn't need to be in a relationship to be happy, but she did want to start a family some day. Her mom and dad were always asking when she would make them grandparents and, each time they did, she felt more and more pressure to find a suitable mate and tie the knot. Her mom had recently pointed out that Susan was already on her second child while Takecia hadn't even gotten married yet. To that, she had responded, "All the good men are taken, so sue me." Her mom had sensed her frustration and dropped the topic. In fact, she hadn't brought it up since then, but Takecia knew she was constantly thinking about it.

Mrs. Verdin pulled away from Takecia and wiped tears from her eyes. "Where is he? Is he bringing back his lawnmower?"

"Well, there's been an accident." Takecia held Mrs. Verdin by the shoulders to steady her. "Your husband's going to make it, but he did get hurt."

"He got hurt?" A scowl played across Mrs. Verdin's face. "What happened? Where he's at?"

"He's on his way to the hospital," Takecia said soothingly. "They're gonna take good care of him. He probably broke a few bones and he's got some bruises, but they'll fix him up."

"That Andy's always getting into trouble." Mrs. Verdin shook her head disapprovingly. "I keep telling him to stay away from the water, but he won't listen. He's hard-headed!"

Takecia smiled. "Look, why don't you grab your purse and come with me? I'll take you to the hospital and we can wait for the doctors to see him. They might need information from you about his health and what medicines he's taking."

"Oh, don't you worry, I got that." Mrs. Verdin hurried into the house and returned a few minutes later carrying a large red purse and a giant Ziploc bag full of prescription bottles. "Okay, I'm ready."

Takecia helped her to the Tahoe, made sure her seatbelt was fastened correctly, and then she sped out of the driveway.

Although she had lost some time at the Verdin residence, she caught up to the ambulance within ten minutes.

"Where we going?" Mrs. Verdin asked.

"Chateau General."

"Oh, I like that hospital." She nodded her head for emphasis. "Last time he hurt himself, they tried to take him to New Orleans."

"What happened?"

"He was setting his traps and one of them closed on his hand." Mrs. Verdin slid her left index finger across the back of her right hand. "It broke all these bones. He couldn't work for a week."

"Wait a minute," Takecia began. "He broke his entire hand and was back to work in a *week*?"

"Mai, he had to trap or we wouldn't get money for food." Mrs. Verdin looked at Takecia as though that should've been understood. "He didn't have time to sit at home and watch the stories. He had to set them traps so he could catch something."

Takecia shook her head in awe. The more she heard about the man, the more she felt comfortable that he would survive and recover.

It took another ten minutes to reach the hospital, and the fact that the ambulance was driving at a modest speed made Takecia feel better. Had they been running lights and siren, it would've spelled trouble for the ninety-something-year-old.

When they reached the hospital, Takecia parked near the main entrance, while the ambulance went around to the ramp that was reserved for them. She helped Mrs. Verdin out of the Tahoe and then ushered her through the sliding doors and into the waiting area of the emergency room. That's when her world stopped.

Takecia had just helped Mrs. Verdin into a chair when she heard a man in a deep Jamaican accent ask, "Is that my World War II veteran coming in now?"

She turned and caught her breath when she saw the owner of that voice. He was dark and handsome and wearing a flowing, white coat, and the name on his lapel read, *Evans*. Her gaze immediately dropped to the left hand that was cradling a patient's file, and she saw that the left ring finger was empty.

"Yes, Dr. Evans," she said, "that's Mr. Andy Verdin that they're bringing in now."

The doctor looked up and she saw his eyes widen a bit. His lips moved as though he was trying to speak, but no words came out. His Adam's apple swam up and down as he swallowed hard and cleared his throat.

"Takecia Gayle, is that you?"

Takecia smiled. "Do you still eat worms?"

Bruce Evans moved closer to Takecia, and it felt to her like the rest of the room melted away. She hadn't seen Bruce since she was a little girl and their parents had rented neighboring cottages off the beaches of south Florida. Both couples had migrated to the United States from Jamaica and, although they'd moved to separate parts of the country, had always kept in touch via the postal service. Takecia had only ever met the Evans that one summer, but she had been immediately smitten by their son, who happened to be the same age as she.

"I quit eating worms when I went to medical school." Bruce flashed a wide smile as he looked Takecia up and down. "I'm not surprised you're a police officer. You do have a strong right cross."

She felt her face flush. Bruce had tried to kiss her that summer, but—too embarrassed to admit she had never kissed a boy before— she had instead punched him in the jaw and dropped him to his knees.

"About that," she said, "I guess I owe you a dinner. If you're not busy this weekend…"

"I'd love to," he said without hesitation, reaching into his coat pocket. "Here's my card."

Takecia took it and put it in her shirt pocket, right over her left breast. She was about to ask him how long he had been in Chateau, when a nurse called out that the patient was being wheeled in. He turned and hurried after the gurney that was being pushed through the double doors leading to the emergency rooms.

"Dear Lord," Mrs. Verdin said, standing beside Takecia and rubbing her neck, "he looked so pale."

Takecia snapped back to the present and put an arm over Mrs. Verdin's shoulder. "He's a very strong man. He'll be fine."

She guided Mrs. Verdin back to her chair and sat beside her.

"Was your husband in World War II?" she asked.

"Him and three of his brothers," Mrs. Verdin said with a nod, "but his brothers didn't make it back. The family never knew what happened to them."

Takecia frowned. She had heard many stories over her years in Mechant Loup from some of the veterans who lived in the area. Some of the stories were horrific, some were humorous, and many were inspirational. Sadly, most of the WWII veterans she had met just a few years ago had already died, and there seemed to only be a small handful of them left in town.

After they had been waiting in the lobby for about twenty minutes, the medics returned with their gurney, and Takecia approached them to ask about Mr. Verdin's status.

"He's in there talking," the young woman medic said, "but we can't understand a word he's saying. I think he's speaking French, but I can't be sure. I took French for four years in high school and two years in college, and I can only understand every third or fourth word he's saying."

Takecia nodded and returned to where Mrs. Verdin sat waiting patiently to see her husband.

"Mrs. Verdin, can you act as a translator for your husband?"

There was a puzzled expression on the elderly woman's face. "What's that?"

"If I ask you a question in English, can you ask it to your husband in French, and then tell me what he says?"

"I'm not good at that," she said with a shake of her head. "You would have to talk to my granddaughter. She usually helps Andy with his paperwork or when he has to talk to his doctors on the phone."

"What's your granddaughter's name?"

"Gretchen."

"Gretchen Verdin?" Takecia asked in surprise. "Sergeant Gretchen Verdin of the Chateau Parish Sheriff's Office?"

Mrs. Verdin nodded her head. "She has a cop dog."

Takecia didn't waste a second. First, she called Clint and told him that Mr. Verdin was trying to talk.

"What'd he say?"

"I didn't speak with him yet," she said. "The medics said he was speaking French, but they couldn't understand him. I'm about to call in an interpreter and you'll never guess who it is."

"Gretchen Verdin."

Takecia gasped. "How did you know that?"

"I just got off the phone with the sheriff," he explained. "He called to ask if we had an Andy Verdin missing. He said his chief deputy had gotten word about it and they wanted to pull Gretchen in privately and let her know what was happening before it became common knowledge throughout the department."

Takecia nodded to herself. Gretchen was one of the best K-9 handlers in the state of Louisiana, and possibly even the country, and she was well respected amongst her peers. If anyone got word that a Verdin was in trouble, they might've automatically assumed she was related and told her.

"Well, they can tell her that Mr. Verdin's fine for now and that we need her to interpret his statement for us," Takecia said, glancing toward the lobby to make sure Mrs. Verdin hadn't wandered off. She hadn't.

"Why don't you call her?" Clint suggested. "She'll be happy to hear the news from you."

"Okay, are you heading this way?"

"Yep, I'll be there in fifteen."

"Oh, and Clint…"

"Yeah?"

"I just found my husband."

Before he could utter a word, Takecia ended the call. She smiled as she scrolled through her contacts to find Gretchen's number. She couldn't remember being this excited about a man in a long time.

CHAPTER 10

Chateau General Hospital

When I arrived at the hospital, I parked my Tahoe next to Takecia's and made my way quickly toward the lobby that was connected to the emergency room. After getting the call from Takecia that Mr. Verdin was alert, I had shut down my search for more surveillance cameras, brought Achilles home, and then headed straight to the hospital. I hadn't had any luck with the cameras anyway, and I was hoping he could give us something useful from which to launch our investigation. As of that moment, we couldn't even put out a BOLO on the suspect's vessel.

Upon entering the lobby, I immediately spotted Takecia in a corner sitting with an elderly woman whom I guessed was Mrs. Verdin. I wanted to pull Takecia aside and ask about the husband comment she'd made right before ending the call, but I knew it had to wait.

I held out my hand and introduced myself to Mrs. Verdin.

"You got a good sheriff right here," Mrs. Verdin said, patting Takecia on the shoulder. "She found my Andy and brought him back home, just like she promised."

I smiled. Many of the older Cajuns referred to anyone in police uniform as a *sheriff*, even though we worked for a police department, not a sheriff's office, and the patrol officers for the sheriff's office were deputies, not the sheriff. But I didn't care what they called me. I had grown fond of the custom, because every person who spoke the term did so with the utmost respect. I only wished that custom and sentiment would trickle down to the next generation.

"Takecia's one of the best we have," I said in agreement, and settled in beside them to wait. Gretchen arrived twenty minutes later, and she joined us in the lobby to anxiously wait to see her grandfather. Mrs. Verdin talked on and on about her husband, and I enjoyed listening to all of the stories.

After nearly two hours of waiting, I heard some bustling from the nurse's station and turned to see a man in a white coat approaching the waiting room. I knew immediately that something was going on between the good doctor and Takecia, because he was obviously walking on air and his eyes were focused like lasers on Takecia, when they should've been focused on Mrs. Verdin.

"Hello, Doctor," I said, stepping forward and breaking through his fog of love. "I'm Clint Wolf."

He lurched to a stop and adjusted his gaze. He glanced down at the badge on my belt and stuck out his hand.

"I'm Dr. Bruce Evans," he said in a thick Jamaican accent. "I've been caring for Mr. Verdin, and I'm pleased to report that he's alert and wanting to talk."

I let out a feigned gasp upon hearing his accent and turned to Takecia. "Take Away, you never told me you had a brother!"

Takecia pursed her lips in embarrassment, but I saw the makings of a smile tugging at the corners of her mouth.

"He's an old friend," she muttered, and helped Mrs. Verdin to her feet. "Doc, is it okay if we all go in with her? Detective Wolf has some questions for Mr. Verdin."

Dr. Evans nodded. As we walked past him, he leaned toward Takecia and I overheard him say, "Please don't call me that. It sounds weird coming from you."

I'd never heard Takecia giggle before, and I wasn't positive she had done it just then, but I would've put money on it.

"What's going on?" Gretchen whispered to me. "Is Takecia dating that doctor?"

"I don't know if she is," I said in a low voice, "but I can tell she wants to."

CHAPTER 11

We followed Dr. Evans down a long corridor until he stopped near one of the rooms and stepped aside to allow us through the door. When we walked inside, Mrs. Verdin instantly broke down at the sight of her husband lying in the hospital bed with both arms and one leg wrapped in casts. There was a large bandage on his right hand, and I knew that was from the injury he'd sustained while making the fire to attract our attention. He no longer wore the neck brace, and I took that as a good sign.

Takecia and I stood silently by while Gretchen and Mrs. Verdin fussed over their loved one. Dr. Evans politely saw himself out of the room, but not before he and Takecia locked eyes for too long of a moment. I thought I heard the good doctor whisper for her to call him, but I couldn't be sure, because Mrs. Verdin was speaking rapidly in French. It sounded like she was fussing Mr. Verdin, but he only smiled and responded with what sounded like jokes. He had seemed to come alive when he saw his bride. Even after all their years of marriage, the two of them were still very much in love.

Finally, Gretchen scooted to one side and waved us closer to the bed.

"He's ready to give his statement," she said. "He wants to get this over with so he can go home."

"Are they releasing him today?" I asked skeptically.

"If they don't, he said he's getting up and walking out of here." Gretchen grinned and patted Mr. Verdin's shoulder. "He's always been a stubborn man, but I think that stubbornness is what's helped him last so long."

Mr. Verdin stared up at Gretchen, and it was obvious he didn't have a clue what she was saying. His face was no longer pale. Instead, it had returned to a more natural and deep olive complexion that befitted the Chitimacha Indians with whom I'd been acquainted, Gretchen included.

"Did he say anything about what happened out there on the water?" I asked.

Gretchen shook her head. "He only complained about not being able to work with those casts on, and he wanted me to tell the doctors to remove them immediately—only, he used the word *carrement*."

I laughed, and Mr. Verdin turned to look in my direction. I smiled and introduced myself. Gretchen made the translation. He smiled back and rattled off a string of sentences. My Cajun French was extremely rusty, but I did recognize a word or two, including the French enunciation for *sheriff*, and I nodded along as I waited patiently for Gretchen to interpret.

"He said he recognizes you from the newspapers," she said. "He said your wife's the sheriff in town and y'all have a young daughter with hair that looks like fire. When he mentioned her hair, he went on to say that he heard y'all searching for him this morning, but he couldn't call out to y'all because of a pain in his back and side. He said it was difficult to breathe, and I'm assuming that's because of his broken ribs. Anyway, he always carries a lighter in his pocket in case of emergencies, and he took it out and started a fire to get y'all's attention. That's how he burned his hand."

I jotted down some notes as I listened to Gretchen. When she was done, I asked her to ask Mr. Verdin about the crash. I didn't need to ask a lot of mundane—albeit important—questions, like what time he left the landing, because I'd already been able to ascertain that information from the surveillance footage I'd obtained from Sam Beard.

There was a bit of back and forth between Gretchen and Mr. Verdin, and I could tell she was asking some follow-up questions to clarify certain issues. At one point, Mr. Verdin grew emotional and had to stop to wipe his eyes. It was hard for him to maneuver his arms with the casts, so Mrs. Verdin had stepped forward and helped him.

Throughout much of the dialogue, there remained a puzzled expression on Gretchen's face, and this had my interest at an all-time high. She asked what sounded like some pointed questions and she used her hands for emphasis but, for the life of me, I couldn't make out what was being conveyed. Whatever it was, it seemed intense, and I couldn't wait to hear what Mr. Verdin had said.

When Gretchen finally turned to me, she still seemed a bit confused.

"Well?" I asked impatiently. "What happened?"

"First, he said he was checking his catfish lines and thinking about T-Bill, who is one of my cousins' kids. They recently moved to Texas. T-Bill used to help my père-père check his catfish lines before school, but he's been doing it on his own ever since my cousin moved his wife and T-Bill to Texas. Anyway, he says if T-Bill would've been with him, he would be dead." She frowned as she paused to take a breath. "That part broke his heart. He started to blame himself and said that if T-Bill's parents hadn't moved him to Texas, he would've gotten his own great-grandson killed."

"Oh, no," I said, "he can't put that on himself."

"That's what I told him," Gretchen said. "I explained that everything happens for a reason, and the reason they left for Texas is because God knew this day was coming. That seemed to satisfy him."

I glanced at Mr. Verdin, who was watching the exchange between Gretchen and me curiously. I wondered if he could understand a little of what we were saying. When I was a kid, I had picked up quite a bit of Cajun French by listening to my grandpa, and I knew he had picked up some English by listening to those of us around him.

"What did he say about the crash?" I asked, turning back to Gretchen. "Did he see the vessel that hit him?"

"That's just it," she said with a scowl, "he claims it wasn't a boat that hit him."

I cocked my head to the side. "What?"

"Yeah, he said something fell from the sky and landed on his pirogue," she explained. "He said he was just sitting there one minute, paddling across the bayou, and then the next thing he knew, he was flying through the air. He said he caught a brief glimpse of something falling from the sky and hitting the front of his pirogue, and that's what propelled him through the air."

"Wait a minute." I shook my head. "He really believes something fell from the sky and landed in his boat?"

Gretchen nodded. "And if he says it happened, then I believe it, too."

CHAPTER 12

Mr. Verdin was not able to tell us more than he already had, so after thirty minutes of using Gretchen as a go-between, I thanked him and ended the interview. I told Gretchen to wish him well for me, and then Takecia and I headed for the parking lot.

Once we had reached our vehicles, I asked her if she believed Mr. Verdin.

"Do you think it's possible he sustained a head injury and is just confused?" I asked.

"I guess it's possible, but you saw how certain he looked," she said. "And Gretchen sure believes him, so that's saying a lot."

I nodded absently, trying to understand how something could've fallen from the sky. "Did you see any large branches floating in the area? It's quite possible a giant limb fell on his pirogue and catapulted him into the air, but I'd think we would've seen some evidence of that—either on the water or on the pirogue."

Takecia shook her head. "I didn't see any branches big enough to destroy a pirogue, and I don't remember seeing any broken trees when I looked up."

I hadn't seen any either. As we stood there, I pulled out my cell phone and called our office. Lindsey answered.

"Hey, did we get any reports of planes or helicopters crashing in the area?" I asked.

"Nope," she said. "You would've been the first to hear of it."

"Can you do an internet search to see if there's been a plane crash or satellite explosion anywhere in Louisiana or the surrounding states?" I asked, realizing that an in-air explosion could leave debris scattered over a stretch of many miles. "Also check to see if there's been any space launches last night or early this morning."

I was leaning against my Tahoe and tapping my boot on the ground as I waited. Movement in my peripheral vision caught my eye, and I looked up to see Takecia heading back toward the hospital. There, coming to meet her, was the new emergency room doctor we'd just met—or, rather, that I had just met.

I smiled warmly. I liked seeing good people happy, and I hadn't seen Takecia this happy since her last relationship had gone south. Sure, she'd always seemed happy enough on her own, but I remembered how excited she had seemed over her engagement. Of course, if I had to compare her levels of excitement from one to ten, her engagement excitement had been a six, while this level of excitement was a twenty.

"Clint, are you still there?" Lindsey finally asked.

"Yes, ma'am."

"There hasn't been a plane crash since the one in China earlier this year," she said. "I can't find anything about a space launch, but if there had been a shuttle crash, that would be big news. I did find something about a UFO sighting in Georgia, but I don't know if that has anything to do with this."

"When was that sighting?" I asked, more curious than anything. I didn't think for a second that it had anything to do with Mr. Verdin's crash, but one never could tell.

"It was last night," she said. "Some man was driving along a country road and saw this flying saucer in the sky. He said it blinded him for a full minute and caused him to drive right off of a dead end road and into a river. The police aren't buying it, though, because they arrested him for DUI."

I shook my head. "Okay, thanks for checking."

I ended the call and waited for Takecia to finish her conversation. I wanted to jump into action and find the person or persons who had almost killed Mr. Verdin, but I didn't know in which direction to go. I had a couple of ideas, but I doubted any of them would turn up something solid.

For one, I could continue driving along Bayou Tail in town searching for homes or businesses that had cameras pointing toward the water, but that ultimately wouldn't do much good. Even if I did catch a boat driving along the bayou, I wouldn't have probable cause, or even reasonable suspicion, to stop it unless there was significant damage to the vessel that was consistent with having blown through a pirogue—and I doubted any surveillance system would produce a video of high enough quality to detect damage to a boat from hundreds of feet away and at night.

I did have another option. Bayou Tail ran like a snake in a northerly direction from the Gulf of Mexico to the northern end of Mechant Loup, where it curved sharply to the west. While it did curve to the west, it also continued flowing to the north, following the length of Chateau Parish. There had been much debate between old timers over the years about whether or not the waterway consisted of one bayou or two, but regardless, the portion that flowed toward the north through the parish was called Bayou Chateau. Along that portion of bayou, there were a number of pontoon bridges that crossed the waterway and connected the two roads that paralleled it to the east and west. Those pontoon bridges were manned around the clock and would have to open for traffic if any boat larger than a pirogue passed through the area. These bridge tenders would be my last hope. I would have to find out everyone who worked the night shift and ask them if a damaged boat came through there around the time that Mr. Verdin's pirogue had been destroyed.

I pulled out my cell phone and called the Chateau Parish Sheriff's Office. I asked the dispatcher who answered if they had a list of all the bridge tenders who worked the night shift.

"No," she said, "but we do have the phone number to every bridge in the parish. I could give you those numbers and you could talk to the person who's on shift now. They would know who worked the night shift."

I liked that idea, and took down the numbers. I was wrapping up my call when Takecia approached. Like the good doctor earlier, she also seemed to be walking on air.

"Did you solve the case yet?" she asked.

I didn't answer for a long minute. Instead, I just stood there staring at her. Finally, I asked, "Is that your husband?"

Even through her dark flesh I could see a hint of red.

"Maybe," she said coyly. "So, what are we doing next?"

I glanced at the time on my cell phone. It was past noon. "Shouldn't you be home and in bed? You've been up all night."

"It's fine," she said with a wave of her hand. "I don't have to work tonight, so I'm good. Besides, I couldn't sleep now even if I wanted to."

"It wouldn't have anything to do with Dr. Evans, now would it?"

She only smiled. "Look, Amy's on her honeymoon, and it looks like you could use some help, so I'm offering."

"I appreciate it." I told her about my idea to call the bridge tenders. "We'll need to call them before we head back to town, in case we need to go by and interview them further."

"I'm in."

I turned the list of names so she could see, and we each began making calls. In all, we were able to reach six of the bridge tenders currently on duty, and four of them were able to provide the numbers of the ones working the night shift. One of them didn't feel comfortable providing the information over the phone, and the other didn't know who worked the previous night shift.

Armed with the names of the night workers, we began calling them. The first woman I spoke with said her night was slow.

"I think I opened the bridge once," she said in an irritated voice from having her sleep disturbed.

"What kind of boat was it?"

"A tugboat. Why?"

"Did you notice any damage to the front of the boat?"

"No," she said. "Now, can I go back to sleep?"

Before I could answer, she abruptly ended the call.

The next bridge tender I spoke with was a man named Rusty. He was more pleasant, but equally useless. He worked the bridge closest to town, but he didn't see a single boat all night.

"It's not to say one didn't pass through here," he said. "Some of those small skiffs can squeeze by without me opening the bridge, and if one came by while I was sleeping, I wouldn't have known."

I thanked him and turned to Takecia, who was ending her last call.

"Anything?" I asked.

"Nope." She frowned and clipped her cell phone to her belt. "What next?"

I was about to suggest knocking on doors to search for surveillance footage when something occurred to me. It was something Lindsey had said.

"What is it?" Takecia asked when she saw the expression on my face. "You've come up with something, haven't you?"

"I'm not sure," I said idly, quickly accessing the internet on my cell phone. "Lindsey said that a man in Georgia saw a UFO last night."

Takecia laughed. "And you think this UFO shot down Mr. Verdin's pirogue?"

"No." I typed the name of our town into the search bar and waited for the page to load. "The man claims he was driving along this road when the UFO appeared and blinded him. According to him, it blinded him and caused him to drive over a dead-end road and into a river."

"I've heard a lot of excuses for crashing," Takecia said with a grunt, "but that's a new one. Did they buy it?"

"No, they arrested him for DUI."

She nodded and waited, probably wondering how the UFO in Georgia factored into our case, but not willing to ask.

Finally, I found what I was looking for.

"Holy shit," I said in a low voice. "Mr. Verdin was right."

"About?" Takecia crowded me, trying to see the screen on my cell phone.

"He said something fell from the sky and landed on his pirogue," I explained, pointing to the map of Back Street in town. "This used to be the old Main Street, and the Mechant Loup Bridge crossed the bayou right here—right over where the crash happened."

"Hold up!" Takecia squinted against the sun's glare on my screen. "You think a car drove off the end of the road and landed on his pirogue?"

"That's the only thing that makes sense," I said, pushing off of my Tahoe and heading for the driver's door.

CHAPTER 13

I raced toward town with Takecia hot on my bumper. It was lunch time for most of the workers in the parish, so there was more traffic than I would've liked on the road, but before long, we were finally approaching the Mechant Loup Bridge. After turning left onto Washington Avenue, we slowed and cruised toward Back Street. There were a few restaurants, a bar, and a bakery along Washington, and it was also where the police department was located, so it was a congested area.

I glanced at the police department as we drove by and saw that Susan's Tahoe was there. I shook my head and smiled.

"That girl's gonna give birth on her office floor!"

The words had barely left my mouth when a sense of fear swept over me. What if I was elbows deep in this—or some other—case when she went into labor? What if I was in the middle of interrogating a suspect or processing a crime scene? I couldn't simply stop what I was doing and leave. Amy and Baylor were driving across the country on their honeymoon, so there was no way she could fill in for me, even if she had wanted to. The last I'd heard, they were doing some rock climbing in Arches National Park and would be heading north from there. They had each taken three weeks of vacation time, and they said they intended to fill every second of that time with adventure.

I turned left when I reached Back Street and headed north. I shook my head once I'd made a block. I could see the old barricades from when the town had closed the road decades ago—long before I had transplanted there—and, although they were weathered and weak, they were still standing. There was no way someone drove a vehicle through them and into the bayou beyond.

I slowed as I passed the last building on the right to allow a red car to turn into the parking lot. The exterior of the building was wrapped in white wooden siding that desperately needed a fresh paint job. It was the new home of our local newspaper, the Mechant Voice, and I recognized Ali Bridges as the driver of the red car.

She waved and I returned the greeting before stopping on the shoulder just north of their building. Takecia parked behind me and we met at the front of my Tahoe. I heard Ali's car door slam and then I heard my name. I smiled. There was no way she would let us walk off without finding out what was going on. After all, it was her job, and she was good at it.

"Detective Wolf and Sergeant Gayle," she said as she approached us with her hand extended. "How are y'all?"

We shook her hand and Takecia spoke before I could.

"We're great," she said, still beaming from her encounter at the hospital. "How are you?"

"It's going good." She pushed her long brown hair out of her face and indicated our vehicles. "Are y'all working a case? Is it anything good?"

I told her about Mr. Verdin going missing and how we had found him clinging to life and a cigarette lighter. "He's in the hospital now, but they're expecting a full recovery," I concluded. "He's a tough old Coonass."

Ali's brow furrowed. "So, do you expect foul play?"

I hesitated, not wanting to give away too much information, but also not wanting to brush her off. She had been good to me in the past, and I wanted to maintain our cordial working relationship while not jeopardizing a case.

"We believe there was some kind of collision, but we don't believe it was intentional," I finally said. "The initial crash appears to have been accidental, but the individuals left the scene of the crash, which is a crime."

"I see." Ali glanced toward the barricades. "If the crash happened on the water, why are y'all up here?"

I smiled. "Ali, you should be a detective instead of a reporter. Amy's out of town at the moment, so we could use the help."

She laughed and waved me off. "Nice try, but flattery will not distract me."

"I promise you this," I said, "if there's anything newsworthy to report, you'll be the first to know."

That seemed to satisfy her for the moment, as she waved goodbye and headed toward the door to her office, but I knew she wasn't done asking questions. In fact, I fully expected her to spy on us from inside the building.

Once she was gone, Takecia and I strode toward the barricades. One of the wooden blockades was facing south and warned traffic approaching along Back Street that the road was coming to an end, while the second blockade faced Bayou Tail Lane. The asphalt leading to the Back Street barricade had been pulled up when the original bridge had been removed, and that patch of earth was now covered in green grass and lined with shrubbery. There was a domineering bulkhead beyond the Back Street barricade that had been part of the support system for the original bridge, but it had now been reduced to a favorite fishing spot for some of the townsfolk.

Wanting a closer look, Takecia and I headed for the bulkhead. I stepped onto one of the creosote pilings that formed the foundation of the bulkhead and glanced down at the bayou beneath us. We were at least fifteen feet above the water, and the elevated position offered a great bird's eye view of the crash site. From memory, I mentally placed the pieces of Mr. Verdin's boat back where I had found them, and compared them to the rest of the debris that still floated on the water.

"The pirogue was farther out that way," I said to Takecia, pointing toward our right in the water. "Even if a car had crashed through the barricade, it wouldn't have hit him. But…"

I paused and glanced in the direction of the two cypress trees that stood ten feet beyond the Bayou Tail Lane barricade. To the east of the trees was a strip of land that stretched from the edge of the embankment southward to the Mechant Voice building. The outer edge of the land nearest the bayou was covered in grass and clovers, but the rest of the property consisted of a shell parking area. I'd parked there myself when I'd gone into the Mechant Voice to speak with Ali, and I'd often seen recreational photographers stop and park there to take pictures of Bayou Tail. During our yearly Mardi Gras parades, folks from town would use the area to set up tents, grills, and folding chairs from which to enjoy the parade.

I wasn't positive if the strip of land belonged to the Mechant Voice or if it was town property, but no one from the newspaper had ever objected to folks using it.

"What're you thinking?" Takecia asked.

"It's quite possible someone drove through that parking lot, over the edge of the embankment, and right on top of Mr. Verdin."

Takecia seemed to like that idea, and we both walked toward the lot to search for evidence.

CHAPTER 14

Takecia and I walked along the asphalt until we reached the Mechant Voice building, and it was there that we intended to begin a methodical search of the parking lot. As it turned out, the evidence found us.

"Look," Takecia said, pointing toward the ground. "Peel-out marks."

She was right. At the edge of the asphalt off of Back Street, and about fifteen feet from the northwest corner of the building, there were distinct tire tracks in the shells. It appeared that someone had raced down the street and then veered into the parking lot, heading straight for the embankment. The tire tracks grew fainter and even disappeared as the vehicle had progressed through the parking lot, but it was plain to see that the grass near the embankment had been pressed down by car tires in recent time. A vehicle had definitely run off the road and driven straight over the embankment at that location.

I quickly strode to my Tahoe and retrieved my camera. After documenting the tracks with photographs, we stayed to the left of them and made our way to the embankment. When we reached it, I grunted.

"No shit," I muttered. We were standing almost directly over the spot where I'd found the largest pieces of Mr. Verdin's pirogue. "He wasn't run over by a boat—he was run over by a car."

Takecia pointed toward the water. "You think the driver survived?"

We had already scoured the banks of the bayou down there, but I scanned them again from our perch above the water. I figured it would've been easy to see if someone had clawed their way up the muddy banks, but I saw nothing.

"It's deep in this area and I don't see where someone came out of the water," I finally said. "My guess is the divers will find him or her at the bottom of the bayou."

Takecia turned and looked back in the direction from which we'd come. "I've worked a lot of vehicle crashes," she said. "Usually, you'll see brake marks before the vehicles make impact. Whoever was driving this car, they didn't even try to stop. They drove right over the edge."

I nodded my agreement. "Either they were drunk or drugged out of their minds, or they intended to die."

"Want me to call the sheriff's office and request some divers?" Takecia offered.

I nodded and mumbled a *thank you* while I surveyed our surroundings. There were no houses along Back Street from the Market Street Bridge to where we stood, so that meant no one would've been present during the night or early morning hours when the incident had occurred.

Directly across the street from the Mechant Voice was a peach-colored two-story building trimmed in red. While it looked nice and had recently been renovated, it was vacant. The lot between the peach building and Bayou Tail Lane was empty. The ground was covered in broken concrete with weeds growing up between the cracks, and it was completely surrounded by a cyclone fence that had some type of privacy barrier interwoven between the links. The building east of the empty lot was another business that had seen better days, and I had no hopes of retrieving surveillance footage from it or any of the other buildings in the area.

Looking across Bayou Tail toward East Main, I could only see trees and portions of the shipyard that operated in that area. It was closed at night and I already knew there were no surveillance cameras on the property, thanks to a case I'd worked where employees were stealing tools from the shipyard and transporting them over the border to Mexico.

As far as crime scenes went, it would've been better if the vehicle had driven into a bayou in the middle of the swamps. At least we might've been able to find a random game camera in the area that could've provided some information.

Takecia was still on the phone, so I pulled some evidence flags from my crime scene box and marked off the pathway that the vehicle took on its way to the embankment. I then pushed a spike into the ground, hooked the dumb end of the measuring tape to it, and recorded a measurement of 150 feet from the road to the embankment.

"The sheriff's office is sending two water patrol deputies and a diver," Takecia called out a few minutes later. "They should be here within the hour."

"Why do y'all need divers?" a voice called from the opposite side of the parking lot. "I thought Mr. Verdin was found alive?"

I couldn't help but smile when I turned and saw Ali standing where I'd pushed the spike into the ground. Her arms were folded across her breasts and she was eyeing me suspiciously, but she was careful to respect the crime scene.

I reeled in my measuring tape as I walked toward her, wondering as I did so how much I should tell her.

"Mr. Verdin was found alive," I said, "but it looks like a car might have been the cause of his accident."

"A car?" She looked down at the evidence flags and then toward the embankment. Her brown eyes widened. "A car drove over the edge and landed on top of his pirogue?"

I nodded.

"How on earth is he still alive?"

"Luck, I guess."

Ali chewed on her lower lip. I could almost hear the gears spinning in her head. I knew she wanted to ask a hundred questions, but I had nothing for her. Hell, I had nothing for myself.

"So, you think there's a car at the bottom of the bayou," Ali began slowly, "and there's a body inside that car, right?"

"That's a strong possibility," I explained patiently. "I didn't see sheen on the surface of the water, but it can sometimes take several hours for gasoline and oil from a car's engine to drift to the top."

"What time do you think it happened?" she asked. "I was here until almost two in the morning and didn't hear anything."

"I'm not real sure," I admitted, "but your information helps."

Ali pointed to the shell parking lot. "Is this a crime scene?"

"Yeah."

"Do you think someone intentionally tried to kill Mr. Verdin?" she asked.

Takecia walked up with a roll of crime scene tape and handed me the loose end.

"No," I said, pausing briefly to tie my end of the tape to the down-spout at the corner of the Mechant Voice building. "We don't know much at this point, but I'm pretty sure we can rule that scenario out. There are easier and safer ways to kill someone."

"Do you think this was an accident or a suicide?"

I simply smiled and said, "Yes."

CHAPTER 15

Takecia and I had been forced to wait forty-seven minutes for the sheriff's office's patrol boat to come roaring down the bayou, but it had given us time to conduct a thorough search of the parking lot. Other than the peel-out marks near the road, we had found a small scuff mark in the shells nearby, but it hadn't appeared to be related. Other things we found that didn't appear to be related to our case were a few dozen cigarette butts, a broken beer bottle, almost a dollar's worth of loose change, a .22 caliber bullet, and a dirty diaper with pictures of the cartoon Batman and Robin printed all over it.

"I think we should recover the diaper," Takecia had joked. "It's definitely evidence."

"Oh, yeah?" I had asked, turning my attention to the bullet. It hadn't been fired and it appeared to have been sitting in the shells for a long time. Although it didn't appear to be a part of our scene, I photographed and recovered it anyway.

"Yeah," Takecia said. "I think the driver swerved to miss the diaper because he didn't want to get baby poop on his new tires, and that's when he lost control and ran off the edge of the embankment."

I had laughed as I'd recovered the diaper, and then we'd continued our search of the parking lot. After we were done, we had removed the crime scene tape and headed for the police department to retrieve the cabin cruiser.

"I guess I'm picking Gracie up from school," Susan had said when she saw us hitching up the boat under the building. "It looks like you'll be working late."

I had nodded and told her everything we knew. She was as

puzzled as we were.

"That's an odd one," she had said. "I'll be curious to see what y'all find at the bottom of the bayou."

I had stopped long enough to kiss her and rub her belly, and then I had jumped into my Tahoe and followed Takecia to the landing. She was backing the cabin cruiser into one of the slipways when the sheriff's office boat arrived. They were also driving a cabin cruiser, and I immediately recognized the deputy who was stepping out of the cabin. He was Paul Rupe and he was checking the gauges on his air tank.

"Paul," I said as the water patrol deputy pulled alongside the dock, "since when do you dive?"

He smiled a warm greeting. He and I had collaborated on a case a little more than a year earlier, and it was one of those cases that stuck with us.

"I'm the newest certified black water recovery diver in the department," he said, puffing out his chest playfully. He then let his shoulders sag. "This'll be my first solo dive. If I die down there, I'll probably be kicked off the team."

I didn't laugh. Paul had suffered a tremendous loss the year before, and I wondered if he had taken on such dangerous assignments in the hopes that he could see his deceased wife again soon.

As Takecia fired up the engine on our boat, I jumped in her Tahoe and pulled it out of the slip for her. Once I'd parked it and we were both onboard our vessel, we led Paul and the water patrol deputies to where the crash had happened. We watched Paul lower himself into the water, adjust his goggles, and then slowly disappear into the blackness below. He was gone for about fifteen minutes before resurfacing.

"I've got nothing," he called out after removing his regulator. "Are you sure the vehicle went down here?"

I glanced overhead and studied the edge of the raised embankment for the umpteenth time. I'd initially thought the vehicle had impacted Mr. Verdin's pirogue farther from the bank, but as I reconsidered, I realized the peel-out marks that Takecia and I had discovered earlier must've meant that the vehicle had begun its acceleration from the edge of the shell driveway, rather than losing traction when it left the asphalt.

"It could've been closer to the bank," I told Paul. "The vehicle would've had about 150 feet to pick up speed, and it was on loose shells, so it might not have been going fast enough to make it very far."

Paul nodded, pulled on his regulator, and disappeared beneath the utter blackness. This time, he was under for a little more than thirty minutes, and we all began to worry.

"How much air does he have in his tank?" I asked one of the water patrol deputies, who glanced at the captain of the boat.

"Those tanks are supposed to be good for an hour under normal circumstances," the captain said, consulting his watch. "According to my estimation, counting his first dive, it means he's got about seven minutes left."

I glanced at the safety line attached to a cleat on the boat. I had seen the captain tug on it once about fifteen minutes earlier—and there had been a responding tug from the depths of the water—but he hadn't tugged on it since. I was about to suggest he give it another tug when the water exploded in bubbles.

I relaxed when I saw Paul's head break the surface of the water. He gathered his bearings and then proceeded to the sheriff's office boat. Once he'd pulled himself aboard and removed his regulator, he took a moment to catch his breath. Finally, he looked over at me and wiped a stream of water from his face.

"I found it," he said. "I found a vehicle down there. I can't tell what kind it is, because it's upside down. All the windows are closed and the doors are locked."

"Are they locked or stuck in the mud?" asked the captain.

"They're locked. When I pulled on the handles, they were loose. They didn't catch on the internal latches. It's too dark down there to see if anyone's inside, so I don't know if it's occupied. If I was to guess, I'd say it is, because no one locks the doors behind them when they escape from a submerged vehicle."

"Why didn't you break a window to check for survivors?" asked the other water patrol deputy.

"There won't be any," I interjected, frowning as I watched Paul changing air tanks. "The car's been down there for hours. It would've filled with water a long time ago and, if someone *is* inside, they've long ago drowned. Paul, how deep would you say it is in this area?"

He was thoughtful. "It's at least twenty feet deep."

I nodded and pulled out my cell phone to call Lindsey.

"We need the next wrecker on the list to respond to the corner of Back Street and Bayou Tail Lane," I said when she answered. I explained the situation and told her to make sure they could handle such a removal.

"And if they can't?"

"Keep moving down the list until you find someone who can."

"Ten-four," she said and hung up.

As we sat there waiting for the wrecker to arrive, I tried to imagine what we would find once we got the car out of the water. I could tell Takecia was wondering the same thing, although she was still floating on air from her encounter with Dr. Evans.

"Why would someone drive straight off the edge of the earth and into the bayou if they weren't trying to kill themselves?" she mused aloud.

I didn't have a good answer for her. Had they run off the road and plunged into the bayou, I could've come up with a few possible scenarios. Perhaps they had been drunk and passed out, or they had been driving drowsy and fallen asleep, only to be rudely roused from their stupor or slumber by a giant splash and muddy water seeping into every crack in their vehicle. However, since it appeared that the initial acceleration had occurred in the shells, it couldn't have been an accident. Whoever had done this had apparently pointed their vehicle directly at the embankment and tried to reach hell in a hurry.

"What if they were trying to jump the bayou?" Paul offered. "Y'all did have that motorcycle try to jump the bayou earlier in the year. Maybe this was some sort of copycat."

I looked up at the embankment to the south, and then turned to the one on the north, which was much lower.

"Only a fool would think that was possible," I muttered, but then shrugged. "We've got a lot of fools in this town, so anything's possible."

CHAPTER 16

It was almost four o'clock in the afternoon before two wreckers had finally arrived, and it took another hour for Paul to dive down to the vehicle and attach the end of two winch cables to the axles of the vehicle. It was a dangerous job, and he had to make two separate dives to attach the cables individually. I was relieved when I saw him resurface the second time and lift up a thumb to let us know the vehicle was secure.

Takecia and I were standing on the edge of the embankment looking down as the winches began to grumble and the slack in the wire ropes was taken out. Once they became taut, the sound of the winches grew louder as they strained under the weight of the submerged vehicle.

"What if they can't pull it out?" Takecia asked.

"That won't be good." I glanced over my shoulder toward the wrecker trucks, and caught movement out of my peripheral vision.

I turned toward the Mechant Voice building and saw Ali standing there with a camera that was outfitted with a large zoom lens. I frowned. I knew I couldn't stop her from publishing any pictures she took out here in the public eye, but I was hoping she would be discreet. The last thing I'd want was for some family member to see their loved one's vehicle being pulled from the bayou before we'd had a chance to make the death notification—*if* there was a body inside.

While I had resigned myself to the belief that we would find a body in the vehicle, there was still a part of me that was hoping it would be empty.

After what seemed like forever, there was finally a large stirring just beneath the dark water, and then we saw a rear bumper emerge. My heart pounded as more and more of the vehicle inched into view. Since the back end was being pulled out first and the winches moved at a snail's pace, it would be a while before we could see if there were any occupants inside.

As more of the vehicle came into view, I could see that it was a small truck. I couldn't be sure of the make and model, but I could see that it was a four-door vehicle and, beneath the thick mud that now coated it, it appeared to be blue.

Once the truck had been pulled against the water's edge below, the tow service drivers had to reposition their wrecker trucks in order to draw the vehicle up along the embankment.

"Look," Takecia said, pointing toward the back of the small pickup, "there's no license plate."

I cursed under my breath. But of course there wouldn't be a license plate. To have one would've been too easy. Paul was still down in the cabin cruiser and he was staring intently at the front of the truck. I saw him reach for his cell phone, and then a few seconds later, mine rang.

"What's up?" I asked.

"There's a body in the driver's seat," he said grimly. "The head's bent forward, but the body's upright. It looks like he's strapped into the seatbelt."

"It's definitely a man?" I asked.

"That's what it looks like from here."

I didn't recognize the vehicle. While that didn't positively mean it wasn't from here, there was a good chance it was an out-of-towner, because I was familiar with most of the people in town.

"Is there a license plate on the front of the vehicle?" I asked.

"Nothing official," he said. "There's a personalized plate, but I can't make out what it says. It's covered in mud."

I sighed and ended the call. As bad as I wanted to know who the mystery man was, I would have to wait—and wait we did.

It took the tow service operators quite some time to get the truck up and over the embankment, but it was finally resting in the shell parking lot. I glanced toward Ali before making my approach to the vehicle, and she was steadily photographing it. I was grateful the back of the truck was facing her. Otherwise, she would've been able to get a clear photo of the victim's face with that lens of hers.

"Can you get a blanket?" I asked Takecia as I started forward. "I want to cover the windshield so Ali won't get a picture of our victim."

Takecia nodded and headed for her Tahoe. I walked past the tow operators and approached the truck from the driver's side. Some of the muddy film had slid from the truck as it had been suspended over the embankment, and I could see through the window on that side. Just as Paul had described, there was a man slouched forward in the driver's seat. He was held upright and in place by the seatbelt.

Before touching anything, I peered through the front windshield and searched the lower dashboard for the VIN plate. To my shock, it was gone. The vehicle was an older model, but wasn't nearly old enough to not have a vehicle identification number, so that could only mean the VIN plate had been removed. And the only reason I could think of for doing that was if the vehicle had been stolen.

I removed a pair of latex gloves from my back pocket and pulled them on. I tested the door. Once again, Paul had been right—the doors were locked. When Takecia walked up with one of the plastic blankets that each of our officers carried in their toolkits for just such an occasion, we wrapped it over the front windshield. I then went to my Tahoe and grabbed my lock-job tool. It had been years since I'd unlocked a vehicle with it, but it turned out to be just like riding a bike. I hadn't missed a beat.

Within seconds, the driver's door was unlocked. After glancing over my shoulder to make sure Ali hadn't approached the truck, I eased the door open. Water spilled from the floorboard and wet my boots, but I hardly noticed. I was fixated on the gentleman seated behind the steering wheel.

Since he had only died that morning, his body was relatively fresh and still easily identifiable, although I didn't recognize him. Using my department crime scene camera, I took a few shots of his face and the front of his body before examining his surroundings.

From what I could see of the front seat, there were several fast food cups and crumpled bags strewn about the area, as well as one sandal—it was for the left foot—and a pair of aviator sunglasses. The console was empty, but that wasn't surprising, as the truck had been found on its roof at the bottom of the bayou. The keys were in the ignition, and they were in the *on* position. There was no sign of life from the battery, and this was also not surprising.

"Can you tell if he's got any injuries?" Takecia asked over my shoulder.

"No." I had examined what I could see of the man's face and exposed arms, but everything looked normal. He had tanned features, thick brown hair, and he appeared to be in good shape.

"He looks like a body builder," Takecia commented wryly. "He's got those swollen but empty muscles. I've sparred men like him in the gym. They're all so easy to beat. Now, those men who earn their muscles with hard work"—she gave a grunt of admiration—"those are a different breed."

I nodded idly and began searching his pockets. The front pockets seemed to be empty, so I reached around to see if there was a wallet in his left rear pocket. It was empty. I said a silent prayer as I leaned across his body and felt for the right pocket. I cursed under my breath. It was also empty.

Since the battery was dead on the truck, I had to reach around to unlock the back door. When I got it open, I saw that there was a suitcase resting in an awkward position on the rear passenger floorboard. Some loose clothes were strung about the seat and floor. There were two empty bags of ice, a leather shaving kit bag, and the right sandal that matched the one in the front seat.

"It looks like he was living out of his truck," I muttered, stepping back to give Takecia a chance to look inside. While she conducted her visual examination, I moved around to the passenger's side, jimmied the front door, and checked the glove compartment. It was empty.

At that moment, I was convinced the truck was stolen, and I was starting to fear we'd never find the owner when Takecia called out that she'd found something. I walked around to her side of the vehicle and found her squatting in the shells, the muscles in her powerful legs testing the fabric of her uniform pants.

"Look there," she said, pointing under the front seat. "It looks like a *For Sale* sign."

She stepped away and I moved forward, looking where she had been pointing. Sure enough, there was a red and white *For Sale* sign. I photographed it and then pulled it out from under the seat. I smiled when I had it out in the light. We finally had a lead.

CHAPTER 17

"There's a phone number on it," I announced, turning the *For Sale* sign so Takecia could see. However, the smile faded when I saw the area code. "It's in the 806. Where the hell is that?"

Takecia pulled out her cell phone and went to work. Within seconds, she had an answer for me.

"Amarillo, Texas," she said. "This man's come a long way to drive to the bottom of the bayou. I'm sure he's passed a hundred rivers, bayous, and lakes on his way here. Why'd he pick this place?"

Instead of answers, this revelation brought more questions. Why had he come here? Why had he chosen this exact spot to die? Had he met with someone in town and gotten some news that pushed him over the edge? If so, with whom had he met? An estranged lover? A child? An old enemy?

And what about the truck? Was it stolen, or was there another explanation for the missing VIN plate? If it wasn't stolen, had our victim purchased it from someone in Amarillo, or was he the one trying to sell it? If he was the one trying to sell it, the number would be his and it would result in a dead end. Such would be my luck, I was sure. Not wanting to wait for an answer, I secured the sign in an evidence bag, removed my gloves, and dialed the number. It only rang once before a man with a Texas drawl answered.

"Godfrey's Automotives," he said. "What can I do you for?"

"Mr. Godfrey, is it?" I asked.

"That's what I said."

"Hi, I'm Clint Wolf," I said. "I'm a detective with the Mechant Loup Police Department."

"The what?" came his confused response.

"I'm a detective with a police department in Louisiana," I explained. "We found a truck in the bayou, and we're trying to identify the man who was in it."

"Why don't you just ask him?" To Mr. Godfrey, this must've seemed like a simple solution.

"He's dead, so he's not talking."

"Oh, I see." There was a pause on the other end of the phone. Finally, Mr. Godfrey asked, "What's this got to do with me, and how'd you get my number?"

"I found a *For Sale* sign in the truck with your number on it, so I was hoping you could tell me more about the truck. It doesn't have a VIN plate, so I was beginning to think it had been stolen from you."

"Nope, I ain't never had no truck stolen from me." He sounded sure of himself. "I've got twenty dogs the size of small steers guarding this place. You can't get to within a mile of here without them getting a bite on you."

"Do you know who might've bought it from you?" I asked, hoping he could help.

"I sell all kinds of cars and trucks to all kinds of folks from here and everywhere, and I deal in cash," he said with a grumble. "So, I don't know that I could help you."

"Well, this one might've been purchased in recent time, so you might remember it," I pressed. "The *For Sale* sign looks sort of fresh. If you don't mind checking your records, I'd greatly appreciate it."

He grunted, and based on what he'd already said, I was betting he didn't keep meticulous records.

"What kind of truck did you say it was?" he finally asked begrudgingly.

I hadn't said what kind of truck it was, but I didn't say that. Instead, I provided the make, model, color, and a description. He grunted again and I could hear some rustling in the background.

"And how long ago did he buy that truck?"

I started to ask how in the hell would I know that, but I refrained. "I'm not real sure," I said patiently, "but I don't think it was too long ago."

"Hold on a minute."

Godfrey must've put his hand over the phone, because I heard his muffled voice holler at someone and ask them about the truck. There was some back and forth, during which a hammer drill screamed intermittently, and then he was back with me.

"Okay, yeah, we did sell that truck to a drifter," he said. "Some man came walking in off the street saying he needed to buy something, because his car had broken down on the interstate. He said he was willing to pay cash."

"How much did he pay for the truck?"

"Oh, it was about four or five."

"Hundred?"

Mr. Godfrey laughed. "What do you think I'm selling, vintage Hot Wheels? Nothing leaves this lot for less than two grand."

I scowled. "He was on foot with four or five thousand in his pockets?"

"Nah, it wasn't in his pockets," Godfrey corrected. "He was carrying a suitcase and a large duffel bag. It looked to be a military issue, so I figured him for a Veteran. Otherwise, I would've charged him more."

"Did he say he was a Veteran?"

"No, I just figured he was because of the bag," Godfrey explained, "and when I thanked him for his service, he nodded his head."

"Did you get his name?" I held my breath, almost afraid of the answer. Within a second, my fear was realized.

"Nope," he said. "He gave me the cash and I gave him the keys. There was no need for me to get his name."

"What about the registration?" I asked. "Don't you have to switch it out of your name and into his?"

"None of the cars on this lot are registered to me, and I ain't the government." I heard him spit. "It ain't none of my business who he is or what he intends to do with that truck. I got my money, so I'm happy. You say he drove it into the bayou down there, well, I say it's his truck and his life and he can do what he wants with both of them."

"Did he say where he was headed?" I asked. "Or mention where he was from? We need to notify his family. I'm sure they're worried sick about him. And if he was, indeed, a military veteran, we'll have to make sure he receives a proper burial—one with honors."

I was appealing to his sense of patriotism, but it didn't matter. He knew nothing.

"He didn't talk much," Godfrey said, "and I didn't ask any questions. Folks around here keep coming back to do business with me and they refer their friends because they know I'm discreet."

I sighed and thanked him for his help.

"Nothing?" asked Takecia, who had been eyeing me curiously. She seemed to read my frustration.

"Nope…not a thing." I shook my head. "We don't know if this guy is from Amarillo—or anywhere in Texas—or if he was just passing through and bought the car. If we can't identify him, we won't be able to notify his next of kin."

"Maybe they'll report him missing and we'll be able to identify him that way," she suggested. "Of course, if we don't know where he's from, it would be like finding that elusive needle."

I couldn't argue with her, so I didn't. Instead, I called the Chateau Parish Coroner's Office to request a transport for the body and an autopsy. After putting me on a brief hold, the receptionist came back on and said Dr. Louise Wong could perform the autopsy first thing in the morning.

"One of the coroner's investigators should be there within the hour to pick up the body," she said after I confirmed that I could attend the autopsy at seven-thirty the next morning.

Since we were dealing with a suicide or accident, it wasn't time sensitive. There were no visible wounds on the man, and his truck doors had been locked, so I wasn't expecting any surprises at the autopsy. However, I was hoping for a breakthrough in the identification process. While a scar or dental records might help us confirm his identity at a later time—should a potential name be discovered—it wouldn't do much good in the initial investigation. No, what I needed was a tattoo that might send us in the right direction. I didn't want to be greedy, so I was hoping for a social security number or a full name tattooed across his chest. An address would also be nice.

I thanked the receptionist and shoved my cell phone in my pocket. I heard shells rustling from somewhere behind me and turned to see Ali moving across the parking lot. She was careful to maintain a respectable distance from the scene of the recovery, but she was definitely trying to gather as much information as possible for what was certainly going to be the next day's top story.

Since Hurricane Ursula had hit a couple months earlier, most of the news stories had focused on the rebuilding effort. We hadn't had much crime in town during that period of time. We also hadn't had many tourists come through, and that was probably due to the national news coverage of the devastation left behind by the monster storm. It was true that we had suffered extensive damage in certain areas but, for the most part, we had weathered the storm and gone right back to rebuilding. Our greatest relief was that we hadn't suffered a single casualty in all of Mechant Loup or the entire parish due to the storm.

I told Takecia about the autopsy and let her know that the coroner's investigator was en route. He would check the liver temperature, snap some photographs, and document his observations in an attempt to more accurately determine a time of death. Since we had Mr. Verdin as an eyewitness to the crash, we were already on solid footing as to when this man had died, unless...

"What is it?" Takecia asked when she saw my brow pucker.

I approached the truck and glanced down at the victim again, staring at the front pockets on his pants. I then squatted beside him and checked under the driver's seat, like I had already done before. I then moved to the passenger's side and checked under that seat. I then moved to the back of the truck and sifted through the items on the floorboard there.

"What're you looking for?" Takecia pressed. "What's on your mind?"

"Something's not right with this picture," I said, straightening to scan the parking lot again. "This might not be a suicide."

"Do you think it's an accident?"

"No." I shook my head slowly, mulling over the discrepancies with the scene. "I'm thinking it's a murder."

CHAPTER 18

"Murder?" Takecia echoed. "No way. He was locked inside his car. In fact, he was still wearing his seatbelt when we found him, and there were no other wounds on his body."

My head swiveled from side to side as I scanned the area, trying to come up with a plan. Finally, I knew what I wanted to do and jumped into action. I started by waving for the wrecker truck operators to join Takecia and me. When they did, I indicated the front and back of the pickup truck.

"Can y'all park one wrecker in front of the truck and one behind it?" I asked. "I want to form three walls around this truck to give us some privacy."

One shrugged and the other nodded his head, and they leapt into action. As soon as the wreckers were in place, I used my Tahoe to cap off the third wall, and then returned to the victim's truck carrying a body bag. I studied my surroundings again, and was satisfied that Ali wouldn't be able to see the body when we pulled it from the truck.

"Give me a hand," I said to Takecia. "I want to stretch him out over the body bag."

Takecia nodded and moved in as I unlatched the seatbelt. I carefully examined the front of the man's shirt. There were no holes in the fabric, and it appeared clean for someone who had supposedly been living in his truck.

When I was satisfied I hadn't missed anything, I grabbed his shoulders and gently pulled him toward me. Hooking my wrists under his armpits, I eased his upper torso out of the truck and waited for Takecia to gain control of his legs. When she did, we pulled him completely out of the truck and stretched him out across the body bag. He was a little stiff from the rigor mortis that had settled, so we had to force him into a supine position.

"I'll get some evidence boxes from your Tahoe," Takecia said as I began to remove his shirt.

She returned a few seconds later with several folded boxes. After unfolding them, she helped me get the shirt off and then I spread it across the bottom of the box to dry. We then removed his shoes and pants and placed them in separate boxes to dry. Now that the victim was clad only in his silk boxers and black dress socks, we could clearly see most of his body, and there wasn't a single wound in his flesh.

"No injuries," Takecia said. "Do you still think this is a murder?"

"It has to be." I grabbed his shoulders, and nodded for Takecia to grab his legs. When she did, we turned him over. I scowled. There were no wounds on his backside either. "Something's not right."

"I don't understand how this could be a murder," Takecia said. "How do you kill someone who's locked inside of a car?"

"You kill him before you put him inside," I said idly, wondering how it had been done. A number of things that had seemed odd early on were now starting to fall into place. "And whoever killed him didn't want us to identify him, which is why they stole his wallet and the paperwork inside the glove compartment. They must've also stolen the duffel bag."

"But the man from the dealership said he didn't provide any paperwork," Takecia said. "So, there wouldn't be any registration or anything."

"Have you ever met an empty glove compartment?" I asked, cocking my head to the side. "Even if this man hadn't registered the vehicle in his name, there would surely be some old paperwork from earlier registrations. Somebody definitely cleaned out the box."

I waved for Takecia to follow me outside of the wall we had formed with the vehicles. Once we were standing over the evidence flags near the peel-out marks, I pointed to the scuff mark we'd located earlier. It was about three feet before the peel-out marks and nearly centered with them.

"Do you know what made this mark?"

Takecia was quiet for a long moment, deep in thought. Finally, she shook her head. "I would say a jack, but it would've been on one side of the car or the other, and closer to the tires."

"It was a car jack," I said with a smile, "but it was one of those old fashioned kinds. You're probably too young to remember the stand-up jacks that attached to the bumpers, but I believe that's what made this mark. They jacked up the back of the vehicle, weighted the accelerator down, and then gave the truck a push. Once the jack toppled over and the rear tires made contact with the shells, they left these peel-out marks on the way to the bayou."

"First off, Mr. Detective Man," Takecia began with a wag of her finger, "you're not that much older than me. Second, the accelerator wasn't weighted down. That was the first thing I checked when I entered the driver's side."

I smiled. "It was weighted down, alright, but in the most unique way I've ever seen. The killer or killers definitely wanted to make it look like a suicide."

Takecia cocked her head to the side impatiently. "Well, how was it done?"

I waved for her to follow me. As we walked back toward the truck, I saw Ali talking to a woman who had walked by pushing a stroller. They were both looking toward my Tahoe, which hid the victim's truck from their view, and Ali eventually pointed toward Takecia and me. I smiled and waved, but didn't stop walking.

Once we'd reached the pickup again, I pulled on another glove and opened the back driver's side door. I reached inside and removed one of the bags of ice. There was water sloshing around in the plastic.

"When I first saw these bags of ice, I just figured they were empty from someone icing down food or drinks, and that they had been tossed into the truck like the other garbage that was scattered around. I figured our victim left it there until he could get to a garbage can to throw it away. It's what I do with my trash." I paused and shook the bag. "But there's still water in this bag and the other one, and they haven't been ripped open."

Realization seemed to hit Takecia just then. "They used the bags of ice to hold down the accelerator!"

"Yeah, it's like the mythical projectile that appeared in a movie I watched years ago," I explained. "The assassin in the movie fired a projectile made of ice to kill the victim, and the evidence just melted away. While that can't happen in real life, it's definitely possible to use two bags of ice to hold down the accelerator. Once the truck goes into the water, all evidence of the accelerator being weighted down would just melt and float away."

"How'd you figure that out?" Takecia wanted to know.

"Too many things weren't adding up, so I knew the scene

must've been staged," I began. "Like you, I looked to see if something had been propped against the accelerator. There was no evidence of scuff marks on the seat opposite the accelerator, and there were no sticks or rods or bricks left inside the truck that could've been used, so I initially ruled it out. That's when I noticed the bags of ice were unopened. I began to wonder why our victim would have two bags of ice laying around his truck, and it dawned on me that someone had used the bags to depress the accelerator."

"Would they be heavy enough to hold down an accelerator?" She seemed skeptical.

"It depends. I did an experiment once when I worked as a detective back in the city. If you were to lay a brick or a ten-pound weight directly on the accelerator, it would simply push the brick or weight back." I lifted a finger. "However, if you depress the accelerator and *then* put the brick or weight against it, it could work. A brick on its own would still be too light and could slide away from the opposing force of the accelerator, but two ten-pound bags of ice would be enough to keep it firmly in place."

Takecia leaned into the driver's side compartment and studied the floorboard. "I guess a twenty-pound bag of ice would be too big to fit between the hump and the brake pedal."

I nodded. "That's why they used two ten-pound bags."

She straightened, but still seemed skeptical. "That's a lot of work just to kill one man. Are you sure he didn't do this to himself?"

"Think of how we found him," I said, pointing to the truck. "He was still strapped into his seatbelt. Had he been alive when he hit the water, he would've fought to get out. Even if he wanted to die, at some point, his survival instincts would've kicked in. He would've gotten the seatbelt off and started fighting to get out of the cab. He might've remained trapped in the cab, but we would've found evidence of him clawing around and trying to escape. He wouldn't have been sitting in the seat like he was on a lazy Sunday afternoon drive."

"That's why they pay you the big bucks," she said with a smile.

I grunted, and added, "Look, I learned a long time ago that you have to keep an open mind and go where the evidence takes you. Could I be wrong? Sure, but if I were a gambling man, I'd bet this man was dead before he hit the water. There's no way he drowned."

CHAPTER 19

"He drowned," Dr. Wong said the next morning as she peeled off her latex gloves and tossed them into the red biohazard waste can.

"It's a good thing I didn't take you up on that bet," Takecia said, flashing a bright smile. After wrapping up the investigation on the previous night, she had asked to tag along for the remainder of the case. Susan had agreed to pay her overtime and let her stay on the case, as long as she could be back to work to cover her night shifts on Wednesday and Thursday. "Had we shook on it, I'd be a rich woman."

I smiled, but I wasn't ready to accept defeat just yet. I always followed the evidence, and while the evidence from the autopsy revealed our victim had drowned, it didn't refute the evidence we had found at the scene. Besides, the autopsy wasn't complete yet, so there was still room for more.

"What's the fastest you can get his toxicology worked up?" I asked, already knowing the answer, but hoping for a break in the case.

"You know the drill." Dr. Wong removed her face shield and nodded for her assistant to begin sewing up our victim. "If I put a rush on it, I might be able to get it to you right at four weeks, but don't hold your breath. You know how it goes with toxicology reports."

I nodded, and began tapping the toe of my boot lightly on the floor. The autopsy had revealed nothing about our victim, other than he had drowned. There were no scars or marks to help identify him. An X-ray had not revealed any broken bones, and there had been no internal injuries of any kind. The only visible injury was a small bruise just above the hairline, and Dr. Wong surmised it had been caused when his head rocked forward and hit the steering wheel upon impact. The airbag had not deployed, but I wasn't surprised. The truck was old and in disrepair.

"Doc, do you think it's plausible that he was incapacitated somehow and his truck was sent over the embankment?" I asked, as a part of me began to wonder if I might have misread the crime scene. Before Dr. Wong had begun the autopsy, I had described everything we'd found at the scene, while at the same time recovering our victim's prints with my cadaver fingerprint kit. Dr. Wong had only listened and geared up as I'd talked.

"Everything you described earlier sounds suspicious," she agreed. "Had he crashed into the bayou by accident or even intentionally, I would've expected to find his fingernails missing or cracked. Even if he wanted to die, he would've involuntarily clawed at his seatbelt or the door handle or the windows in an attempt to free himself, but his fingernails were in pristine condition. It was as though he simply sat there and allowed himself to drown. He didn't even reach up to claw at his throat, which is atypical for a person who can't breathe."

Dr. Wong paused for a moment, seeming to consider everything we knew so far, and then shrugged.

"Sure, I believe it's plausible that he was incapacitated," she finally said, "but you know I can't rule it a homicide unless I have some evidence to support it. I'll classify it as *Undetermined* for now, but if the toxicology workup says different or you bring me something solid, I'll change it. And while you're at it, please find a name for this man. I don't like strangers in my morgue."

I chuckled and, after thanking her and her assistant, led the way down the long corridor and out into the parking lot, where the morning sun was shining brightly.

"Where to now?" Takecia asked once we'd climbed into my Tahoe. She wore dress slacks, a loose-fitting blouse, and her tactical boots. Her pistol was tucked into a leather paddle holster on her belt. I only rarely saw her out of uniform, so it was different seeing her dressed as a detective. "It's too early for lunch."

"To be honest, we're kind of at a standstill until the toxicology report comes back," I said slowly, firing up the engine and turning up the air. "Even if his blood comes back dirty, I really don't know what more we could do. We've already canvassed the area where the truck was found for witnesses and searched for cameras, but that turned up nothing. After you left last night, I jumped on the computer and went through every recent missing person case in the tri-state area, but turned up nothing. Other than going to the press and asking for the public's help, I don't know what more we could do."

Takecia nodded and pointed ahead, where I'd turned and headed away from town. "So, where are we going?" she repeated.

"The sheriff's office crime lab to drop off our victim's fingerprints, and then we're off to the hospital," I said. "I want to check in on Mr. Verdin. He's had a night to sleep it off, so maybe he'll remember something helpful."

Takecia immediately sat a little straighter in her seat and caught her breath.

I didn't comment or acknowledge her change of posture in any way. Whatever was going on between her and the emergency room doctor, I was hoping for the best. Takecia was a good woman and she deserved a good man. I didn't know if Dr. Evans was that guy but, for his sake, I was hoping he was, because if he hurt Takecia like her last boyfriend had, I knew Susan would come out of retirement to rearrange the furniture on his face.

We stopped at the sheriff's office first and I met with Vanessa Comeaux, who was a scientist in their lab. I signed over the cards containing the victim's known prints, and I asked if she'd been able to do any work on the victim's truck yet.

"We processed it for prints, DNA, and fibers," she said. "We did recover legible prints from the steering wheel, rearview mirror, passenger's side window, the tailgate, and one of the ice bags."

"You got one from the bag of ice?" I asked excitedly.

"We did." Her blonde ponytail bobbed up and down as she nodded her head. "We ran all the prints through AFIS, but we didn't get any hits back. I'll compare everything we recovered against your victim's prints. Let's hope some of them don't belong to him."

I agreed. After a brief conversation, we left and headed for the hospital. It was a little before ten when I parked my Tahoe in the emergency room parking lot. Takecia beat me to the pavement and was already halfway to the entrance by the time I shut my door and hit the lock button on the key fob.

I caught a glimpse of Gretchen's K-9 cruiser parked near the front of the building and was glad to see it. I would need an interpreter to speak with Mr. Verdin again, so her presence was definitely appreciated. Not only was she helpful in relaying my questions to Mr. Verdin and his responses back to me, but it seemed her grandpa was in better spirits when she was around. That the elderly man was proud of his granddaughter was obvious, and it was plain to see how much she loved her pépère.

Takecia had hurried through the sliding doors and disappeared from my view when they slid shut. I smiled. I was glad that she had tagged along on my case—not only because she was a tremendous help to me, but because she had run into Bruce Evans.

My smile faded a little as I strode through the sliding doors and saw her speaking with the head nurse at the counter. She looked so excited at the moment. Sure, if things went well between her and Bruce, I would continue to feel good about her tagging along. However, if things didn't work out, I would feel somewhat responsible.

When Takecia heard me approach from behind, she turned from the counter. She had that same starry-eyed expression on her face from the previous day, and I knew she was smitten.

"They said we could go straight up to Mr. Verdin's room to see him," she explained, "but I asked if they could call Bruce to give us an update before we meet with him and Gretchen."

"I'm sure you did," I said with a wide grin. "Why don't I head up to see Mr. Verdin, and you wait here to get a status report from Dr. Evans? We can meet up again later."

Her face was beaming as she nodded, but then something suddenly caught her attention behind me. Her brow furrowed and her face fell. She lurched forward and pushed past me, stopping only when she'd reached the newsstand in the waiting area.

"Oh, shit, Clint," she muttered, lifting a newspaper from the top slot of the rack, "you need to see this. You won't like it."

CHAPTER 20

I hurried to where Takecia stood and looked at the newspaper in her hand. There, above the fold, was a picture of her and me standing in front of our victim's truck. It was in full color and it took up the entire top half of the page.

"Not a bad picture," I mused aloud.

She tapped the headline with her middle finger. I groaned when I read it.

Unidentified Man Pulled From Bayou, Police Baffled

"Baffled is a very strong word," I said with a grin and a shake of my head. "Couldn't she just have mentioned that we were seeking information from the public?"

Takecia only nodded. She had begun reading the article, so I joined in with her. Ali had done a decent job of relaying the facts as she understood them, and she did make a public appeal for anyone with information to contact the police department. I was almost finished reading the piece when I caught movement from behind us. Before I could turn, Dr. Evans offered a greeting—and it was directed toward Takecia.

"Bruce," Takecia said, shoving the newspaper into my chest. "How are you?"

Bruce made no effort to hide his appreciation for Takecia's appearance in civilian clothes. It was only then that I understood why Takecia had dressed more for court or church rather than for attending autopsies and chasing bad guys—of course, the jury was still out on whether or not a bad guy was involved. I still wasn't sure if ours was a murder case, an accident, or a suicide, but I was going to treat it as a homicide until I could prove otherwise.

I knew Takecia was excited to work this case with me, but at that very moment, Dr. Evans had her undivided attention.

"Look, why don't y'all catch up," I said smoothly, "and I'll check in on Mr. Verdin."

Takecia started to object, but I waved her off. "Nonsense, I'm a big boy," I said. "I think I can handle this one alone."

She let out a hearty laugh and I walked away to find the elevator to Mr. Verdin's room. On the way up to the third floor, my phone started to ring, but it disconnected when I answered. I waited until the elevator reached the third floor, stepped out, and checked the number. It was one I didn't recognize. I was about to call it back when I heard my name. I glanced up to see Gretchen strolling down the hallway carrying two cold drinks and a bag of Cheez-Its.

"These are my pépère's favorite," she said, holding up the bag of Cheez-Its. "He asked me to sneak him a bag when the nurse wasn't looking. He thinks they'll fuss him for eating junk at his age."

I laughed and followed her to Mr. Verdin's room. They had him propped up in a seated position, and it seemed to agree with him. All the color had returned to his face and he was speaking with more fervor.

"How's he doing?" I asked.

Gretchen posed the question to her grandpa in French, and then turned to me. "He said he wants to go home. He's tired of sitting here doing nothing. He wants to go back and run his catfish lines, because the best of the season is about to be over."

I admired the man's determination and his work ethic. I asked Gretchen if she could ask if he had remembered anything new about the night of the accident. She asked, but she didn't have to relay his response. I knew by the shake of his head that he hadn't remembered anything. I had known it was a long shot, but knew I had to try. If someone didn't give us something soon, the case might drag out for weeks, months, or even years—and the one thing I didn't have was time. While Susan wasn't due for a few more weeks, the doctor had warned us that the baby could come at any time, and I did *not* want to be working a case when my child was born.

"I saw the article in the paper," Gretchen said with a sly grin. She knew how much I didn't like attention. "Nice picture. I was thinking maybe you could autograph one of my pépère's casts. I mean, since you're famous and all now."

"I thought I'd get a break from being teased about my age since Amy was off on her honeymoon," I said with a grunt. "Did she pay you to take over while she was gone, or are you doing it for free?"

"She didn't want you to lose your edge."

I shook my head, told her to tell her grandpa to call if he had any problems, and then I left the hospital room. As I made my way to the elevator, I looked up the number of an old friend of mine in town. When he answered, I asked if he could build me a pirogue with two seats, and I gave him the dimensions of Mr. Verdin's pirogue.

"What happened to the other one I built you?" he asked. "Did you destroy it already?"

"No," I said, pausing outside the elevator door to finish the call. "It's a gift for a friend."

"Would it have anything to do with the pirogue that got smashed up when that truck took a dive on the north end of town?"

"Thanks a lot, Ali," I muttered under my breath. To my buddy, I said, "Yeah, I'd like to replace Mr. Verdin's pirogue. He'll need a new one to run his catfish lines."

"Well, that's all you had to say," he said. "It's on me."

"No," I said more forcefully than I meant it to come out. "I'd consider it an insult if you took this from me."

He hesitated for a moment. "What if we go half and half?"

I sighed. "Fine, that'll work. And thanks. I really appreciate it."

"No problem."

I ended the call, rode the elevator to the first floor, and looked around for Takecia.

"If you're looking for your partner," the head nurse called from the other side of the glass, "she's in the cafeteria with Dr. Evans. And it looked like things were going *pretty* good."

I wondered if I should just leave and come back later. I didn't want to intrude on their time alone. As I stood there mulling it over, my cell phone rang. I glanced at the screen. It was the same number from earlier.

"This is Clint," I answered, ready to shut down a telemarketer in a hurry. "What can I do for you?"

"Is this Detective Clint Wolf?" asked an uncertain voice.

"Yes, it is," I said, growing curious. "What's up?"

"This is Rusty…Rusty Dantin. I work on the bridge. I talked to you yesterday about a boat crash."

"Oh, yeah, I remember you," I said. "Did you remember something?"

"No," he said, "I didn't remember anything about a boat, but I did see your picture in the newspaper."

I groaned again. "Well, they didn't have my permission to print that picture. They took it from my bad side."

He laughed at that. "Yeah, well, I was looking at the picture and I read the article, and I think I saw that truck before."

I froze in place. "The truck in the picture?"

"Yes, sir," he said. "I'm pretty sure I saw that truck before—the one that y'all pulled out of the water. It came over the bridge one day."

"Do you remember when it came over the bridge?" I was trying not to sound overly excited, but I wasn't doing such a great job.

"Yes, sir. It was about two weeks ago."

"And did you see the person driving the truck?"

"Yeah, it was a man. In fact, I even talked to him."

"Can you describe what he looked like?"

"Sure," Rusty said. "He had brown hair. It was thick. And he had brown eyes, too. It looked like he was a weightlifter or something. He was nice."

"Really?" I scowled. "How do you know that?"

"Know what?"

"That he was nice."

"Oh, because I talked to him," Rusty explained. "I had to open the bridge for a boat to pass and he was the first car that stopped. He got out of his truck—the same one I saw in the newspaper—and started talking to me. In fact, he gave me something."

"What?" I began walking swiftly toward the cafeteria to find Takecia. "What'd he give you?"

"I don't really know," he said hesitantly. "It was some kind of little book. I didn't read it or nothing, so I don't know what it was about."

My mind was racing through the possibilities as I strode down the long corridor that led to the cafeteria. What if our victim was an author and it was his book? That would be the best-case scenario. If he wasn't the author, he might at least have scribbled his name inside the book—or someone else might have, and that would give us a place to start looking. If it was a library book, there should be a stamp, which would point us toward an address where someone might recognize a picture of our dead guy.

"Where's this book now?" I asked.

"Well, it should still be in the shack on the bridge. I...is it important?"

"Yes, everything's important at this point."

I thought I heard him gulp on the other end.

"What is it?" I asked. "What's wrong?"

"I…I threw it away."

"You did what?" I lurched to a stop, my left hand on the door to the cafeteria. "Where'd you throw it?"

"In the garbage can near the bunk," he said. "I'm not a reader and I didn't think anyone else would want to, so I just chunked it."

"When do y'all do garbage pickup at the bridge?"

"What day is it?" he asked.

"It's Tuesday."

"Oh, the trash goes out today."

Of course it does! I wanted to shout.

Instead, I asked if he could call the bridge tender on duty and have him or her check the trash. He said he would, I ended the call and pushed through the door. After a quick scan of the large cafeteria, I saw Takecia and the doctor sitting all alone at a table in the corner of the room. They were both laughing heartily.

I hesitated. I couldn't remember seeing Takecia so happy before, and I hated to be the one to ruin the party. I thought about leaving and returning later for her, but then she turned in my direction and saw me standing there. She said something to Dr. Evans, they both stood to their feet, and then she hugged him. She seemed to float as she headed in my direction.

"We might have a lead," I said when she reached me. I didn't need to ask how things were going with the doctor, because it was written all over her face.

"Let's go!"

Neither of us said anything until we were out in the parking lot, and it was she who spoke first.

"You know what's crazy?"

"What's that?"

"Bruce and I haven't seen each other in decades, but it's like we just spoke yesterday." She stopped near my Tahoe and turned to look at me. "He looks a lot different as a man, but he's still that young boy I fell in love with so long ago."

CHAPTER 21

The outer walls of the bridge shack were greasy and in desperate need of a paint job, and the bridge tender on duty looked disheveled and disoriented when she came to the door.

"What's going on?" she asked, rubbing sleep from her eyes.

I explained who we were and why we were there, but it didn't seem to register. I was about to repeat myself when I heard a voice shouting from the eastern side of the bridge. I turned to see a man with long red hair jogging toward us.

"I'm Rusty," he said when he reached us. He stood panting for a few seconds trying to catch his breath, and then he turned toward the bridge tender. "Hey, Delores, I need to check the trash can."

The woman stepped aside and Rusty dipped into the shack. I could hear him shuffling around inside, and then I heard a cry of triumph. I glanced at Takecia. She hadn't stopped smiling since the hospital, so I couldn't tell if she was as happy as I was that he had found the book.

"Here it is," Rusty said when he reappeared. "This is the book he gave me."

I frowned as I stared down at the object in his hand. It was more like a small pamphlet than a book. I took it from him and immediately knew what it was when I saw the cover. It was a gospel tract—a small booklet used to spread the Word of God through stories—and it appeared fairly new. I'd seen my mom with similar tracts when I was a kid.

"What'd he say to you?" I asked as I skimmed through the pages. "Did he give you his name?"

"He called himself a father or something," Rusty said, his brow furrowed. "Father Carlos, I think it was? Or maybe he said brother. Brother Carlos? I can't be sure. I just know it sounded weird."

"Father Carlos or Brother Carlos?" I looked up from the tract. "Was he a priest?"

"I mean, he wasn't dressed like one, but I don't know if they always dress like that or not." Rusty shrugged. "He was just wearing jeans and a shirt with a collar. He was a smooth talker, though, that I know. Come to think of it, he didn't sound like a priest. He sounded more like a car salesman, and that kinda turned me off. I don't like being pressured, and it felt like he was pressuring me to be religious."

"What was he saying?"

"He was asking me if I went to church and if I believed in God," he said. "I told him I did believe in God, but that I hadn't been to church since I was a kid. My parents were Catholic and they made us go to church a lot, so I kind of got tired of it. When I said that, he looked at me like he didn't approve of me. That's when I felt like he was judging me."

"Did he say if he was a preacher of a church?" I asked. "Or did he invite you to a specific church?"

"He didn't say for sure if he was a preacher and he didn't give a name of a church, but he did say something about starting a church here, or that he had started a church somewhere else." Rusty shook his head. "I can't be sure. I wasn't really paying a lot of attention to what he was saying. My dad's always preaching down to me and it felt like he was doing the same thing, so I kinda shut him out. I don't like being preached to, so I just kinda nodded while he was talking, and then when the boat passed, I told him I had to close the bridge so the cars could cross the bayou. By that time, there was a line of traffic waiting to cross. That's when he pulled out that book and gave it to me."

"I thought you said he was nice?" I asked, confused.

"He was nice, but I didn't like the way he was talking to me."

I had noticed Takecia listening intently to Rusty as he spoke, and once he was done, she gave me a nod.

"I might know who can help us," she said. "I met a new preacher in town yesterday morning when I was running radar. It was right before I got the call about Mr. Verdin being missing. The preacher called himself Father Reggie Hamilton, so he might be connected to this Father Carlos fellow."

I was thoughtful. I'd remembered seeing a utility truck erecting a new sign at the old car dealership toward the southern end of town, and I remembered thinking it was for a church. I asked Takecia if it was the same church, and she nodded.

"The preacher was real nice," she said. "He told me I could run radar from his parking lot anytime, and he even offered me some coffee. I'm sure he'll be helpful if he knows anything."

I turned back to Rusty. "Did this Father Carlos say anything else to you?"

"No, sir. That was it. I closed the bridge, he waved as he drove on by, and I never saw him or that old truck again until I read the newspaper yesterday afternoon."

I thanked him and headed for my Tahoe.

"That was yesterday's paper?" I asked Takecia as we strolled across the bridge.

"Yep," she said with a smile. "Ali didn't waste any time."

A car drove by and the bridge dipped in the water and made a loud, rattling sound. I smiled to myself. There was no other sound that made me feel more at home than that of a vehicle driving over a pontoon bridge.

I continued flipping through the tract as we continued our stroll across the bridge. The message was an interesting one, and I found myself reading the text. I was just flipping to the last page when we reached my Tahoe.

"Well, this was a dead end," I said, closing the tract. I was about to open my door when something on the back page caught my eye. I stopped and pulled it closer.

"Hey, wait a minute," I said to Takecia, "this thing has a stamp on it."

She had been rounding the front of my Tahoe, but she stopped and walked over to where I stood. I held the tract so she could see the back page. The stamp was faded, but it looked to be an address.

"Can you see this?" I asked, tilting it more toward her.

Takecia took it and pulled it close to her face. She squinted and moved the tract to the right and then the left, trying to catch the most sunlight. Finally, she held it still and stared intently.

"Yeah," she said, "there's definitely an address on here, but I've never heard of this place. It's 777 Spirit Way in Sandy Knobs, Nevada."

"Sandy Knobs, Nevada?" I asked. "Where in the hell is that, and what in the hell is this man doing here?"

"Maybe that's just the address for the publisher of these tracts," she offered with a shrug. "It doesn't mean he's from there."

"That's true," I said. "Let's go talk to your preacher. Afterward, we can pick up some lunch and head to the office to research this Sandy Knobs place."

As I drove away from the bridge, I began to worry. My investigations had taken me across the country on more than a few occasions, and I was completely fine with it. I loved my job and I would drive to the end of the earth to solve a case. I actually considered it a perk of the job. However, my baby boy was due to be born at any time, and I did *not* want to be on the road when that happened.

I started to say a silent prayer for a speedy resolution to our case, but then thought better of it. That would be a waste of a prayer, and it would be a selfish request. There were people out there with real problems who needed His help, and they didn't need the airwaves clogged up with needless chatter.

I decided I wouldn't worry about it. I would follow the evidence wherever it led, and if it would require me to take a trip to Sandy Knobs, Nevada—wherever the hell that was supposed to be—I would decide at that point what to do about it.

Until then, I would just keep plugging away at the investigation, and hopefully find a local link to the man in the blue truck that we'd pulled from the bottom of the bayou.

CHAPTER 22

When Takecia and I made it to the Mechant Life Church, I grabbed the envelope with the gospel tract inside and we walked into the lobby. We made contact with a secretary who smiled pleasantly and pushed a lock of blonde hair away from her forehead.

"Hey," she said, pointing to Takecia, "aren't you the officer who was in the parking lot yesterday morning?"

"Guilty as charged," Takecia said. "I was trying to ruin someone's morning, but people must think it's a sin to speed past a church, because everyone was on their best behavior. Are you Laurie?"

"Guilty as charged," the secretary echoed, laughing as she did so. "I guess you're here to see Father Reggie."

Takecia and I nodded in unison.

"We just need to ask him if he knows someone," I explained. "It's for a case we're working."

"Oh, wow, is it about the body that was found in the bayou?" she asked, her eyebrows arching. "I heard he was cut to pieces, shoved inside his truck, and then pushed over the edge."

The dead guy in the bayou was the most excitement we'd had in town since the storm had blown through two months earlier, so I knew it would be futile to deny it. However, I wasn't going to confirm or deny her street gossip.

"Yes, ma'am, we're here about that case."

Her sky blue eyes sparkled and she rose from her chair. "Follow me," she said, opening the door to the receptionist area. "He's in the tabernacle."

As we followed Laurie, she spoke in hushed tones, explaining what she had heard from one of her neighbors. None of it was even remotely accurate, but neither Takecia nor I corrected her. We simply walked behind her and let her rattle on about the case.

Even before we reached the door to what she had called the *tabernacle,* we could hear a man's shouts echoing from inside.

"It's Father Reggie," she explained. "He's getting ready for tomorrow night's service. We have church on Wednesday nights and twice on Sundays. Y'all should come."

I only nodded and smiled when she looked over her shoulder to make the invitation, and then we were stepping through the door and into a large sanctuary. A cross hung on the wall above the stage. There were three rows of pews stretching from the stage to the rear of the room, and red carpet covered the floor between the rows.

Father Reggie had been shouting his sermon—his eyes closed and his face turned skyward—but he immediately clamped his mouth shut when we entered. How he knew we were there, I didn't know, but I didn't even have a chance to make sense out of what he was saying. He smiled and carefully placed a rope book mark across the pages of his open Bible, and then closed it.

"Sergeant Gayle, am I right?" he asked, walking down from the stage still holding on to the Bible. "To what do I owe this pleasure?"

Takecia shot a thumb in my direction. "This is Detective Clint Wolf, and he's working the case where that man was found in his truck. He needs to ask you some questions."

Father Reggie turned his attention to me. "I have the utmost respect for law enforcement officers," he said sincerely. "You guys have a thankless job and are most often unappreciated, yet you perform your duties with the gusto of someone representing their country in the Olympics."

I never did like compliments or praise, so I simply nodded my thanks and got right down to business.

"Do you know a man who calls himself Father Carlos?"

Father Reggie scowled. "Father Carlos who?"

"We don't know," I admitted. "We're trying to identify a man who was pulled out of the bayou yesterday, and we received information that he goes by Father Carlos."

"Is this the man who was found cut to pieces?" he asked, glancing at Laurie for confirmation.

Laurie nodded. Her eyes were wide with excitement.

"Well, he wasn't found cut to pieces," I corrected. "He was just found in his truck, all intact."

This seemed to disappoint Laurie, but she didn't say anything.

"Father Carlos," Reggie repeated. "Hmm…it's not ringing any bells. Do you know what church he attended?"

"We don't, but he did give this to a bridge tender in the parish." I pulled the gospel tract from the envelope and turned it so he could read the address on the back. "The address is hard to see, but it's 777 Spirit Way in Sandy Knobs, Nevada."

"Where's Sandy Knobs, Nevada?" he asked, leaning close to study the tract.

"I'm not sure," I said. "We haven't had the chance to research it yet."

He asked to see the front of the tract, and I obliged him. After reading the cover, he nodded.

"I recognize this tract," he said. "There's a Christian publisher that publishes a whole line of these, but they're not headquartered in Nevada. They're somewhere in the south. I guess whoever's handing these out put the address to their church on it in an attempt to attract some new followers."

I sighed, glanced at Takecia to see if she had any questions.

"The people who make this tract," she began, "with what religion are they affiliated?"

"They would be of the Christian faith," he opined, "most likely from a non-denominational church. I mean, you can look over there by the door. We have tracts from this same publisher on the rack, but we don't push them on people. I don't like the used car salesman approach to ministering the gospel."

I nodded my appreciation, and thought of another question. "Are there any other non-denomination churches in this area?"

Father Reggie was thoughtful. "We're the only one in town, but there's another church like ours in Magnolia Parish. Being in law enforcement, you guys might've heard about all the commotion that happened over at that church a bunch of years back. It made all the national news stations and was discussed on every talk show in the country."

"What was the name of the church?" I asked.

"It was called the Magnolia Life Church—and still is to this day—but it's under different spiritual leadership." He nodded for emphasis. "They've definitely cleaned things up since then, thank the Lord. That place was full of sin, from the top down."

"How long ago was that?" I asked, wondering if there might be a possible connection to our victim. "I've only been in town for about eight years now, and I don't remember seeing or hearing anything about a church in the news."

"I've been here less time than he has," Takecia joined in, "so I definitely haven't heard of it either."

"Oh, that was about seventeen years ago," he said. "I was pastoring a church in Alabama at the time, and I wasn't intimately familiar with the situation, but I did see nonstop media coverage, and a number of us pastors from different denominations got together to discuss how it would impact the public's perception of what the rest of us were doing. It was a dark time for everyone in the faith, that's for sure."

I did the math in my head. Seventeen years earlier, I had been set to marry my first wife, Michele Landry, and I was working as a homicide detective for the La Mort Police Department. I had only been in homicide for a year when the church incident would've happened in Magnolia Parish, and I remembered things being hectic in the city, so there was no wonder I had missed it. Between visiting wedding venues, helping to decide what food to serve at the reception, and chasing down the worst of the city's populace, I'd never had time to watch television or read the news. I had been too busy making the news myself.

"What actually happened back then?" I asked the pastor, my curiosity thoroughly aroused.

Father Reggie sat at the edge of the stage and began telling the story. Some of it sounded familiar, but I couldn't be sure if I had heard about it or imagined it. I had worked too many of my own cases over the years to pay attention to what other detectives were doing, and I tended to tune out most of the noise if it didn't pertain to something I was working.

When he was done talking, I straightened from where I'd been leaning against a support column and rubbed my chin thoughtfully. His history lesson might actually be of use to us. While I was certain there was no connection between the Magnolia Life Church incident and the drowning of our victim, I was hopeful that Carlos might somehow be tied to that church and that someone over there might be able to identify him.

As it stood at that moment, we had a dead man whose family knew not where he was, and we had not a clue as to his identity, except that he called himself Father Carlos. I had not been able to find a missing person report matching his description, but it was quite possible he hadn't been reported missing yet. After all, he had been dead for less than forty-eight hours and it appeared he had been traveling, so there was a good chance his family hadn't started to miss him yet.

I frowned as I considered his family. At the least, he was someone's son; at most, he was a brother, a husband, a father, and an uncle. Hell, he could have even been a grandpa, considering he appeared to be in his mid-fifties.

I hesitated for a moment, and then pulled out a photo I had printed up the previous night. It was a close-up of our victim's face.

"I know the name doesn't sound familiar to you," I said to the pastor, "but would you mind looking at this photo to see if you recognize him?"

Father Reggie nodded somberly, knowing he was about to look at a dead man. I handed him the photo and he studied it intently. My cell phone buzzed in my pocket while he was examining it, but I ignored it. After a long and careful moment, Father Reggie handed back the picture.

"No, sir, I don't recognize him."

I thanked him for his time, and was about to leave when Father Reggie called out to his secretary.

"Laurie, can you have a look at this picture?" He turned back to Takecia and me. "She has family who attends Magnolia Life and she visits there from time to time. If he's affiliated with them, she might recognize him."

Laurie approached us and stood with her hands clasped against her stomach. "Is…um, is the man in the picture dead?"

I frowned. "You don't have to look at it if you don't want to."

"Is it scary looking?"

Takecia stepped forward and put a hand on Laurie's shoulders. "It looks like he's sleeping," she said gently. "Have you ever been to a funeral?"

"Oh, yeah, both of my grandparents passed away last year, and I went to their funerals."

"It looks like that," Takecia said.

Laurie swallowed and nodded. "Okay, I'm ready."

I turned the picture so she could see it. I was ready to flip it back around if she reacted harshly to it, but she didn't. She only frowned.

"I don't know," she said. "It's hard to say for sure, but he does look familiar."

"Really?" I asked excitedly.

"It's no one that goes there now, and I'm not even positive it's even him, but it does look like a man who used to go there. Of course, that would've been years ago when I was small, and he looks a lot different in that picture, but it could be him."

"Do you know his name?"

"No, sir. I was a little kid back when we first went there, so I didn't really know all the grownups." She shuddered. "We quit going after all the drama happened, but—if he's the same man I'm thinking of—he wasn't even there at that time. I think he left a few years before that whole thing with the baby. That wasn't unusual, though. A lot of people came and went there, and they do the same thing here."

Reggie nodded his agreement. "It happens everywhere."

After asking a few more questions and giving Takecia an opportunity to ask some, we thanked them and then made our exit. Once we were in my Tahoe, I checked my cell phone to see who had called me. I grunted and turned the screen so Takecia could see.

"Why would Amy be calling? She hasn't been on her honeymoon for three whole days yet and she's already calling work." Even as I asked the question, a thought occurred to me. "Oh, shit, what if something's wrong?"

This got Takecia's attention. "Quick, call her back."

CHAPTER 23

Provo, Utah
Earlier…

Amy rolled to her stomach and draped an arm over Baylor's bare chest. She used his body to shield her eyes from the bright rays that flooded in through a crack in the hotel room curtain.

"What time is it?" she asked.

"It's a quarter to nine." He sounded wide awake. "I've been up since the sun came over that mountain over there."

"What time did we go to bed?" Amy asked, trying to burrow deeper into the soft mattress.

"Four o'clock."

"Utah time or Louisiana time?"

"Utah time," Baylor said.

"Does that mean we would've gone to bed at three in Louisiana?"

"No, five."

Amy bristled. "I can't get used to this damned time zone. I want to go back home."

Baylor slipped his warm hand under her thin shirt and ran it slowly up her stomach. "Are you sure about that?"

"No." She arched her back to give him room to remove her shirt, suddenly fully awake. "Three weeks of uninterrupted sex and room service is starting to sound really good right about now. Let's just stay here until it's time to go back home. To hell with Yellowstone."

"Sounds good to me."

Amy Cooke Rice pulled her new husband close and they made

love for the third time since arriving at the hotel on the previous evening. When they were done thirty minutes later, Baylor slipped out of bed and pulled on his jeans.

"What're you doing?" Amy asked. "You're not pulling a hit and run, are you?"

"Nope, I'll be bringing you breakfast in bed again."

Amy smiled and stretched lazily on the soft mattress. Although they had been living together for a while prior to getting married on Saturday and he had always brought her breakfast in bed when he could, she kept up the game. "You're gonna spoil me, Mr. Rice!"

"That's the plan."

Once Baylor had left, Amy closed her eyes in an attempt to go back to sleep, but sleep wouldn't come. She pulled on her shirt and turned on the television. The hotel's logo popped up. She tried to navigate to the screen that displayed a list of channels, but she couldn't figure out the remote.

Cursing, she killed the power and tossed the remote on the bed beside her. She glanced at her cell phone. She hadn't touched it since the wedding. Well, except to check the time. Her mind had drifted a few times on the long drive from Louisiana to Utah, and she had found herself wondering if anything was going down in town. Since she was on her honeymoon, she figured no one would bother her if a major crime occurred. She thought back to the last thing Clint had said when she and Baylor were about to abscond with a giant piece of wedding cake: "Don't look back, and don't think about this place for a second. Your job will still be here when you get back—well, unless Shade wants it."

She had laughed and allowed herself to be taken by the hand and whisked away by Baylor. They had been on the road since then, and they were supposed to leave later this afternoon to continue toward Yellowstone National Park. She figured she would lose cell service again once they got into the middle of nowhere, so she decided to give in and check her phone.

Sitting up in bed, she accessed the internet and searched the social media pages of several people she knew from town. No one had posted anything of interest, and that made her feel better. She was about to close out the app when she thought about the local newspaper. Short of calling someone at the police department, checking the Mechant Voice's social media page would be the best way to find out if anything was happening in town, so she did just that.

"What the hell?" she blurted out loud when she saw a picture of

Clint and Takecia standing next to a busted-up truck that had been pulled from the bayou. She quickly scrolled through the article, hanging on every word. Ali Bridges, who had written the article, didn't have a lot of details about the incident, but Amy wasn't surprised. Clint would've only provided that information which was absolutely necessary to disseminate, and it was not enough to satisfy Amy's raging curiosity.

Sliding her thumb across the screen, she accessed her contacts folder and pressed the button that displayed Clint's name. It rang and rang and rang, but Clint didn't pick up.

"You little shit!" she hollered.

"What'd I do?"

She hadn't heard Baylor enter the room, and she jerked in her skin when he spoke. She quickly explained that she hadn't been talking to him. She saw that he was struggling to get through the door without dropping something, so she hurried to help him.

"There's been a murder in town," she explained as she reached for a cup of coffee and a plate. "A truck was pulled out of the bayou and a body was found inside."

Baylor used his boot to kick the door shut. "Have they made any arrests yet?"

"I don't know." Amy put the food on the table in the kitchen area of the suite and then retrieved her phone from the bed. She quickly accessed the article and turned her phone toward Baylor. He put down the food and read it.

"It doesn't say anything about murder in the article," he said. "They say it might've been an accident or the man might've been drunk."

"Nah, it was a murder." Amy enlarged the photo until only Clint's face was visible on her screen. "See the look on his face?"

Baylor grunted. "I think you might be right."

"I know I'm right," she said. "I've seen that look on his face too many times not to recognize it. It's the '*who killed this man?*' look."

No longer hungry, Amy had to force herself to eat. Her mind was 1700 miles away. While she was enjoying her time with her new husband, she missed work. Being a detective was a large part of her life, and she had been afraid that something big would happen when she was gone.

"You want to call the office, don't you?" Baylor asked between bites of scrambled eggs and pork sausage. "Go ahead, I don't mind."

"I already did." Amy took a drink of coffee to wash down her food. "Clint didn't answer. I think he ignored the call because we're on our honeymoon—"

Just then, her cell phone screamed to life. It was Clint! She picked up on the first ring.

"Are you shitting me?" she asked before Clint could utter a greeting. "There's a murder in town and you don't even call to tell me about it?"

"What?" he asked.

"Yeah, I had to read about it on the Mechant Voice social media page, of all places." Although Clint couldn't see her, Amy shook her head. "This betrayal is astounding."

"But how'd you know it was a murder?" he asked, seemingly confused. "There's no mention of a murder in the article. I know, because I read every word to make sure."

"I could see it on your face in the picture of you and Takecia," she explained, "and by the way, I thought you said my job was safe."

"It is."

"Then why's Takecia wearing detective clothes and working crime scenes?"

"She's just helping me for a few days," Clint said reassuringly. "She'll be back on night shift by tomorrow night."

Amy laughed. "I know…I can never be replaced."

"You've got that right," Clint said sincerely. "We might someday add another detective, but you'd better never leave. I need you."

Amy felt her cheeks redden, but she didn't waste much time feeling flattered. She was extremely interested in finding out about the case. "So, what happened?" she asked eagerly. "Tell me everything."

CHAPTER 24

Mechant Loup, Louisiana

When I returned Amy's call, she picked up on the first ring. After some back and forth, I explained everything that had happened from the moment Takecia received the call about a missing boater until we had stepped out of the Mechant Life Church.

"What're you doing next?" she asked after a moment of silence, at which time I knew she was pondering everything I'd relayed to her.

"Well, they're serving shrimp spaghetti with garlic bread at Seafood Sarah's, so we'll probably pick up a few plates and meet Susan at the police department for lunch." I paused for a second as I waited for a car to drive past the exit to the church. Once the traffic was clear, I pulled onto Main Street and headed north. "After that, the plan is to head to Magnolia Parish. I want to show Father Carlos' picture around to see if anyone remembers him. From the sounds of it, there was an overhaul at the church, so I'm not holding my breath that anyone will recognize him."

"If no one recognizes him, then what?"

"I haven't thought that far ahead," I admitted, "but I'll most likely do some research on that Sandy Knobs address. If it looks promising—hell, even if it doesn't—I'll probably call the police over there and ask them to make contact with someone at that address. Maybe there's a connection between them and Brother Carlos."

"He's a *Father*," Takecia corrected. "He's not the brother."

"That's right—*Father* Carlos."

"I've got a better idea," Amy said. "Why don't you have Baylor and me head out to Sandy Knobs and see what we can dig up?"

"Hell to the no!" I said in exasperation. "You're on your honeymoon! I'm not about to ask you to go to work."

"Look, it's only two and a half hours from Provo," Amy argued.

"How do you know that?"

"I checked on my phone while you were talking."

"No!" Although she couldn't see me, I shook my head like I had done a few days earlier when I'd caught Grace throwing shells at a large wasp nest. "I would never ask you to go to work on your honeymoon. You need to go enjoy your time with your husband."

"Duh, Baylor would come with me. And besides, we're dying for a little excitement over here. I mean, rock climbing is cool, and so is whitewater rafting, but we want to do something awesome like wrestle bears or run with bison."

"I'm pretty sure it's illegal to wrestle a bear," I said idly, slowing down on our approach to the Mechant Loup Bridge. "At least it is in Louisiana."

"Well, if we can't wrestle bears," Amy pleaded, "at least give us a chance to be a part of this murder investigation. Come on...don't make me beg."

I glanced over at Takecia. She was smiling.

"Let her do it," she said. "It's their honeymoon. They get to spend it however they want."

"You would say yes to anything right now, thanks to Dr. *Evans*," I mumbled, emphasizing his last name.

"Who's Dr. Evans?" Amy asked from the other end of the phone. "And why'd you say his name like that?"

"I'll let Takecia tell you all about it when y'all get back." I took a breath, feeling guilty, but realizing it was a battle I couldn't win. I was very aware that having Amy and Baylor two and a half hours from the Sandy Knobs address was a Godsend and it would probably save us a ton of time. However, even if we hadn't been able to contact someone from a neighboring sheriff's office or police department, I would've never asked them to give up their honeymoon time for an investigation. "Okay, I'll agree to it under one condition."

"What's that?" Amy asked.

"You have to promise to stay on your honeymoon for an extra day, because we'll count today as a work day," I began. "Also, you have to let me pay for your hotel room tonight."

"You said one condition," she argued, "but that's two. We'll stay the extra day, but we won't take your money."

Before I could argue, she ended the call.

"I guess that's settled," I said, continuing north of town until we reached Seafood Sarah's.

We walked inside, ordered five plate lunches, and then headed for the police department. Once we arrived, we called Shade in off the road and told Susan and Lindsey to join us in the lunch room. I brought my laptop with me and began researching everything I could find on the Magnolia Life Church. I found some old newspaper articles that referenced what had happened seventeen years earlier, but the details were sketchy. The entire incident seemed to have been shrouded in mystery, and one of the reporters even warned of a cover-up.

"I remember hearing about that church," Shade said around a mouthful of spaghetti.

"You were two years old and living in Tennessee when it happened," Susan countered with a scowl. There was a suspicious expression on her face, as though she expected a punch line from a joke. "How could you have heard about it back then?"

"No, I heard about it during the police academy," he insisted. "Someone asked Captain Berger about a case involving some church and zombies, or something. It didn't sound like he wanted to talk about it, though, so it must've been bad. Judging by the little bit he did say, I got the feeling he worked the case. I think he even got shot over it—at least, that's what a firearms instructor said when we were at the range one day. I never heard it from him directly, so don't quote me on it."

I leaned back in my chair and considered this. I remembered hearing that Brandon Berger used to be a detective with the Magnolia Parish Sheriff's Office years earlier—long before I joined the force in Mechant Loup—but I'd never known what had led to his transfer to the police academy. Not only was it none of my business, but I had never even thought to ask about it. Officers transferred from one division to another within an agency for all sorts of reasons, so there was nothing odd about that. However, the fact that he didn't want to talk about it might speak to the impact it had had on him.

I drummed my fingers on the table. Although the church was under new leadership and had probably taken a beating in membership after the incident, I was willing to bet there were still members of the congregation from seventeen years earlier. Someone from there might recognize our victim, but would they be willing to talk?

My best option would've been to speak with the detectives who worked the case, but if Carlos wasn't attending the church at the time of the incident, they might not recognize him. Besides, if Shade had read the situation correctly—and I trusted his instinct—then Brandon didn't want to talk about the case. And if he didn't, who was I to impose?

Still, I needed some information on the church and its members. While there was seemingly no connection between my case and Brandon's old case, I still wanted to know what kind of people we were dealing with before Takecia and I went nosing around the church. What had happened seventeen years ago was no joke, and before I walked blindly into that place, I needed to know if they were apt to cooperate with law enforcement, or if they would clam up at the first sign of a badge.

The advantage that Takecia and I held was that we weren't from the area, so—if need be—we could attend a church service incognito and try to gather information that way, but it might take time to gain the confidence of someone there and have them open up, and that was a luxury we didn't enjoy. I was sure our victim had been murdered, and the more time and distance that came between the killing and the suspect, the greater the chances were that the case might go unsolved.

It suddenly came to me. If there was one man who would know what had happened and who might be able to guide us forward, it would be my old friend London Carter, who used to be a detective and a sniper with the Magnolia Parish Sheriff's Office. He had recently moved to the mountains of Tennessee to finish out his law enforcement career, but he'd invited me to call if I ever needed anything. I decided to take him up on his offer now.

CHAPTER 25

"How's the weather down there?" London asked when I got him on the phone.

Takecia and I were seated in my office leaning over my desk phone, which was on speaker.

"Hot as ever," I said, "but I love it. What about over there?"

"It's nice. We finally get to experience all four seasons." He paused for a brief moment to tell Dawn who was on the phone, and then he addressed me again. "Dawn wants to know if y'all had that baby boy yet."

"It should be any week now."

"She said if you want to name your boy after a handgun, you should call him Smith."

I could hear laughter in the background.

"She said it's just wrong to name your kid Baretta," he continued. "Personally, I think it's cool, and I would've named Brandon Accuracy International Carter if I would've thought of it."

"Over my dead body!" Dawn hollered.

I smiled. I'd never been able to surprise Susan with anything, but I really had her going with the naming of our son.

After more small talk, I told London that I needed his help.

"I can be there in eight hours," he said without hesitation. "Just let me make a few phone calls."

"It's not like that," I explained. "We're working a case and I need to approach the new pastor at the Magnolia Life Church to see if he can identify a victim of ours."

I went on to relay everything we knew up to that point about our case, and explained how I was hoping for some guidance regarding how to approach the members of the church.

"I wouldn't have given it a second thought," I admitted, "but we're just finding out that the church was embroiled in some heavy stuff back in the day, and I'd like to know what kind of people we're dealing with before we head out there. I thought about asking Brandon Berger, but I'm hearing he might not want to discuss the case."

"He'll talk to you," London said, "but you're right, he doesn't talk openly or publicly about it. He was actually ambushed and almost killed during that case. Had Dawn not been there, he wouldn't have made it."

"Wait a minute...Dawn worked the case with him?"

"Yeah. She's right here if you want to talk to her."

"Absolutely!" I looked up and gave Takecia a nod.

"Hey, Clint, how's Susan?" Dawn asked when she got on the phone.

"She's ready to have this baby," I said with a grunt. "You know her; she likes going twelve rounds with her fighting equipment, and she can't do that when she's nine months pregnant."

"I hear that." She took a breath. "So, it sounds like you need some info on the Magnolia Life Church. What can I tell you?"

"I was gonna bring a photo over there to see if someone could identify our murder victim, but I was hoping you or Brandon might be able to guide me a little," I explained. "When I worked in La Mort, I investigated a couple of cases involving members of one particular church, and the congregation there circled the wagons around their brethren. On the other hand, the elders in one church grabbed a parishioner who was accused of a sex crime, forced a confession out of him, and then delivered him to me with his hands and legs tied in knots."

"Yeah, unfortunately, the mentality of most of the folks at Magnolia Life is to cover for each other. Brandon and I went undercover into the church during one of their services, and I thought we'd have to fight our way out." Dawn sighed. "That was one hell of a sad case. I don't know how much things have changed over the years at the church, but I never had any more dealings with them after that night."

I repeated everything I'd told London about the case, and I asked if she had any informants who might speak freely to me.

"We had one informant," she said, "but they excommunicated him from the church after he provided Grand Jury testimony against the pastor and some of the elders."

"Oh, wait, that might work." I leaned closer to the phone. "According to the secretary of the Mechant Life Church, she thinks this guy would've attended the church long before the case you and Brandon investigated. If your informant was a long-time member, he or she might remember our victim."

"His name's Ray Broussard. I kept a digital copy of all my old reports when I left the sheriff's office, so I can give you his date of birth, address, and phone number. He actually worked for the sheriff's office at the time."

"Really?" I asked. "What did he do?"

"Courtroom security." Dawn paused, and then asked how sure the secretary was about our victim's identity.

"She wasn't positive."

"Send the picture to London's phone," she suggested. "Even if he had already left the church by the time we investigated them, London and I might've seen him around the parish."

I quickly pulled out my cell phone, snapped the picture, and sent it to London's phone. Almost immediately, I heard the chirp on the other end of the line.

"Got it," Dawn mumbled. After a moment, she grunted. "Nah, I don't recognize him. Look, I'll pull up Ray's info and give it to you. Check with him before going to the church. If someone over there was responsible for your murder, they'll get spooked and go into hiding. That church has connections all over the country, and they can make a member vanish into thin air if they want to."

Takecia and I asked her a dozen or so more questions about the church and its members, and then she turned the phone over to London while she searched for the contact info on Ray. It only took her about five minutes to find it. When she did, she relayed it to London, and he provided it to us.

"She says it's possible he moved or died," London said, "because this was more than seventeen and a half years ago, and he wasn't in the best of health."

After a few more questions and some small talk, I thanked him and hung up the phone.

"Let's see if we can find Mr. Ray Broussard," I said. "If he can't help us, I guess we'll head to the church afterward."

CHAPTER 26

As Takecia and I began the long drive to Ray Broussard's house on Ditch Boulevard, which was located in the northern part of Magnolia Parish, I found myself doubting the church connection. After all, the only thing that had led me to check with Mechant Life was the gospel tract that had been given to the bridge tender, and the fact that our victim called himself *Father*. It just so happened that Father Reggie's secretary, who couldn't have been more than thirty, might have recognized Carlos from when she was around thirteen years of age. That was it. We had nothing more to go on.

"This is it," Takecia said two hours later when we reached the end of Ditch Boulevard. She held up a computer printout of the license inquiry she had run before we'd left the police department. "The address matches and so does the truck in the driveway. He still lives here."

I was relieved, but not convinced that he would be able to help us. Before I could park my Tahoe in the driveway, the door to the house opened. A man walked out carrying a large key ring and a respirator. He stopped when he saw us and raised his hand to block the sun.

I stepped out of my SUV and walked around the large flatbed trailer that was parked in front of us. A zero-turn lawnmower and two push mowers were secured to the trailer, and two weed eaters protruded from the back of the truck. Thanks to the sticker on the side of the F-250, I knew that Ray was the CEO of Broussard's Lawn Care and Kutz. Judging by the types of mowers and the condition they were in I was willing to bet business was booming for the man.

"Can I help y'all?" Ray asked as we neared the front steps. He was a lot thinner than I'd expected, and his head was shaved, so it was hard to judge his age.

"How's it going, Mr. Broussard?" I asked, extending my hand. "I'm Clint Wolf and this is Takecia Gayle."

"Y'all are detectives," he said, taking my hand first and then Takecia's, "but y'all aren't from here. I might be retired, but I'm still on the Reserve Squad and I know every officer in the parish."

"We're from Mechant Loup," I acknowledged. "Former Detective Dawn Luke told us we could find you here. She said you might be able to help us with something."

"You talked to Detective Carter?" he asked, his face beaming. "You know she's a Carter now, right? She married London Carter. He was the best sniper we ever had. They moved away to—"

"The mountains of Tennessee," I finished. "Yep, I know London well. He's saved my bacon on more than one occasion."

Ray stepped back and waved us toward his front door. "Come on in. Any friend of London and Dawn is a friend of mine."

"I don't want to interrupt whatever you had going on," I said, hesitating. "We just had a few questions about the Magnolia Life Church."

The mention of the church caused his face to blanch.

"I was just heading out to cut the yard at the high school, but I'm early," he explained. "I've got time."

Takecia and I followed him inside and found ourselves in a tidy living room. He directed us to a sofa and he took the recliner next to it, but he didn't relax into it. Instead, he leaned forward and fixed us with intent eyes.

"What's going on over there?" he asked. "Are they up to their old tricks again? I knew it would only be a matter of time before they once again became corrupted by greed and power."

"No, nothing like that." I lifted my hands to let him know it wasn't as bad as he feared. "We just pulled a man out of the bayou in our town, and we were wondering if you could identify him. Someone told us he might have attended the church way back before the incident with the baby happened."

"Oh." Ray took a breath and relaxed. "That's a relief. Um, yeah, I was going there a few years before all that stuff went down with the baby. I knew most of the people there, so I might know him. What's his name?"

"We only know his first name," I explained. "He spoke with a bridge tender in our parish and he called himself Father Carlos."

"If he's considered a father, then he's the head of a church," Ray mused, "but he's definitely not the head of Magnolia Life. I've heard that the new pastor is better than what they had before, but I'm a little skeptical. It's kind of like a bad relationship—once you've been burned really bad, you get a little gun shy."

I nodded and pulled the printed photo from my manila folder. "Keep in mind the man's deceased," I cautioned, "but this is only a photo of his face, and it's rather peaceful."

Ray nodded and reached for the photo, seemingly unbothered by the prospect of it being of a dead man. As soon as his eyes came to bear on the photo, he let out a grunt.

"Yeah, I know this man. This is Carlos Marcella. He was the principal of Magnolia Life Christian School."

I traded glances with Takecia before turning back to Ray.

"Magnolia Life had a school?" I asked.

"Yeah, but it only lasted for two years." Ray shrugged. "Some of the parishioners figured Father Nelson only opened the school as an experiment to see if he could increase his income stream and when it didn't prove profitable, he shut it down. I defended him at the time, but after everything else that's happened, I wouldn't argue it anymore."

"Are you positive that this guy"—I tapped the photo—"was the principal of the Magnolia Life School?"

"Yes, sir. I'm absolutely positive it's him. I'd never forget that man."

"Was there something that made him unforgettable to you?"

"Well, he was a bit of a proud man," Ray said slowly, staring down at the floor as he spoke. "Wherever he went, he looked down on other people. He thought he was better than everyone, including Father Nelson. He was pretty rough with people. Like, the way he talked to everyone was kind of mean, you know? I was always taught that pride was the worst of the seven deadly sins and, after seeing the way he treated people, I believe it. He was a bad man."

"What do you mean?"

"He was just bad, you know?"

"Other than being a prideful man, what else did he do that makes you think he was a bad man?" I pressed. "Can you give me some examples of what he did?"

"I couldn't really give you any specifics. I just heard he was a bad man. It...well, it was just common knowledge amongst the church members that he was bad news." Ray shook his head, still refusing to look up at us, and I could tell he was holding something back. "I can't give any specifics. I wish I could, but I really can't."

"Do you know if anyone had a problem with him?"

Ray grunted. "Everyone had a problem with him, especially those who attended the school."

"Some of the kids in the school had a problem with him?"

"They all did," he said. "He ruled the school with a rod of iron, and he used that rod excessively. There was barely a kid he didn't hit with that stick. He even had a name for it. I think it was Jezebel. He told some story about it once, something about his grandfather used it on his dad, and his dad used it on him, and now he uses it to rear up God's little servants. He was obsessed with that thing. Carried it everywhere. He said his grandfather carved it by hand from a large sycamore tree, and that it was his most prized possession."

"How big was this stick?"

Ray held out his hands to indicate a length of about two feet and then four inches. "When the kids were bad, he beat them with it. He...um, well, some of the kids described it as more than a spanking. They said he would rear back, holding the rod in both hands, and then swing it like he was going for a strike. They said it hurt worse than anything they've ever felt. I've heard him brag openly about making the kids cry. I think he got off on it. It fueled his arrogance. He...he was an evil man."

I was thoughtful. "Mr. Broussard, do you know of anyone who would want him dead?"

"Sure," Ray said simply. "Everyone who knew him."

CHAPTER 27

"How do you know everyone wanted him dead?" I asked. "Did people say that?"

"No, not in so many words," Ray acknowledged. "It's just that the kids were all scared of him and they hated him for beating them. And there was talk that most of the parents wanted him gone, but everyone was too afraid to say anything to Father Nelson about it. They all knew Father Nelson would tell him what they had said and...well, and then Carlos would come after them. He was a vengeful fellow. If you said or did anything to make him angry, you would be in his crosshairs and he wouldn't stop until he got revenge."

Ray shuddered. He opened his mouth to continue, but clamped it shut. I got the sense there was something he wasn't telling us, but I decided to let it go for the moment. I didn't want him to shut down. I needed him to tell me as much as he could about Carlos and his evil ways, and in order to keep him talking, I needed to get his mind off of whatever was bothering him.

If a lot of people wanted Carlos dead, then that would present some challenges. I needed to narrow down the suspect list—if, indeed, I was looking in the right place—and Ray might just be the person to help me do that. It was also possible that someone unrelated to the church had followed him to Louisiana and killed him, but I felt like I needed to ride this church angle until the wheels fell off.

"When did the school close down?" I asked, holding my pen poised over my notebook.

"Two years before the incident with the baby."

"We spoke with someone who said Carlos left the church before the incident happened," I began. "Did he leave around the time the school shut down?"

"Yeah, he left a few months after it closed." Ray took a deep breath and let it out slowly. He glanced again at the photo of Carlos. "I knew he would come back some day—he even said he would—but I can't believe he's dead. You asked if anyone wanted him dead. Is that because he was murdered?"

"We're not sure," I said, deciding to go with the story in the newspaper. "It looks like he might've lost control of his truck and crashed into the bayou. However, being a retired cop, you know we have to look at every possibility. Now, let's get back to the school. Why'd it close down?"

"It wasn't making the money Father Nelson thought it would, so he shut it down."

"What happened to the students?" I asked. "Did they head back to public school?"

"Oh, no, Father Nelson forbade it. He said it was the job of the parents to—as the Bible says—*teach their children the way they should go.*"

"Were they forced to home school the kids?"

Ray nodded. "I never had any kids, but from what I heard, not only were they forced to home school, but they were also forced to buy the school books from the church—and they were *expensive*! A couple of families rebelled and put their kids in public school. They were immediately excommunicated."

"Is that a bad thing?" I asked.

"I used to think so, because it meant you were shunned from the church and no one could have any dealings with you. You lost all of your friends and even family if they attended the church. It was like being in exile." Ray shrugged. "But after the baby incident, I was excommunicated. I thought my life was over. I was lonely. I had no friends. I even contemplated suicide, but then one of the fellas from the DA's office invited me to a book club meeting he held at the library. I went and, before I knew it, everyone there became my friend. They offered me encouragement about a lot of things, including losing weight and getting healthy again."

Ray's chest seemed to swell with pride as he talked about his transformation to a healthier man.

"I started having more energy and was able to do more at work, and I was promoted to the rank of sergeant before I retired," he said.

"And now I have my own grass cutting business, so everything's going great for me. Had it not been for the excommunication, I would still be living in a rut."

"Do you know why Carlos left the church?" I asked. "I know the school closed down, but was there something else that prompted him to leave?"

There was a long moment of hesitation before Ray answered. When he did, his tone was noncommittal.

"I heard he left because he wanted to be a principal again. If you ask me, he had gotten a taste of being in control, and he was addicted to it." He bristled. "I'm not surprised he's a pastor. He has a way of entering a room and taking control over it. We all knew he wanted Father Nelson's church, but Father Nelson was too powerful for anyone to take on. He had followers who would've killed Carlos at the snap of his fingers."

I glanced down at my notepad. "Do you know where Carlos went when he left the church?"

Ray shook his head.

"What about family?" I asked. "Did Carlos have a wife?"

"He did. Her name was Kari. She was older than him by quite a few years."

"Did they have any kids?"

"They had a son and a daughter together, but Kari had a son from an earlier marriage."

"What were their names?"

As soon as I asked for the names, the arteries in Ray's neck began to throb like a frog was trying to jump through his flesh.

"They, um...well, the stepson was Dean..."

Ray shifted on the edge of his recliner as his voice trailed off. He opened his mouth a few times to say something, but closed it each time. He was holding something back, of this I was sure. His eyes shifted from side to side, and I caught him looking up at Takecia once or twice.

Takecia noticed, too, and she gave a knowing nod, cleared her throat, and stood. "Excuse me, Clint. I have to step outside to make a phone call."

I watched Takecia leave. Once she was gone, I turned back to Ray. "Mr. Broussard, what did this man do to you?"

He swallowed hard. "What do you mean?"

"I can tell something happened between you and Carlos Marcella," I said softly. "He did something bad, didn't he?"

Tears welled up in Ray's eyes. His chin was trembling. He once again tried to speak, but couldn't, so he only nodded.

"What was it?"

A long moment of silence followed. Finally, he coughed and cleared his throat.

"How...how did you know?" he asked. "How can you tell?"

Instead of answering him, I leaned forward and stabbed the photo that was still clasped in his hands. "What did this animal do? What's got you so upset?"

I thought I was prepared for anything, but I was wrong. When he told me what Carlos had done, I involuntarily sucked in my breath. I did manage to keep my jaw from dropping, but he noticed my initial reaction and his face burned red.

CHAPTER 28

Twelve County, Nevada

Amy shook her head and tossed her cell phone to the dashboard of the Jeep Wrangler she and Baylor had rented for their honeymoon.

"I can't find any reference to a police department in Sandy Knobs," she said. "Twelve County has a sheriff's office. It's about two miles up the road, on the right. Think we should stop there first?"

Baylor checked his side mirror and eased into the left lane to pass an eighteen-wheeler that was creeping along the highway.

"Yeah," he said. "They might know something about these people. Sandy Knobs didn't look very big on the map. It might be an unincorporated community. Maybe that's why it doesn't have a police department."

"Probably."

"Has Clint sent another update yet?"

Amy leaned forward, snatched her phone back from the dash, and checked her text messages for the thousandth time since they'd left Provo. There were no updates. Thus far, all they had was a first name and an address from some gospel tract that Clint had recovered from a bridge tender. Their primary mission was to find a family member and make a death notification, and secondly, they were to try and determine who might want to kill the mysterious Father Carlos. Since there was no guarantee that the address belonged to the victim, it was quite possible they were wasting time.

"No updates from Clint," Amy said, turning her face toward the open window.

The country through which they traveled was beautiful. Off in the distance, mountains rose majestically toward the sky, while the area along the highway was flat and salty—or so it appeared. They hadn't stopped to check that particular stretch of highway, but when they were driving through West Wendover they had stopped at the Bonneville Salt Flats.

Amy smiled. Even if 777 Spirit Way was a dead end, it certainly wouldn't have been a waste of time. They had seen some interesting places already, and she had never been to Nevada before, so it was another state she could cross off her bucket list.

"Who do you think would win in a fight," Baylor began, flipping his blinker on. "Wendover Will or the Big Texan in Amarillo?"

"It depends." Amy sat up and tamed her blonde wind-blown hair. "If it's straight boxing, Big Texan wins. If it's MMA, then my money's on Wendover Will, but only if he can get a take-down before Big Texan knocks him out."

Baylor laughed and followed Amy's directions to the sheriff's office.

"Did you know Independence Day was filmed in Wendover?" Amy asked. "And so were The Core, Hulk, and Pirates of the Caribbean."

"Yup." Baylor nodded. "I was right next to you when you were reading the signs."

Once Baylor parked in front of the sheriff's department, Amy opened her door and stretched for a long second before walking around to Baylor's side of the Jeep. The building was constructed of solid brick and it was called the Twelve County Law Enforcement Complex, because it appeared to house all divisions within the sheriff's department, including the jail.

Amy hesitated before approaching the entrance. "I didn't bring my badge. Do you have yours?"

"No, it's pinned to my uniform back home, but I have my commission card."

"I guess that'll have to do." Amy headed for the door. "Here goes nothing."

The lobby was small and sterile. Amy rang a doorbell that was attached to an inner wall next to a set of wooden shutters and waited. After a few seconds, a woman in uniform pulled the shutters open and peered through the window.

"How can I help you?"

"I know we don't look like it," Amy said apologetically, "but we're a couple of cops from Louisiana. We're heading to Sandy Knobs and we'd like to speak with someone about the place. We need to make a death notification."

The deputy's brow furrowed. "Sandy Knobs, you said?"

Amy nodded.

"Yeah, sorry, but that's out of our jurisdiction."

"Is there anyone we can talk to about the place?" Amy pressed. "We'd like to gather a little intel before dropping in blind. We've got an address of 777 Spirit Way. Do you know if anyone's familiar with that address or if y'all have ever been called out to it?"

"Do you have a badge?" the deputy asked.

"No, but we've got our commission cards." Amy produced hers while Baylor pulled out his. They pressed them against the window so the deputy could get a good look.

She nodded and the door to the right buzzed. "Come on through. I'll talk to you guys out back."

Amy glanced at Baylor and headed for the door. Once they pushed through it, they saw the same deputy step into view about twenty feet down a long hallway. When they drew nearer, Amy saw that the name plate on her uniform read, *A. Ready*.

"Right down here," Deputy Ready said. "You guys caught me just in time. It's been slow, so I was heading out back to grab a cigarette break while I had the chance."

Amy and Baylor followed her to the door at the end of the hall, which she opened, and then they found themselves standing behind the building in a large courtyard. Fifty feet away was a tall fence topped with razor wire, and on the other side of that fence were several prisoners weightlifting under an overhang.

"So, why are you going to Sandy Knobs again?"

"A man was found dead in our parish, possibly murdered."

A puzzled expression fell across Ready's face. "What's a parish?"

"It's the same thing as a county." Amy shrugged. "Louisiana just has to be different—the whole Napoleonic Code and all that."

"Oh, yeah!" She snapped her fingers. "I heard about that. Don't you guys have different terminology in the law, too? I once had a friend who wanted to move to New Orleans and practice law there, but he went to law school in California. He said the law was too different in Louisiana to just transfer over. He ended up moving to Texas."

Amy nodded patiently. When Deputy Ready had finished speaking, she cut in. "So, this guy who was found dead, he might be some kind of preacher or something. The detectives working the case were able to link him to a gospel tract with the Spirit Way address on it. Do you know anything about the place?"

Deputy Ready lit her cigarette and took a long drag before answering. When she did, her voice was low and foreboding.

"I know enough to stay away from there," she hissed. "If I were you, I'd forget about that dead guy and head back in the other direction. It's not worth the trouble."

Amy scowled. "Why are you whispering?"

"Folks around here, they like to pretend that place doesn't exist— our sheriff included. And it's not hard to forget, because it's almost eighty miles in that direction"—she pointed toward the south—"in the middle of nowhere. Those people come to town about once a week for supplies, and when they do, people steer clear of them. Whatever they don't buy here in town or over in West Wendover, they make themselves. They grow most of their own food—and that's not easy out here, but they're successful at it—they have their own meat source, and they've got their own power grid. They even have their own cell tower that's linked to some private service. It's like they're their own country."

"Well, we don't want any trouble with them," Amy said. "We just need to deliver a death notification."

"They don't like outsiders."

"Would it be better if we had a police escort?" Amy asked. "Maybe someone who was familiar to them could introduce us and let them know we're not there to cause problems."

"We have no control over that area."

"When I looked at the map, it showed that the address on Spirit Way was well within the county lines." Amy cocked her head to the side. "Why wouldn't y'all have control of that area?"

"Look, Sandy Knobs is definitely within the jurisdiction of Twelve County, but we have no control over it," she explained in an even softer voice. "Those people govern themselves—kind of like sovereign citizens, but worse. They believe they only answer to God, and that his law is supreme over man's law."

"Is your sheriff afraid of them?"

Deputy Ready winced. "If I were you, I wouldn't go around here saying things like that. The sheriff isn't afraid of any man or woman—except his wife and two daughters—but he doesn't want to be responsible for the massacre of nearly a thousand people, most of them women and children."

"Why might there be a massacre?" Amy asked, although she was starting to get the picture.

"Since they don't recognize our laws, they have been known to violate them," Deputy Ready explained. "About two years ago, one of our narcotics boys purchased drugs from one of the Knobsters—as we call them—and he got an arrest warrant for him and a warrant to search his house. He got the SWAT team together and converged on the compound. Well, when they arrived, every woman and child from the compound was lying across the roadway refusing to move. Some of the officers said they saw men with guns in the windows of nearby houses and buildings. A couple of the agents wanted to press forward and force the issue, but they knew it would look bad if they plowed through the women and children. While they were trying to decide what to do, the sheriff showed up and ordered them to stand down. Apparently, someone had told the sheriff what was happening, so he shagged ass over there."

"Why didn't he just radio them or call their cell phones?"

"The service out there is spotty, at best." She shook her head. "The sheriff was livid. He fired the narcotics agent who made the drug buy, and he suspended the lieutenant of the narcotics division and the commander of the SWAT team for conducting an unauthorized raid. After that, a directive went out ordering us to stay away from Sandy Knobs unless they invite us in."

Amy considered everything they'd just heard. "And y'all won't send a deputy with us to deliver a death notification?"

She shook her head. "They haven't invited us in."

CHAPTER 29

Magnolia Parish, Louisiana

"He *spanked* you?" I asked Ray Broussard incredulously. "With a stick?"

Ray nodded his head, tears of anger and resentment streaming down his face. "And he did it in front of the entire church."

I sat aghast. I had so many questions, but I felt like it would be cruel to ask them, so I just remained silent as Ray cried softly. Finally, after about three long minutes of neither of us saying anything, he cleared his throat once more.

"It was my own fault," he began in such a low voice that I could barely understand what he was saying. "Kari's son for her first husband was named Dean, and everything happened because of him. I mean, he didn't cause it, but it was over him."

"Do you know the boy's last name?" I asked when Ray had paused for a breath. "Or his biological dad's name?"

"No, I never knew it. Dean was just a little boy when I first met them, so I don't even know if he knew his real dad. And I've never heard him called by anything but Dean."

"How old do you think he was when they first joined the church?" I asked.

"Two, maybe three?" Ray shrugged. "It's hard to tell when they're that young. I just know he was around five or six when they left the church. He was running around like a normal boy and he could hold his own in a conversation. He was pretty witty—maybe too much, because his mouth would get him in trouble with Carlos. I talked to him a few times and he was really funny. Everyone in the church loved him, and I don't think Carlos liked that at all."

"What were the family dynamics like?"

"Right away, I could tell that Carlos resented him. He was always fussing the kid for no good reason. I saw him spank the kid when he was still in diapers—and that was during a church service. It got worse as Dean got older. He would do things like jump off the church steps like all the other boys did, and Carlos would spank him. It was never enough to fuss him—Carlos had to hit him. There was this one time when Dean picked up a pine cone and threw it across the yard. It didn't hit anything and didn't bother anyone, but Carlos gave him the rod."

"When you say *give him the rod*, you mean he beat him with the sycamore stick?"

Ray nodded. "I don't believe in hitting any kid with a stick, but that boy was way too young to be spanked. The older he got, the harder Carlos would hit him. Oh, and Carlos didn't care who saw it. He would do it in front of everyone. When the pinecone incident happened, he beat Dean right there in the front yard of the church, with everyone watching. I bet you could hear that poor boy screaming all the way across town. I felt so sorry for him."

"Did any of the church members try to step in and stop him?" I asked, wondering how other adults could watch that type of abuse and not get involved.

"Oh, no, everyone was afraid of him."

"What about Father Nelson?" I countered. "I thought he was too powerful for Carlos? Didn't he try to stop him?"

"He wasn't outside during that spanking, but I don't believe he would've stopped it. He preached corporal punishment. He used to say something like, *Wield the rod, spare the child*. It meant that if you whipped your kid, it would make them better and they could get into Heaven."

"What about the spanking Carlos gave you?" I asked tentatively, still unable to wrap my mind around a grown man spanking another grown man—and in a public place, no less. "Did the preacher approve of that beating?"

"I think Father Nelson thought I deserved it at first, after hearing everything that Carlos had said about me," Ray explained. "I...well, if I'm being honest, I think I thought I deserved it, too."

"What exactly happened?" I didn't want to ask the question, but I was beginning to realize that I might very well be sitting in front of Carlos' killer. The man was still deeply traumatized by what had happened. "What led to the spanking?"

"Well, like I said, I didn't like what he was doing to his stepson, so I went to Father Nelson to complain." He frowned. "That was the first time I was disappointed in Father Nelson. He basically said the disciplining of a child was between the parents and God, and he said that it was no one else's business. I then pointed out that Carlos was also spanking other kids in the school, and that some of the parents didn't approve. I asked if it was Carlos' business to decide how to discipline those children."

"Good point." I cocked my head to the side. "What did he say to that?"

"He said that when the children were at the school, they were wards of the church, and that Carlos—as the principal—assumed the role of the parent, and it was between him and God to determine how best to discipline them." Ray sighed. "Father Nelson had an answer for everything."

"Did Carlos find out about your conversation with Father Nelson?" I asked, wondering if that was what had prompted Carlos to publicly torture Ray. As I waited for his answer, another thought began to creep into my mind, and I started to grow suspicious.

"I don't think so, because he never said anything to me. And believe you me; I was worried about it getting back to him." Ray took a haggard breath. "There was another day after church that I walked into the men's room, and I caught Carlos beating Dean. The boy was screaming and wriggling around on the bathroom floor. His pants were down around his ankles and…and I could see bruises up and down the back of his legs and on his butt. It…it was the most horrible thing I'd ever seen up to that point."

I settled back in my chair, the hate rising up from the depths of my stomach like bile. Suddenly, as a man, I didn't much care about what had happened to Carlos. As a law enforcement officer, I had a duty to find his killer and bring that person to justice, but at the same time, if I were to have an unsolved murder on my record, I could think of none better.

"What'd you do?" I asked.

"I…I wasn't thinking, you know?" Ray swallowed hard, as though reliving the moment. "I just rushed forward and tackled Carlos. He was a strong man—much stronger than I was—but I was a lot heavier at the time. I had lap band surgery several years ago and lost more than 100 pounds, but back then I weighed about 300, and even Carlos was no match for that kind of weight. Like I said, I rushed forward and tackled him. He was caught by surprise and went down hard. I knocked the wind out of him. I think he even hit his head on the floor, because he didn't move afterward. I was afraid I'd killed him. Dean, he took off running and screaming. Other people saw the bruises, but they were all too afraid to do anything."

I had a sudden respect for Ray. That the man would risk the wrath of a person such as Carlos was admirable, and I said as much.

Ray only sighed. "I'm glad I did it, but I paid dearly. When I got off of Carlos, he didn't say anything. Like I said, he wasn't moving and I was scared. I think I was in shock. Anyway, I ran outside and told some people what I had seen. By that time, someone was tending to Dean, so I ran to my truck and went home. I…I talked to my supervisor at work about it the next day, and she told me I was a mandated reporter, and that if I knew about an abuse taking place, I had to contact someone in the juvenile division."

"Did you?" I asked when he paused for a moment. "Did you report him?"

"I did." He licked his dry lips. "Apparently, Carlos was expecting that I would, because when the juvenile detectives went to his house, they found a boy with no bruises. He must've gotten someone else's kid to pretend he was Dean, because the boy said his name was Dean and he said he was Carlos' son. The juvenile detectives came find me and they began asking me all kinds of questions. At first, they began asking me if I was sure about what I had seen, and then it started to sound like they were accusing me of lying. I realized much later that Father Nelson was very good at covering up things in the church to help protect his people and himself from the authorities."

I nodded thoughtfully. "And you went back to church after reporting him to the authorities?"

"Yes, sir, I went back the following Sunday morning." Ray was visibly trembling now. "I had skipped the Wednesday service because I was scared, but one of the elders called me and told me that I needed to be back in church on Sunday. They usually do that when someone misses a service. They want to make sure you didn't backslide."

"That sounds pretty controlling."

"They were very controlling," he said with a nod. "Anyway, on that next Sunday, I was sitting in the back pew trying not to be noticed. After the worship service—that's when everyone sings before the main service begins—Carlos stepped up to the cordless microphone and said he had a word from the Lord. That wasn't unusual. Someone would do that almost every service. They would usually have a prophesy from the Lord or a testimonial they wanted to share."

Ray paused and took a few deep breaths. I was starting to think he wouldn't go through with it, but he finally continued.

"Carlos, he then started talking about there being a demon in our midst, and how the enemy of God was infiltrating the church, and how heathens had been sent to his house to bring his children into darkness. The whole time he was talking, he was walking down the aisle, heading right for me. I tried to sink deeper into my pew, but I couldn't hide. When…when he got to the back, he, um, he reached over and grabbed me by the arm. It was really rough and he had a strong grip. He dragged me to the stage like I was a little kid who had done something wrong. On the way up, he whispered that I was gonna pay for what I had done, and that I'd better pray for God to spare my life."

"Did you try to resist?" I asked.

"I…I told him to stop and to leave me alone, but he just dragged me forward." Ray shook his head. "I thought if I tried to resist it would be worse, so I just went along and tried not to trip. Once we were up on the stage in front of everybody, he stuck a finger in my face and told everyone that I had sent the heathens to his house to steal his children."

He paused again to take a trembling breath, and I asked him what the preacher was doing while Carlos was dragging him to the front of the church. On the one hand, I couldn't imagine such a scene playing out and someone not interceding on his behalf, but then I remembered what Dawn Carter had said about the time she and Brandon Berger went undercover at the same church.

"Father Nelson was just watching at first and listening to what was being said," Ray explained. "Once Carlos made his accusation, Father Nelson stepped forward and took the mic from him. He asked me if it was true, if I had really summoned the heathens to Carlos' house. I…I told him it was true and he…"

Ray's voice trailed off.

"He what?"

"He looked so disappointed." Ray sucked in a trembling breath. "My dad used to look at me like that when I would do something terrible. He wouldn't yell or punish me. He would only look at me with that disapproving expression, and it would rip my heart out. I'd rather get a whipping instead of that look."

Well, you got both, I wanted to say, but didn't. Instead, I nodded sympathetically and encouraged him to go on.

"Well, when Carlos saw the way Father Nelson was looking at

me, it was like a bomb went off inside of him—like he had Father Nelson's blessing to do whatever he wanted with me. He began calling me a Judas and saying that I had betrayed the Word of the Lord. He grabbed me and...and he spun me around. He...the crowd was yelling at me as he pushed me face-first over the altar. I don't know where he got his rod, but all of a sudden I felt an excruciating pain on my backside. It...I could hear the loud smack as he spanked me again and again. He just kept whipping me, the entire time screaming at the top of his lungs that I was a Judas. The crowd, they...they were screaming for more. Someone even shouted for him to kill me. I..."

Ray broke out in uncontrollable sobs and covered his face with the picture of Carlos that he still clutched in his hands. He was trembling as though he had a high fever. Not knowing what else to do, I just leaned forward and put a hand on his shoulder.

CHAPTER 30

Still crying hysterically, Ray continued his story, but most of his words were unintelligible. From what I could understand, he was shocked and embarrassed, and he broke down crying in front of the entire congregation. He said Father Nelson commanded Carlos to stop, but he wouldn't. That was when Father Nelson excommunicated Carlos on the spot and ordered his men to remove him from the church. Ray said it took several men to get control of Carlos and drag him off the stage.

"That was the last time I ever saw him," Ray said between fits of sobs. "As they dragged him out, he screamed that he would be back, that he wasn't finished with me. He ordered God to bring hell down upon me."

As Ray took a break to try and get his sobs under control, I sat there staring awkwardly at the ground, not wanting to make him feel even more uncomfortable. After several more minutes, he finally spoke again.

"Father Nelson put me on my knees and prayed over me to cast out the demons of betrayal. I don't know what happened next. I kind of blacked out and when I came to, he was standing over me with a smile on his face. He said I had been delivered from the demon of Judas. He said he forgave me for what I'd done, and he told the church that I had been through enough, and that they were to also forgive me." Ray scrubbed a fist across his watery eyes. "I loved Father Nelson like he was my own dad from that moment forward. I owed him my life. There's no doubt in my mind that Carlos would've beaten me to death had Father Nelson not intervened."

I only nodded. I gave Ray a few more minutes to get better control of his faculties. When I felt he was strong enough to continue, I asked him if he knew where I could find Kari Marcella.

"We need to notify his family that he's deceased," I explained, thinking it would be easy now that we had his last name. A quick name inquiry might reveal everything we needed to know inside of a minute, but it wouldn't hurt to have as much information as possible at our disposal.

"No, I don't know where they went when they left. I tried to put him out of my mind. Every now and again—even now—I would remember his promise to come back and get me, and it would cause a tingle to go up and down my spine." He handed back the picture he had been clutching. "I'm glad he's dead. At least now I can rest in peace knowing he'll never make good on his promise."

I studied Ray thoughtfully. "Mr. Broussard, do you mind telling me where you were and what you did between Sunday night and Monday morning?"

Ray blinked. "Please tell me you don't think I did this! I didn't even know he was back in town."

"I'm just asking." I shrugged absently. "You know the drill. I have to ask everyone who knew him."

"Yeah, I know where you're coming from." He sighed heavily, and then scrunched his face. "Let's see, I went to the Chinese restaurant in Payneville, ate there, and then stopped at the store on the way home. I needed milk and bread for the week. I then came home and didn't leave until I went to work yesterday morning."

"What time did you get home Sunday night?"

"Oh, it was early. Probably seven-thirty."

"And what time did you leave on Monday morning?"

"A little after eight."

"Can anyone verify that you were here all night?" I asked, feeling I already knew the answer.

"Other than me?" He shook his head. "I was here alone, so no one else can."

I studied Ray Broussard carefully as I considered the story he'd told. While he appeared visibly distraught over the beating that Carlos had purportedly handed down to him, I had to remind myself that it could all be a ruse. It was quite possible that Carlos had been a decent man who had never wronged anyone, and that Ray had murdered him for some unknown and selfish reason. What if Carlos was the reason he had been excommunicated? If he thought that action had ruined his life—even though he now claimed it had been a blessing in disguise—it might be motive enough to want someone dead.

"Mr. Broussard," I began after a moment, "can you provide the names of some of the folks who witnessed the beating you endured at the hand of Carlos Marcella?"

It was his turn to be thoughtful. "Wow…um, everyone in the church saw it."

"Can you name a few of them?"

"I mean, none of them are around here anymore." He rubbed his shaved head. He named a handful of people who had witnessed the incident, but then stated they were all dead.

Based on what Dawn had told me, I'd already known all the people he mentioned were dead. I thought that it was rather convenient for him that the witnesses he mentioned were no longer available, because he might have fabricated that horrible story to justify the murder of Carlos. Of course, if no one could verify the beating he'd suffered, then his justification might be destroyed, and so might my motive for him wanting to kill Carlos Marcella.

And was that really Carlos' last name? I hadn't had a chance to run a name inquiry yet, but what if he was sending us down a rabbit hole? Every bit of information we'd received to that point came from Ray, who might turn out to be the killer, so I would have to approach him like President Reagan approached the Russians: trust, but verify.

"Are there any witnesses to the beating from back then who are still alive?" I asked. "I mean, out of a church room full of people, you can't think of one witness who's still living?"

Ray's brow furrowed. He started to shake his head and then froze in place.

"Wait a minute!" he said with a snap of his fingers. "Mia Foret was one of Father Nelson's assistants back then, and she was there! I saw her in the grocery store the other day. She's all grown up and has a newborn, but you couldn't tell by looking at her. Anyway, she mentioned that she still goes to the Magnolia Life Church, but she said things are much better now than they used to be. But she was there when Carlos did that to me, and she can tell you all about it!"

"Do you know where she lives or works?"

"No." Ray frowned. "I didn't think to ask for her phone number or address. I didn't think I'd need to prove to the police that the most humiliating experience of my life actually happened."

"I'm sorry, Mr. Broussard." It was my turn to frown. "I just need to verify the things you're telling me. It's potentially a homicide investigation, so I can't take anything for granted or take anyone at face value."

"Does that mean I'm a suspect?" He asked. "Do I need to worry? Should I hire a lawyer?"

"I have no evidence to suggest you killed Carlos Marcella, so you're not a suspect at this time." I stood to my feet. "As the investigation unfolds and more evidence comes to light, that could change, so I can't tell you that you shouldn't worry and I can't tell you if you need a lawyer or not."

"I…I don't know what to do." Ray was visibly shaken. As though it weren't enough that I'd just convinced him to recount his most embarrassing moment ever, he now had to worry about going to prison for murder.

"Did you kill Carlos Marcella?" I asked pointedly.

Without hesitation, he said that he had not. "I have never killed anyone, not even in the line of duty."

"Then you have absolutely nothing to worry about and you don't need a lawyer," I explained. "I'm not in the business of arresting innocent people."

He let out a long sigh of relief that seemed genuine, but I wasn't willing to rule him out as a suspect just yet. He had a very compelling reason to want Carlos Marcella dead, and he didn't have a witness who could vouch for his whereabouts during the time of the murder. While that didn't make him a suspect, it also didn't clear him, and it made my job a little more difficult.

CHAPTER 31

When I exited Ray Broussard's house, I found Takecia standing on the opposite side of his work trailer staring toward a large tool shed. I approached her.

"What's up?" I asked.

She pointed toward the open door to the shed. "Do you see what I see propped up against the wall inside that shed?"

I followed her finger and grunted. There, leaning against the wall, was a three-ton farm jack. It wasn't the same type of old-fashioned jack I'd had in mind, but it could've definitely been used to lift the back of Carlos' truck while the killer put it in gear and weighed down the accelerator with the bags of ice.

I glanced back toward the house and saw Ray standing inside the closed door, staring through the window at us. He looked nervous, but that still didn't mean he was our killer. Most people got nervous when the law started digging around in their business.

"Did you get a picture of it?" I asked.

"You know I did."

I nodded. "Okay, let's get out of here before he realizes what we're looking at. If he becomes a suspect at some point, we're gonna need that jack, and I don't want him throwing it in the bayou in the meantime."

Once we were in my Tahoe, I called Lindsey and asked her to run a name inquiry on Mia Foret. While waiting for her return call, Takecia told me she had sent Amy a text message and relayed the information we'd received from Ray, the most important of it being that the wife's name was Kari Marcella. When trying to notify a wife about her husband's death, it was always good to have a first and last name.

"I also got Lindsey to run a name inquiry on Carlos and Kari Marcella. Their last known addresses were here in Magnolia Parish, and their last driver's licenses were also from Louisiana. Carlos' DL expired fifteen years ago and Kari's was expired before they left town."

"Did Lindsey run them in other states?" I asked, confused.

"She ran them in every state." She glanced at her notepad. "I also ran the name Dean Marcella, but nothing came up. Do we know his biological father's last name?"

"Ray didn't know it," I said, "but he thought the boy was five or six years of age when they left the area nineteen years ago."

As I pulled out of Ray's driveway and turned onto the highway, I began to tell Takecia everything that Ray had said. Once I was done, she nodded thoughtfully.

"If any man ever had a motive to murder someone, it would be this Ray Broussard," she began, "but we can't rule out the little boy. If he was five or six at the time of Ray's whipping, he would be twenty-four or twenty-five by now. That's old enough to kill a piece of shit stepfather."

As I mulled over what she had said, I found a small strip mall along the highway and parked at one end of the lot. Since I wasn't sure where Mia lived, I didn't want to drive too far in the wrong direction.

"What if the boy never made it to twenty-four or twenty-five?" I asked. "What if Carlos eventually beat him to death? It wouldn't be the first time that's happened."

Takecia frowned grimly. "If he did survive his stepdad, that kind of abuse would've either made Dean a very strong men or it would've broken him down over time. It's hard to survive a lifetime of torture unless you're built for it."

She was right. And if Dean had survived growing up with Carlos Marcella, it would be easy to imagine him wanting some payback. I suddenly caught myself.

"What if this is all a lie?" I asked. "What if Carlos never beat anyone, and Ray is lying to justify murdering him?"

"I guess we'll find out soon enough," she said when my cell phone rang.

"What's up, Lindsey?" I answered. "Anything good?"

"I've got a home address and the address to a florist shop that Mia Foret owns," she said triumphantly. "I also know her favorite vacation destination, her favorite country music artist, and who her man of the hour is—judging by her posts over time, it seems she goes through a lot of boyfriends. Anyway, most importantly, she's got this really cool bikini that I want. So, when you talk to her, ask her where she bought the red and white striped—"

"Can I just have the addresses?" I asked with a chuckle and a shake of my head.

"You're no fun." Lindsey provided the work address, which was for the florist shop Mia seemed to own, and the home address for good measure. "It looks like her shop is open until seven tonight, so you're good to go."

Lindsey also said she had tried to find a social media presence for Carlos and Kari Marcella, but they were ghosts. "It's really weird, because everyone's on social media nowadays—even my great grandma. If they're not on any of these platforms, they've got to be running from something."

I was starting to get the same feeling. Since there was no record of their existence after they'd left Louisiana, it could mean one of two things: they had never applied for new driver's licenses when they had moved, or they had changed their names, and neither option bode well for them. According to Detective Dawn Luke Carter, the people of the old Magnolia Life Church had been known to lie about their identities when they were up to no good.

"Lindsey," I said, thinking as I talked, "can you search those social media sites by location?"

"Yep."

"Can you do a search for Sandy Knobs, Nevada and see what names pop up from there? Maybe we'll get lucky and find a Carlos or a Kari with a different last name."

"Sure thing."

I could hear her fingers dancing across the keyboard as she ran her search.

"I've got nothing," she said. "It's saying the place doesn't even exist."

"Can you search for Dean Marcella on social media?" I asked. "Maybe Carlos adopted the boy and gave him his last name."

There was another pause on the other end of the phone while she searched. When she came back on the line, she said there were three men named Dean Marcella, but none of them were from Nevada or Louisiana.

"Maybe our guy moved," I suggested. "Is there any way you can contact each of them to find out if their mom's name is Kari or if they have a stepfather named Carlos? I think you can send messages through those sites even if you're not friends with someone, right?"

"I can do one better than that," Lindsey said idly, obviously working in the background. "I can check their familial statuses on their pages. If I send them a message without friending them first, it'll go to some hidden folder, and they might not see it for weeks, if at all."

I left the strip mall parking lot and began heading toward the florist shop, which was about five minutes away. I was about to tell Lindsey that I'd have to call back when she let out a grunt.

"Never mind, it's none of these guys."

Flabbergasted, I asked, "How could you possibly know that already?"

"Easy. They all have their profiles completely filled out and neither of them has a mother named Kari or a stepdad named Carlos."

Impressed, I thanked her and told her I might have to look into the whole social media thing.

"Don't bother…it's the devil," she said. "It'll suck out your soul and steal most of your time. Read a book instead. At least then you'll learn something."

"But you just got through saying everyone's on social media nowadays, even your grandma."

"I don't like my grandma, so I don't care what happens to her," she said flatly. "You, on the other hand, you're pretty cool, so I'd never want anything bad to happen to you."

I felt my face redden. "Thanks, Lindsey, that's really nice of you."

"You want to be nice in return?" she asked coyly.

I saw the sign for the florist shop up ahead and slowed down, but my mind was distracted by something in her voice. It set my warning bells off. "What do you mean?"

"If you want to be nice in return, then don't name your son after a gun."

"Did Susan put you up to this?" I asked.

I heard a burst of laughter in the background and recognized my wife's voice.

"Tell Susan his middle name's gonna be 92FS."

"What does that even mean?" Lindsey asked through fits of laughter.

"It's the type of Berretta he's gonna be named after."

As Susan continued to laugh in the background, I told Lindsey I had to go, and she promised to keep digging for more information on Carlos, Kari, and Dean.

CHAPTER 32

Somewhere North of Sandy Knobs, Nevada

As Baylor drove, Amy stared out at the expansive wasteland all around them. She hadn't seen a source of water since they'd left the Twelve County Sheriff's Department twenty minutes earlier. The road on which they traveled was worn and bumpy, and although they were surrounded by mountains, the stretch of highway they were on was mostly flat. She hadn't seen any connecting roads or signs telling them how far they were from Sandy Knobs. Had it not been for the GPS navigational system on her cell phone, she would've felt disconnected from the rest of the world. She no longer had cell service, and she knew if she interrupted the route on her phone, she'd never be able to get it back.

"I wonder who owns all this property," she mused aloud. "There're no houses or animals out here. And where're the trees? The grass? Everything's so gray. How does anything survive out here?"

"We're in the desert," Baylor said. "If this Jeep broke down on the road, we'd be screwed. I doubt another car's been through here in the last week."

Amy scrunched her nose and glanced at her new husband. "Would you drink your own urine to survive?"

"It depends."

"On what?"

"If I could add strawberry powder to it or not."

"Strawberry urine?" Amy feigned a gag and slapped his shoulder.

"That's disgusting! I'd rather die."

Baylor laughed, and then in a knowing voice said, "Yeah, I'd do it to survive."

Remembering his time in the military, Amy gasped. "Wait...did you have to do it already? Was that part of your training for Afghanistan?"

"It's all in a day's work," he said with a firm nod. "You know what would be worse than drinking your own urine?"

"What?" Amy asked curiously.

"Drinking your buddy's."

"Enough!" Amy really gagged that time. Before she could say another word, her cell phone beeped loudly. "I've got service!"

She snatched up her phone and glanced at the screen. The display showed that she'd received a text from Takecia, but it had been sent fifteen minutes earlier. She checked the indicator bar at the top of her phone.

"I'm out of service again," she declared, using her thumb to access the text message. She gave a triumphant shout when she read the message. "We've got a last name! The victim's name is Carlos Marcella and his wife's name is Kari."

"Anything else?"

"Just that this Carlos fellow might've had a lot of enemies," she said, reading as she talked. "He was a principal of a church school and he believed in corporal punishment. According to this fellow named Ray Broussard, who used to be a member of the Magnolia Life Church, everyone who knew Carlos wanted him dead."

"Damn, if a lot of people knew him, that'll be a large suspect pool."

"Yeah," she agreed. "Takecia said Carlos and Kari had two children together, but she had a son from a previous marriage. They should be grown up now, considering they left Louisiana about nineteen years ago."

"Any names on the kids?" Baylor flipped the Jeep's visor down to block the relentless rays of the afternoon sun.

"Just the stepson—it's Dean." Amy chewed on her lower lip. "Takecia thinks something happened that involved the stepson, because Ray began acting all weird when he mentioned the boy's name. She'll text me when she knows more."

Amy checked again to see if her cell phone had any bars, but it didn't, so she tucked it into the console. She went back to staring out the window as she made small talk with Baylor. She had never been to the desert, and it was much different from what she'd expected.

For one thing, she had never imagined it would be so lacking in color. It was like they were driving through a black and white television set from the sixties.

Finally, after nearly an hour had passed, a sign loomed ahead. It was hard to read at first because of the shimmering heat waves, but when they drew closer, she could finally see what it said.

Sandy Knobs Church of Life: 25 miles

Baylor grunted. "I guess the church is more important than the town to these folks."

"What if the church is the town?"

"Could be."

Amy saw Baylor reach under his seat with his right hand to feel for the pistol he'd concealed there when they'd left the hotel. She did the same and felt the reassuring grip of her Glock where it was tucked just out of sight under her own seat.

Prior to them leaving Louisiana, a number of people had asked both she and Baylor why they hadn't decided to fly out west for their honeymoon rather than wasting days on the road driving, and their response had been the same: "How in the hell are we gonna get two AR-15s on an airplane?"

Having witnessed the evils of the job and endured their own trials and tribulations throughout their careers—including an ambush that had almost killed both of them—they treated their firearms like most people treated their American Express cards: they never left home without them.

While they hadn't been expecting any trouble with their death notification initially, their conversation with Deputy Ready had raised their alert level to orange.

Amy reached over and cupped her left hand over Baylor's right, which was resting on the gearshift. Their eyes met and she smiled. "I can't think of a better way to spend my honeymoon."

He returned the smile, beaming like a high school boy about to step on the football field for the first time.

"And I can't think of a better woman to spend my life with," he said. "Not only are you beautiful, smart, sexy, good in bed, and good with a gun, but your taste for adventure is probably a little spicier than mine—and that's hot!"

CHAPTER 33

Seasville, Louisiana

Takecia and I parked in front of the florist building and were soon standing inside a cluttered room waiting on a robust woman to finish paying for some kind of flower arrangement. Takecia leaned over and told me what kind of flowers they were, but I didn't care. Flowers were all around us and I could feel my allergies starting to protest.

When the lady had finished making her purchase, I stepped back and held the door for her. Her hands were full and she seemed to appreciate the help. I then turned and approached the counter with Takecia. The name tag pinned to the woman's apron told us she was Mia Foret.

I smiled and introduced myself and Takecia. Her eyes drifted down to our badges and pistols. She seemed apprehensive. It must've been obvious we weren't there to buy flowers.

"Is something wrong?" she asked. "Am I in trouble?"

"No, ma'am, we're from Mechant Loup, so we have no jurisdiction over here," I said with a grin and a shrug. "You can break any law you like and there's nothing we can do."

She chuckled. "Where's Mechant Loup?"

I shot a thumb over my shoulder. "It's over in Chateau Parish, down near the swamps."

"Oh, yeah, I think I've heard of that place. Isn't that where the giant alligator almost killed that man?"

I frowned, and nodded. "That's the place."

"I don't know where it's at, but I've definitely heard of it." She glanced at Takecia and then back at me. "What can I do for y'all?"

"We just need some help verifying a story," I explained. "It's regarding an incident that happened at the Magnolia Life Church about nineteen years ago."

I noticed immediately that Mia's hands froze in place and her face lost a shade of color.

"Is this about the baby?" she asked in a hushed voice. "I thought that was all over and done with. I wasn't even going to that church when it happened."

"No, ma'am, like I said, we're not from Magnolia Parish, so we had nothing to do with that case." I cleared my throat. "It's about an incident that happened during one of the church services. It involved two men named Ray Broussard and Carlos Marcella, and it happened a couple of years before the baby incident."

"You mean the public whipping?" Mia put a hand over her mouth. "Is that what this is about?"

I nodded and shot a glance at Takecia.

"So, it was true?" I asked Mia. "It really happened?"

"Oh, yeah, it happened. I couldn't believe what I was seeing." Mia indicated a bench toward the front of the shop. "Would y'all like to have a seat? This might take a while."

I shrugged, but followed her to the seat. She sat wearily and smoothed out her apron. Takecia sat beside her and I stood in front of them.

"What do y'all need to know?" Mia asked.

I asked if she remembered what had initiated Carlos' attack on Ray, and she nodded.

"It all started when Ray jumped on Carlos in the men's bathroom one day after church," she explained. "I was walking from the church building to the school when I heard a lot of commotion in the courtyard between the two buildings. I…it was so shocking and disturbing."

She paused and swallowed. "I looked toward the noise and saw Dean. He was just a little boy. The back of his underwear was pulled down, exposing his rear end. He had bruises from his butt all the way down to the back of his knees. I…I've never seen anything so horrific."

Mia continued to describe what she saw, and I began wishing for a chair of my own. I felt dizzy with anger. As a man, I was glad Carlos was dead. As a cop, I knew I had to find his killer—if, indeed, he had been murdered. I found myself hoping the toxicology would come back clean, and that I had been wrong about the bags of ice. If only the fingerprints would come back to Carlos, I could put this case to bed and move on, never to look back at it again.

"What happened next?" I asked, my voice sounding like it was underwater.

"One of the parents ran over and pulled up Dean's pants," Mia continued. "A little bit later, Mr. Broussard came out of the bathroom yelling that he had witnessed Carlos beating Dean with that stick he loved to carry around. He looked scared, and he didn't hang around. He took off running to his truck and drove off. We knew he must've done something to Carlos. Three of the church men went into the bathroom and they came out a little bit later with Carlos. One of the men was helping Carlos walk. His clothes were dirty and there was a red mark on his head. He looked embarrassed and angry."

"Did Carlos say anything?"

"Oh, yeah." She nodded for emphasis. "He was roaring mad. He demanded for someone to tell him where Ray was, and when someone said he had left, he ordered two men to go after him and bring him back immediately."

"Did they?"

"No, Father Nelson stopped them. He had come outside to see what was going on, and when he realized what had happened, he told his men to usher Carlos into his office. He told everyone standing around that everything would be fine, and for everyone to just pray about what they had seen and he told them to go home."

"When did the spanking happen?" I asked, feeling weird about referring to the beating in that manner.

"It was the following Sunday." Mia scowled. "That was another weird day in the church."

"How old were you at the time all of this took place?"

"I had just turned sixteen."

"Did you attend the church's school back then?"

"I did attend the school, but the school was closed when this happened, and we were all being homeschooled," Mia said. "At the time, I was working as an assistant to Father Nelson. In fact, I heard some people complaining to Father Nelson about Carlos one day."

"What did they complain about?"

"About the way he was treating Dean. They said they thought Carlos had been drunk on power when the school was running, but that he began going through withdrawals when he couldn't beat the other kids anymore. They said they thought he was taking his frustrations out on Dean—and I believe it. I know he used to love hitting the kids at school, and he was always mean to Dean, so I could see him getting worse."

"What did Father Nelson say?"

She frowned. "He told them that the correction of Dean was between Carlos and God."

I cursed under my breath. The more I heard about Carlos, the more I disliked the man, and I certainly wasn't a fan of this *Father* Nelson.

"Did Carlos ever spank you?" I asked after pausing long enough to relax my tightening jaw.

"No, he never bothered me." She frowned. "He did spank some of the other girls, but it was mostly the boys he went after. He was downright brutal. I still can't believe the parents let that happen. If that would've been me, I would've never let him spank my kid. Had he even tried, I would've had him locked up so fast the black dye would've flown off his hair."

"He dyed his hair?"

"Oh, yeah, it was jet black." She shook her head. "It was way too dark to be natural. And he was only in his thirties back then, but I think he was starting to get some gray hairs. My mom used to say Mrs. Kari and their kids didn't need to love him, because he loved himself enough for the whole family. He was a creep, too. He was always flirting with the young girls and trying to show off by pushing the boys around. He was a horrible person."

"How'd he treat his biological kids?" I asked, wondering if he favored them over his wife's son.

"They could do no wrong," Mia said. "He treated Dean like a pariah, but he treated his flesh and blood like God-kissed angels from Heaven."

I sighed. I had been afraid of that. While it was a good thing he'd at least spared the other two, it must've made things that much worse for young Dean.

"Go on and tell me about this public spanking, if you don't mind," I said, leaning against a nearby shelf as I listened.

CHAPTER 34

Mia described the spanking incident almost exactly the same as Ray had, only she said he started crying the moment Carlos grabbed his arm at the back of the church, and she said he was begging and slobbering over his words all the way to the stage. Tears welled up in her eyes as she told the story.

"It was really sad to watch," she said, brushing a tear from her face. "It was the last straw for my dad. After we left the church that day, we never went back. Father Nelson and some of the other elders called several times and even came by the house to pressure him into going back, but he wasn't changing his mind. The last time they showed up, he answered the door with his shotgun. He told them he'd shoot the next one of them that stepped foot on his property."

"Did anyone show up at your house after that?"

"Nope," she said, "and he didn't go back until long after the stuff with the baby had happened and Father Nelson was long gone. I had already moved out of the house and was married by the time he started going back to church there. He tried to get me to go back for a few years, but that whole thing I'd heard about Father Nelson and the baby had left a bad taste in my mouth. When I got pregnant, I decided I wanted my baby baptized in a nondenominational church, so my husband and I gave the new preacher a shot."

"How is it now?"

"I haven't been to church a lot lately, because I got real behind with work when I took some time off to have my baby. I've been using my weekends to catch up, but it has definitely been different the few times we did go to church. When my baby was baptized it was awesome and uplifting." Her face beamed. "The new pastor and his wife are so amazing and loving and nurturing."

I nodded, and then got right to it. "When was the last time you saw Carlos Marcella?"

"Oh, wow." She scrunched up her face. "Let's see…the last time I saw him was when he attacked Mr. Ray Broussard, but my mom did see him a few days later. Where was that again?" She paused and snapped her fingers as she tried to remember. Finally, she shrugged. "I don't remember where—maybe the post office—but she said he had his family in a station wagon that was all loaded up with a U-Haul trailer attached to the back. She said it looked like they were leaving town. It must've been true, because no one's seen them since."

I was thoughtful, wondering if it would be worth pursuing the Magnolia Life Church angle. Other than finding out that Ray Broussard might be our guy, it seemed to be a dead end. "What's your preacher's name?"

"Brother Baxter."

"He doesn't call himself a father?"

"No, he says he's our brother in the Lord, so he prefers everyone to call him brother." She pursed her lips. "Carlos and Father Nelson could've used some of the same humility. And you know what else?"

"What?" I asked, playing along.

"He doesn't take money from the church to pay his bills or to live his life," she said. "He has a regular job like the rest of us. He uses the church's money to help those in need."

"Really?" I was impressed with the man already. "What does he do?"

"He's a plumber."

Even more impressed. I asked a few more questions, but didn't learn anything that would help us solve our mystery. I finally glanced at Takecia and asked if she had any questions.

"Yeah, do you know Dean's last name?" Takecia asked.

Mia's brow furrowed. "I used to know it, but it's been so long ago. Dean…Dean…" After a minute of contemplation, she said, "You know what? I bet my dad remembers it."

She got quickly to her feet and hurried to the counter.

"What about the other kids that Carlos and Kari had together?" I asked while she searched the counter for her cell phone. "Do you know their names and ages?"

"Oh, yeah, there was a little girl named Star and a boy named Abel," she said. "Star was a year younger than Abel, so that would put her around twenty-one now, and Abel would be about twenty-two. Obviously, they had Carlos' last name."

Mia was sliding her fingers across the phone when she suddenly stopped. "Hey, do y'all mind telling me what this is about? I know my dad's gonna ask what's going on, and I won't know what to tell him."

"Carlos is dead," I explained. "We're trying to find his family to make the notification."

A puzzled expression fell across Mia's face. "And y'all said y'all are from Chateau Parish?"

I nodded. "Mechant Loup, to be exact."

"If y'all are from Chateau and looking for his family to notify them," she asked slowly, "does that mean he was in Chateau?"

"I'm afraid so," I said.

"Do you mean to tell me this animal has been living in Chateau Parish all this time?" She seemed flabbergasted. "I can't believe he was that close to us! I...we all thought he was long gone, that we were safe from him."

"Well, we believe he *has* been long gone," I explained. "There's some indication that he might have just arrived in town from Texas or somewhere farther out west. We don't think his family came with him, but we can't be sure. That's why we need to talk to anyone who might've seen or heard from him in recent days."

"My dad would know if he's been around here," she said with a grunt. "He knows everybody and everything that goes on up and down the bayou in Magnolia."

Mia turned her attention back to her cell phone and was soon talking to her dad.

"Hey, Dad," she said after answering his questions about how she was doing and how the business was going, "remember Carlos Marcella?"

There was a pause and I could hear a man's voice asking her what was going on.

"Some cops are here asking about him," Mia explained. "They need to find his stepson, Dean, or his wife, Kari. Wait...what?"

Mia's expression turned to one of shock. "Here? In Magnolia Parish? When? No way!"

I couldn't hear what else was being said, but Takecia and I didn't have to wait long to find out what was going on.

Mia cupped a hand over the phone. "My dad says Dean is here in Magnolia, and that he even went to church a few times. He said he thinks he's down here to stay."

"What?" I figured my own expression was one of shock at that moment. "Can I talk to your dad?"

She handed me the phone. I quickly introduced myself and asked, "Sir, are you sure Dean was here?"

"I'm positive," said Mia's father, his voice confident. "I would know that boy anywhere. He hasn't changed a lick since the last time I saw him, except he's grown taller and his muscles filled out a bit. He walked right into church about a month ago and sat down in the front pew right next to this pretty girl. I don't know who she is—I don't know any of the younger crowd—but she's been coming to church for quite a while."

"Do you remember what day that would've been?"

"Oh, let's see...that would've been around August the twenty-first, I believe. He's come back nearly every week after that, and he always sits next to that same girl. It looks like they're dating or something. I don't think I saw him last week though, but I'm sure he'll be back. My wife talked to him a few times over the past month, and he told her he was moving here to stay."

"Did he say anything about his stepdad?"

"No, but the last time he was here, he did tell my wife he was worried about Kari—that's his mom—because he hadn't heard from her in a couple of weeks. He said she calls him every weekend, but she missed the past two or three."

"He's worried because she hasn't called?"

"Well, that and there was something about an interrupted conversation. He told my wife he was on the phone with his mom and he heard some noise in the background and then the line went dead."

"When did he tell your wife this?"

"Um, hold on a second."

There were some scratching sounds over the phone and then I heard his muffled voice call out for his wife. There was some discussion back and forth—with him having to explain in great detail why he was asking the question—and then he finally got back on the line.

"It was the Sunday before last, she said." He grunted. "You know what?"

"What's that?"

"The funny thing is...that's the last time we saw him. He didn't show up for church this past Sunday. I wonder if it's because he was lying about the whole thing. People do that, you know?"

I nodded absently. "Has Carlos been to your church recently?"

"Not that I've seen," Mia's dad said. "I don't think he'd be welcome here. He's hurt too many people."

I was thoughtful. The fact that Carlos had been killed in our parish around the same time that his stepson had moved back to Magnolia could *not* be a coincidence. According to what I'd just learned, Dean had moved back down here for a girl, but what had brought Carlos to the area? Had he been tracking Dean? If he was hunting Dean and had found him, it hadn't ended well for the older man. I then considered Kari Marcella. The fact that Dean was worried about his mom had to mean something to the case, but what? I needed to know more about that interrupted phone call, and I would only be able to get that from one man.

Behind me, I could hear Takecia asking Mia a few more questions, and then a customer entered the shop and interrupted them. I was pacing in a corner of the shop, trying to figure out what everything meant while Mia's dad's voice droned on in the background. He was talking about the church and what had happened between Ray and Carlos, but I was barely listening. I was trying to figure out how Dean or Ray or whoever had killed Carlos could've incapacitated the man without leaving a mark on his body. I also wondered about his other children. Did they know anything?

"Do you know where I can find Dean?" I finally asked.

"No, but Brother Baxter might be able to help you."

"Do you have his number?"

"I sure do." He gave me the preacher's cell phone number and told me it would be best to wait until after five to call him. "He's a working man like the rest of us, and that's what we like about him."

I pulled Mia's phone from my ear and glanced at the screen. It was a quarter after four. I decided I wasn't gonna wait forty-five minutes. I would call him as soon as I had the chance.

I was about to end the conversation when I remembered the all-important question. "Sir, do you know Dean's last name?"

"Um, I'm pretty sure he was a Fletcher. I never knew it before, but I thought I heard him introduce himself recently as Dean Fletcher." Mia's dad paused and was quiet for a moment. It sounded as though he might have something on his mind. I didn't have to wait long to find out what it was. "Say, can you arrest Carlos for the things he did in the past? I know it was a long time ago and I've heard that y'all have time limitations on arresting people, but he needs to be punished for what he did. He's pure evil—kin to the devil himself."

"Carlos will never go to jail for his crimes," I said slowly.

"That's a damned shame."

"Yeah, but he's already burning in hell."

"Really?" he asked.

"Yes, sir," I said. "That's why I was looking for his wife or next of kin."

"Well, now, that's the best news I've heard in some time."

CHAPTER 35

Sandy Knobs, Nevada

After having driven more than seventy miles on the rough highway and not seeing any sign of life—not even a single vehicle—Amy noticed some sort of tower sitting high above an outcrop along the road. Unless aliens had taken up residency in the desert, the tower had been put there by humans, so they were finally reaching some semblance of civilization. She grabbed her cell phone and checked it, but there was still no signal. She sighed and wondered if Clint or Takecia had been trying to contact them.

"This must be the private cell tower Deputy Ready told us about," Baylor said.

Amy nodded. "We should've brought a SAT phone. We knew we were heading to the National Parks and there wouldn't be any service. What were we thinking?"

"Wasn't that the point?" Baylor asked. "To get lost in each other and leave everyone else behind? You said it was the only way you could disconnect from your job."

"Yeah, and then I went checking my cell phone the first time we had service," she said with a frown. "I'm sorry for doing that. It...it's just so hard to turn it off, you know? Being a detective is different than being on patrol. When we're home, I'm always thinking about the cases on my desk and I'm always wondering when I'll be called out again. I'm gun-shy now. When I was on patrol, I'd get off and not think about work until the next morning. But now, it's all I think about. Remember how I jumped and nearly fell out the bed when I heard sirens Friday night?"

Baylor laughed.

"I just knew I was being called out and the wedding was gonna be ruined." Amy also laughed.

"It might've been postponed, but it wouldn't have been ruined." Baylor suddenly scowled. He cast a sideways glance in her direction. "Are you thinking of leaving detectives?"

"Never—I love it. I just need to learn to turn it off." She reached over with her left hand and rubbed the back of Baylor's dark hair. "After we make this death notification, I'll throw my phone in that Salt Lake we drove by in Utah."

"Stop worrying about it," he said. "This is the most fun we've had since we left home. Don't get me wrong, every second I spend with you is fun, but to go to a place where the local cops won't dare to tread? That's my kind of assignment."

Amy nodded her agreement. She had felt a surge of adrenalin earlier when they had talked to Deputy Ready, and that feeling was starting to return as they rounded a bend in the road and the mountains on their immediate right melted away, revealing a smattering of homesteads in the distance. The homes appeared to be in a valley that stretched toward the west, where other mountains— made of rock and lacking in greenery—loomed on the distant horizon.

Baylor slowed the Jeep as they approached an exit ramp. The highway they were traveling along continued to stretch deep toward the south, but the approaching intersection bore a sign that informed them they had reached Spirit Way. The letters to the sign were silver and the background was blue.

"It's a private road," Amy said, trying to see around the sheared rock face to their right that cropped up from the earth. There were a lot of similar outcrops and rocky hills scattered all around, and she could only imagine what evil might lurk beyond them.

Amy could tell Baylor was on high alert. His eyes kept shifting from his rearview mirror, to each side mirror, and then to the front. Afterward, he would start the process all over again.

"There's no traffic," he said when they reached Spirit Way, "which seems weird."

Spirit Way ran from east to west, but it appeared there was nothing to the east except an expanse of dry desert. To the right, Amy saw her first tree in over an hour. There was actually a half dozen of them, and they were healthy and green.

"Is that grass or a mirage?" She pointed to an apartment complex up ahead where bright green grass sprouted from the ground. "This looks like paradise in the middle of Hades."

"But something's off," Baylor said, driving slowly past the complex on Spirit Way. "Something's not right."

"Yeah, there aren't any kids on the playground, no one walking their dogs, no cars driving around." Amy reached under her seat and pulled out her Glock. She set it between her legs. If their bad feelings did pan out, she wanted her pistol in easy reach. "Although I don't see anyone, I get the sense we're being watched."

Baylor's head bobbed up and down in agreement, but his eyes never left their surroundings as he continued driving along Spirit Way.

After passing another apartment complex and more houses, the road took a sharp bend to the left, and at the top of that bend, there was a driveway leading to a large metal building. A few cars were in the parking lot, but there was no sign of life.

Amy had immediately noticed that there were no mailboxes lining the street, but there were ascending numbers accompanied by what appeared to be a last name marking the various buildings.

Baylor eased the Jeep to a stop and asked, "Do you see any numbers on that metal building? It could be a business. Is it 777 Spirit Way?"

Amy shook her head and pointed to a placard attached to one of the columns at the front of the building. "We're still in the 500 block."

They continued through the sharp curve, passed three houses on the right, five on the left, and then the street curved back to the right. The hair stood up on Amy's neck. The ragtop to the Jeep had been down all day, and suddenly she was wishing for a hardtop. She looked up through the opening, but there were no drones flying overhead and no cameras on the street poles. She scanned the windows to the buildings that they passed. The curtains were drawn.

Get a hold of yourself, she thought. *No one's watching us. I'm just being paranoid.*

As quickly as the thought entered her mind, it disappeared. Baylor was also feeling the same thing, so she was not simply being paranoid. Something was definitely not right about this picture.

Amy was about to tell Baylor to stop the Jeep so she could get her AR-15 from the back, but she gasped when a five-acre plot of land came into view on the left. It was along a straight stretch of Spirit Way and it was hard to miss. The rich green grass that carpeted the area was in sharp contrast to the surrounding desert wasteland,

and even the air through which they were driving felt cooler.

Baylor pointed to a placard on the largest building that squatted on the lot. "777 Spirit Way," he said. "This is it."

There was a horseshoe driveway that connected to a large concrete parking lot, and Baylor accessed it. A four-by-four Dodge Ram was parked near the entrance to the building. Baylor parked beside it and shut off the engine.

"Here goes nothing." Amy shoved her pistol inside her waistband and concealed it with the tail of her shirt. She and Baylor had stopped at a mall in Salt Lake City and purchased more appropriate attire for the job. Baylor had protested a little, but relented when Amy promised to rip his clothes off in the middle of the desert after their work was done. She had purchased blue jeans and an orange blouse to replace her shorts and tank top, and he had purchased blue jeans and a Polo shirt to replace his cargo shorts and T-shirt.

Amy waited while Baylor shoved his pistol under his shirt. He gave her a nod and they both stepped out of the Jeep.

The wind blew warm against their faces as they approached the front door to the church building. A monument near the entrance informed them that they were about to enter Sandy Knobs Life Church, and that it had been founded by none other than Carlos Marcella.

"This is definitely it," Amy whispered, indicating the monument. She didn't know why she felt the need to keep her voice down, but it somehow felt appropriate.

"Should we knock or just go in?" Baylor asked when he reached the door. They had approached the front of the church as casually as they could manage, while also keeping a little distance between themselves in case of an attack.

"It's a church. Everyone's welcome." As she said the words, Amy realized how ridiculous she felt to approach a house of prayer with tactics on her mind. She had scanned the windows on the second floor carefully, and kept her left hand on the front of her shirt so she could pull it away in the event she needed to quickly draw her pistol. Somehow, she felt that God would frown upon starting a shootout in the middle of His church, but then she also wasn't sure to which god Carlos prayed.

Baylor hesitated for a second, gave Amy a nod, and then he grabbed the doorknob.

CHAPTER 36

Seasville, Louisiana

I called Lindsey as soon as I fired up the Tahoe and turned up the air. She barely said hello when I began talking.

"Lindsey, we've got a last name on Carlos' stepson and we know the names of his biological kids," I said excitedly. "The stepson's last name is—"

"Fletcher," Lindsey interrupted before I could finish. "His name is Dean Fletcher and he's all grown up now. He's twenty-four, he left the Marine Corps two years ago, and his relationship status is *single but complicated*. Oh, yeah, and he lives with his grandparents in Alexandria, Louisiana, where he runs a tire shop outside of town along Old Highway 1."

"Wait a minute," I began, confused. "How could you possibly know all of these things?"

"I know a lot more than that." Her voice grew more excited as she talked. "And you're not going to believe what I found out about Kari Marcella. I think I might've cracked your case wide open and figured out why that asshole was killed."

I pulled the cell phone from my ear and stared at it for a quick second. I couldn't remember the last time I'd heard Lindsey curse, if ever, so I knew she must've been really excited. I glanced at Takecia, who only shrugged.

"What'd you find out?" I asked, putting the phone back to my ear.

"On the fourth of September, Dean Fletcher puts up a social

media post asking for information about his mom. He said he hadn't heard from her in almost two weeks and he thought something might have happened to her. He asked anyone in or around Sandy Knobs to let him know if they've seen her. He said he's called the police in Nevada, but they aren't much help."

"He put all that information on a social media post?"

"Yep," she said, "and he even offered a reward of two thousand dollars for anyone who could get him in contact with his mom. He posted his cell number online and said they could call him day or night. He also posted a picture of him with his mom—it was an old picture, back when he was a kid—and he listed her name as Kari Marcella. He said she was last seen with his stepdad, Carlos Marcella, in Sandy Knobs, Nevada."

Lindsey finally paused for a breath, but it was a short one.

"In the comment section of his original post," she continued, "more than two hundred and fifty people offered well-wishes and prayers, and the post was shared seventy-eight times. I clicked on each of the shared links. Some were hidden, so I couldn't see what was said about it, but I did find a comment on one of the shared posts that was from someone who claimed to be a former member of the Magnolia Life Church."

"So, someone from the old Magnolia Life Church is communicating with Dean Fletcher?"

"Yeah," she confirmed. "There was a whole side discussion about what Carlos used to do to kids of the school that was affiliated with the Magnolia Life Church, and many of them were telling him how sorry they were, and that he was the one who had it the worst, because he had to live with that monster every day."

"So, what did this comment from the former member say?"

"It was from a woman who used to go to the church, and she wrote that if Kari went missing, then Carlos had definitely murdered her. A girl named Starry Night asked if the woman had any firsthand knowledge, but the woman said no, and then Starry Night told her to shut her mouth or she would be sued for slander. When I checked out Starry Night's profile, I realized her real name was Star Marcella, and she's the daughter of Carlos and Kari Marcella. She's twenty-one and works as a waitress at a Walk-On's in Arizona."

"Did anyone respond to her?"

"Dean did," she said. "He told Star that everyone was just trying to help, and that's where the conversation died. Next, I checked out Star's familial connections, and found out that, in addition to being Dean's stepsister, she also has a brother named Abel, who's twenty-two and in the Marine Corps. It looks like Abel is following in Dean's footsteps, and that they like each other, because there're a lot of photos of them together."

"Hold up," I finally said. Although my head was spinning from the huge information dump, I had a good handle on what I'd just been told. However, I didn't understand how Lindsey could have come by that information so quickly. "I thought Kari Marcella wasn't on social media?"

"She's not."

"Then how'd you find her on there and how'd you discover that Dean's last name was Fletcher?"

"I found her because people were talking about her," Lindsey explained. "After my earlier search didn't turn up anything, I did a new name search for Kari Marcella, but instead of just searching for social media profiles under that name, I searched for any mention of her."

"So, anytime someone mentions her name, it's possible to find it by doing a name inquiry?"

"Yeah," she said. "I found the name mentioned several times. Some of them were really her, while some were of a different Kari Marcella, but when I found the missing person poster, that's when everything started coming together. And since the post was linked to Dean Fletcher's profile and he had identified her as his mother and Carlos as his stepfather, I knew I had the right person."

I shook my head. I wasn't sure if I liked that much information being easily accessible to stalkers and other evil people online, but I couldn't argue with it being helpful. I made a mental note to never allow my kids on social media until they were thirty-five, and then asked, "Can you make screenshots of everything you found, and then send a picture of Dean and Kari to me, Takecia, Baylor, and Dawn?"

"The screenshots are already done. I printed them out, stuck them in a yellow envelope, and put them on your desk. I'm sending the digital photos to everyone right…about…now!"

My phone buzzed almost instantly, and I knew I had received them. I was about to tell Lindsey what a great job she had done when she spoke up.

"Look, detective work is your job, but Dean definitely saw that comment about Carlos murdering his mom, because he responded to it," she said. "I think he believed it, he hunted Carlos down, and then he killed him."

"You might be right," I said idly, wondering where I might find the younger man, "but we're hearing that Dean recently moved to

Magnolia Parish. Maybe Carlos was hunting the kid and bit off more than he could chew."

"Do you want his cell number?" she asked.

Although she couldn't see me, I nodded. "You know it, *Detective* Savoie."

I could almost feel her beaming through the phone as she called out his cell number. It had a 318 area code, which was consistent with the Alexandria area, but it was impossible to tell if it was a landline or cell phone by the number.

"Where'd this number come from?" I asked.

"It was on the information for the tire shop," she explained. "He claims to be available twenty-four/seven, so I'm guessing it's a cell phone."

"Thank you," I said. "I owe you big time."

"You don't owe me a thing. Just don't bother me for the next hour or so. I'm in the middle of The Faithful Spy, and I'm about to start crying."

"Is that another Vince Flynn book?" I asked, remembering that she had been working her way through the entire Mitch Rapp series.

"No, I'm finished with that series for now. This one's by Alex Berenson. It's the last book in his Wells series, and it's breaking my heart. I don't know what I'm gonna read after I'm done."

I stifled a chuckle as I ended the call and turned to Takecia, who was sitting with her arms crossed, staring impatiently at me. "Well, what's going on?"

I told her everything I'd learned. She listened without interruption. When I was done talking, she asked if I thought Dean was the one who had killed Carlos.

"It's quite possible," I began, thinking through the evidence. "He was here at the same time Carlos was here, so he has opportunity. He hated Carlos, so he has the motive. Hell, he might've found out what happened to his mom, and if Carlos did something to her, my money would definitely be on him. But…there's just one thing that doesn't make sense."

"What's that?"

"The way Carlos was killed," I explained. "Thanks to the bridge tender, we know Carlos was alone, so that must mean he did something to Kari. If Dean found that out, he would've ripped Carlos to shreds. He would've destroyed him. He wouldn't have calmly made it look like an accident."

"Unless he's been planning this for a long time," Takecia suggested. "I'm sure he's not interested in going to jail, and he would have to know he'd be named as a suspect, so maybe he kept his cool and did it right. Only, how would he incapacitate Carlos and seatbelt him into the truck?"

"That's the million-dollar question." I fired up my Tahoe and pulled out my cell phone. "We know he wasn't shot with a dart gun because there were no marks on his body. I doubt he'd eat or drink anything that Dean would give him, so that's probably out of the question. I guess the only way Dean could've incapacitated Carlos without leaving a mark would've been to sneak up behind him with chloroform or a similar drug."

As Takecia mulled this over, I dialed Brother Baxter's number.

CHAPTER 37

"This is Larry," a man said in a strained voice when he answered the phone. I heard metal clanking against metal in the background and he grunted. There was a sigh, and then he spoke again, but this time his tone was more relaxed. "How can I help you?"

I introduced myself and explained that Takecia and I needed to speak with him about a case we were working from Mechant Loup.

"Mechant Loup?" he asked. "A friend of mine is a pastor down there."

"Would that be Father Reggie," I asked, "of the Mechant Life Church?"

"It would be."

I didn't want to get into it over the phone, so I asked if we could meet him face-to-face to talk about our case.

"Sure." He paused for a second and then gave us an address to a business in the town of Seasville, which was in the southern portion of Magnolia Parish. "Somebody's been flushing wet wipes down the drain for about ten years at this place. It backed up the sewer system and clogged about ten yards of pipe, so I'll be here for a while."

I thanked him and gave Takecia a nod as I headed out of the parking lot. "We're working late tonight."

She didn't seem to mind. As I drove, I asked her to call Amy and update her on the information we'd learned.

"They should be close to the Spirit Way address," I said. "They need to know that Kari might be missing."

Takecia nodded and pulled out her cell phone. A minute later, she shook her head. "Their phones go straight to voicemail. They must be out of range."

I nodded, but a sense of dread began to form in my gut. "Can you call the sheriff's department up there and see if they can send someone to check on them?"

"Yeah." Takecia got back on the phone and made the call. After a moment, she shook her head. "No one's answering."

I frowned, hoping I wouldn't regret asking Amy and Baylor to make the death notification. While they were well-trained and would never walk blindly into any situation, they had been expecting to make a simple death notification, not stumble into a missing person case that might end up being a murder.

"At least Carlos is dead and won't pose a threat," I mumbled to myself, hoping that he didn't have any accomplices who might cause problems for Amy and Baylor.

Once we reached the address in Seasville, I parked near a white van with a sign that read, *Baxter's Plumbing Service, LLC.* Before we could dismount, a man wearing blue coveralls lumbered around the building carrying a motorized drain snake. He placed it on the ground near the back door of the van and straightened wearily. There was a brown smudge across his left cheek, but he didn't seem to notice.

Takecia and I met him near the van and we nodded a greeting. Brother Baxter lifted a gloved hand apologetically.

"I would shake hands, but I'm a bit of a mess," he said.

I waved him off, trying not to appear as grateful as I felt. He indicated a shaded spot under a nearby oak tree, and we followed him to it.

"We need to ask you some questions about Dean Fletcher," I said, watching him closely for a response. "I understand he started attending your church recently."

"He did." Baxter smiled. "He's an interesting fellow, that's for sure."

"Do you know what brought him to Magnolia Parish?"

"Yeah, I do. He met a young woman in our church through the internet and they started dating. Her name's Lily Pierce. She's a nice young lady." He paused and frowned. "She's been through a lot, but she's doing well. Dean's been through a lot himself, as I hear it, and I think they're good for each other."

I asked him about the timeline regarding Dean's church attendance, and it corresponded with the one we'd gathered from Mia's dad.

"Do you know where he was this past Sunday?"

"No, but I did find it curious that he wasn't in church, considering."

"Considering what?" I asked, eagerly awaiting the information.

"Wait a minute…" Brother Baxter carefully removed one of the dirty gloves and reached for his face, going straight for the brown smudge. He scowled as he studied the substance that had transferred to his hand. "That was on my face—and it's not mud."

CHAPTER 38

I took an impatient breath as Brother Baxter felt around to see if he'd gotten all of the excrement off of his face.

"You said you found it curious that Dean wasn't in church," I began as his face twisted in disgust. "Why is that?"

"Because his stepfather showed up," he said matter-of-factly.

I shot a glance at Takecia and saw that she was equally alert.

"Carlos Marcella went to your church?" I asked, stepping closer. "Are you sure it was him?"

"Oh, yeah, it was Carlos Marcella, alright. When I first became the pastor of the church, his picture was hanging in the study hall, honoring him for being the first principal of the Magnolia Life Christian School. I took it down and burned it, but I still remembered what he looked like. He's a little older now, but I'm good with faces, and it was definitely him."

I gave an approving nod when he mentioned burning the picture. "What was he doing at your church?"

"I didn't know at first, but I found out later that he was looking for his stepson." He sighed. "I don't know how much you know about Carlos, but he's an abusive man. He beat his stepson and he beat nearly every student that attended the old school that the church used to run. His favorite Bible scripture was—"

"He that spareth his rod hateth his son: but he that loveth him chasteneth him betimes," I said, quoting Proverbs 13:24, a scripture my mom had mentioned many times when I was growing up.

Brother Baxter's eyes lit up. "You know the Bible?"

"I've forgotten more than I know, but I remember that scripture well." I shook my head. "While I think God's a fan of discipline, I don't think for a second that He meant for people like Carlos to beat children the way he did. That's pure evil."

"I wasn't here back then—I wasn't even a believer—but I heard the stories."

"We heard the stories, too."

"As you can imagine, I wasn't about to let him anywhere near Dean or any of the other people in my church."

"What'd you do?" I was getting a sense that something happened between the good preacher and Carlos.

"I was preaching when I first saw him walk in," Brother Baxter explained. "I immediately recognized him, so I kept my eye on him. He sat in the last row and he scanned the room the entire service. It was obvious he was looking for someone, and I knew it had to be Dean. When the service ended, I lost him in the crowd. When I found him again, he was outside in the parking lot near the basketball goals. I approached him and introduced myself."

Confronting a man like Carlos was a bold move for a preacher, and I got the sense that being a plumber and a preacher weren't the only jobs this man had ever held.

"He must've been perturbed."

"He was," Baxter admitted. "I told him I wanted to speak with him in private, but he immediately dismissed me. He was scanning the faces of everyone leaving the church. I already knew Dean hadn't shown up, because he wasn't in his usual spot—parishioners have a way of claiming their seats—and I would've normally been worried that Carlos had already found the kid and hurt him, only he was searching too hard for it to be an act. When he brushed me off, I asked if he was scared to be alone with me."

I chuckled. "That was all it took, wasn't it?"

"Oh, yeah, I'd heard of his prideful ways, and I knew I could easily manipulate him." Baxter's eyes sparkled as he continued the story. "Once we were seated in my office, I asked what he was doing in my church. I don't normally refer to it as *my* church—it's the people's church—but I wanted to make my challenge very clear. He told me he was looking for his son. He said he knew Dean was attending Magnolia Life Church, and he demanded to know where he was. I told him I knew about his abusive past and he wasn't welcome in my church. I told him that he would never get close to Dean or any other child in my church, and that he was to leave and never return."

"What did he say to that?"

"Oh, he jumped to his feet and started yelling threats and

pounding the desk." There was a hint of humor and a faraway look in Brother Baxter's eyes, and I could tell he was reliving the moment. "He was threatening to run me out of town and take over the church. He said I was a weak pastor who didn't command respect."

I knew Brother Baxter hadn't always been a preacher. The man carried himself with a quiet confidence that only came with being in deep shit and coming out in one piece—and I didn't mean the kind of shit that was smeared on his face and hand.

"What'd you do?" I asked pointedly. "I can tell by that smirk on your face that you did something."

He turned his attention back to his contaminated hand, and then indicated his face. "I really need to get cleaned up so I can finish this job."

"Don't leave me hanging, preacher," I said.

He chuckled, looked up at me, and said, "I did what any self-respecting pastor would do. I calmly pulled my Springfield 1911 Government from my desk and pointed it right at his face. I dropped the safety and told him that if he ever stepped on church property again or went around Dean, I would shoot a hole through his head big enough to fit my thumb."

I smiled inwardly, but then frowned. Had this preacher killed Carlos? Had Carlos gone after Dean, forcing Baxter to make good on his promise? Baxter seemed to be a man of his word, and he was comfortable talking about killing Carlos. It would've also been a lot easier for two men to stage the scene to look like a suicide, rather than it being just Dean or Baxter. Maybe the two had colluded?

"Have you seen Dean since your confrontation with Carlos?"

"No, but one of the assistant pastors saw him at a gas station. They didn't talk long, but Dean said he would be coming back to church soon. He said he's been busy trying to buy a house."

"Do you know where I can find him?"

"Dean?"

I nodded.

"He's staying at the Payneville Motel north of here…" Brother Baxter's voice trailed off and he scowled. "You're asking how to find Dean, but not Carlos. Is it because you already have Carlos locked up, or is it because he's dead?"

"The latter," I said without hesitation.

Baxter mulled over this bit of information. "You think Dean killed him." He said it more as a statement than a question, but when I didn't confirm or deny anything, he raised an eyebrow. "You think I killed him?"

I shrugged knowingly. "You know how it goes."

"I do." He sighed. "Look, I'll save you a lot of time. If Carlos is dead, I didn't kill him, and I don't know who did. Had he come back to my church acting the fool, it would've been different, but he didn't. I haven't seen him since Sunday and, as far as I know, Dean never found him."

"You said you haven't spoken to Dean in a couple of weeks, so how do you know he didn't find Carlos?"

"I said, *as far as I know* he didn't find Carlos." He was thoughtful. "But if everything I heard about Carlos is true and Dean did find and kill him, then I wouldn't blame him, and I hope you go easy on the kid."

I couldn't argue with the preacher, so I didn't. Instead, I regarded him with curious eyes. "Where'd you work?"

He grinned. "Is it that obvious?"

"Yep."

"I was a detective in a small town called Galliano," he said. "It's in Lafourche Parish."

"I know the place." I thanked him for his time, resisted the urge to shake his hand, and then Takecia and I turned to walk away. We needed to head north to Payneville to find Dean Fletcher.

I glanced toward the sky as I slipped into my Tahoe. It was getting late and we hadn't heard from Amy or Baylor yet. I was starting to get worried.

CHAPTER 39

Sandy Knobs, Nevada

Amy and Baylor made a quick sweep of the church and found it empty.

"Where in the hell is everyone?" Baylor asked when they were back on the sidewalk in front of the rental Jeep.

Amy shook her head. She didn't have an answer, so she remained silent. They walked back to the Wrangler without another word passing between them. Once they were inside, Baylor backed the Jeep toward the middle of the parking lot to give them some room to maneuver in case of an attack.

After mulling over their situation, Amy indicated the street. "Let's finish checking Spirit Way. If we don't find a house with the Marcella name on it, we'll get the hell out of here."

Baylor nodded his agreement and headed for the entrance to the parking lot. Although they already knew there wouldn't be any traffic, he stopped, looked both ways, and turned left to head toward the end of the street. They could already see that the road didn't continue very far past the large compound that housed the church buildings, and they reached the last cross street within seconds. Straight ahead, there was a large gate that blocked off the end of the street, and it appeared that a gravel road continued past the gate. Along the cross street, there were four houses to the right and one to the left. The houses at the intersection didn't bear the Marcella name, so Baylor turned right so they could check the four houses in that direction. Nothing.

"Go back to the intersection and turn right on Spirit Way," Amy said. "There's a sign on that gate. I want to see what it says."

Baylor nodded and whipped the Jeep around in the middle of the cross street. When he reached the intersection again, he stopped and they both surveyed their surroundings.

Amy felt a chill reverberate up and down her spine. She whipped her head around and checked the road behind them. When she glanced toward one of the houses on the cross street, she noticed a curtain swaying slightly against the window.

"Someone was in the window of that white house," she said, not looking directly at it. "Pull up to the gate for just a second and then let's get the hell out of here."

Baylor nodded and looked left along Spirit Way before committing to approaching the gate. He sped to the end of the street and lurched to a stop. Amy pointed to the sign that read, *900 - Marcella.*

"This is it," she said. "This is where they live."

She studied the gate. It was a rusted, twelve-foot tube gate with six bars running across it. The hinges were on the right side and a thick chain secured it to an old-fashioned fence post that had probably been in the ground for decades. Four strands of barbed wire were attached to the posts that supported the gate, and they extended in either direction, seemingly making it impossible to access the property by car.

"This is a big plot of land," Baylor said, pointing to the homestead an eighth of a mile away. "There's no way we're getting over there in the Jeep."

Amy chewed on her lower lip. To abandon the Jeep and their AR-15s would be foolish, but she would feel equally as foolish approaching the house with her rifle in her hands. What if the people in that community posed no threat at all to them? What if they simply wanted to live their lives in peace, without interference from the outside world? Had they been able to make contact with someone from the commune, they could've quickly explained their reason for being there and all would've been fine. However, everyone seemed to have run for cover as soon as they turned off the main highway.

"I'm gonna walk to the house," Amy finally said. "Why don't you stay here with the Jeep? If I run into trouble, get your rifle and come after me."

"I don't like that idea, Cooker."

Amy smiled. Baylor had taken to calling her that when he realized she couldn't cook well, although her last name argued otherwise.

"I'll be fine," she promised. "You can see the road all the way to the house, and I'll make sure not to let anything obstruct your view of me. I'll go straight to the front door and knock. If no one answers, I'll come back and we'll leave."

Baylor twisted around and squeezed between the seats. She heard the zipper retract on his rifle case. When he pulled himself back to the front seat, he was holding his AR-15. Amy knew it was fully loaded—like hers—because it would've been useless otherwise.

"It's a little over 200 yards to the front door of the main house," Baylor said, pointing toward an outcrop near what they believed was Carlos Marcella's residence. "If something goes wrong, get behind those rocks and I'll take out any threats from here."

Amy glanced in her side mirror. The street behind the Jeep was clear. "And what if you run into trouble?"

"I'm gonna drive right through that damned gate and meet you behind those rocks."

Amy reached for the door handle, but then hesitated. "Do you think these people are really dangerous?"

"I've got no clue," Baylor admitted. "Something feels off, but I don't know if it's real or just based on what Deputy Ready told us. It is weird that no one's around, but that might have something to do with their leader being gone."

Amy hadn't considered that, but it seemed logical. If they weren't accustomed to outsiders showing up, their first instincts might be to take cover until they knew the intentions of those outsiders. With their leader gone and out of reach, there might be some confusion and indecision on the part of current leadership—if any existed—and they might be waiting to see what might happen next.

After checking her cell phone one more time and confirming that she didn't have cell service, she gave Baylor a nod. "Okay, I'm heading to the house."

Amy opened the door and stepped out into the warm air. It was a little after four in the afternoon and there was plenty of daylight left, but she didn't know if it was a good thing or bad thing. She didn't like the idea of walking into an unknown situation while out in the open, but she had no choice. She began moving forward, keeping her left hand against the front of her shirt. If she needed her pistol, she would jerk her shirt upward with her left hand while simultaneously reaching for the Glock with her right hand, but she was hoping there would be no need for gun play.

Once Amy reached the gate, she paused and listened. There were no sounds from anywhere, and no movement on the homestead. She wasn't sure if there were dogs, and she knew they would present one hell of a dilemma. If there were dogs and they attacked her, she would be in a bind. She wouldn't be able to outrun them and it wouldn't be right to shoot them, because she was trespassing on private property.

Thinking quickly, she decided to make a little noise to attract any dogs that might be guarding the property. Grabbing the chain that secured the gate, she tapped it sharply against the gate and waited. Nothing happened. She glanced over her shoulder. Baylor was watching her carefully, but he kept checking his side mirrors.

Satisfied there were no dogs on the property, Amy grabbed the top bar of the gate and easily pulled herself over. She dropped lightly to the ground on the other side and began walking toward the house at a quick pace. She tried to remain as casual and unassuming as possible in case Kari Marcella was watching from the house. After all, she was there to deliver bad news, not frighten the woman.

On her approach to the house, there had been no sound except for the rattling of a loose piece of aluminum gutter, and she had seen no signs of life. She stepped to one side of the door and rapped sharply on it. She waited. Nothing happened. She knocked again and waited for a few more seconds, but still nothing.

She was about to knock a third time when suddenly it dawned on her that something wasn't right. For the last few seconds, she had heard the sound of an engine humming in the distance, but the meaning of that sound hadn't registered. It was such a common occurrence in her everyday life that she'd forgotten it might spell trouble here.

A car engine meant that people were coming—it meant the hidden people were making their move. She whipped around and saw a large truck come into view far up Spirit Way. It had rounded the sharp bend in the road and entered the straightaway. It was about 375 yards behind Baylor, but it was closing the distance fast. Movement from her right and almost even with the truck caught her eye. It was another vehicle—a dark colored Hummer—and it was pulling out from behind the church. It raced through the parking lot and turned onto the street, also heading in Baylor's direction.

"Oh, shit," she said, whipping out her pistol. She didn't know what the people wanted, but it didn't look good. Three more vehicles pulled out from the driveways of various homes around the compound, and they all converged on Baylor's location—or, rather, where Baylor had been moments before.

True to his word, her husband hadn't wasted any time. As soon as the first truck had rounded the bend in the road, he had punched the accelerator on the Jeep and drove it directly into the gate. The wooden posts were no match for the rugged four-by-four, and the one on the left snapped and folded over like a matchstick under the weight of a bowling ball.

Baylor was racing straight for her, the five vehicles in hot pursuit. She couldn't see him in the glare of the windshield, but she could tell by the rate of speed and the sheer reckless abandonment with which he traveled over the rough terrain that the situation was desperate.

Remembering what Baylor had told her, Amy turned and made a mad dash for the outcrop of rocks near the front of the house. Even as she ran and Baylor sped toward her, she didn't fully know what was going on. What if they were simply coming to tell them to get off of their private property? They were, after all, trespassing, and the townspeople would have every right to make them leave.

As she ran, she shook her head. No, something more was going on. Baylor would not have crashed through the gate if he thought the people were only concerned about them trespassing. He didn't scare easy, either, so he must've seen or heard something that had prompted his desperate action.

She was still two leaps from the rocks when she stole a glance over her left shoulder. Baylor was closing fast, but it looked like the five vehicles were still gaining on him. She figured that would change once they left the smooth surface of Spirit Way, but they were still way too close for comfort.

Just as Amy dove behind the nearest rock, she heard something that caused her stomach to clutch—it was the sharp and distinctive sounds of gunfire. Baylor's actions suddenly made sense, and she knew they were in real trouble.

CHAPTER 40

Payneville, Louisiana

Takecia and I arrived at the Payneville Motel a little after six in the afternoon. We had grabbed a quick lunch at a drive-thru and wolfed down the food on the ride to the motel. The parking lot was full of cars, but one vehicle stood out from the rest. Not only was it an odd-looking thing, but there was a standup jack mounted to the front quarter panel, just forward of the driver's side mirror.

"What in the hell is that?" I asked Takecia.

She shook her head in awe. "It looks like a Jeep Wrangler and a pickup truck had a baby."

She was right. The front part looked like a Jeep Wrangler, but there was a truck bed attached to the back of it. It was black and red, with a lift kit, tactical bumpers, large tires, and a winch on the front bumper. The tires had to be thirty-fives and the rims were red to match the accented parts of the vehicle.

"If that's Dean's vehicle, he just moved up to the number one suspect," I said, driving around so I could see the back of the vehicle. When the license plate was in view, I called Lindsey and asked her to run the number through NCIC. She was pleasant, but distant, and I knew she was probably upset over reading the last book by one of her favorite authors. I decided not to mention anything about it.

When she came back on the line, she was in a better mood. "That's Dean Fletcher's vehicle!" she said. "You found him!"

"Yeah, we're at the Payneville Motel," I explained. "It's in Magnolia Parish. We'll be attempting to make contact with him."

"Do you need backup?"

I thought about it. We had no evidence that Dean was armed, or that he had even killed Carlos, but that didn't mean he wasn't or hadn't.

"No, but keep the number to the Magnolia Parish Sheriff's Office handy," I said. "I won't call unless we need them in a hurry."

She told me she would be waiting, and I ended the call.

The Jeep-truck child was parked between two rooms, and I asked Takecia which one she thought was Dean's.

"We've got a fifty-fifty chance of getting it right." She shrugged and indicated the crowded parking lot. "Unless he was forced to park far away from his room."

She had a good point. I pointed to the door on the right as we stepped out of my Tahoe and approached the sidewalk. "You knock on that one, and I'll knock on the one to the left. We'll go on the count of three."

Takecia moved beside her door and I moved beside mine. I gave a low count to three and then we knocked in unison. I didn't hear anything from inside my room, but she called out that she had movement. A second later the door pulled open and there stood Dean Fletcher.

The young man took one look at Takecia and then at me, and I saw his countenance fall.

"Is it about my mom?" he asked. "Did y'all find her? Is she okay?"

I sized him up for a long moment. In my mind's eye, I was replaying the images of this same young boy being beaten by Carlos Marcella as had been described by Ray Broussard earlier. From the outside, there was not even a hint of what he had endured as a child. It was remarkable. Working in law enforcement, I had learned early on that one could never tell what a person had been through in their lifetime simply by looking at them, any more than one could pick out murderers based on the way they looked.

What I saw in Dean Fletcher were not the eyes of a survivor, but, rather, the eyes of a warrior. That he was physically strong was plainly obvious, but I detected much more in his eyes. He was also mentally tough, and I knew it wasn't the military that had done that to him. People who possessed that type of mental resiliency were born, not made.

I stuck out my hand. "I'm Clint Wolf and this is Takecia Gayle. We work for the Mechant Loup Police Department. We'd like to ask you some questions about Carlos Marcella."

Dean's eyes hardened, but he didn't say anything. He looked confused.

I glanced past him into the motel room. It appeared to be empty. I didn't want to interview him inside the room or out on the sidewalk, so I asked if he would accompany us to the police department.

"It would be better that we didn't have this discussion on the streets," I explained.

"You know something, don't you?" The young man was cautious. "Is...is it about my mom?"

"We don't know anything about your mom," I assured him, "but we've got some information on Carlos. I know you're looking for your mom. I was hoping we could help each other."

Dean was thoughtful. Finally, he asked, "How far away is your office?" He hadn't committed to accompanying us, but I could already tell he would.

"It's about forty minutes from here."

"Do I have to ride in the back with y'all?"

I shot a thumb over my shoulder toward the spawn of the Wrangler and pickup truck. "Is that your vehicle?"

He nodded.

"You could follow us." I lifted a shoulder. "It shouldn't take more than an hour for us to ask our questions, and we'll certainly answer any you might have."

"Okay, I'll come. Just let me lock up."

I nodded and stepped to the left side of the door while Takecia sidled over to the right. We had no legal authority to force him to come with us, so we had no right to follow him into his room. All we could do at that point was remain wary and try to follow his movements through the open door.

Although I didn't have my eyes on him the whole time, I saw him when he stepped out of the bathroom a few minutes later, and I could tell his hands were empty. He stopped near the dresser to grab a set of keys and a wallet from the countertop. He then scanned the room, nodded, and headed for the door.

Once he had rejoined us, I pointed to my Tahoe and asked him to follow us.

CHAPTER 41

"It's like when you buy a new car," Takecia was saying on the drive back to Mechant Loup. "My first car was a green Miata. Before I bought it, I had never seen one like it before, but then suddenly they were everywhere. It's like those standup jacks. I never noticed them before, but now they're popping up left and right."

I nodded and glanced in my rearview mirror. Dean was still following us. While his face looked a little tense, he didn't look too bothered by the fact that he was going to the police department.

"What do you think?" Takecia asked when she saw where I was looking. "Did Dean kill Carlos?"

I turned my attention back to the road in front of us. "I don't know, but somebody did, and it would be one hell of a coincidence to have Dean in town at the same time Carlos was murdered."

"Are you gonna get his fingerprints?" Takecia asked. The question reminded me of the prints from the bags of ice and the tailgate of the truck.

"We don't have enough for a warrant, so we'd need his consent." I reached for my cell phone and handed it to Takecia. "Speaking of prints, can you call Vanessa and put her through the car speakers?"

Takecia did and Vanessa's soft voice soon called out to me. "What's up, Clint? Did you catch the bad guys?"

"Not yet, but we're working on it," I said. "Were you able to compare all the prints from the scene?"

"We did," she said. "The prints on the bags of ice and the tailgate of the truck matched each other, but they didn't match the victim, so it looks like your theory is a sound one. We ran the prints through

AFIS, but we didn't get a match. Chances are, your suspect has never been arrested. We dusted the rest of the truck and came up with some partials and a few smudges that won't do us much good. We also found three fulls that matched your victim. One was on the door handle, another was on the rearview mirror, and the third was on an empty water bottle we dug out from under the seat."

Finding a full fingerprint at a crime scene was not as common as Hollywood made it out to be in their movies and television shows. Additionally, it was not as easy as they made it seem to identify an unknown print. Had we been lucky, our suspect would've had a criminal record and his prints would've been in the system. As it turned out, we worked in the real world, and it wasn't going to be that easy.

I thanked Vanessa, and Takecia ended the call. Without saying a word, she used my phone to dial another number. It went immediately to voicemail, and I heard Amy's voice: *"Don't bother leaving a message. I know who you are. If I feel like calling you back, I will."*

I frowned. "What time is it over there again?"

Takecia glanced at the dash clock. "It would be almost six in the afternoon."

We were approaching seven in the evening. The sun was going down and lights were starting to come on under the porches that lined the highway. I wondered if it was dark in Nevada, and figured it mustn't be.

Takecia tried calling Baylor's phone next, but met with the same results.

"Can you call the sheriff's office again?" I asked.

Takecia nodded, made the call, and it rang about twenty times before she finally gave up. "Something's not right, Clint. I think they're in trouble."

I hoped she was wrong, but in my gut, I felt she was right. "Can you dial our office?"

Takecia did and I waited until Lindsey answered.

"What's up, y'all?" she asked cheerfully. "It looks like I'll be working a double shift. Karla called in sick. She thinks she got food poisoning."

Karla McBride was our nighttime dispatcher. While she hadn't been with the department as long as Lindsey had, she was a good dispatcher and a likeable person.

"I hope she gets better," I said, and then got down to the reason we'd called. "Can you find a number to the Nevada State Police? We need to have someone go out to 777 Spirit Way in Sandy Knobs and check on Amy and Baylor. We called the sheriff's department, but they don't answer."

"Do you think they're in trouble?" she asked, her voice suddenly dripping with concern.

"I don't know," I admitted, "but we haven't heard from them in a couple of hours."

"I'm on it. Do you want to hold the line?"

"Yeah."

I waited while Lindsey searched for the number and made the call. As she did, I tried to imagine what was happening out there. I'd seen a lot of evil in my time working in law enforcement and I had a vivid imagination. I didn't like the images that were flashing through my mind. I remembered the time Amy and Baylor had been ambushed, and when that night flashed in my head, I shook it violently and focused like a laser on the road in front of me.

Lindsey had gotten in touch with someone, and I said a silent prayer as she talked with them. I could only hear her side of the conversation, and it only took a few moments to know I didn't like what was happening. When she hung up the phone, her voice became louder and clearer.

"The desk sergeant suggested we contact the Twelve County Sheriff's Department," she said. "When I told him we already did and they didn't answer, he said he would try calling someone he knows from the area. He said Twelve County is a remote place located hours away from their nearest regional command and there isn't much traffic out there, so they don't patrol the area."

"Does he find it strange that the sheriff's department doesn't answer the phone?"

"No, he said the phones are usually turned off after hours," she explained. "People have to call the shift commander's cell phone to get service, and he'll try to find it and call it. Outside of that, he said he could send someone out there first thing in the morning."

"First thing in the morning?" I gripped the steering wheel until my knuckles were white. My mind was racing. "Can you see if Twelve County has a constable? If so, try to contact him or her and see if they'll go to Sandy Knobs. Also, see if the sheriff's department has a social media page. Maybe you can contact someone through there. If that doesn't work, see if you can find a county mayor or president or whatever in the hell they call their county leaders. If you can, let them know we need a deputy to go to Sandy Knobs."

I paused for a breath, wondering what else we could do. I then had another idea, but I didn't know if it was a good one. "Lindsey, were you able to find anyone on those social media sites who were from Twelve County?"

"I only checked Sandy Knobs, but I can check the whole county. What's the plan?"

"Try to connect with somebody from there," I suggested. "Tell them we've got officers who might be in trouble in Sandy Knobs. See if you can find anyone willing to drive out there. We need eyes on the ground. I'll pay them personally for their time. See if they have a community page on social media. Hit up anyone with thin blue line flags or military emblems on their profiles. They're the ones most likely to get involved and help out a former soldier and two current law enforcement officers."

"You want me to organize a posse," Lindsey said excitedly. "I'm on it!"

Once she was gone, I glanced over at Takecia. She was staring intently at me.

"How worried are you?" she asked.

The question was a fair one, because I usually remained stone-faced on the outside even if I was deeply concerned on the inside. I didn't know if my eyes betrayed me, but I was worried.

"On a scale of one to ten?" I asked.

She nodded.

"I'm at a twelve right now," I admitted. "If we don't hear something soon, I'm gonna get to twenty."

Takecia's face tightened and she settled into her seat, staring straight ahead. Inside, I was kicking myself in the ass. If Amy and Baylor were in trouble, it was my fault. They were supposed to be enjoying each other on their honeymoon, celebrating the most joyous day of their lives to that point. It was a day that would only be bested by the birth of their future children and—

I swallowed a huge lump in my throat at the thought of their future children. If the worst had happened—I couldn't even bring myself to internalize what that would be—they would never have children, and that would be on me.

CHAPTER 42

Sandy Knobs, Nevada

Amy could hear bullets whistling through the air as they ricocheted off the hard-packed sand and whizzed past her location. Some of them splattered against the walls of the Marcella home, which were constructed of brick and cinder blocks, while others flattened against the rocks behind which she crouched.

She could hear that the Wrangler was almost upon her, so she hurried to the right side of the rocky outcrop and stuck her pistol out from behind cover. Her plan had been to fire on the vehicle nearest to Baylor, but she cursed and pulled her pistol back when she saw that the lead truck was about two hundred yards away. That distance was grossly outside the effective range of her handgun, and she desperately wished for her AR-15.

Within seconds, the rental they'd been driving appeared around the corner of the outcrop and Baylor screeched to a stop. He lunged toward the back seat and was out of sight for a few seconds. When he reappeared, she could see that he held two AR-15s in his hands. He pushed his way out of the Wrangler and tossed one of the ARs in her direction.

With deft hands, Amy caught her rifle in mid-air and rushed back to the right side of the outcrop. She saw Baylor head to the left side as they prepared to battle the oncoming gunmen. Judging from the sounds of their engines, they had closed to within fifty yards. Within seconds, the vehicles would be rushing by their hiding spot.

Once she had propped her knees into a stable firing position,

Amy quickly lifted her rifle to sight along the barrel through the opening that a V-shaped formation had created in the rocks. The lead truck was larger than life now, with two men shooting over the cab of the truck, spraying their position with automatic gunfire. She quickly realized that only one man was firing at a time. When he would run dry, the other would begin firing while the first reloaded.

These men are well trained, she thought, and fired three quick shots at the second man, who was now shooting toward the left, where she'd heard Baylor's rifle open up. One of her bullets hit the windshield of the truck, the other whizzed harmlessly past the shooter, but the third hit the man in the left shoulder. He cried out in shock. Before he could make another sound, a bullet from Baylor's rifle caught him in the throat and dropped him for good.

The first man was just lifting his rifle to return fire, when Baylor cut loose and Amy saw three spider webs the size of silver dollars appear in the windshield where the driver's head had been. The front tires turned sharply to the left—Amy's right—and the first man lost his balance and tumbled from the bed of the truck and onto the hard ground. As he rolled end over end, Amy sent three bullets in his direction. Once he stopped rolling, he lay writhing in pain and she could see that her bullets had found their marks.

The out-of-control truck raced forward and slammed into the opposite face of the rocky outcrop behind which Baylor and Amy were hiding. Not knowing if it would hold up to the impact, Amy threw herself back and away from it, but it was an unnecessary move. The outcrop didn't even quiver.

"Get to the house!" Baylor suddenly hollered. "They're flanking us!"

As gunshots continued to ring out, Amy gave a quick-peek around the right side of the outcrop and saw that the remaining four vehicles had fanned out, two of them heading around her right side and the other two around the left. Baylor was firing rapidly as the vehicles rounded the outcrop. She knew he was laying down cover fire for her to make it to the house, so, instead of arguing, she broke from cover and began running for all she was worth.

Bullets ricocheted off the hard-packed sand at her feet and whistled past her body, and she found herself flinching with each near-miss. Reminded was she of the bullet wounds that had left her severely wounded not so long ago, and fear began to squeeze at her throat and threatened to take away her breath.

Instead of succumbing to the terror of the situation, her instincts kicked in and she began firing as she ran. Although her shots were far from perfect, they were much improved due to her utilizing a tactical run, where she remained in a crouched position while advancing by rolling from heel-to-toe on the soles of her feet. It helped to limit the up and down movement of her body, and her bullets slammed into the sides of the two passing vehicles, one of which was the Hummer she'd seen earlier.

The house loomed large in her path. She quickly turned her attention away from the vehicles, which had disappeared around the side of the house and were circling around for another assault, and headed straight for the front door. She wasn't sure how stout it was, but she was running too fast and was too close to slow down, so she sped up and threw her shoulder into the center of it.

Just as she crashed into the door and through it, the Hummer had reappeared around the opposite side of the house and a hail of bullets followed her into the room. Baylor had begun to return fire on the Hummer when one of the other trucks opened up on him from behind. Amy quickly righted herself and fired half a dozen rounds at that truck, hitting the driver and one of the men in the bed.

Amy's counter-attack provided Baylor the opening he needed, and he cleared the short distance between the rocky outcrop and the house and was soon beside her on the floor. With a thrust of his boot, he slammed the door shut, but it sprung back, its locking mechanism destroyed by Amy's shoulder. Amy looked around for something to prop against it. Her eyes fell on a sofa a dozen feet away, and she quickly dragged it into place while Baylor ran to a window.

"How many rounds did you fire?" he asked in a tone that most would've found surprisingly calm under the circumstances, but having known him as long as she had, Amy was not surprised.

She quickly dropped the thirty-round magazine from her AR and hefted it. "Shit! I've only got a couple of rounds left."

"I've got a few." Baylor moved quickly from window to window in the front room, and then he disappeared deeper into the house to check the other windows. When he returned, he shook his head. "It doesn't look good. They've got us surrounded. There's a truck on each side, and there're at least three men with each truck. It sounds like more are coming."

Amy cursed under her breath. "What in the hell do they want?"

"It looks like they want to kill us," he said. "I don't know why, but that's their plan."

As they crouched near opposite windows contemplating their next move, shots rang out intermittently. One impacted the wall several feet from Amy's face, and she readjusted her position, trying to get low and behind any amount of cover she could find.

"We need to find a way out of this house," Baylor said. "But in the meantime, they need to know we're still a threat. If they think we've run out of ammo, they'll storm the place and it'll all be over."

Amy nodded her agreement. "What do you want me to do?"

Baylor's brow furrowed like he did when he was deep in thought. She watched as he raised his head and peered out the front window. He remained several feet inside the dark room so they couldn't see him, but she could tell he saw something he liked, because his eyes lit up. "Give me your 5.56 rounds," he said, extending his hand. "I'm gonna move around the house and drop one or two of them. While I do that, I want you to find a way out of this deathtrap."

Amy nodded and tossed him her nearly empty magazine. She headed for the nearest inner door. She glanced over her shoulder as she walked away, and she saw Baylor take careful aim from the darkness of the room and through the already shattered window.

"Going hot," Baylor breathed. "Keep your head low."

Although her ears were already ringing from the earlier gunfire, she slung her rifle and cupped her palms against the sides of her head. She heard the muffled shot, saw the rifle gently buck against Baylor's shoulder, and then heard a barrage of gunfire in response.

Baylor dropped behind a sofa and glanced in her direction. He gave her a wink and a nod, and she knew he had gotten one of them. Bullets sprayed spots on the walls above them, and she hurried through the door. She found herself in a small room. There were no windows and only the one door, so she quickly exited and crawled to the next door along the far wall of the living room.

When she squeezed through the opening, she hesitated. There was nothing but utter darkness in front of her. She reached out with her hand, but only grabbed air. Leaning back, she removed her cell phone from her pocket and turned on the light. When she turned it to face the room, she let out an audible gasp. Baylor heard it and asked what was wrong.

"Stairs," she said. "They go down into a basement. I think I just found our way out of here!"

CHAPTER 43

Using the poor lighting from her cell phone, Amy made her way carefully down the ancient stairs. Each wooden step creaked under her weight, and she kept expecting to fall through them at any moment. She had probably taken her tenth step when one of the aged boards popped. She froze in place and held onto the rough wooden wall to her right. There was no railing to the left and she couldn't tell how far she had left to go, so that added to her trepidation.

Finally, after only a few more tense moments and a half dozen more steps, she was on solid ground. She aimed the light at the floor and saw that it was constructed of uneven squares of stone, with each square measuring roughly twenty-four by twenty-four inches. She put her weight on the one directly in front of her and bounced a little. It seemed solid.

Gunshots continued to ring out above her, but she could tell it was coming from the opposing forces. *What do these people want?* she wondered. Sure, Baylor was right that they wanted to kill them, but why?

Amy aimed her light up and around her. The glow was swallowed up by the utter darkness to the left. She wished for her flashlight. Turning the phone to the right, she saw a light switch. Saying a silent prayer, she flipped it upward. *Yes!*

A pale, yellow glow appeared and beat back the darkness. She turned and inspected the basement. Cobwebs, wires, and ductwork dangled overhead. Unsure if any of their attackers had breached the basement, she tucked away her phone and drew her pistol. From what she could see of the room, it was cluttered with old furniture and there were no openings in the cinderblock walls. The room appeared L-shaped, and she couldn't see what was just ahead and to the left, so she made her way carefully in that direction, careful not to trip on the edges of the uneven stone squares. She didn't know how thick they were, but they seemed solid as she stepped from one to the other. Even the few that were cracked were unwavering.

When Amy passed a wall of cardboard boxes that were stacked almost to the ceiling, she saw a washer and drier off to one side. A laundry basket was parked next to the washer, and it was filled with what appeared to be dirty clothes. Just past the washer, an old weight bench was situated in the middle of an open space. A barbell with two fifty-pound plates on either side rested on the rack. She grimaced.

"Ain't no way I'd ever work out down here," she mumbled. "I can almost feel the radon seeping up through the cracks—"

Something rustled in the darkness to her left, and Amy whirled in that direction, sweeping the area with her pistol, ready to snap off one or more shots if necessary. She gasped when she saw a woman cowering against the far wall. Her hands were up in a defensive position, and her eyes were wide with fright.

Amy immediately lowered her pistol. She could see the rest of the room now, and there didn't appear to be any threats present. Other than a broken dresser, a deep freezer, and a refrigerator, nothing but small odds and ends occupied the open space.

"Who are you?" the woman asked. "Why are you here? What's going on?"

Amy shoved her pistol in her jeans and slowly approached the woman. She wore a long blue jean skirt that was covered in dust, a white blouse that was tattered and dirty, and she was bare-footed. A small plate and a cup were on the ground near her.

"Good Lord, ma'am," Amy said as she reached the woman. "Who did this to you?"

The woman stared up in confusion. Above them and over the intense ringing in her ears, Amy could hear Baylor's boots shuffling across the wooden boards. They stopped and then she heard a thump, as though he had taken a knee. Suddenly, she heard another muffled gunshot. It was followed by more shots from outside. She sucked in her breath and said a silent prayer that he was out of harm's way. The shooting continued until someone from the group began hollering at the others. He seemed to be the one in charge.

"Keep your heads down and don't shoot unless you see something!" he bellowed. "They're trying to make us waste our ammo! Don't fall for that shit!"

"What's going on?" the lady asked again, the words grating against her obviously dry throat. "Who are you?"

"I'm Amy," she said, reaching for the woman's wrists to examine the chains that held her. "I'm a detective from Louisiana. I came here looking for Kari Marcella. I have some news to deliver."

The woman gasped and pulled her hands away from Amy and covered her mouth. "Oh, no! It's Dean, isn't it?"

Amy cocked her head to the side. "Ma'am?"

"Did he find Dean?"

"Did who find Dean?"

"Carlos." Her hands were trembling now, and the words began spewing almost unintelligibly through her cracked lips. "Carlos was going after Dean. Someone…someone called him and said they saw Dean at church, and he…he said he was going after him. I tried…I…I tried to warn him, but Carlos caught me. Oh, God, is it Dean?"

"No, I'm not here about Dean," Amy said, trying to understand what might be going on. She knew that Carlos was found dead, but there had been no talk about Dean's status. As far as she knew, Clint and Takecia were still trying to find info on Dean. "Are you Kari Marcella?"

The woman nodded.

"I'm here about Carlos," Amy said, frowning. "I'm here to inform you that your husband is dead."

"Dead?" Her face twisted in confusion. "But how? Did Dean do it? Did Dean kill him?"

Amy didn't know the answer to that question. "All I know is he was found dead in his truck," she explained. "The truck was pulled out of a bayou in Louisiana and they found him inside, still strapped in the seatbelt."

"Carlos doesn't have a truck," Kari said. "He drives an old Monte Carlo. Are you sure it's him?"

Amy dug out her cell phone and fumbled through her files until she found the picture of Carlos that Clint had sent over. She turned it so Kari could see. "Isn't this Carlos?"

Kari recoiled in horror.

CHAPTER 44

"Oh, no, where'd you get that picture?" Kari asked once she regained her composure.

"It was taken at the scene where Carlos was found," Amy explained. She pulled up the screenshot of the truck from the newspaper article. "He was driving this truck."

"I've never seen that truck before."

"What did you mean earlier about a church and Dean?"

"My son's name is Dean." She lifted her hands and the chains jingled. "The last time I saw him, he was wearing these. Carlos locked him down here because he ran away from home. Somehow, he escaped this place. I still don't understand it, but he did. We hadn't seen or heard from him in years. And then one day my youngest son gave me a note that he said he got from Dean. There was a phone number on it. I…I memorized the number and burned the note on the stove. The next time we went to town, I called the number from a payphone. It was Dean. It was really him. All along, I thought Carlos had killed him and buried him in the desert. I thought he made up the story about Dean escaping to appease me."

Kari stopped talking and tears glistened down her face.

"Before that first phone call, it had been years since I'd heard his sweet voice." She didn't even try to wipe the tears away. "He told me he had enlisted in the military and that he was doing well. He wouldn't tell me how he escaped or where he had been, but he told me everything had worked out for the best. I called him every week or two for the past six years, but that all changed after Carlos received that phone call."

"Tell me about the church and the call," Amy said, trying to move the conversation along.

"I thought Dean was living in Alexandria with my dad, but someone from the old Magnolia Life Church called Carlos and said they had seen Dean at the church. They weren't sure, but they thought he had moved down there and would be attending the church regularly." She paused to take a trembling breath. "Carlos has been threatening to find Dean and bring him back ever since he escaped from the basement. He…he was so excited when he got that phone call. All he would talk about was what he would do to Dean when he got his hands on him. I begged him not to go, but he wouldn't listen. I…I had no choice but to try and warn Dean. So, one evening when Carlos was showering after weight-lifting, I snuck into the bathroom and got his cell phone. I didn't think he had heard me, but Dean had just answered and I was just starting to tell him to run away when Carlos hit me over the head."

"What'd he hit you with?"

"I don't know, but it hurt a lot," she said. "It dazed me. He hung up the phone and immediately dragged me to the basement. He doesn't believe in cursing, but he was cursing me all the way down here. He chained me up and told me I had just killed my son."

"How long have you been down here?"

"Two weeks." She scowled. "Maybe three? What day is it?"

"It's Tuesday, September the twentieth."

"Oh, wow, it was Monday, August twenty-second that Lester called Carlos to say he'd seen Dean," she said. "I've been down here almost a month!"

"What happened after that?" Amy asked impatiently.

"Carlos wanted to wait until the following weekend to see if Dean returned to the church. He must've heard back from Lester, because during one of my feedings the following week he told me that Dean would be back with us soon. He was supposed to leave the week after that, but then—"

A loud crashing sound overhead caused Kari to yelp and clamp her mouth shut. Amy froze in place, waiting and listening. Every muscle in her body was tense. Finally, she heard Baylor's boots shuffling across the floor again and she sighed in relief. From the sounds of it, he was directly above her. She looked up, but there was nothing except exposed wire and hanging insulation overhead, so she couldn't tell exactly what was going on in the house. If she were to guess, it sounded like someone had tried to crash a vehicle into the outer wall of the house.

As for Baylor, she figured he was moving to the different rooms upstairs and using the last of the ammo from their AR-15s to take out as many of the bad guys as possible from as many different locations. That way, the bad guys might think there were more than two of them, and they would also think they were heavily armed.

Amy scowled. She knew Baylor was down to one or two shots in his AR. If the bad guys rushed the house, they would be left to fight rifles with handguns, and that was never a winning strategy, and now they had this woman to think about. She needed to find a way out of the basement...

Her thoughts trailed off as she scanned the walls that surrounded her, and shook her head. If they did make it out of the basement, they would fall right into the arms of the men trying to kill them. She remembered that the four exterior walls of the house were planted firmly on the hard-packed earth, which meant the basement was entirely underground. So, even if they were able to break through the concrete walls, they would encounter the same problem.

She cursed out loud. There were no two ways about it—they were trapped.

"We came under attack when we approached your house," Amy quickly explained to Kari as she began looking around for a tool to cut through the chains. Whatever they decided, they couldn't just leave the woman down there. "Why would they do that?"

"They work for Carlos," she explained wearily. "He runs this community, and they do whatever he tells them to do. The man who was yelling earlier? That's Eagle. He's the second in command. He's the one who comes check on me. He brings me food and water once a day. He...he tried to touch me once, but I told him I would tell Carlos, and he got scared. They won't let you take me. I belong to Carlos. Well, I used to belong to Carlos. Now that he's dead, there's no telling what they'll do to me. I'll probably belong to Eagle."

"They won't do anything to you," Amy said, but she knew her voice lacked conviction. "We're taking you with us."

"They'll kill you and whoever you've got with you." Kari's gaze drifted toward the deep freezer. "I know they will."

Amy stopped digging through a tool box she'd found and followed the woman's stare. "What's in the freezer?"

"Go see for yourself." Kari lowered her head. "You shouldn't have come. You're as good as dead. Eagle won't let you leave."

Amy turned and approached the freezer. She reached for the latch and jerked the lid open. "Oh, shit!" she said when the light from the freezer illuminated the contents.

CHAPTER 45

Amy heard another shot from Baylor's rifle overhead, and as the spent casing clanked across the floor, with it went their hopes of ever getting out of that building alive. She knew if she could hear the bolt locking back on an empty chamber, then the men outside could, as well. She heard Baylor manipulating the rifle and switching magazines, but it was only for effect. He was out of rounds. They were down to their handguns—with less than one magazine each—and they were facing a group of determined and heavily armed individuals who were not there to prevent a trespass against their property, but to protect a secret—a deadly secret.

Wait here, Amy almost said to Kari, but then thought better of it, remembering the woman was chained to the wall. "I'll be right back," she said instead. Spinning from the freezer, she hurried upstairs to check on Baylor. She saw him crouched down in the living room facing the front window when she lifted her head over the landing.

"Bay," she said in a hoarse whisper, "how's it going?"

He turned to her and shook his head. His expression was grim, and she knew what he was thinking, because she was thinking the same thing. He was wishing he were alone in that jam, and she was wishing she were alone. Neither wanted to lose the other.

"There's a dead man in the freezer and Kari Marcella's chained like a wild animal," she said, shooting a thumb over her shoulder. "The man's been murdered—shot full of holes."

"This makes sense now," Baylor said in a low voice. "I found it hard to believe they would get this excited over a simple trespass."

There wasn't much noise from outside, and Amy wondered what the men out there were doing.

"What's the plan?" she asked.

He glanced down at his pistol. "I've got eleven rounds left. There's no way I can keep them from breaching the house. They've already driven a truck into the back wall. I fired a shot at the driver and he backed away before completely breaking through, but it's only a matter of time before they get in. Between the both of us, we can't watch every door and window. We need to retreat to the basement. At least we'll only have to guard one point of entry."

Amy frowned. "The basement's a trap. The walls are solid cinderblocks with no windows. If they come down in full force, we'll die down there for sure."

"We'll take a bunch of them with us," Baylor said wryly, "as long as we have some ammo left."

Amy nodded, not liking their options. "Is there anything up here I can use to cut some chain?"

"There's a pair of bolt cutters leaning against a rolling tool box in the garage." Baylor pointed out the way. "Hurry. I'll keep them busy while you get them."

On her hands and knees, Amy crawled rapidly toward the garage. She expected to hear a shot from Baylor, but it didn't come. Instead, she heard the hoarse voice of the leader of the Sandy Knobsters—she now presumed it to be Eagle—calling out a compromise.

"If you throw down your guns and come out, we'll let you live!" he said. "You've got no business in that house. You guys are trespassing. If you just vacate the premises and take your Jeep with you, we'll forget this whole thing happened. If not, we'll be forced to come in after you."

Baylor didn't respond, but Amy could hear him moving around in the living room.

Suddenly, there was another loud booming sound from behind her and the building shivered. Dust trickled from the ceiling and spurred her on. She had just reached the garage when a quick burst of gunshots barked out. A man screamed in pain, another cursed.

Amy lifted her own pistol and scanned the dark room. She couldn't hear any movement from outside the garage door, but she knew it was only a matter of time before someone crashed through it and tried to enter.

She spotted the bolt cutters—and large red tool box—and quickly went for it. Staying low and shoving her pistol in her waistband, she scurried out of the garage, down the hall, and into the basement entrance. She got up to her feet at that point and rushed down the stairs.

"You'll be free in a second," she said to Kari.

"What was that noise?" the terrified woman asked as Amy fed a link of chain between the teeth of the cutters. "It sounds like the house is falling down!"

Boards creaked above them as boots pounded the wooden floor. Amy couldn't tell if it was Baylor making his way across the house, or if the men had gained entry. She just knew she needed to hurry and cut Kari free so she could move the woman to a more secure spot in the basement. Left where she was, she would be susceptible to ricochets from bullets launched into the basement.

After the first link had snapped free, Amy got set to cut another one. "What about the guy in the freezer?" she asked after she'd dropped the bolt cutters and removed the chains from Kari's wrists. The hard metal had left deep indentations in her flesh. "What happened to him?"

"Right before Carlos left to go get Dean, that man showed up looking for me."

"Looking for you?" Amy asked, her brow furrowing.

"Yeah, I could hear them talking upstairs and he asked for me," Kari explained. "Carlos was saying that he hadn't seen me in a couple of weeks and that he thought I left him. The man said Dean and my dad were worried about me. He said Dean had heard a struggle in the background during our last phone conversation, but Carlos said it was nothing, that I had dropped the phone and it broke. I couldn't hear what the man said after that, because a car drove up and Eagle started yelling from outside. There were some gunshots and then I thought I heard something fall to the floor. Everything got quiet after that. A while later, Carlos and Eagle dragged that man down here and emptied the freezer of all the food. They stuffed him inside."

While Kari rubbed the feeling back into her wrists, Amy returned to the freezer and opened it again. Shoving her hand under the man, she fought to remove his wallet from the back pocket. After a bit of shoving and jerking, she managed to wrestle it free. Before she had a chance to look inside, there was another crash upstairs and she heard some men yell in triumph.

Baylor!

Shoving the wallet in her pocket and drawing her pistol, Amy quickly ushered Kari into a safe corner of the room. "Don't move!" she hissed, and then made her way toward the opening to the basement.

When she reached the landing on the main level, she immediately smelled smoke. It was wafting in through an opening in the front wall, but she couldn't tell what was on fire. She could, however, see their Jeep rental, and she winced when she saw the damage to it. *I'm glad we got the extra insurance,* she thought wryly.

As she tried to determine Baylor's location from the chaotic noise that surrounded them, she heard another crashing sound from the garage. A man gave a triumphant shout. It sounded like they were making entry into the home from multiple points. Gunshots erupted from the opposite side of the house, but she headed for the garage. She knew it was important for the men who had them under siege to know they would face resistance.

As soon as she reached the entrance to the garage, she saw a man squeezing through the twisted metal of the overhead door. She immediately lifted her pistol and snapped off two rounds. He screamed in surprise and then his face twisted in shock as he looked up and saw her standing there with her pistol trained on him. He then glanced down at the crimson liquid that spilled from the holes in his chest.

Someone shouted a question from behind the man, but Amy waited and watched as he relaxed into death's icy embrace. His body clogged up the opening. That, and Amy's gunshots, had backed the men off for the moment, but she knew it wouldn't last long.

Before she could turn to leave, angry gunshots erupted just beyond the dead man and bullets peppered the soft metal of the garage door, letting in bright stabbing fingers of sunlight. She quickly retreated toward the stairway to the basement. She had just reached it when Baylor suddenly appeared out of the gray cloud of smoke that had enveloped the living room. He gripped his pistol in his left hand, and she saw blood dripping down his right arm.

Bullets began pelting the exterior walls of the house with relentless determination, and she quickly descended the steps to give Baylor room to escape. Once Baylor squeezed through the opening and pulled the door shut, they rushed down the stairs and skidded to a stop at the bottom.

"Did you find a way out of here?" he asked, his breath coming in excited gasps.

"No," she said with a shake of her head. "We're trapped."

Baylor's expression was grim. "They've got us surrounded and they've breached the wall. We need to guard this opening and hold them off for as long as we can."

Amy cursed and glanced up at the narrow stairwell. "So, it's only a matter of time before we run out of ammo and they get us?"

Despite the hopelessness of their situation, Baylor smiled. "This is one hell of a honeymoon."

CHAPTER 46

Mechant Loup Police Department

When Takecia, Dean, and I walked through the door at the police department, I went straight to Lindsey while Takecia led Dean to an interview room.

"Anything?" I asked, looking over her shoulder to see what she was working on. She had the internet pulled up and was actively searching for anything related to Twelve County.

"I called the county manager's office, the assessor's office, the jury commissioner, the county clerk, but nothing. Hell, I even called the county planning and zoning office, but it's after five o'clock over there, and no one's open. I can't find anyone on any of the social media sites claiming to be from there. It's like the place doesn't exist."

I took a breath and shook my head. I thanked her and asked her to keep trying. I was hoping Dean would have some answers for us. If not, I would be on the next flight to Nevada.

"Thanks for agreeing to meet with us," I said when I entered the interview room. I grabbed the chair on the same side of the desk as Dean, and sat facing him. "I don't have a lot of time to waste, so I'm gonna get right down to it. I know you haven't heard from your mom in a couple of weeks and you're worried about her."

"How…how'd you know about that?"

"I spoke with the preacher at your church and we also saw your social media post. It seems you suspect Carlos might have done something to her."

"I mean, he's the only one who could have. She was always under his thumb. He never let her out of his sight except for a few minutes at a time when they would go to town. She called me randomly on the twenty-fifth from a cell phone. It had to have been from Carlos' phone, because he doesn't let anyone else on the compound have one. Anyway, when I answered, she told me to run, to get away. Before she could say anything more, I heard some crashing noise and then the line went dead."

"What do you think she was talking about?"

"I had no idea at the time, but now I think she was warning me about Carlos." He took a breath and blew it out forcefully. "He showed up at my church this past Sunday. I was running late and was looking for a place to park when I saw him walking toward the back door. I couldn't believe what I was seeing. I...I just kept driving. My girlfriend asked what was going on, but I didn't tell her. I just brought her home and told her I had to work."

I frowned. Even at the age of twenty-four and having served in the military, I could see that Dean was still fearful of Carlos. Of course, fear was a powerful motivator, and there was no getting around the fact that Dean had seen Carlos first, and thus would've had the advantage over the older man. Afraid or not, I knew he could very well be our killer.

"Dean, I have to tell you something. We pulled a truck out of the bayou yesterday morning and Carlos was inside." I paused to measure his reaction, but there was none. "He's dead. He was murdered."

Dean scowled, and then slowly shook his head. "It can't be Carlos. He doesn't have a truck. He drives an old Monte Carlo. He's been having it since we moved to Nevada. It's all he ever drives."

"Was Carlos driving the Monte Carlo Sunday when he went to church?"

"I...I didn't see his car. He was walking up the steps to the back door when I saw him."

I pulled the photo of Carlos from my folder and turned it so Dean could see. "Is this Carlos?"

Dean's eyes widened. "Is...is he dead? I mean, is he really dead?"

"Yeah."

"But...how? And if he's dead, where's my mom?"

I shook my head. "I don't know, son. Like I said, we pulled him out the bayou yesterday morning. He was alone and buckled into the driver's seat of a small truck." I saw his face twist in pain, but I quickly held out a hand. "Both doors were locked and closed, so we know there was no one else in the truck with him. He was alone. Your mom wasn't there."

"Are…are you sure?"

"We're positive."

Dean's shoulders slumped and he leaned far over, almost falling out of his chair. "She's dead."

"Why do you say that?" I asked.

"Carlos was too controlling to let her out of his sight for more than a few minutes. Unless…" Dean's voice trailed off. He straightened a little, his eyes shifting back and forth as he tried to figure something out in his mind.

I leaned closer. "Unless what, Dean?"

"The basement," he said. "She might be in the basement. Yeah, that's got to be it."

"What basement?"

"At home—in Sandy Knobs," he explained. "When Carlos got mad at my mom, he'd either spank her or punish her, and one time—"

"Hold up a minute." I lifted a hand. "Did you just say Carlos would spank your mom?"

He nodded.

I frowned, trying to wrap my head around that statement. I was old enough to know that some adults liked to be spanked during sexual intercourse, but for a man to discipline his wife like he would a child? It was barbaric and grossly illegal. I shouldn't have been surprised, considering what I knew about Ray Broussard, but it still shocked my conscience and angered me to no end. If Kari was the one who had killed Carlos, I was certain we could make a case for self-defense. However, I believed that scenario to be highly unlikely. My hopes of Amy and Baylor finding Kari alive were starting to diminish.

"Have you witnessed this?" I asked, still unable to fathom it. "Carlos spanking your mom?"

"Yes, sir…many times. He loved hitting people with that stick of his." He tightened his fists and an evil glint appeared in his eyes. "Jezebel, he called it. He used to say his grandfather carved it by hand from a giant sycamore tree one day when his dad had set the neighbor's garbage on fire. One good whipping from that stick was all it took for his dad to become a brand-new boy. His grandfather mounted Jezebel to the wall above the fireplace to serve as a reminder to his children to toe the line. Carlos said his dad did the same to him, and he claimed he was carrying on the tradition, but he wasn't."

Dean grunted. "I never met his grandpa or his dad, but I'm willing to bet they were nothing like the monster he is. He didn't beat me one time, he beat me every chance he got—and for dumb reasons. I forgot the hose pipe on once, and that was a beating. I didn't clean the Monte Carlo as nice as he would've liked—a beating. I accidentally broke a glass while washing the dishes—I had to drop my pants. He was relentless."

"Let's get back to the basement," I said. "Why do you think your mom's down there?"

"One time, when I was young, she stepped between him and me when I was about to get a bad beating." He shrugged. "I don't even remember what it was for, but I knew it was gonna be bad. Anyway, she grabbed Jezebel and pulled it out of his hands. You would've sworn she kicked him in the nuts—" Dean quickly clamped a hand over his mouth and turned to Takecia. "I'm sorry, ma'am."

Takecia laughed and waved him off. "No worries. I've kicked lots of men in the nuts."

Dean relaxed, but there was still tension in his eyes from reliving the incident. "Anyway, he slapped her in the face and knocked her down. I lunged at him to protect my mom, and that was the first time he punched me. I went down hard. I was choking on my blood and crying as he dragged my mom by the hair to the basement. He chained her up for three days, with no food or water."

"Hold up." I raised three fingers and leaned forward. "He starved your mom for three days?"

"Yes, sir. He said she was lucky God hadn't sent two she-bears to destroy her like He did in the Bible when those kids mocked Elisha." Dean grunted. "He was always quoting scripture that benefitted his arguments, but when my mom would use the Bible to correct him, she would either get spanked or punished. Every time he did something to her, I would pray to God to help me grow big and strong so I could kill him."

I nodded slowly, thoughtfully. I wanted to ask if he had finally lived out that fantasy now that he was a grown man and well-trained, but there were more pressing matters at hand. I needed to get in touch with Amy and Baylor and tell them to search the basement.

I pulled out my cell phone and made the call. First to Amy's cell, and then to Baylor's. Still nothing.

CHAPTER 47

I placed my cell phone on the desk beside me and explained to Dean how we had sent two detectives to Sandy Knobs to notify his mom of Carlos' death. "The last we heard from them, they were leaving the Twelve County Sheriff's Department and heading into the desert," I said. "Can you tell us more about that place? I don't know if they're in trouble or if they got lost, but their cell phones go straight to voicemail."

Dean's shoulders slumped as he sank into his chair. "They're in trouble."

My heart rate quickened. "How do you know?"

"The sheriff of Twelve County, he's in bed with Carlos and that cult." He stabbed his chest with his thumb. "I know it for a fact. When I was twelve, I'd had enough of the beatings, so I ran away from home. I made it off the compound without being seen and started heading north on the main highway. I had been to town a few times, so I knew how to get there. I ran as fast as I could. I was on the run for about an hour when I heard the first truck from the compound come up behind me. I got off the road and hid in some tumbleweeds until they passed by. When they were gone, I kept running, but I stayed off the road in case I'd have to hide again."

Dean paused for a breath, and I could tell by the redness seeping into his face that he was reliving the moment in vivid detail.

"I had taken a water bottle with me. I knew I'd have to conserve it, so I took a sip every hour or so," he continued. "I ran out of water before it got dark. I don't know, I must've run and walked for five or six hours before I saw a cop car. It had pulled over a speeder and had just finished writing the ticket when I saw it. I ran into the road yelling and waving my hands. I was tired, hot, thirsty, my feet hurt. I was a mess. Anyway, the cop ran over and helped me to his car. He gave me some water and an energy bar, but I wasn't hungry. I was just real thirsty.

"While I was sitting in the back seat drinking the water, I heard him get on the radio and talk to some lady. She was quiet for a while, and then she came back on and told the cop that the sheriff said to bring me back to Sandy Knobs, that I was a runaway and Carlos Marcella wanted me back home."

"And he brought you back?" I asked.

"Yes, sir. Even though I told him how Carlos would beat me and my mom. I even showed him the bruises on the back of my leg, but he didn't care."

I rubbed my chin. "What did he say when he saw the bruises?"

"He said orders were orders." Dean leaned forward and propped his elbows on his knees. "What's more, I saw that sheriff come to the compound more than one time after that. He even called Carlos one time and told him a raid was about to happen. It was about a year after I'd run away. He told Carlos to get as many women and children as possible and have them lay in the streets to stop the vehicles from entering the compound. He said he was on his way to stop his men, but it would take him an hour to get there."

"Why didn't he just call his men on the radio or by phone and tell them to back off?"

"Phones and radios don't work out there," Dean explained. "There's a cellular tower right when you drive into Sandy Knobs, but Carlos has the only phone that operates from that tower. He's got everybody on lockdown. A lot of the men there are ex-convicts who converted to his version of Christianity. I don't know if they'd die for him, but I'm sure they'd kill for him."

The more I heard about Sandy Knobs, the more my heart sank. I felt relieved to have an answer for Amy's and Baylor's phones going to voicemail, but I didn't like that the sheriff was in bed with Carlos and his cult. What if he had taken our officers into custody? I glanced at Takecia, and she nodded knowingly.

"I'll call the Nevada State Police again," she said, jumping up to leave.

"Sergeant Gayle," Dean said, stopping Takecia near the door. "If you get in touch with someone over there, can you ask them to check on my private detective?"

Takecia and I both frowned.

"What private detective?" she asked.

"When I didn't hear from my mom, I called my pawpaw and told him I was worried about her." He pulled out his wallet and produced a business card, handed it over. "He put me in touch with this man, who used to work for the Cote Blanche Sheriff's Office where I used to live. My pawpaw said he used to be a good detective and he had experience with cults. He's a P.I. now and runs his own business."

I took the business card and read the name. *Oscar London*. I scowled. I knew that name. Where had I heard it before?

"My pawpaw gave him money to make the trip to Nevada," Dean continued. "He left about two weeks ago, but we haven't heard anything since."

I leaned back in my chair and stared wide-eyed at the card, remembering where I'd heard the name. Dawn Carter had mentioned it when she'd told me the story about the Magnolia Life Church. I looked at the number on the bottom of the card.

"Have you tried calling him?" I asked.

"A hundred times." Dean shook his head. "I haven't heard from him since he stopped to eat at a casino in West Wendover."

I handed the card to Takecia and she hurried off. While she began making the phone calls, I turned back to Dean. "What did Carlos do to you after the deputy brought you back home?"

"He told me I was nothing but a rabid dog that didn't deserve to live." Dean's knuckles turned white as he clenched his fists. That evil glint I'd seen earlier returned to his eyes. "He treated me like an animal after that. He chained me to a post in the basement so I couldn't escape again. He'd come down once a day to bring me bread and water and to beat me. I refused to cry, and it infuriated him. He hit me until he was too tired to hurt me anymore, and I would laugh at him. He was always calling himself a lion amongst mere men, so I began goading him. I'd tell him that lions were fierce warriors and they never got tired, so I assured him that he was no lion."

"Why would you do that?" I asked. "Why provoke him when you were tied up and helpless?"

"I might've been tied up, but I wasn't helpless. You see, Carlos was an arrogant man. The way to hurt him was to attack his pride, and that's exactly what I did."

"Were you worried he would kill you?"

"I thought about it, but it didn't worry me," he said. "Nothing could be worse than living with that asshole."

"How long were you locked down there?"

"The basement's underground, where there's not even a flicker of light, so it was hard to judge the days. After locking me down there that first time, he began doing it more often, and each time the sentence got longer and longer, but the last time was the longest. I think he wanted me to die down there." He stared down at his hands, remembering something. "One day, when he brought me some bread and water, he turned on the light just so I could see that the water was brackish and the bread molded. He asked if I was feeling sick, and said he'd been giving me water from the toilet and feeding me old bread. I told him I didn't care where he got it, that it was delicious. I was determined to outlast him. I planned on getting out of there someday and killing him." Dean paused. "I still can't believe he's dead. Are you sure?"

"You saw the pictures, so you know he's dead."

"It's just so hard to believe." He shook his head. "After all this time...he's finally dead and can't hurt anyone anymore."

I studied Dean's face carefully. He had been through a lot, and he was still fearful of Carlos, but it was obvious he hadn't been broken. If anything, he had been made stronger by the abuse.

"Son, did you kill Carlos?"

CHAPTER 48

Sandy Knobs, Nevada

While Baylor kept an eye on the stairway, Amy hurried to the broken dresser and dragged it away from the wall. She slid it toward where Baylor waited, hoping to create a barricade of sorts to slow down Carlos' men, but she froze when she saw the expression on Baylor's face.

"I think the structure's on fire." He indicated the stairway. "I don't know if they intentionally set it or if it was an accident, but they might be trying to burn us out."

Amy cocked her head to the side. From the sounds of the shouts overhead, it appeared the fire was accidental and they were trying to put it out. At least that might keep them busy for a while—hopefully long enough for them to figure a way out of their situation. She walked deeper into the basement and saw Kari cowering in the corner where she had left her, only she was fumbling with something. Amy stared for a second before realizing she had dropped the wallet she'd taken from the man in the freezer, and Kari was now going through it. Suddenly, Kari dropped the wallet and looked up in horror.

"That man's a cop!" she yelled. "Carlos and Eagle killed a cop!"

Amy hurried forward and snatched up the wallet. When she turned it over, she found a retired commission card that pictured a man in uniform. "He's retired," Amy called over her shoulder so Baylor could know what was going on. "His name's Oscar London. He's a retired detective from the Cote Blanche Sheriff's Office."

"Where's Cote Blanche?" Baylor asked.

Amy looked up and studied his face before answering. If they were lucky, they had about an hour left to live, but she couldn't detect a single worry line on his face. She quickly stepped forward and kissed him fully on the mouth. When she pulled away, her heart was pounding.

"Baylor Rice, if we die down here today," she declared, "I'll die the happiest woman on earth, because I'll be dying as your wife."

"Are we gonna die?" Kari cried from behind Amy. "Are they gonna kill us?"

Amy ignored the question. She could either spend her last moments feeling sorry for herself for not being able to spend a lifetime with Baylor, or she could spend it being productive. She chose the latter.

After telling Baylor where Cote Blanche was located, she hurried back to the freezer, pulled the lid open, and began rummaging through the ex-cop's clothes, hoping to find a pistol or a loaded magazine inside. His body was frozen solid, so it was difficult to maneuver around him, but she finally searched enough to know that Carlos had stripped the man of any weapons.

Outside, she could hear the shouts and jeers of the mob that surrounded them. Intermittently, something would crash into a wall overhead, and she would jerk involuntarily. She was expecting a full-on assault at any moment, but she chose to block it from her head. She knew she was gonna die, but she was determined to do so bravely and without making a sound.

As Baylor continued to barricade the staircase, Amy jerked the freezer plug from the wall and slid the freezer deeper into a corner of the basement that would be sheltered from gunfire.

"Kari," she said when the freezer was in place, "get behind this and don't move. Those men don't want to kill you—they want to kill us. Just keep your head down and don't come out. Once everything's over, they'll find you and they should take care of you."

"But what about you guys?"

Amy guided Kari to the corner. "Don't worry about us. We'll be fine."

When Amy turned around, Baylor was scanning the floor. In search of what, she wasn't sure, but he was determined to find it. She watched him disappear behind a wall of cardboard boxes. She glanced toward the stairwell, but there was no movement up there at the moment. Suddenly, a gunshot exploded from behind the boxes. She gasped and rushed toward the sound.

"Bay!" she hollered.

Outside, laughter erupted and some of the men popped off shots of their own, no doubt thinking either Baylor or Amy had committed suicide rather than face their bullets.

Before Amy could call Baylor's name again, there were six more shots, all fired in rapid succession. She dipped behind the boxes and stopped short when she saw Baylor crouched near the wall, pulling at chunks of a cinder block.

"It's no use," he said with a sigh. "I thought I might be able to shoot through the cinder blocks, but the hollow spaces are filled with solid concrete. We're stuck down here, and I just used the last of my ammo."

Amy dropped to her knees in front of Baylor and placed a hand on his face. "There's no one else I'd rather spend eternity with than you."

He smiled back, and she knew it was genuine. There were no regrets in that smile.

As they made their way back to the staircase that led to the top level, Amy removed her last magazine and counted her bullets. She had ten left. Removing five rounds, she handed them to Baylor, and then reinserted the magazine into the well of her pistol.

Baylor hesitated, staring down at the rounds in his hand.

"Put them in your magazine," Amy ordered. "We're gonna fight side-by-side to the end."

A sly grin tugged at the corners of his mouth. "You know what they're not expecting?"

"What's that?" Amy asked, growing curious.

He indicated the stairway. "They're not expecting us to launch an attack on them. Sure, they've got more guns and ammo than us and there's no way we can win, but if we can take them by surprise, we can take out more of them before they get us."

Amy set her jaw. "I like the sound of that."

CHAPTER 49

Mechant Loup Police Department

The question hung in the air for a long moment. I never took my eyes off Dean, who remained thoughtful.

"Well, did you kill Carlos?" I asked again. "It's a simple question that requires a simple answer."

"It's not so simple," he finally said. "In my heart, back when I was a young boy, I killed that bastard a thousand times. I made a number of elaborate plans to kill him when I grew up. I wanted to make it look like an accident, because I didn't want to go to jail for him. He wasn't worth my freedom." He sighed. "As I grew up, I learned to let go of the hatred. Now, if he did something to my mom and he was still alive, I couldn't promise you anything."

I scowled as a thought occurred to me. "Why didn't you go to Sandy Knobs yourself to see about your mom? You're an adult now and you can take care of yourself."

"On that compound, he's untouchable." Dean shook his head. "There's no way I'd ever get close enough to do anything to him, and there's no way he'd let me leave there alive. I know too much about him. My mom said he's been gunning for me ever since I left."

"And you swear you didn't kill him?"

"I swear I didn't kill him."

I hated to admit it to myself, but I believed him. If he was right and he hadn't killed Carlos, then we were back to square one—or Ray Broussard.

Dean was quiet for a long moment. When he didn't say anything,

I broke the silence.

"Where'd you get that determination to survive?"

He thought about it for a long moment before answering. "When I was being homeschooled, I learned a lot about the Holocaust. I read a lot of stories from some of the survivors." He looked up with sorrowful eyes. "There was no comparison between what happened to them and what happened to me. I was in Heaven, they were in hell. All during the time when Carlos was beating me in the basement, I kept thinking about those who survived. I thought about everything they went through. It gave me the strength to hang on—to endure everything he could throw at me. I knew it would never get as bad as it had been for them, and that gave me the strength to outlast him."

Dean paused, was thoughtful, and then gave a nod. "My pawpaw was right. When I was real little, before my mom met Carlos, he used to say, *No matter how bad you think you've got it, somebody's got it worse.* Those words and the stories from the Holocaust survivors kept me strong. They helped me survive—mentally and physically. I kept that same mentality through boot camp, and it helped."

"What did your mom do while you were in the basement?" I asked. "I guess there wasn't much she could do, considering how domineering Carlos was."

"She didn't like it, but, like you said, there wasn't much she could do about it." He smiled warmly. "When Carlos would leave the house, she would sneak downstairs and bring me food. Other times, like when my mom and Carlos made their weekly trips to town, my step-siblings would sneak downstairs and bring me snacks. Mostly cookies and candy. They hated their dad as much as I did, and they felt bad that I was down there."

"Did he beat them like he beat you?"

"Oh, no, they were his pride and joy," Dean said without a shred of resentment. "I guess he beat me because I wasn't his biological kid. Whatever the reason, I'm glad he didn't touch them. Some people can handle that kind of treatment, and others can't."

I sensed his statement had something to do with others who were abused by Carlos, so I asked about it.

"My mom once mentioned that some of the kids Carlos had beaten when he was the principal at the Magnolia Life School were still messed up really bad." He shook his head. "Even though it's been years, it still haunts them. She said they're not messed up physically, but emotionally and mentally. She said one boy even killed himself. It's really sad. Did I murder Carlos? No. Am I glad he's dead? Yes. At least I know he'll never hurt another kid."

I couldn't argue with him about Carlos being dead, but I also couldn't understand how he could've possibly forgiven Carlos. "At what point did you let it go—the hatred and resentment for Carlos? When did you forgive him?"

"Saying I forgave him is taking it too far," he said with a chuckle, "but I did let it go. It was a few days before I escaped. He had come down to the basement to give me my daily whipping, only I decided I wasn't gonna take it anymore. He told me to bend over and grab my ankles, but I told him to go to hell. It shocked him. He lifted Jezebel over his head and said he would bash my skull in if I didn't obey. I was sitting on the ground against the wall, and I had secretly wrapped some of the chain around my fist. I told him to pounce if he felt like a lion. He did, and I jumped up and punched him as hard as I could. He stepped right into my punch, and that chain caught him right on the jaw. It put him out cold."

I grinned widely. "You knocked him out?"

"Yes, sir." He nodded for emphasis. "When he woke up a few seconds later—blood pouring down his face—I hollered something I'd read in the Bible. *A living dog is better than a dead lion, and you're a dead lion, bitch!*"

"I don't imagine that last part is in the Bible—the part about him being a bitch?"

"No, sir." He chuckled again. "I added that part. He was so embarrassed that he ran straight up the stairs. I was able to escape before he came back down, and I think that's a good thing. I'm sure he would've killed me at that point."

"How'd you escape?"

"I was sleeping on the floor a couple of days later and I heard a noise that woke me up," he explained. "It was a scratching sound coming from under the ground. All of a sudden, the floor under me started moving. At first, I thought it was an earthquake, but I realized nothing was moving except the piece of square concrete under me. I rolled off the square and just stared at it, petrified. It was dark, but when the square moved, an orange glow lit up a hole in the ground."

CHAPTER 50

"Wait a minute," I interrupted. "How big was this square tile?"

He held his hands out to indicate approximately two feet.

"And this square concrete block just started moving on its own?" I asked.

"Yeah, it scared the shit out of me."

"I guess it did."

"Anyway, when it was pushed aside enough to see under it, I found myself staring into some large brown eyes. I don't know who was more scared, me or him, but it turned out to be a Shoshone Indian who I had seen out on the prairie a few times. I recognized him right away. He was about my age, and he had a scar that ran from his forehead, down over his left eye, and onto his cheek."

"Is there a reservation around there?" I asked.

"Yeah, and it begins on the opposite side of the main road from the compound," Dean explained. "Carlos and his people would trade with the Indians on a regular basis, so I wasn't surprised to see one—I was just surprised to see him under the basement."

"But...what was this kid doing under your house?" I asked, scrunching up my face as I did so. "He couldn't have burrowed under it, right? How in the hell did he get there?"

"He went through this underground tunnel he found."

"Huh?" I cocked my head to the side. "This kid just randomly found a tunnel that led up under your house?"

"Yes, sir, but I didn't know it at the time," Dean explained. "He told me later that he had been rummaging through his grandpa's barn a few months earlier looking for something to help him change a flat tire on his tractor. He found a large rock in the corner and figured he could use it as a fulcrum to lift one end of the tractor. So, he got his horse, tied a rope to the rock, and dragged it across the barn and out into the yard. He said he changed the tire and later, when he went back into the barn, he noticed a dark shadow where the rock had been. When he looked, he saw that there was a large hole in the ground. He knew it was too big to have been made by an animal, and when he saw old support beams around the opening, he knew it had to go somewhere important. He made a torch and decided to explore it."

"And this tunnel led to your basement?"

Dean nodded. "He said he had been going back and forth all that time before he made contact with me. He said he hadn't been sure exactly where the spot was located above ground, but he could hear us talking fluid English, so he figured it was somewhere on the compound, because no one on the reservation spoke that way."

"He would just go back and forth from his place to yours?" I asked. "I mean…what for?"

"Yeah, he would, and he told me he was just curious about how we lived our lives," Dean said. "He said he would sit there for hours and listen to us. He said he enjoyed it, but then one day he heard Carlos screaming at me. He said he heard loud clapping noises—it was Carlos giving me the rod—and then he heard me crying. He said he could tell I was about the same age he was, and he felt bad for me. He wanted to help me—to be my friend."

Dean paused and stared wistfully at the floor. I figured he was probably wondering what had ever become of his Shoshone friend, and I asked him to go on with his story.

"Well, he said that was when he realized Carlos was a bad man, and he thought I was in danger," Dean explained. "He said he was listening when Carlos first locked me in the basement, and he was listening the night I knocked him out. He thought Carlos would retaliate in a vicious way, so he decided he would break me free and bring me to live with his people."

"Go back to the night you first saw those large brown eyes," I said. "What happened after that?"

"I smiled and he smiled back. He came in real cautious like, first poking his head up through the hole and then taking a good, long look around. He pointed to the chains and asked if I could get out of them, but I told him I couldn't. He told me he would be back the next night, and then he and his torch disappeared. I heard some latching sounds, and then it was dark again."

"Did he go back the next night?"

"He did, and he brought some tools with him." Dean rubbed his wrists as though he could still feel the iron against his flesh. "He cut through the chain and then told me to follow him, so I did—and I took Jezebel with me."

"You did what?"

"Carlos had dropped it when I knocked him out, and he hadn't come down there to pick her up yet, so I took her so he couldn't use her on anybody else." Dean seemed proud of himself. "I still have her in a box somewhere at my pawpaw's house."

I laughed and then asked if he had been scared on the night of the escape.

His brow furrowed. "You know, I don't remember feeling anything but relief. I just wanted to be away from Carlos, so I guess I felt anything would be better than living with him. I knew I would miss my mom and my siblings, but I had a chance to escape, and I was taking it."

"Were you worried that Carlos would find the tunnel and come after you?"

"No, it's impossible to open the hatch from inside the basement," he said. "Underneath, there's this ancient locking mechanism that keeps it secured. Once the latch is pulled down and the lock put in place, there's no opening it. The hinges and the locking mechanisms are anchored to the hard rock under the floor."

"What happened next?"

"We crossed the tunnel. Irvin—that's my friend's name, Irvin Fillmore—he figured it was about four or five hundred yards long, and I believe him. It took us a while to crawl through to the other side. My knees and palms hurt on the rough surface, but I didn't care. I was glad to be out of there. When we got to the end of the tunnel, we were in his barn and I was safely on the reservation."

"How did that tunnel get there?" I asked.

"Irvin's pawpaw believed it was built by white settlers who lived in our old house." Dean shifted in his chair. We had been there a while, and he seemed to be getting restless. "His pawpaw figured the settlers would leave the trap door open in case they were attacked by marauding Indians. If that happened, he figured they would run down the hatch, lock it behind them, and escape into the mountains that were beyond the prairie. Irvin thought they probably had supplies like guns and ammo waiting for them in the tunnel, because he found evidence of that when he explored it for the first time."

I nodded and considered everything I'd just heard, while also worrying about Amy and Baylor.

"How long did you stay with Irvin's family?" I asked after a moment.

"I lived there for a few years, right next door to where Carlos lived, but he never knew it. No one did. I attended school with Irvin on the reservation, and then, when I was old enough, I left and joined the Marines."

"What about your mom?"

Dean's eyes misted over. "My biggest regret is leaving her behind, but I knew she'd never come with me. I used to always beg her to leave Carlos and take us with her, but she said she couldn't. Said she loved him. Can you believe that? Despite everything that monster did to her, she actually loved him. I never could understand it."

"Did you ever go back through that tunnel?" I asked.

"Only once. I was afraid Carlos would somehow find it and come after me, so I convinced Irvin to keep the bucket of his pawpaw's tractor resting on the rock that covered the hole." Dean took a haggard breath. "I spent every waking hour of those years looking over my shoulder. I just knew Carlos would find out and storm the reservation with his men."

"You said you went back through the tunnel once," I said when he didn't elaborate. "Tell me about that."

"Sometimes, I would climb up on this giant outcrop near Irvin's house and look toward the compound. It was about a thousand feet in the air. On a clear day, with field glasses, I could see into the compound and right to the front yard of my old house." There was a dreamy look in his eyes, and I wondered if he would ever answer my question.

"I used to sit up there for hours and watch Star and Abel play," he continued. "I'd see Mom sometimes, and she always looked sad. I wanted desperately to communicate with her—to let her know I was okay—but I didn't know how. When I was eighteen and about to leave for the military, I knew I needed to let her know, so I got Irvin to take me back through the tunnel. It was a Saturday afternoon after Carlos and my mom had left for town. I'd seen Abel working on a dirt bike in the back yard. There was no one else around, so I figured it was safe."

"It must've been weird going back through there," I said when he paused for a long breath.

He nodded. "When I came up through the basement, I was surprised to see that it was pretty much the same way I'd left it. The only thing that had moved was Carlos' weight bench. He was obsessed with his body. He weight-lifted every day. Anyway, I made Irvin wait by the trap door so it wouldn't shut, and then I made my way through the house and out into the back yard. Abel freaked out when he saw me. He just stood there staring at me."

"Did he recognize you?"

"Oh, yeah, right away," Dean said. "He just kept saying over and over that he thought I was dead. I gave him a piece of paper with my cell phone number on it and told him to memorize the number and give it to Mom. I told him not to say anything to Carlos. Before he could say anything more, I heard a car coming up the road, so I turned and ran back toward the house. Irvin was waiting for me near the tunnel. We locked the trap door shut and left out of there. I've never been back since."

"I assume you eventually heard from your mom, considering y'all have been communicating over the years."

"Yeah, she called about three weeks after I'd given the note to Abel. It was a brief conversation and she said it was from a payphone outside a women's restroom in West Wendover. She told me she had to hurry, because Carlos was nearby, but she told me not to worry about her and not to come back. She told me Carlos was obsessed with finding me and he wanted Jezebel back. She said he couldn't understand how I'd escaped, and he blamed her and my siblings for assisting me. She said he beat Star and Abel after I was gone, trying to get a confession out of them."

I gritted my teeth. After taking a few calming breaths, I opened my mouth to ask Dean where he had gone after leaving the military, but the interview room burst open and Takecia rushed in.

"Clint, you need to come here quick!" Her voice was laced with concern. "Something's going down in Sandy Knobs, and it doesn't look good!"

CHAPTER 51

I reached the radio room a step behind Takecia. My eyes were immediately drawn to the large television that was mounted on the wall. It was tuned to one of the national news channels and the aerial footage seemed to be coming from a helicopter. I stepped closer to make sense out of what I was seeing.

The first thing that grabbed my attention was a line of dark smoke billowing up toward the sky. Its source was a damaged vehicle protruding from the back wall of a large brick home that was situated at the edge of some kind of compound. It appeared to be its own little town.

In addition to several other vehicles parked at various angles facing the house, I saw a disabled Jeep Wrangler near an outcropping of rocks in front of the home. Every tire appeared to be flat, and when the chopper circled overhead, I saw that the front windshield was blown out. I wasn't positive, but there appeared to be tiny holes in the side panels—bullet holes.

I squinted and leaned closer, not believing my eyes. It appeared that there were bodies—at least three or four of them—strewn about the yard. A dozen or so men had taken up positions of cover behind the vehicles, and four of them were moving toward a busted garage door. The men appeared to be heavily armed.

"What's going on?" I asked Takecia. "What am I looking at?"

"I called the Nevada State Police and gave them the update," she explained. "They said they were sending a team right away, but that it would take about an hour for them to arrive. I didn't know what else to do, so I called a local news station and told them we had two officers in trouble with a cult out in the desert, and I asked if they had a news helicopter available. They said they had one doing a traffic report nearby, and they agreed to send it to Sandy Knobs." She pointed toward the television. "This just popped up as breaking news."

"Hey, that's my old house!" called a voice from behind me. It was Dean and his mouth was wide open. "What in the hell is going on?"

"We don't know that Amy and Baylor even made it there," I said, the lack of conviction evident in my voice. "Maybe they never found the place."

"Clint," Lindsey began, standing to stab a slender finger at the disabled Jeep Wrangler on the screen, "that's the Jeep they rented for their honeymoon."

My heart jumped to my throat. I leaned even closer, trying desperately to make out the figures lying on the ground. They were all men, so they couldn't be Amy, and none of them were built like Baylor. A sense of dread gushed over me like a flash flood—the men approaching the garage door had their rifles pointed forward. I knew then that Amy and Baylor were inside the house, and if the men were approaching across the open ground, things couldn't be good on the inside.

Suddenly, the helicopter dipped violently and the pilot yelled that the men on the ground were shooting at him. He sped away, banked sharply to the left, and then circled back. His cameraman tried to zoom in, but the footage was not as clear as earlier.

I sank to my knees and stared up in despair at the television footage. Amy and Baylor were there because of me. While I knew Amy had insisted on going, I could've stopped it. I didn't have to give her the information. I could've waited to get in touch with the local police or even the state police—officers who were familiar with the area and the people.

Takecia had dropped into a chair, her eyes transfixed on the screen. Lindsey stood there crying. None of us moved until Dean stepped forward and pointed to the television.

"What's that?" he asked.

I looked where he was pointing. Off in the distance, along a strip of four-lane highway, there was what appeared to be a line of ants heading toward the compound. Lindsey wiped away her tears and jumped forward.

"That's the Mors Umbra Motorcycle Club from Elko!" she screamed. "I found them on GETTR and told them we had two officers in trouble in Sandy Knobs! The vice president told me they had members in the area and would send them right away! That's them!"

"What's Get Her?" I asked, watching as the helicopter swooped down on the highway, enabling us to see a line of about eight or nine motorcycles racing toward the compound. I was familiar with the Latin term, *mors umbra*, which meant *death shadow*, but I'd never heard of Get Her.

"It's *GETTR*, not *Get Her,* and it's a new social media website," she said, jumping up and down with excitement. She was oblivious to the fact that the club members were too late. At least a dozen men had filed through the busted garage door of the house. If Amy and Baylor were inside—and all indications pointed to them being there—they were either already dead or taken captive, because they seemed to be offering no resistance.

Feeling numb from my toes to the brown hair on my head, I watched the bikers close in on the compound. They turned off the main road and headed down a long street that led through the center of the compound. I figured that was probably Spirit Way. The bad guys still out in the yard had either seen or heard the bikers, because they turned their attention away from the helicopter, jumped into some trucks, and headed for what appeared to be the town square.

Working like modern-day cowboys, the four bikers at the front of the line laid their bikes down and sprawled out behind them, using them as cover. They then produced long guns and began opening up on the approaching trucks, the occupants of which were already firing on the bikers.

"Holy shit!" Dean said in a stunned voice. "Is this really happening?"

I didn't acknowledge him. I simply watched as the two sides exchanged gunfire. Suddenly, I realized I'd been listening to it for a full thirty seconds before recognizing what it was—my cell phone was ringing. I lifted it to my ear without taking my eyes off the television.

"Are you seeing this shit on the news?" Susan asked. "Isn't Sandy Knobs the place where Amy and Baylor were headed to do that death notification?"

"Yeah," I said weakly.

"Is that the Jeep they rented in the front yard?"

"Yeah."

"Dear God, Clint!"

"Yeah."

CHAPTER 52

Sandy Knobs, Nevada

Amy heard thunderous footsteps above them and she knew the cult members were flooding the house. She glanced at her pistol and wished for more ammunition. Letting out a silent prayer, she eased to the right side of the dresser and took aim at the top of the stairway. Baylor was on the left side, ready to spring into action. They would have to make each bullet count, but she knew even if they did, they would run out within seconds. It would all be over soon...very soon.

They were about to rush the stairs when everything suddenly grew deathly quiet above them.

She traded glances with Baylor, who shrugged and mouthed that he was ready to go. She nodded. This was how her brief, but happy marriage to Baylor would end. She gritted her teeth, crouched low. Just as she was about to spring forward, a loud screech sounded from the back of the room. She and Baylor both whirled around to see Kari staring across the basement, her eyes wide with horror.

When Amy turned to see what had startled Kari, her own eyes widened. There, coming up from a hole in the rock floor, was a dark human shadow that appeared to be holding a rifle. Before Amy could react to the threat, someone let out a battle cry from upstairs and gunfire exploded in the confined space,

Bullets peppered the dresser and other items within the basement and ricocheted off the floor. Amy quickly dropped to the ground behind the dresser and Baylor joined her. Instinctively, they stuck their pistols around the wooden frame and returned fire. Within a split second, they had shot their pistols dry. The men upstairs seemed to sense this, because they began descending the stairs as they continued shooting.

In the explosions and chaos of the ongoing attack, and through her ringing ears, Amy heard what sounded like muffled screams from Kari. She turned to see the stranger dragging Kari toward the back of the basement. Once he reached a certain point, he shoved her into the hole in the floor and then slammed a large slab of rock down on top of her, closing off the hole.

"Shit!" Amy said aloud, worried for Kari. A bullet whizzed past her face and she dropped even lower on the ground, but she knew it would only be a matter of seconds before one got her. She could still feel Baylor moving beside her, so she was confident he hadn't been shot yet. She turned, expecting to get shot from behind by the new stranger who had entered the fight, but he was lost in the shadows somewhere.

Stealing a peek around the corner of the dresser, Amy saw the first man make the landing. He carried a pump-action shotgun and he was headed straight for the dresser they were pinned behind. She braced herself for the blast that would end her life, but it never came. Instead, the man took two stumbling steps and fell forward, a startled expression plastered on his ugly mug.

That's when Amy realized the man behind her was firing at their attackers. She turned again and caught a glimpse of him in his muzzle flash. He was crouched behind a narrow column. He had braced his AR-15 against it and was snapping off shot after shot, his brown eyes narrowed into slits and the muscles in his jaw bulging.

Someone screamed for the men to retreat, and Amy felt Baylor lunge to his hands and knees. She followed his lead, rushed to where three men lay dead on the floor. Baylor grabbed up a rifle and she grabbed a shotgun. They started to head for the stairway to pursue their attackers, but stopped dead in their tracks when they saw several cylindrical objects bounding down the steps toward them.

"Flash bangs!" Baylor yelled, and they both turned and rushed for cover. Although the flash bangs were harmless in that they weren't filled with projectiles, they did emit a brilliant flash and concussive explosion that could leave them blind and deaf for several seconds—and that would be enough time for the men upstairs to rush back down and take over the basement.

As soon as they rounded the corner, Amy dropped to her knees, closed her eyes, and covered her ears. Baylor and the stranger followed suit, and they were just in time to ward off the deafening explosion and brilliant flash that followed.

Before the explosion had completely died out, Amy was spinning around to face the front of the basement. She didn't know how many shells were left in the shotgun, but she was hoping for at least a few. Baylor had moved to the opposite side of the room and had leveled his newly-acquired rifle toward the danger zone. They were out in the open and vulnerable, so they would have to make their bullets count.

Nothing happened.

As the seconds ticked by, Amy heard a sound like thunder from somewhere above them. It was followed by shouts, the roaring of engines, and then some distant popping sounds that had to be gunfire. She wasn't sure what was happening, but whatever it was, it had been enough to grab the attention of the men above them. She turned to the stranger. "How in the hell did you get in here?"

"There's a tunnel over there," he said, pointing to the spot in the basement floor from whence he'd appeared.

"A tunnel?" Amy asked. "Where does it go?"

"It crosses under the highway and comes out in my barn on the reservation."

"Let's get out of here!" Amy started to head for the slab of rock under which she'd seen Kari disappear. "We can circle around and catch them by surprise."

"There's no getting out of here," the man explained. "The door latches shut when it closes. Even if Mrs. Kari could figure out how to spring it, it's way too heavy for her to open."

Amy cursed. "Is that the only way out of here?"

The man nodded.

"Then why'd you close it behind her?" Amy asked.

"I thought all was lost and I wanted her to be safe." The young man, who appeared to be in his early twenties, frowned. "Her son and me, we were friends. I came because it looked like there was trouble, and"—the man pointed to Baylor—"I saw you running toward the house. I thought you were my friend. I thought you had come back to rescue your mom. I knew you would want her to be safe."

"She's not my mom," Baylor said, sticking out his hand, "but we're definitely friends now. My name's Baylor and this is my wife, Amy."

"I'm Irvin...Irvin Fillmore." He shook Baylor's hand and nodded at Amy.

Amy wanted to ask him a dozen questions, but the gunfire

outside seemed to be intensifying. She could hear angry shouts from the men upstairs, and she thought she detected a hint of panic in their voices. That they had thrown the flash bang grenades down the stairs and not followed up with an assault could only mean one thing: they had been surprised by an opposing force.

She could tell Baylor sensed the same thing, because when their eyes locked, he nodded and said, "Let's take the fight to them. Catch them in a crossfire situation."

"But what if the other side of that crossfire is hostile to us?"

He shook his head. "We'll just have to figure it out as we go."

Amy nodded and quickly checked the twelve gauge. There were four shotgun shells in the tube and one in the chamber—all of them 000-aught buckshot. Irvin removed an extra magazine from his back pocket and tossed it toward Baylor, who had armed himself with an M-16 he'd found on the ground.

"I'm ready," Irvin said, gripping his own AR-15 tightly. "I never did like the way these people treated Dean and Mrs. Kari, and if you guys are here to stop them, I'm going with you."

Before Amy could object, Baylor stepped in front of her and took the lead. She followed and Irvin trailed behind her. When they were halfway up the stairs, she thought she could hear a helicopter circling outside, but that didn't make any sense. *Unless these cult assholes have a chopper*, she thought.

They had almost reached the landing when a man suddenly appeared in front and above them. He held the business end of a flame thrower and his eyes were wide with excitement. It immediately occurred to Amy that he was there to burn them and all of the evidence in the basement.

CHAPTER 53

In the same instant that fire belched from the throat of the flame thrower, Amy and Baylor fired in unison. Baylor snapped off two shots that caught the man high in his chest, and Amy, who was two steps lower and slightly to Baylor's right, let go with a buckshot blast that sent eight sixty-eight-grain lead balls into the man's groin and upward through his torso and out his back.

The heat from the flame was intense and Amy felt her nose hairs singe, but the man fell from the gunshots and the flame petered out. As they continued their rush up the stairs and past the downed man, Amy saw that the "flame thrower" was actually a brush burner attached to a propane tank that was secured in a makeshift pack on the man's back. The man lay writhing in pain. Blood sprayed from his mouth as he begged for help, but Amy didn't even slow to acknowledge him. Thanks to him, she had almost been barbecued, and she knew she'd lost most of her eyelashes, so he could go straight to hell.

They met no more resistance as they rushed through the living room and toward the front door, but the fighting outside had grown more intense. Bullets smashed against the exterior walls of the house, and a few even found their way inside through the windows and open front door.

With a wave of his hand, Baylor indicated for Amy and Irvin to get low and take cover. Amy rushed toward the hallway to the left while Baylor flattened out near the sofa. Irvin dropped down beside Baylor and they were just in time. Three men rushed into the house with bullets chasing them and tearing up the airspace where Amy,

Baylor, and Irvin had been milliseconds before.

The men somehow made it inside without getting hit, but that's where their luck ended. Amy immediately recognized them as part of the group that had tried to kill them, and she emptied her shotgun into them, firing first one blast and then the next and the next until her firing pin hit on an empty chamber. Baylor and Irvin had also engaged the men, and they were soon lying harmlessly on the hard floor.

When the shooting was over, Amy scrambled to one of the downed men and relieved him of his weapon, a worn and battered SKS semi-automatic rifle. She cursed silently when she saw that the bolt was locked back on an empty magazine, but rejoiced inwardly when she noticed a loaded stripper clip resting in the man's lifeless and bloody hand. Ignoring the blood, she grabbed the clip, inserted the rounds into the magazine, released the bolt, and pulled herself to her feet.

Baylor was already at the front door and Irvin was beside him, each of them engaging targets from the opening. Amy rushed to the living room window and peered outside, searching for something to shoot. A man was running backward toward the house while firing a Thompson submachine gun in the direction of a man crouched behind a motorcycle. Amy didn't know the man behind the motorcycle, but if he was an enemy of Carlos' cult, she considered him a friend.

Without so much as a blink, she lifted the SKS and shot Tommy Gun in the back, twice, right between the shoulder blades. He took two more stumbling steps and then collapsed to the ground. The man behind the motorcycle locked eyes with Amy and gave a grateful nod. When he stood to his feet, Amy noticed his right arm dangling helplessly at his side, and blood poured down the front of his leather vest, covering up most of the insignia. The only word she did see—and it was one she recognized—was Elko. She remembered seeing the name of the nearby county on the map back when she had service on her cell phone. She sighed. That seemed like such a long time ago.

Amy swung the muzzle of her rifle around, sweeping the front yard of the compound in search of more threats. Thankfully, there were none. The only remaining cult members were being herded by a group of heavily armed bikers toward the rock where their destroyed Jeep was located. There had to be a dozen or more cult members remaining—some of them injured—and although they outnumbered the bikers, they were no match for the group.

Amy lowered her rifle and headed for the door. Baylor and Irvin had already stepped out into the front yard. Just as she made her way outside, she saw Irvin jump into a vehicle that was idling near the garage door of the house. Without wasting a second, he sped off toward the gate that Baylor had busted through, and Amy knew he was heading for the other end of the tunnel.

"Bahía de los Cochinos!" a man suddenly shouted from the group of bikers. He broke from his buddies and slung a rifle over his right shoulder. "Bay of Pigs, is that really you?"

Amy watched curiously as the man approached Baylor and threw an arm around him.

"How the hell are you, brother?" the man asked, leaning back and giving Baylor a once-over. "It's been years!"

"I've been trying to find you," Baylor said. "You fell off the map."

"What can I say? I've got warrants. I was in Denver one night and saw this asshole slapping a girl around. When I told him to try that on a man, he took a swing at me. I dropped him and, as it turned out, he takes a punch like a bitch. He ended up with a brain bleed and had to have surgery." The man grunted. "What's more, his dad's a federal judge. As you can imagine, my face has been plastered all over Colorado. I have to take the long way around when I head east." The man paused, nodded his head at Baylor. "What'd you need? Were you in some kind of trouble?"

"Nah, I just needed some groomsmen." Baylor indicated their surroundings. "I'm on my honeymoon."

"I appreciate the thought, but you know I don't dress up." The man turned to his fellow bikers. "Guys, this is my brother from another mother I'm always talking about—Baylor Rice from the mountains of North Carolina. He saved my bacon more than once in that hellhole of a place they call Afghanistan."

"You saved my ass, too." Baylor turned and waved Amy over. "Amy, this is Grant Cole. Grant, this is my wife, Amy Cooke."

Amy smiled and shifted the SKS to her left hand, stuck out her right. "It's a pleasure to meet you," she said. "Baylor's talked a lot about you."

Grant's eyes widened. "Are you shitting me? You really got married and this is really your honeymoon?"

"Yeah. We're cops out of Louisiana. Someone got killed and we were trying to deliver a death notification." Baylor regarded one of the dead men on the ground nearby. "These assholes had other ideas. Anyway, I tried your old number and I even called all of your old haunts. No one's heard from you in years. I started to think you were dead."

"Man, I'm gonna live forever, you know that." Grant shot a thumb toward the other bikers. "I did some merc work for a few years, and after I got in that trouble in Colly, I started hanging with these boys. I don't carry a cell phone anymore. It doesn't work where we go anyway, so it's really only a tracking device for the government." He shifted his gaze back to Amy, looking her up and down. "Damn, Bahía, you found yourself a tough one. She can fight, that's for damn sure. I see why you married her. Someday, maybe I'll find a—"

Grant's mouth clamped shut when the sound of sirens reached them. They were still some distance away, but obviously growing closer. Grant cocked his head to the side, listening intently. "They should be here within ten minutes," he said. "If they run me, they'll take me in, so we need to hit the road."

Baylor nodded his understanding and shook his friend's hand. "Be safe out there."

"If you need anything, call," Grant said, and headed for his Indian parked nearby. His men followed suit, taking their wounded with them. Luckily, none of their men had been killed during the fighting.

As the bikers rode away, Baylor tilted his rifle toward the cult members who were lying prone on the hard ground. "Don't even think about moving," he said.

Amy was about to head for their damaged Jeep to grab an extra pistol magazine when she saw the truck that Irvin had borrowed come barreling back toward the house. It stopped a dozen yards away. Through the cracked windshield, she could see Kari staring wide-eyed at the chaotic scene that surrounded her house.

"Dear Lord," the woman said when she stepped out of the vehicle. "What on earth happened out here? Who did this to them?"

"We got a little help," Amy said, glancing up at the helicopter that circled overhead. "I don't know who called it in or how they got through to anyone, but we definitely had an angel looking out for us."

"Does...does this mean I can leave?" Kari's voice trembled. "Am I free of this place?"

Amy smiled. "Yes, ma'am."

Kari fell to her knees and wept.

CHAPTER 54

Mechant Loup Police Department

As I watched the gunfight unfold on live television on the opposite side of the country, I remained on my knees, too weak to move. Men came and went inside the house at the center of the chaos—taking fire and returning it—and through it all I saw neither hide nor hair of Amy or Baylor. At one point, a man entered the house carrying a brush burner, and I expected to see the building totally engulfed in flames within minutes.

And then something odd happened. A cult member had a biker pinned down behind his motorcycle and was moving in for the kill. Suddenly, the cult member stumbled, lurched forward, and lay still. The helicopter was moving as it filmed, so the footage was shaky, but it appeared the man had been shot from behind, and the shot appeared to have come from the house. Had it been an accident? Or…?

I jumped to my feet as more cult members began to fall. I pointed. "Something's happening!"

"That's Baylor!" Melvin shouted.

I jerked my head to the left, surprised at the sound of his voice. I was even more surprised to see Shade, Regan Steed—one of our other patrol officers—and Mayor Pauline Cain standing amongst us. I had been so absorbed in what I was watching that I hadn't heard the rest of them enter the room.

I turned back toward the television and my emotions almost got the best of me when I saw Amy, Baylor and another armed man exiting the house. Baylor was favoring his right arm, but the trio seemed otherwise unscathed. A group of bikers had rounded up the remaining cult members and were leading them to the center of the clearing near a large outcropping of rock.

Before I could say a word, my cell phone rang. I picked it up, thinking it was Susan, and said, "Are you seeing this?"

There was a pause. "Seeing what?"

"Oh, I'm sorry, Vanessa." I swallowed hard and took a breath, trying to control my voice. "I thought it was Susan. What's up? You're working late."

"I've got a hit on the diaper."

I was confused for a second, but then remembered the dirty diaper Takecia and I had recovered out at the crash site. "What kind of a hit?"

"A fingerprint," she said. "I know y'all said y'all weren't sure if it was related to the case, but I printed it anyway and got an AFIS hit on a left thumb print we recovered. It's for…"

Cheers from all around me drowned out Vanessa's voice, and I looked up to see police cars approaching the compound. I stepped away and cupped a hand over my ear.

"Say again."

"Her name's Lauren Gaubert."

"Lauren Gaubert?" I scowled. "Her name never came up in this investigation. What do you know about her?"

"She was arrested for felony theft twelve years ago," Vanessa said as she read from the woman's criminal history report. "She was twenty-three at the time."

I quickly did the math in my head. She would be thirty-five now.

"Let's see," Vanessa continued, "she was sentenced to five years probation, had to pay a fine of $2,000, and had to do a ton of community service. It looks like she walked the straight and narrow after that. She's got no other record that I could find."

"In what jurisdiction was she charged?"

"Magnolia Parish."

"Do you have a mugshot?"

"I'll send it to your phone now."

"Thanks a bunch!" When I ended the call, I waved Takecia over. I glanced at the television screen briefly and saw a large state police presence. I couldn't make out Amy or Baylor, but I knew they were doing well at that point.

When Takecia had pushed her way through the crowd gathered around the television, I told her we had a break in the case and I explained what I'd just learned from Vanessa. My phone dinged before I could finish telling her everything. I accessed the text message from Vanessa and waited as the mugshot loaded.

"Hey!" Takecia said, stabbing at the screen with her index finger. "That's Laurie from the church!"

I grunted. She was right. Lauren Gaubert was the woman named Laurie that we'd interviewed earlier at the Mechant Life Church. She looked a lot younger in the mugshot, but she was definitely the same woman.

"We need to bring her in right away," I said, shoving my cell phone in my pocket. "She lied when she was acting unsure about whether or not she knew him. She knew exactly who he was—she killed the bastard."

I felt a tap on my shoulder. I turned. It was Dean Fletcher.

"Detective Wolf, did you say Lauren Gaubert?" he asked, a curious expression on his face.

I nodded. "Do you recognize that name?"

"Yes, sir. I was five or so when we used to go to Magnolia Life Church, but I remember this older boy who used to go there. His name was Rory Gaubert and he was always nice to me. He had a sister named Lauren. She was really pretty. I remember being embarrassed every time she came around. Anyway, is she somehow involved in everything?"

I hesitated. While he might still be a potential suspect, I saw no harm in giving him a little information. "Her fingerprint was found at the crime scene," I said. "She might've had a hand in killing Carlos."

Dean nodded, lowering his head. "That makes sense," he muttered, almost too low for me to hear.

"What's that?" I asked, leaning closer.

"It makes sense that she would want him dead," he said in a louder voice. "Carlos used to beat Rory a lot—more than some of the other boys—and he even dunked his head in a toilet once."

"Wait...what?" I asked incredulously. "He dunked the boy's head in a toilet?"

Dean nodded.

"What in the hell for?"

"Because he stood up for me," Dean explained, his voice taking on a surly tone. "Carlos hated it when anyone stood up to him, and he especially hated it when someone defended me. I...I think that's what sent Rory over the edge. That's what did him in."

I glanced at Takecia and then back at Dean. "What do you mean?"

"I saw him at church after the toilet incident, and he was never the same. He used to be proud, defiant, but after that day, it was like he was broken." Dean scrubbed a hand across his eyes. "I feel like it's my fault that he's dead."

I could almost feel my ears perk up. "Rory's dead?"

"Yes, sir. My mom told me he killed himself."

"When was this?" I asked, my mind racing. Not only did we have Lauren Gaubert's fingerprints at the scene, but we now had a clear motive for her wanting to kill Carlos, and we could prove she was lying about not knowing him. Of course, we still needed to establish that she had the opportunity to commit the crime, because a fingerprint on a dirty diaper at a crime scene did not necessarily mean she had killed him. There could be a number of explanations for it being there. She might've randomly driven by that area and thrown the diaper out of her vehicle. She might've stopped to change her kid in the parking lot one night and the diaper fell out in the parking lot. The diaper could've been dropped from a sanitation truck during garbage pickup if, indeed, her residence was along the same route.

While all of these options seemed farfetched and I didn't believe her fingerprints being there was a coincidence, we couldn't take anything for granted. We had more work to do. If we could prove that she had been in the area around the time of the murder, her goose was cooked.

Dean was thoughtful. "I think it was about ten or fifteen years ago. Carlos and my mom had heard about it through the church. Carlos made a joke about the toilet incident when they found out. I remember my mom crying and telling him how cruel he was, but he only laughed at her. Hell, I cried, too. Rory was the only teenager who ever stood up to Carlos."

I gritted my teeth. Did I want to find out if Lauren had killed Carlos? Was this a case I really wanted to solve? I glanced at the television screen and instantly made up my mind. Amy and Baylor could've been killed out at that compound, and whoever had murdered Carlos had set the whole thing in motion. Vigilante justice wasn't justice at all, and it often led to more damage.

As sick a man as Carlos was, I had to pursue his killer and bring that person to justice. The fact that he could no longer hurt another child was just lagniappe.

CHAPTER 55

"Do you see what I see?" Takecia asked when I shut off my headlights and parked along the street in front of Lauren Gaubert's house. It was dark and everything was graveyard quiet on the street.

I nodded. Attached to the side of Lauren's Jeep Wrangler was a standup jack. Of course, we'd been seeing them everywhere since first discovering one was involved with our murder, so we knew it would take more than a jack to wrap up the case. Still, it was one more piece to a puzzle that was shaping up to look like Lauren Gaubert had killed Carlos.

We weren't sure how Lauren had incapacitated Carlos and we figured she must've had an accomplice, so we kept our heads on a swivel as we exited my Tahoe and made our way stealthily through her front yard, keeping a tree between us and the front door as we made our approach.

After getting the information from Vanessa Comeaux earlier, I had received a call from Amy, who had borrowed a SAT phone from one of the state troopers on the scene. She had filled me in on everything that had happened in great detail, and my heart had pounded in my chest as she'd described their harrowing experience down in the basement of Carlos Marcella's house. She and Baylor had come very close to dying, and it was probably the fault of the woman we were about to confront. I knew I needed to keep my emotions in check when we came face to face with her, but I was angry that our officers—our dearest friends—had almost died because of what this woman might have done.

I indicated the right side of the door when we reached it and moved in that direction. Takecia took the left side. Keeping my hand close to my pistol, I depressed the button for the doorbell and waited.

"What if she runs out the back?" Takecia asked, glancing toward the far side of the house.

"I doubt she'll get far," I whispered. "She didn't look like much of an athlete at the church. I doubt she'll be able to jump the fence back there without hurting herself."

Takecia chuckled and nodded.

I rang the bell again.

After a long minute or two, a light came on in the foyer. "Who's there?" called a familiar voice. I recognized it immediately as Laurie from the church. "It's late at night. If you don't state your business, I'm calling the police."

"It is the police," I said. "It's Clint Wolf and Takecia Gayle. We spoke with you at the church this morning."

There was a moment of hesitation, and then the storm door sucked in as the main door opened. Lauren stood there in a thick robe, staring through the glass at us. I could tell she was nervous. The main vein in her neck jumped like there was a frog stuck in her throat.

"Um, what's going on?" she asked. "It's late. I was sleeping. I have work in the morning."

There were bags under her eyes. She might've been in bed, but she hadn't been sleeping. The makeup she'd worn earlier had concealed the stress she was under, but I could now see that she was struggling. Sure, killing Carlos might've sounded righteous at the time she had hatched the plan, but everything changes once it becomes real.

"We need to talk to you about Carlos Marcella," I said. "We need you to come down to the police department with us."

She hesitated. "Who?"

"The man in the picture," I said patiently. "The dead man, remember? We showed you his picture and you said you might've recognized him."

"What's that got to do with me?"

"We'll talk about it down at the station."

"I...do I have to come?"

"If you don't," I said in a low and serious voice, "we're prepared to swear out a warrant for your arrest."

"Arrest?" She gasped and grabbed at her throat. "For what?"

"Second degree murder."

Whatever shade of red was still present on her face after initially seeing us now faded to a sick pale color that made Carlos' deathly complexion look ruby.

"Can...can I at least put on some clothes?"

I glanced past her. "Is anyone in the house with you?"

She shook her head. "I'm alone."

I indicated Takecia with a nod of my head. "She'll accompany you to make sure you don't do anything stupid."

CHAPTER 56

Once Takecia and I had arrived at the police department with Lauren Gaubert, I advised Lauren of her Miranda rights and handed her the rights form to sign. She studied it for a long moment.

"I don't understand why you're asking me about this murder." The color had returned to her face and she seemed to be in better control of herself. "I told you everything I knew this morning. There's nothing more to tell."

"You have a right not to talk to us," I explained, hoping she wouldn't take me up on the offer. "We have a few questions for you. If you want to know what those questions are, sign the form and we'll get started. You can stop talking at any time."

She took a breath and then nodded, signed the form. "I don't know what I can tell y'all, but whatever."

After she'd signed the form and slid it across the desk toward me, I put it to the side and studied her. "Can you tell me what you did on Sunday, beginning with that morning when you woke up and leading up to when you went to bed that night?"

"Oh, that's easy," she said. "I went to church and then went home. I was home all day until Monday morning when I went to work." She turned to Takecia. "You can verify that, because I saw you in the parking lot when I arrived at work yesterday."

"That's right," Takecia said. "I did see you pull up in your Jeep yesterday morning."

Lauren nodded smugly. "Told you."

"What time did you leave the church?"

"Let's see…" She twirled a lock of brown hair with her left index finger. "It must've been around twelve fifteen. The service ended at noon, and I left shortly afterward. There's usually a mad dash to the parking lot right when the service is over, and I like to wait for that to die down."

"Did you stop anywhere on your way home?"

"Nope."

"What time did you get home?"

"A few minutes later." She regarded me with suspicious eyes. "You know where I live, so you know it's not far from the church."

I nodded, but repeated the question.

"Um, a few minutes later." She waved a hand. "Like...twelve-twenty or something. Before twelve-thirty."

"What'd you do when you got home?"

I could tell she was growing impatient with the questioning. "I changed my clothes. Would you like to know what I put on?"

"No, ma'am, but I would like to know what you did after you changed clothes."

"I worked in my garden for a few hours, took a shower, changed again, cooked a frozen pizza, watched television, and then went to bed." She crossed her arms when she'd finished, indicating she was done.

"What's your cell phone number again?" I asked suddenly, randomly, staring down at my notepad.

It caught her off guard, and she blurted it out. I jotted it down and scowled as I studied it.

"What's the matter?" she asked.

"Nothing," I said with a wave of my hand. "And you're sure you never left your house?"

"That's right."

"Not even for a few minutes?"

"Not even for a few minutes."

"If a neighbor said they saw you leave your house at some point during the night, what would you say—?"

"They'd be lying," she said abruptly, cutting me off. "I never left my house."

I decided to change direction. "Are you married, ma'am?"

"No."

"Do you have any children?"

"How can I have children if I'm not married?"

I wanted to explain the many different ways that would've been possible, but refrained. I was wondering how her fingerprint got to be on a diaper if she didn't have children. While it was obvious it was someone else's child, I needed to find out whose child it was.

"Do you have any nieces or nephews?" I asked.

She shook her head.

"Any siblings?"

She hesitated, and then shook her head again. "I used to have a brother. He passed away. It was a long time ago, but it still hurts so much."

I frowned. I felt genuinely sorry for her and hated that I had to interrogate her, but Amy and Baylor had almost been killed because of what she had done—if indeed, it had been her. At this point, I was sure I was on to something, but I needed her to start talking. Since the prints on the ice bags and the vehicle didn't belong to her, it meant she'd had an accomplice, but unless she talked, I might never know who that was.

"Do any of your friends have babies?"

"Why do you keep asking about children and babies?" Her eyes narrowed. "What's going on?"

That she was lying about something was obvious to me, but I had to be careful about pressing too hard. I could sense her frustration and impatience, and it was only a matter of time before she would shut down or ask for a lawyer. I didn't want either of those things to happen.

I gathered up my file folder and stood. Takecia followed suit. Lauren looked surprised and seemed about to rise herself, but I raised a hand.

"Is there anything I can get you?" I asked. "We have to step out for a second, but we'll be right back."

"Um, some water would be nice."

After bringing Lauren a glass of water, I headed for my office and Takecia followed me, a curious expression on her face. Once I was seated behind my desk, I accessed a digital map of Mechant Loup, zoomed in on the parking lot where we had found the diaper, obtained the coordinates for that spot, and then placed a star over it. Next, I inserted a text box and entered the coordinates, Lauren's cell phone number, and a note that read:

Aforementioned cellular number, assigned to mobile device registered to Lauren Gaubert of 333 Library Way, Mechant Loup, LA, was positioned at said coordinates on Monday, Sept. 19 at 03:13 hrs. Degree of certainty: 100%

I leaned back and studied my handiwork. It was a con job, but it just might work. Takecia whistled and nodded as I shoved pink paper into my printer and then hit the *print* key. I studied the official-looking, but unofficial, document one last time and then placed it on top of the file folder. As we hurried to the interview room, I stopped briefly at Lindsey's desk.

"Can you knock on the door and interrupt the interview in five minutes?" I asked. "Call my name and say it's important, that there's been a major break in the case."

She was busy with something on her computer, but she gave a nod to let me know she'd heard me.

When Takecia and I entered, I placed the folder on the desk and took my seat.

"Let's see," I began, idly grabbing my notepad. "Where were we?"

Lauren's eyes were immediately drawn to the pink document that now lay exposed atop the file folder. It was turned away from her, so she couldn't read what I'd printed in the text box, but the map had definitely gotten her attention.

"You mentioned watching television," I said, trying to remember what might've been playing on Sunday evening. I didn't have time for television, but I knew a simple internet search would help me verify or disprove whatever she claimed to have been watching. "What show did you watch?"

For a very brief moment, I could see the panic in her eyes, but then it faded away and a subtle smile formed at the corners of her mouth. "I watched the latest episodes of Ozark on Netflix," she said smugly. "For the third time. It's the final season and I'm having a hard time letting go of it, so I've been watching it over and over."

I cursed inwardly, as there was no way I could disprove what she had said. Before I could ask another question, there was a sharp rap on the door.

"Clint!" Lindsey called excitedly. "I need you to come quick! There's been a break in the case, and it's a major one!"

Takecia and I jumped to our feet and rushed out of the room, leaving Lauren alone with her thoughts and the pink slip that lay staring at her from across the desk.

CHAPTER 57

Takecia and I went straight to the observatory room, where we could watch what Lauren was doing through a two-way mirror. Lindsey hesitated in the doorway. I waved her forward. With an excited gasp, she rushed inside to join us.

"Regan's watching the radio and phone," she whispered.

I only nodded. My focus was on Lauren, whose focus was on that pink piece of paper beckoning from the opposite side of the desk. She kept glancing from the paper to the door. After a full minute or two, her hand shot out and snatched up the page. She read over it quickly. As she did so, I could see her eyes widen.

"She's falling for it," Takecia said in a low voice.

"She didn't act alone," I explained. "Lindsey, I need you to work your magic. I want to know everything you can find out about her on social media."

"I was already on it," she said. "She's got two pages—one old and one new. The new one's privacy settings are high, so I haven't been able to get much information other than what restaurants she recommends and what music she likes. I'm about to start checking her old page. If she lists her friends and family on the old one, maybe I can find out more about her that way. People are always posting things and tagging their family members."

Before I could respond, Lauren tossed the pink sheet back to the desk and reached for her pocket, no doubt going for her cell phone.

"Let's go," I hissed, and led the way back into the interview room. When I stepped inside, I could've sworn I'd walked in on Lauren using the bathroom. She shrieked and threw up her hands.

Her cell phone went tumbling through the air, bounced off the desk, and landed at my feet.

I studied Lauren for a long moment, wanting the tension to build in the room, before I bent and picked up the cell phone. The screen was still locked, so she hadn't been able to make any calls or text anyone. While it was good that she hadn't alerted anyone, I desperately wanted to know who she wanted to contact. That person would most likely be her accomplice.

"What's going on?" I asked, taking my seat. I placed Lauren's cell phone on top of the pink slip. I was not surprised that she didn't object or demand to get it back. She knew she was busted. I could see it in her eyes. She realized she had no bargaining power. When she said nothing, I repeated my question.

"Nothing's going on." She swallowed hard. When she spoke again, her voice trembled. "I was just checking the time. I'd like to go home now. I have to work in the morning."

I sighed. "That's not gonna happen. You see, we have reason to believe you murdered Carlos, and we know you didn't act alone. Someone else handled the bags of ice."

Her shoulders sagged to the point that she almost slid out of her chair. I let the silence grow in the room.

"Who was it?" I asked after a minute had ticked by. "Who helped you kill Carlos?"

She opened her mouth to speak, but then closed it again. She licked her lips and swallowed several times. Finally, in a hoarse voice, she said, "I...I want a lawyer. I don't want to make a statement anymore."

"Very well." Although I sounded like I didn't care, I was cursing on the inside as I gathered up my case file and her cell phone. I needed her statement. I needed to know who had helped her, and I needed a confession or more evidence. Her fingerprint on a diaper just wouldn't cut it. While the cell phone trick had worked to an extent, it had also backfired and caused her to shut down.

Sure, I could now apply for a search warrant for her cell phone coordinates, but they would be almost useless. She lived so close to the scene that her cell phone would've pinged off of the same towers from both locations. And without her passcode, I wasn't getting inside the phone to view her messages—warrant or no warrant.

"We'll be right back," I said, and led the way toward the radio room.

"I really thought she would break," Takecia said. "She looked ready to talk."

"I think she would have, but she's protecting someone," I said. "Someone very close to her."

"I bet her dad was pretty angry at Carlos," she mused.

I nodded as we approached Lindsey and Regan, who were huddled over Lindsey's computer. Neither woman looked up.

Shade was on patrol and the last I'd seen of Melvin he was keeping Dean distracted in the break room. I still couldn't positively rule Dean out as a suspect, but even if I could, I figured he might be helpful. I also wanted to arrange for Amy to get his mother on the phone so they could talk. I knew he would like that.

"What do we do now?" Takecia asked.

I dropped the file folder to the desk and rubbed my face with both hands. I was tired and exhausted from the rollercoaster of emotions that had haunted us earlier. Truth be told, I wanted to go home and get some sleep—forget Carlos Marcella ever existed—but I knew I couldn't.

"Well, we can apply for an arrest warrant," I said. "The judge will probably sign it, as there's enough probable cause to arrest Lauren, but we don't have enough to convict her. We'll need to keep digging." I turned to Lindsey. "Got anything, Detective Savoie?"

"I'm still working on it," she called over her shoulder.

I walked over to where she was pecking away at her keyboard. She pointed to the screen, where a social media profile picture of Lauren Gaubert was displayed, but she wasn't alone. Sitting beside her in a boat was Rory Gaubert, and there was a caption on the photo mentioning how much she missed her brother.

I frowned as I read her heartfelt message. She didn't mention Carlos in the post, but she did allude to some form of abuse and how it had contributed to her brother's waning mental health. They were both much younger in the picture and the post was from five years earlier.

"This is her old profile," Lindsey explained, "and the picture of her and her brother is the last thing she posted to it. While that doesn't help us much, the fact that this profile is public helps me go back through her old friends. I couldn't find anyone with the last name of Gaubert, but she tagged some friends in a bunch of photos."

"What does *tagged* mean?" I asked. I had played that joke on Amy once and it had worked, but Lindsey didn't fall for it.

"If you don't know what it means by now," she said with a smirk, "you don't deserve to know."

We all laughed and watched as her fingers continued to fly across the keyboard. I glanced up at the television screen, but nothing more was happening in Sandy Knobs. They were showing the same footage over and over while commentators were trying to tell their viewers what they had just seen, as though the footage hadn't spoken for itself. I shook my head. I didn't like people trying to tell me what I had just seen or heard. I was quite capable of processing that material on my own.

"I'm searching through the profiles of Lauren's friends now to see what I can find out," Lindsey was saying. "Most of her friends have public profiles, so it's giving me a backdoor glimpse into her life."

"Can you go back to her old profile and sort through her pictures?" I asked. "Check Father's Day and Mother's Day to see if she posted anything on those days. We might find out who her parents are."

"Good idea," Lindsey muttered, and backed out of the profile she'd been perusing. When she returned to the older profile, she moved to the photo folder and clicked on it. She began scrolling through the photos, looking for anything that might stand out. Sure enough, she came to a photo with Lauren and an older woman with a caption that read: *Best Mom Ever*. Lindsey moved the cursor until it hovered over the picture of the older woman. A bubble displaying the name *Denise Gaubert* appeared over the picture. Lindsey clicked on it and was taken to another user account.

I stiffened when I saw the profile picture associated with the new account. It was of a shirtless baby boy in a high chair with his face covered in oatmeal. Beneath the tray, and in plain view, was his diaper, and it was covered in pictures of the cartoon Batman and Robin.

Takecia had noticed the diaper too and slugged my arm. "That's the same diaper we found at the scene—the one that caused the crash!"

I laughed at her reference to our earlier joke about the reason for the diaper being at the scene, but only briefly. "Lindsey, we need to find out whose baby that is."

"I'm on it," she said. The image immediately disappeared, a page displaying some profile information popped up, and then more pictures came into view. The speed at which pages appeared and disappeared was blinding, but not so fast that I didn't instantly recognize the woman in a photo that flashed by.

"Lindsey, wait!" I said. "Go back to the picture of the woman holding the baby."

She stopped and maneuvered back to where she had recently

been. When the picture of the woman and the same baby from earlier filled the entire monitor, I leaned forward and tapped it triumphantly.

"That's Lauren's accomplice!"

CHAPTER 58

Midnight...

It had only taken thirty minutes for me to type up a search warrant for Lauren's sister's residence and her fingerprints, but it had been another hour before a detective from Magnolia Parish named Rachael Bowler could present it to a judge in her parish and get it signed. While waiting for that to happen, I had also obtained a warrant from a judge in our jurisdiction to search Lauren's house and cell phone. I had put Melvin and Regan on that search, and they had taken Lauren out to her residence to search for drugs that could incapacitate a person, Carlos' wallet, his cell phone, the standup jack, and anything else that might be related to our case.

After Melvin and Regan had left the police department, Takecia and I had traveled to Magnolia Parish and met with Detective Bowler at her office. It was eleven-forty-five before the judge signed the warrant, and we were finally making our approach to the target residence.

The fact that Lauren had earlier denied having any living siblings—along with the diaper from the crime scene matching the kind her sister used—was all the proof we needed to develop her sister as a suspect, but I wasn't ready to apply for arrest warrants just yet. Although I could demonstrate that Lauren had lied to protect her sister, whose fingerprints would surely match those found on the bags of ice and the rear of Carlos' truck, I still wanted more. I wanted to know how they had gone about luring Carlos away to kill him, and I wanted to know why. However, that would only come if one of them confessed. Since Lauren had already asked for a lawyer, we couldn't question her anymore about the case, so that meant her sister was our only hope. The trick would be getting her to talk without pushing her to invoke her right to an attorney.

"How do you want to approach her?" Detective Bowler asked when Takecia and I had slipped out of my Tahoe and met her and two patrol deputies at the front of her unmarked unit.

"If you don't mind, I'd like for Takecia and me to knock on her door and see if she'll agree to talk to us before showing her the search warrant," I explained. "I'd like her to feel at ease with us and get her talking. If we show her the warrant and start interrogating her, she might lawyer up."

Rachael nodded her agreement and took a portable radio from one of the deputies. "We'll wait here on the street," she said, handing me the radio. "Call if you need us."

I thanked her and set off across the damp grass of a neighboring yard. Other than the sounds of mosquitoes buzzing in our ears and a dog barking in the distance, all was quiet in the neighborhood. Standing each to one side of the door, I gave Takecia a nod and waited as she rang the doorbell. We could hear the chimes echoing throughout the house. The front door was made of textured glass, and I could see into the foyer. A dim light was glowing from somewhere deep inside the house.

Within seconds, a shadowy figure approached the door. As the woman drew closer, I recognized her as Mia Foret, a woman we now knew as Mia Gaubert Foret—Lauren Gaubert's sister and her most likely accomplice in the murder of Carlos Marcella.

Mia recognized us through the glass and opened the door. She wore only a thin T-shirt and loose-fitting shorts, but she made no attempt to cover up. She was obviously perplexed to see us on her front stoop.

"What's going on?" she asked hesitantly. "It's past midnight. Why are y'all here? Is something wrong?"

"It's your sister," I said slowly. "Can we come inside and talk?"

"Lauren?" Her eyes switched from mine to Takecia's, and then back. "Is she okay? Was she in an accident?"

"No, she's fine," I explained, "but she's being arrested."

"Arrested?" She echoed the word loudly. "For what?"

"Can we come inside and talk?" I repeated. "I'll explain everything, but I don't want to do it out here where we might disturb the neighbors."

With a reluctant nod, she stepped aside and let us through the entrance. She shut the door behind us and I waited for her to lead the way into the house. She didn't stop in the living room. Instead, she took us to the kitchen, where she sat at a glass table and folded her arms in front of her.

"What happened?"

I sat across from her and Takecia took the seat to my right.

"She'll be going to jail for murdering Carlos Marcella."

"Murder?" She tried to sound shocked, but it was obvious she wasn't. "But…I don't understand."

While it was legal for police officers to lie to suspects in order to elicit confessions, I didn't like doing it. If I happened to be wrong and they knew it, then I would lose credibility. If they knew I was fishing, they would not feel compelled to talk. At the moment, I needed Mia to start talking, so I decided to offer some baiting questions.

"What would you say if I told you she confessed to murdering Carlos?" I offered. "Would that make any sense to you?"

Mia opened her mouth and closed it. Shaking her head, she said, "I…I just can't believe it. There's no way she killed anyone."

"Can you think of any reason why she would confess to killing someone if she didn't do it?"

"No, not at all." She shook her head for emphasis. "That's so unlike her."

"Your sister certainly doesn't look like the killing type, but I've seen stranger things." I studied her carefully. "When's the last time you saw Lauren?"

"Oh, wow, let's see…" Her brow furrowed as she stared up at the ceiling. "It must've been last week sometime, probably Wednesday or Thursday."

"Did you see her this past Sunday?"

Mia shook her head.

"Did you talk to her on Sunday?" Before she could answer, I waved a dismissive hand. "If you can't remember, that's okay. We've got detectives searching her cell phone, so we'll be able to find out."

Although Lauren's cell phone was locked and she had refused to give us the code to search it, Mia didn't know that, and I saw the color drain from her face.

"I…um, I might've talked with her on Sunday." She licked her lips. "I don't really remember. We usually talk on the phone every day."

"Has she said anything about seeing Carlos Marcella lately?" I asked.

"No, sir."

"Strange." I furrowed my brow and glanced down at my notes. I was quiet for a long moment, wanting Mia to feel the pressure. Finally, I asked, "Do you know if Lauren has a best friend? Like, if she wanted to kill someone, who would help her?"

Mia shifted in her seat. That she was uncomfortable was plain to see. Although it was cool in her house, there was a line of sweat on her upper lip. "I don't know."

"We know she committed the murder, but we also know she didn't act alone, because we found two sets of prints at the scene." I stared intently at her, and noticed her hands slowly ball into fists, as though trying to hide her prints from my view. I pressed on. "She refuses to give up her accomplice and I don't think it's fair for her to go down alone. Do you have any idea who this other person might've been?"

"No, sir."

Are you saying you're willing to let your sister take the rap for this? I wanted to ask, but didn't. Instead, I asked if Lauren had a boyfriend.

Mia shook her head. I wasn't surprised. It wasn't a boyfriend who had helped Lauren, or any other friend. No, it had to be Mia—right? I remembered how surprised Mia had acted when we'd shown up at her florist shop to ask about Carlos. Either she was a great actress or she'd had nothing to do with the murder. I mulled it over for a second, but then dismissed the doubt in my mind. She was the link to the Magnolia Life Church and her child's diaper was the link to the crime scene. It had to be her.

I suddenly frowned as I remembered her baby, glanced around the room. Where was the child? No doubt he was sleeping. Who would care for him once we took Mia into custody? And where was his father? Surely, the man wouldn't have slept through the doorbell and the commotion we were making.

"Is your husband home?" I asked.

"No, sir. He's offshore."

"How long's he been gone?"

"Almost two weeks. He'll be back on Friday." She shook her head. "I still can't believe my sister would do something like this. It's so not like her."

I nodded thoughtfully, glanced down at my notes. It was time to make my move. Mia was starting to relax. She didn't think we had anything on her. She thought she was in the clear.

"Mrs. Foret," I began, looking her directly in the eyes, "is it your fingerprints we found on the bags of ice?"

"No, sir," she said quickly—too quickly. She instantly realized her mistake.

CHAPTER 59

"Wait, wait, wait!" Mia stammered. "That's not what I meant to say. I mean, what bags of ice are you talking about? I don't know anything about any bags of ice."

I sighed and pulled the search warrant from my case file. I slid it across the table. "Ma'am, we've got a search warrant for your fingerprints. We've also got a search warrant for your house. It's over. You helped Lauren kill Carlos Marcella, and y'all did it because he's responsible for your brother's death."

Mia's mouth fell open as she studied the warrant. "I...I don't know what you're talking about."

"It might be better if you just explained everything that happened and throw yourselves at the mercy of the court," I suggested. "We can prove Carlos was a piece of shit. While that didn't give you and your sister the right to kill him, it might weigh heavily in your favor when it comes down to the actual charges you'll be facing."

Mia was quiet for a long moment. Finally, tears began to slide down her cheeks. Her head hung low. "What about my baby?"

I wanted to tell her that she should've thought about that before bringing her little boy on a joyride to murder a man, but thought it would be cruel.

"Your baby will most likely live with your husband until you get out of prison."

Her head shot up. "You think I'll get out someday? You don't think I'll spend the rest of my life in there?"

"I can't make any promises or predictions," I cautioned. "I'm just saying I think this case is a little unique. Never before have I worked a case where a murder victim had been so cruel to so many people. I can't see a jury having much sympathy for him."

Mia nodded and wiped the tears away. "Okay, I'll tell you whatever you want to know—if you think it'll help."

"It's not about what I think," I said, suddenly feeling sorry for her and her situation. "You have to make this decision on your own. If you'd like to speak with an attorney before making any statements, that's your right."

She shook her head. "I'm ready to talk. It's been eating me up since it happened. Every time I close my eyes, I see his ugly face. Maybe if I talk about it, I'll finally get some sleep."

"We've got some officers waiting outside to search your house," I explained. "We'll let them in while you tell me what happened."

"What're y'all looking for?" she asked. "Will it disturb Rory?"

I sighed inwardly as I realized she had named her son after her brother. "No, ma'am, they won't disturb him. We're looking for Carlos' wallet, cell phone, and any other property he might've had on him."

"It's all at Lauren's house," she said quietly. "I wanted nothing brought here because of Rory."

"We'll have them search your house just the same," I explained, and gave Takecia a nod as I pulled out a rights form. Takecia stepped outside briefly to let Detective Bowler know it was clear to enter and search. When she returned, I advised Mia of her rights and we began questioning her.

"Just start from the beginning and tell me what happened," I said. "All I ask is that you tell me the truth and you leave nothing out."

"Everything actually began about twelve years ago." She took a haggard breath and exhaled forcefully. "Lauren and I have been planning to find Carlos and kill him for as long as Rory's been dead. And we would've done it, too, but Lauren got arrested and ruined everything."

I cocked my head to the side. "I don't understand."

"We found out from somebody in church that Carlos was living at this commune in Nevada," she explained. "I had a fast car and Lauren had a good job, and we hatched a plan to go find him and kill him. We were young, but we were old enough to know we didn't want to spend the rest of our lives in prison, so we knew we needed to make it look like an accident."

"How were y'all planning on doing that?"

"We figured that when we found him, we would drug him and then drown him in a toilet—just like he tried to drown Rory in a toilet."

I was struck by the nonchalant way in which Mia described their plan. I could tell she really hated Carlos, and I didn't blame her one bit.

"What did Lauren's arrest have to do with the plan to kill him?" I asked. "How'd that ruin everything?"

"She bonded out of jail, and part of the condition of bail was that she not leave town." She shook her head. "I couldn't do it alone. I needed her help."

"What was the plan?"

"For some reason, Carlos was always fascinated with me," Mia explained. "I would often catch him staring at my breasts. He would make lewd comments when no one could hear him. He would never discipline me at school, even when I deserved it. In fact, one time when another teacher heard me curse out another student, he took me into the sanctuary—that was where he would spank the kids—and told me to pretend he had hit me, but he promised he would never do anything to hurt me. He said I was his favorite and he would take me away if he could."

Mia paused and shuddered. A sick paleness fell over her. "That animal gave me the creeps," she said. "I never told my mom or dad about any of it. I thought my dad would confront him and then something bad would happen to my dad. So, for the most part, I ignored it. But after my brother died…"

Her voice trailed off and she stared down at her hands.

"You decided you would use the attraction against him," I said, finishing her thought.

"Oh, yeah," she said. "If he wanted me, I would offer myself to him—and then we would kill him."

"Is that what happened?"

She nodded. "Like I said, we never could carry out our murder plot because Lauren got arrested and then life got in the way. But when he showed up at church Sunday, I knew we had to do something."

"Wait—so you did see him at church?"

"Yes, sir." She frowned. "I'm sorry for lying to you. I was scared—hell, I'm still scared. I don't wanna go to prison."

"Go on," I coaxed when she didn't continue. "What happened?"

"I was late, as usual, and was trying to get my baby out of his car seat when I saw Carlos walking through the parking lot. Our eyes locked and it startled me. I…I just kinda froze in place. He immediately smiled and walked right up to me, so I went along with it. He asked how I had been and if the baby was mine. After we talked for a few seconds, I asked him why he was there. He said he'd heard that Dean was back at church and he wanted to reunite with what he called his *Prodigal Son*. I lied. I told him I hadn't seen Dean."

"Why'd you do that?" I asked.

"I knew how much Dean hated him and I knew he would make Dean's life miserable."

That made sense. I asked her to go on.

"As he stood there talking to me, I was overcome with this feeling of intense rage. Not just for what he had done to my brother, but for what he had done to everyone else—and for what I was certain he was still doing to other kids." She took a trembling breath and blew it out through her mouth. "I decided at that moment to carry out our plan. I flirted a little with him. I was really subtle about it, but he understood. All it took was for me to say that my husband was offshore and I was lonely, and how he looked just as young as he did when he was the principal. He did the rest."

I cocked my head to the side. "Meaning?"

"Meaning, he invited himself over to my house," she explained. "The biggest part of the plan was getting him there. The rest was easy. I told him where I lived and that I would cook the best dinner he'd ever eaten. He said he missed seafood, so I told him I had some shrimp in the freezer and that I could make an etouffee. He was real excited, and that got me even angrier. He had to have known what happened to my brother, but he never once said he was sorry or asked about him."

"Is that why you killed him?" I asked. "Was it for revenge?"

"No, I didn't do it for revenge." Her jaw was set and there was a look of determination in her eyes that I had to admire. "I did it to prevent more abuse. Every child that comes into contact with that animal is doomed beforehand—only they and their parents won't realize it until it's too late."

CHAPTER 60

Takecia and I listened as Mia Foret continued explaining how she and her sister had killed Carlos Marcella.

"I was wearing a short skirt and a low-cut blouse. I wanted his mind on me and nothing else." She shifted uneasily in her seat. "Anyway, we had agreed to meet at my place for eleven o'clock. I told him it would have to be late because of my nosy neighbors, and I told him I'd leave the garage door open for him. I told him to park inside, because I didn't need anyone telling my husband a strange man had visited in the middle of the night. He arrived a little later than eleven, but he parked in the garage like I'd planned. When I heard him drive up, I immediately went out and closed the garage door."

My heart was thumping in my chest as I listened to her story. "This was pretty daring of you," I said. "Carlos was a dangerous man."

"I know, but I knew it had to be done. He had to be stopped."

I couldn't argue with her about Carlos having to be stopped, and part of me didn't blame her for what she had done. However, the cascading effects of her actions had almost taken the lives of two people very close to me, so I remained unhappy with the whole situation.

"What if he would've attacked and raped you?" Takecia interjected. "You might've been killed."

"We were prepared for that and, looking back now, it might've actually been better. You see, Lauren was waiting in the other room with my pistol. If he would've attacked me, she would've shot him dead, we could've claimed self-defense, and we wouldn't be in this mess." She paused and scrunched up her face. "Of course, I don't think I would've called the police. I think we still would've dumped his body."

"Why's that?" I asked.

"How on earth would I explain to my husband that I was having dinner alone in our home with a strange man in the middle of the night dressed the way I was?"

It was another good point, so I only nodded and asked her to continue.

"Well, I had dinner ready for when he arrived. He gave me a hug when he first came inside, and he held it for a long time, moaning and saying how good it felt to finally have me in his arms. He said he'd been dreaming about that moment since he first saw me, which was sick, because I was a teenager back then. He even smelled my hair, which really creeped me out." She shuddered as she apparently replayed the scene in her mind. "Anyway, I gently pushed him off and told him he'd get his dessert after dinner, and that I'd worked really hard preparing a meal for him. He said he'd been eating fast-food for the past few days, and that he was craving a home-cooked meal. I told him to sit at the head of the table, where he belonged, and then I set out to serve him."

"You knew what you were doing, didn't you?" I asked, studying her with a critical eye. A simple thing like telling Carlos he belonged at the head of the table would've stroked his ego so loudly that he would've been oblivious to anything else happening around him.

"I played him like the fool that he was," she acknowledged. "He was saying inappropriate things about my legs and breasts while I was serving him, but I only giggled. I know how to pull his strings. He never suspected anything. I put his plate in front of him and he began eating immediately, even before I'd served myself. He was almost finished by the time I'd taken my first bite. He asked for a second plate, so I stopped eating and served him again."

"Aren't you leaving something out?" I asked. "The part where you poisoned him?"

She sighed, nodded. "I drugged his food. I don't know if it'll help my case or not, but he didn't feel anything when he died. I gave him just enough to render him unconscious, so when he drowned, he didn't even know it was happening."

"What'd you use?"

"Methylmorphine."

"What's that?"

"Codeine," she explained. "It's a pain medication. I had crushed up some codeine phosphate tablets and put the powder in the salt shaker before he got here. When my back was to him, I sprinkled a lot of it in his food. I stirred it around really good to mix it in with the etouffee so he wouldn't taste anything strange."

I glanced toward the countertop. "Do you still have the salt shaker?"

She shook her head. "I gave everything to Lauren. She should have it with Carlos' wallet and phone. She lives alone, so she doesn't have to worry about anyone stumbling upon something like that."

"Where'd you get the codeine?" I asked. "You can't get that without a prescription."

"It was left over from when Lauren got arrested," she said. "Back when we first planned to kill Carlos, she was working at a pharmacy and stole a handful of drugs that we wanted to use to knock him out, but someone at the pharmacy noticed some drugs were missing. They suspected her right away and she was arrested a few days later. She was charged with felony theft. It was in the newspaper and everything. They told her if she returned what she'd stolen they wouldn't charge her with the drug possession, so she brought back everything except the one packet of codeine tabs that she'd already given to me."

"Did they notice it was missing?"

Mia nodded. "But she swore up and down she'd returned everything she'd stolen and that it must've been someone taking advantage of the fact that she had been busted. I guess they believed her, because they didn't charge her with the drug possession."

"And that's what you used to incapacitate Carlos?"

"Yes, sir. It was actually easy—much easier than I would've thought."

I leaned back in my chair and crossed my arms. I considered all the times I'd eaten food that others had prepared. Never had I given consideration to anyone poisoning or drugging my food. Now that I thought about it, I realized just how vulnerable I was, and it was frightening to think that my next bite of food could be my last. Shaking off the feeling, I asked Mia what happened next.

"It was while I was serving his second plate that Carlos started to slur his speech. He said something was wrong and he tried to stand up, but he lost his balance and sat back down. He knocked his glass over and it fell to the floor and broke. That's when Lauren came out from the back room holding my pistol."

"Did he suspect he had been poisoned?" I asked.

"I'm not sure what he thought at first, but we wanted him to know what was happening," she said. "We weren't sure how long he would be alert, so Lauren pointed the pistol at him and told him we were gonna drown him like he had tried to drown Rory. She told him that he would never hurt another woman or child again. She had heard all the disgusting things he'd said to me, so she also told him to take a good look at me, because my ass and breasts were the last he would ever see."

"What'd he do? Did he try to fight?"

"He struggled several times to stand up, but he ended up falling on the ground. He was very drowsy, but it took him a long time to pass out. He fought it hard." Suddenly, and for the first time since we'd arrived at Mia's house, she smiled. "He was terrified. He begged for his life—well, at least it sounded like he was begging. We could barely understand him. I'm not gonna lie, it felt good to watch that pompous asshole beg for his life. I didn't feel an ounce of sorrow for him, and I don't regret what we did, except for the fact that I may never see Rory again as a free woman."

I nodded and listened as she continued describing how they had loaded Carlos in the back of his truck after he finally passed out.

"He was still breathing, but he was out like a light," she explained. "We covered him with a blanket and then headed for this place that Lauren had scouted. It was next to some business on the side of the bayou not far from where she lives. She said it would be the perfect place to run the truck in the bayou and make it look like an accident. I drove Carlos' truck and Lauren drove my van. Thank God we thought to put the ice in an Igloo, because there was a car at that business and we had to wait a couple of hours for it to leave."

I rubbed my chin, remembering Ali Bridges saying she had been at the newsroom until two in the morning, and then I asked, "At what point did you get the bags of ice?"

"Oh, I got them earlier in the day—long before Carlos showed up at my house. I had everything ready to go when he stepped foot in my garage."

"Where'd you get the idea to use the ice?" I asked. "It was brilliant. We almost missed it."

She shrugged. "I've thought of a million ways to kill that man and get away with it, and that was just one of them. Right when I saw him in that church parking lot, I knew what Lauren and I would do. They say when you make a plan God laughs, because things never go the way you expect them to go. Well, God must've wanted him dead, too, because everything went according to plan. Once we dragged him into the driver's seat, I lifted the back of the truck with the jack from Lauren's Jeep, cranked up the engine, put the truck in gear, placed the ice bags on the accelerator, and then gave the truck a shove. The rest, as they say, is history."

I was thoughtful. "Where was Rory when all of this was going down?"

Mia hesitated for a long moment—too long. She tore her eyes away from mine and stared up as the two deputies walked by, heading toward the front door. Detective Bowler was a few steps behind them. She paused and shook her head to let me know they hadn't found anything. I turned back toward Mia.

"Rory was in the van, wasn't he?" I pressed. "In fact, Lauren changed his diaper at some point while all this was happening."

"No," Mia said. "He—"

"He what?" I interrupted. "He stayed home alone? No matter how you slice it, you endangered your baby. You either left him here alone, which is neglect, or you took him to a murder. Which is it?"

Mia swallowed. She shifted in her chair again. Finally, she licked her lips and spoke. "Okay, look, he was in the van, but he was only at the scene for a second while Lauren helped me get Carlos in the front seat. We never took him out of his car seat."

"At what point did she change his diaper?"

"I...I don't know. If she did, it must've been earlier when I was driving around waiting for that red car to leave. I know she pulled in at the park for a while, but I didn't ask if she changed Rory." She scowled. "How would you know if she changed my son or—"

Suddenly, the stillness of the outdoors erupted in automatic gunfire, and the glass from one of the front windows in the kitchen exploded into tiny shards as a bullet whipped through and blew a tiny hole in the cabinet behind Mia.

CHAPTER 61

As quickly as the automatic gunfire had begun, it was over...but only for a few seconds. I had just jumped across the table and taken Mia to the ground when the gunman started firing again. A few *popping* sounds could be heard from the front of the house, and I imagined these shots were coming from the handguns of one of the deputies.

Detective Bowler, who had thrown a chair through the front living room window and shut off the interior lights, called for backup and reported that they had one officer down with another pinned under heavy gunfire.

Mia struggled under me, screaming for her baby, but I didn't let her go. I dragged her squirming body across the kitchen floor and toward the opposite side of a thick island.

"Stay down!" I shouted. Movement to my right drew my attention and I saw Takecia low-crawling across the kitchen floor. She was headed toward a hallway, beyond which I could hear the terrified screams of a small child. "Takecia's going after Rory. She'll take care of him."

That seemed to calm Mia a little, and it allowed me the opportunity to move off of her and toward the edge of the island, pistol in hand. From the sounds of it, the shooter had switched from full-auto to semi-auto, and was now delivering select fire to various targets along the front of the house. Every now and then a bullet would break a window and splat against a far wall inside the residence. It served as a reminder for us to keep our heads down.

I was just easing my head out from behind the kitchen wall and into the foyer when I saw a bloody hand reach into the open doorway. I scooted farther out and saw that it was one of the deputies from earlier. His eyes fixed on me and he opened his mouth to speak, but a sick *splat* sounded and he let out a throaty gasp. His body relaxed and he lay still. I heard the gunshot a split second later.

"He's a hundred yards out!" Detective Bowler called from the living room. "I think he's in the trees across the street. Can anyone see him?"

I scooted across the foyer and into the living room, and it was then that I realized why Detective Bowler had busted out the window and killed the lights. She was stretched out in a prone position atop the coffee table and was aiming her pistol in the direction of the broken window.

"Both deputies are down," I called from where I was perched on the floor just beyond the foyer and inside the living room. "What do you need me to do?"

"Can you draw his fire?" she asked. "I think I've got him, but I need to see his muzzle flash to be sure. I'll only get one shot at this."

I gingerly stuck my head from behind the foyer wall and peered out the doorway. I could see the first deputy in the driveway near a squad car, and the second was several feet from me where he had just been shot. Directly across the street, I only saw a house.

"I can see a light under the carport of a blue house across the street," I said. "Where is he in relation to that house?"

"He's to our right, between two houses. His position is set way back toward the trees. This'll be a long shot, but I can get him if I'm sure of his location."

"Get ready," I said, taking a deep breath. "I'll rush out the door and dive behind that oak tree in the front yard."

"Go fast, because his sights are locked on the doorway."

I nodded, said a prayer under my breath, and told her I was going. Just as the words left my mouth, I sprang from the ground like a panther pouncing on its prey. My legs pumped three or four times and then I was out the doorway and into the warm night air. Instead of running down the steps of the stoop, I dove off the platform. Just as I went airborne, I heard a bullet splatter against the brick wall to my left. Before the sound of the bad guy's shot could reach me, I heard a shot from Rachael's Glock 22.

As the authoritative bark of Rachael's .40 caliber bullet faded into the night, I landed headlong on the palms of my hands and collapsed my arms into a ninja roll. I could feel the coolness from the damp grass seep through the back of my shirt, and for a brief moment I thought that was the last thing I'd ever feel. But then I rolled to my knees and scrambled behind the oak tree. Everything was deathly still except for the pounding of my heart and the distant sound of sirens heading in our direction.

After several long and tense seconds, I heard Rachael's voice again. "I got him."

I stood shakily to my feet and joined Rachael in cautiously checking on the two deputies. They were both injured badly, but alive. We moved them out of the line of potential fire and waited until an ambulance arrived to attend to them. Once they were being cared for, I followed Rachael across the street. Just in case the gunman was still alive, we took advantage of every piece of cover and concealment between our location and his, but when we arrived at the tree line, we realized it had been unnecessary.

We found a tall man with grayish hair slumped over an M-16. He was in a seated position with his back to a tree. His head hung low, so we couldn't readily identify him, but we could tell by the thick red drops of blood that fell through the beam from Rachael's flashlight that he was a goner.

"I can't believe you shot him in the head with a pistol from 100 yards," I said incredulously. "How in the hell did you do that?"

"A great man once said that 100 yards is just a distance," she explained, "like age is just a number."

"Who said that?"

"London Carter, my former sniper leader." She sighed. "He up and left us. Moved to Tennessee."

"I know London well," I said, my voice betraying my excitement. "He saved my bacon more than once."

"When he was here, he'd have us making head shots out to 100 yards with every type of gun we owned, including an old snub nose revolver I got from my grandpa. You'd be surprised what you can do with a handgun."

Holstering her pistol, Rachael reached forward, grabbed a handful of the man's hair, and lifted his head until his face came into view. There was a dark bullet hole through his left eyebrow, and a surprised expression on his face.

"Do you recognize him?" she asked.

"Not at all." I shook my head. "But it can't be a coincidence that he's here."

Careful not to disturb the scene, Rachael squatted beside the man and eased a wallet from his back pocket. She flipped it open and read the name on the driver's license. "Lester Smith, from right here in

Magnolia."

I scowled. When I'd spoken with Amy earlier, she'd said that a man named Lester had contacted Carlos to tell him that Dean was attending Magnolia Life Church again. I passed that information on to Rachael, and surmised that he was there to seek vengeance for Carlos' murder.

"Makes sense," she said.

After calling for one of the responding deputies to stand guard near the body, Rachael and I headed back to the house, where we met with Takecia and Mia in the driveway. Mia was holding her son and Takecia was on her cell phone. When Takecia ended the call, she pulled me aside.

"Melvin and Regan found Carlos' cell phone and his wallet," she explained. "They also found a half empty pack of codeine tablets and a salt shaker just like Mia described."

"Did they recover the jack from Lauren's Jeep?" I was watching Mia as we talked. She was speaking softly to her son and there was resignation in her eyes.

"Yep."

Rachael joined us as the first ambulance raced off with one of the deputies. A second ambulance had arrived and they were prepping the second deputy for transport to the hospital.

"I don't know how that bastard didn't kill them. He had them dead to rights." She shook her head and then indicated Mia Foret. "Did you arrest her yet?"

I shook my head.

"Wanna do it in your jurisdiction?" Although it was a question, it was also a suggestion. "I've got my hands full here, and I know it'll streamline things for you."

"Sure." I pulled out one of my business cards and handed it to her. "I'm sure your shoot team will need a statement from us at some point. This is my cell number."

She took it and handed me one of hers. "I'll let you know what I turn up on this Lester Smith idiot."

CHAPTER 62

Takecia and I drove Mia Foret to her parent's residence so she could ask them to watch her baby. They had lots of questions, but Mia didn't tell them much. She promised to explain everything to them later. It was a sad moment watching her say goodbye to her baby for what could've been the last time as a free woman. It made me think of Grace and my little boy who would be here within a few weeks. How would I feel if I had to go the rest of my life seeing them through prison bars or in some crowded visitation room?

Mia cried softly in the passenger seat beside me as I drove us to the Mechant Loup Police Department. Although we didn't expect any trouble from her, Takecia sat behind me so she could keep an eye on her. After all, she was a murder suspect, and she had killed in an especially cunning way, and with very specific intent.

Once at the police department, I fingerprinted Mia and emailed the cards to Vanessa, whom I'd called earlier and asked if she could make the comparison. It had been five in the morning when I'd made the call, and Vanessa had sounded wide awake. After I'd sent the print cards to her, it had only taken a few minutes for her to call and positively say that it was Mia's prints that were on the ice bags and the tailgate of Carlos' truck.

With that information in hand, I began typing up the arrest warrants for Lauren and Mia. I let them visit in an interview room while I worked. I had all the information I needed for trial, so it didn't matter what they said to each other.

Although I finished the affidavits by six, I wanted to wait until eight to contact the duty judge, because I didn't want him in a bad mood when I called. In the meantime, I contacted Amy and Baylor and we compared notes on the case. They were in a hotel in Salt Lake City when I got a hold of them. The Nevada State Police had finished interviewing them and let them go, and they had taken Kari Marcella with them.

"It was weird not having to work the crime scene," Amy said. "It was a mess, Clint. It's gonna take them days to process it."

"What're you gonna do with Kari?" I asked, not wanting them to interrupt their trip. "You can't take her on your honeymoon."

"No, we got her a plane ticket out of here," she explained. "We're gonna drop her off at the airport in the morning and Dean's gonna pick her up in New Orleans."

Dean had left while Takecia and I were at Mia's house, but I'd spoken with him by phone to let him know we would be arresting Mia and Lauren for Carlos' murder. He had asked if I could let them go, but I told him it was out of my hands.

"What'll happen to the bikers who helped y'all?" I asked Amy.

"What bikers?" she asked coyly. "Bay, did you see any bikers?"

I heard Baylor laugh in the background.

"I can't imagine the state police will just let it go."

"No, they won't," she acknowledged, "but we can't help them. I didn't go around taking names while we were being shot at. I'm sure they're gonna use the news footage to try and make some identifications, but those bikers acted in self-defense of us, so I don't think they'll mess with them if they find them."

We talked for a while longer, and then my cell phone rang. I glanced at the screen. It was Detective Rachael Bowler.

"I have to go, but I'm glad y'all are okay," I said. "Thanks for everything. Enjoy the rest of your honeymoon and don't call again."

"I'll try not to."

"If you do, I won't answer." Before she could respond, I hung up my desk phone and answered my cell. "Rachael, what's up?"

"Hey, Clint, I just finished interviewing Lester Smith's wife, Ann," she said. "It seems Lester and Carlos were best friends and they've kept in touch over the years. A month ago, Lester calls Carlos and tells him that Dean showed up at church. Carlos has been looking for Dean for years, and Ann thinks he wanted to kill the boy for attacking him in the basement of their home in Nevada. When Lester told Carlos he'd seen Dean, Carlos asked him to call back if Dean showed up again. The following week, Dean shows up and Lester makes the call."

"Did Lester know that Carlos wanted to kill Dean?" I asked. "Or did he just think Carlos wanted to find Dean to reconnect?"

"Oh, no, they all knew Carlos wanted to kill Dean." Rachael grunted. "I asked Ann why she didn't alert the authorities, and you know what she said?"

"What?"

"She said Lester was her authority."

"I don't guess I'm surprised."

Rachael took a breath before continuing. "Anyway, on the day that Carlos shows up at church, Dean's nowhere to be found. Next thing they know, Carlos disappears. He stops answering his cell phone and he doesn't answer the door at his motel."

"He was staying at a motel?"

"Yeah, here in Magnolia," Rachael said. "We searched it, but it was empty. He didn't even have any clothes in it."

That made sense, considering we had found his suitcases in the back of his truck. "Did Ann know why her husband was at Mia's house shooting at cops?" I asked.

"Ann says Lester saw Mia talking to Carlos in the parking lot at church on the day he disappeared, and Carlos also texted him to say he was gonna be having sex with Mia that night, so Lester was certain Mia had something to do with his disappearance. When word got out that Carlos was dead, she said Lester became incensed. He started watching her house, just waiting for her to mess up." Rachael sighed. "She claims she doesn't know why Lester shot at our deputies. My best guess is he thought Mia was walking out with them, and he wanted to kill her before she could be taken to jail. Once she's in prison, he would've known there was no getting at her."

I nodded. It was getting close to eight, so I wrapped up the conversation and reached for my desk phone to call the judge. I couldn't believe how nervous I was for Mia and Lauren. Although they were murderers, I was hoping for a low bond in the moment and a reduced sentence in the future.

"Here goes nothing," I mumbled, and dialed the number for District Judge Zachariah Lamb.

CHAPTER 63

Wednesday, October 12

It was six in the evening and the Mechant Life Church was crowded and noisy. I hoisted Grace on my shoulder so she could see above the people in front of us.

"Where's Mr. Andy Verdin, Daddy?" she asked.

"He should be sitting close to the front," I explained. "He'll be in a wheelchair. Can't you see him?"

"Oh, yeah, I do! He's got a big smile on his face!"

I did, too.

After wrapping up the murder of Carlos Marcella three weeks earlier, I had taken Grace to visit Mr. Verdin in the hospital. There was something about children that helped cheer up a body, and it had worked in Mr. Verdin's case. After we'd visited with him for about twenty minutes that first time, I told him we had to leave. He'd begged us to return. We did—four or five times before he was released from the hospital the previous week—and Grace came to enjoy our visits as much as he did. Today would mark his first return to church since that fateful morning last month. Although he wasn't able to walk just yet, he was at least back home where he wanted to be.

Father Reggie took to the stage and a hush fell over the crowd.

"As you might've noticed, tonight's service will be a little different," he began. "Instead of hearing from me, you'll be fellowshipping with each other and partaking in God's wondrous blessings. We've got food and drinks in the back to help us celebrate this special occasion, which is the return of our young Brother Andy Verdin. Brother Verdin, get up here!"

The crowd cheered as Mrs. Verdin pushed her husband's wheelchair to the front of the church. Grace drummed her hands against my head in delight. Once everyone had settled down and Mr. Verdin was on the stage, Father Reggie walked toward a large object that was cloaked in a drop cloth. After talking into the mic for a while, he jerked the drop cloth from the object and presented Mr. Verdin with a brand new pirogue that my friend had built.

Not wanting any credit for my half of the donation, I'd asked my friend to coordinate the presentation with the church, of which the Verdins were members.

I craned my neck to see Mr. Verdin's reaction. My heart swelled when I caught sight of him. He was smiling and tears were streaming down his face, but I only saw him for a brief moment, as the crowd broke from their ranks and rushed the stage to congratulate him.

Susan took the opportunity to drop to the pew and catch her breath.

"How're you feeling?" I asked.

"I feel ready."

I was about to ask what that meant when I felt a hand on my arm. I turned to see Lauren Gaubert standing there.

"Detective Wolf, can I talk to you for a second?" she asked tentatively, as though she were afraid that I'd snap at her.

I glanced at Susan, who nodded and waved me off. I pulled Grace down off my shoulders and told her to wait with her mom.

"What's up?" I asked when we had stepped into the empty aisle. The noise was mostly toward the front of the large tabernacle, so we didn't have to raise our voices to be heard.

"I wanted to thank you for everything you did for Mia and me," she said. "I know you went to bat for us, and that's why everyone has been so kind and forgiving."

I shifted my feet. While Carlos' toxicology had provided the evidence we needed to confirm that he had been drugged prior to being strapped into the front seat of his truck, and thus bolstering a second degree murder charge, Mia and Lauren had been aided greatly by the fact that text messages between Carlos and Lester confirmed our belief that Carlos was in town to kidnap Dean. It also didn't hurt that Carlos was wanted in Amarillo for a hit and run involving injuries. Once Amy had learned from Kari that he'd left Nevada in his Monte Carlo, I'd contacted Amarillo PD to see if they'd located a vehicle matching that description in the area where

Carlos had acquired the secondhand truck. As it turned out, a Monte Carlo that Dean later identified as having belonged to Carlos had been involved in a crash with a postal van. Although they hadn't been able to identify the driver at the time, they did have fingerprints that matched up to the cadaver print cards I'd recovered from Carlos, and they'd been able to close their case.

"It wasn't me," I said to Lauren. "It was the situation."

"No, it was you," she said, her voice growing stronger. "Our lawyers met with the district attorney's office on Monday and the DA said the only reason we got such a low bond was because you convinced the judge we weren't a flight risk and we weren't a danger to anyone, and that we only did what we did because of the evil things Carlos had done to us and Rory. She said that's also the reason she's charging us with manslaughter instead of second degree murder."

"Was there any talk of a deal?" I asked, genuinely concerned for the two women—especially Mia, considering she had a small boy. While it was early in the process, the new district attorney didn't waste time, especially when it came to murder cases, so I wasn't surprised to learn that they were already in talks.

"Our lawyers both think they can get us off on temporary insanity or an outright not guilty verdict," she said. "They believe once they present the evidence against Carlos to a jury, there's no way they'll convict us."

"They're probably right," I said.

"Yeah, but we weren't insane. We knew what we did was wrong, but we still did it anyway."

I scowled. "So what are y'all gonna do?"

"We're gonna do what you suggested—we're gonna plead guilty and throw ourselves at the mercy of the court." She shrugged. "Our lawyers think we might have to do five to ten years in prison. While that's a scary thought, it's much better than life without parole."

I was about to agree with her when I felt a small hand jerking on my wrist.

"Daddy, come quick!" Grace screeched. "Mommy peed on herself!"

CHAPTER 64

I snapped my head around and saw Susan pulling herself to a standing position. On the pew where she had been sitting, there was a puddle of clear liquid.

"We need to get to the hospital," she said calmly. "My water broke."

My heart began to pound in my chest and the room spun. Images of Susan giving birth to our baby boy right there on the church floor flooded through my mind and I felt my lunch coming up.

"Clint," Susan said, apparently recognizing the fear in my eyes. "It's okay. We've got time."

I nodded, took a breath, and reached for her.

"My water broke," she said with a grin, "not my back. I can still walk unassisted."

"Daddy, it's okay," Grace said, grabbing my hand. "I'll protect you."

I smiled as Grace and I hurried toward the door, clearing a path for Susan. I caught Amy's eye from across the room and yelled, "It's time!"

Her face instantly lit up and she slugged Baylor's arm and said something to him. He began scanning the room and calling out to the rest of the gang. Takecia was in attendance with Doctor Evans. Regan and her husband were there, as was Melvin, his wife, and his daughter, and Shade and his girlfriend. Lindsey was also there and had recognized the urgency of my movements. She beat us to the door and held it open.

"Good luck, Chief!" she said, her face beaming. "I can't wait to meet the little guy!"

Susan stopped and hugged her. "Thank you so much, Lindsey."

I was almost hopping up and down at that point. "Honey, we have to go!"

Susan only laughed and took her time crossing the parking lot. Lindsey rushed to her own car, and it was then that I saw the others piling through the doorway and heading to their respective vehicles. My heart swelled as I held the door to my truck for Susan and watched everyone spreading out across the lot. These weren't just our co-workers or our friends—they were our family.

"Shit!" I blurted, suddenly remembering our family.

"Daddy, don't say that in front of Baretta!"

I laughed and lifted Grace into the back seat. I made sure she strapped herself in and then rushed around to the driver's side, calling my mom as I did so.

"Mom, call Lisa," I said quickly. "The baby's coming!"

Lisa Wilson was Susan's mom. Tragically, Susan's dad had passed away after a boxing match when Susan was young, so he wasn't there to enjoy the moment. She spoke of him often, and I knew it had been hard for her to grow up without a dad. Still, he had done a good job for the years he had been around her, because, aside from being the most beautiful woman I'd ever laid eyes upon—I was certain she hadn't gotten those qualities from her dad—she was also very independent and strong. If he was up there looking down on her right at that moment, I knew he was proud of her.

As soon as I'd jumped into my seat, I tossed the phone aside and raced out of the parking lot. I drove a little faster than the speed limit, but I was very careful. I kept glancing at Susan to gauge how far along we were in the process, but her face revealed nothing but excitement. She and Grace talked about what they would do when we brought him home for the first time, as though they were heading to the grocery store and not the hospital. At one point, she calmly took out her cell phone and called her doctor to say the baby was coming.

Me, I could hardly talk. My hands trembled and my heart pounded in my chest. I was waiting for her to suddenly lurch over in pain and declare that the baby was coming and that I needed to give birth. While I had been in the birthing room twice before, everything had been a bit of a blur that had ended in a state of dizzying euphoria, and I knew I wasn't capable of delivering a baby anywhere, and especially not on the side of the road.

I didn't breathe a sigh of relief until we pulled into the parking lot of Chateau General. I was heading straight for the emergency room doors when Susan stopped me and directed me to park in a regular space.

"I can walk," she said. "We've still got time."

I hesitated, but then realized it would be faster to do what she said than to argue about it. I knew my wife well and, although she was calm, I noticed a little tightness around her mouth that only appeared when she was experiencing pain.

I had just parked and jumped out of my truck when Amy and Baylor appeared from out of nowhere.

"Want me to take Gracie?" Amy asked.

"Yes!" I said, jerking Susan's door open. "Thank you!"

"Daddy, will I get to meet my baby brother?" Grace asked as she watched me take Susan's arm and walk away with her.

"Yes, Pumpkin," I called over my shoulder. "They'll let you in just as soon as he's born."

When I made that statement, I was unaware that the time would come a lot sooner than expected. A nurse met us at the sidewalk with a wheelchair and whisked Susan down the hall. I kept up, but just barely. I was breathless and weak with anticipation.

While the first nurse wheeled her into the delivery room and began prepping her, another nurse brought me into a separate room and made me put some kind of hospital garments over my clothes. I didn't object. I wanted to get in the room with Susan as quickly as I could, regardless of how goofy I looked.

When the nurse finally ushered me into the delivery room, we were almost too late. I heard Susan let out a grunt, and then I moved into position just in time to see the crown of our son's head appear. In another blurry moment, I watched him being born. Within seconds, the doctor was holding a nine-pound, eleven-ounce baby boy in her gloved hands.

In that moment, in my mind, it was as though every living thing paused for a split second to joyously and quietly celebrate a new life being brought into the world. It felt as though the earth had stopped spinning. My heart became still. The blood in my veins ceased to flow...and then our baby boy belted out a cry that I knew could be heard way down the hall, because cheers erupted from that direction.

The doctor placed him in Susan's arms briefly while one nurse worked to clean up Susan and the other waited to accept our son for his cleaning.

Once everything had calmed down and our baby was back in Susan's arms, the doctor gave me a nod to bring Grace in. Without hesitating, I hurried out of the room. I was met with hugs and excited slaps on my back. I couldn't see myself, but I knew I was beaming. It would've taken two crowbars and a dozen strong mules to break the smile that was plastered across my face at that moment.

I grabbed Grace's hand. "Come meet your brother."

"Can I hold Baretta?"

"That won't be his name," I said with a laugh. I was about to turn away when I saw my mom and Lisa hurrying through our extended family.

"How is Susan?" Lisa asked. "Is she okay? Is it really over?"

"They're both doing great," I said. "He came out fast."

Lisa let out a long sigh of relief.

"I called your dad," my mom said. "He's flying in from offshore. He's so upset he couldn't be here."

"I understand," I said, giving a knowing nod. "It's only luck that I made it. Had I been working a scene or in the middle of an arrest, I would've been too late." I indicated the delivery room. "I need to get back inside."

"Can I go in?" Lisa asked tentatively.

I smiled. "Follow me."

Grace and I led the way down the hall and back into the delivery room. Susan was still holding our baby boy. She looked up when we entered. Her eyes were locked on mine, and I knew what time it was.

"Well?" she asked, a twinkle in her eye. "What did you decide to call this precious little man? And you'd better not say Baretta!"

I walked over and knelt beside her, looking down into the wide brown eyes of my son. With Grace squeezing close so she could see her brother, I said, "No, it's not Baretta." I paused and looked at Susan. "I'm gonna name him Isaiah…Isaiah Wilson Wolf."

Susan immediately burst into tears. "You're naming him after my dad?"

I bit back my own tears. Unable to speak, I only nodded. Behind me, I could also hear Lisa crying softly.

BJ Bourg

BJ Bourg is a former professional boxer and a lifelong martial artist who retired as the chief investigator for a district attorney's office. A thirty-year veteran of law enforcement, he has worked as a patrol cop, detective, detective sergeant and police academy instructor. He has investigated thousands of felony cases and trained hundreds of law enforcement officers in self-defense, firearms, and criminal operations.

Throughout his career, Bourg has served on many specialized units such as SWAT, Explosives Search Team, and Homicide Response Team. He founded his agency's sniper program and served as its leader and trainer for nearly a decade. A graduate of seven basic and advanced sniper schools, he deployed as the primary sniper on dozens of call-outs, including barricaded subjects, hostage rescue operations, and fugitive apprehensions. He also served as the sniper instructor for the 2001 Louisiana Tactical Police Officers Association's Conference.

Bourg has been the recipient of numerous awards, including Top Shooter at an FBI Sniper School, the Distinguished Service Medal, and Certificates of Commendation for his work as a homicide detective. In addition to speaking at numerous law enforcement and writer's conferences, he has written dozens of articles for leading law enforcement and tactical magazines covering a wide range of topics such as defensive tactics, sniper deployment, suspect interrogation, report writing, no-knock search warrants, and more.

Above all else, Bourg is a father and a husband. The highlight of his life is spending time with his beautiful wife and wonderful children. Originally from Louisiana, he now proudly calls Tellico Plains, Tennessee home.

www.bjbourg.com

Made in the USA
Columbia, SC
29 March 2024

33811416R00159